LEIF BEILEY

VOYAGE
to
CRUSOE

PART I

CHAPTER 1

CLIFF DEMONT EASED his silver Porsche off the two-lane black-top road and onto the rutted gravel driveway. The car bounced along the ruts a hundred yards and came to a stop near the concrete foundation of an old farmhouse that had burned down long ago. It was mid-November and dappled morning sunlight filtered through the leaves of a magnificent oak tree that stood in the middle of what had once been the home's front yard. Beyond the tree, the land sloped downward toward Highway 101, a quarter mile away.

Wearing jeans and work boots, he got out of the car and zipped his jacket against the cool morning breeze. He wanted to walk the entire property and feel the land before the bulldozers and contractors arrived to transform this pasture into the new headquarters of Evergreen Scientific Corporation.

He envisioned a glass and stone building with wide overhanging eaves nestled among the trees. Its façade would be a gentle S-shape, with the recessed part of the "S" accommodating the oak. The big tree would provide afternoon shade and frame the view from the lobby of the building, a panorama of the valley below. That's what he envisioned, but the plans actually specified a concrete tilt-up, designed for maximum efficiency and little regard for the beauty of the land. *What a shame*, he thought.

An old red pickup truck turned into the driveway and rattled to a stop next to the Porsche. The woman who climbed out of the truck looked about sixty, dressed in denim and cowboy boots, with an old Stetson on her head.

"You the bastard whose gonna cut down these trees and pave Buffum ranch?" She pointed a hostile finger at him as she spoke.

"Not exactly. I'm the architect for the building that's going up here." Cliff sucked in his gut and hooked his thumbs in his jeans, unconsciously trying to look more like a rancher than an architect.

"See that house up there on the ridge?" She pointed toward an old ranch house across the road a quarter mile up the hill. "That's my house, and that property on the other side of the road there, that's my ranch, the Hilliard ranch. My name is Alice Hilliard. I grew up on this land and I don't think you ought to be puttin' up any goddamned buildings in Buffum's pasture." She stared at him in disgust. "You oughta know better than to cut down these trees and pave this good grazing land."

"It surely is beautiful," Cliff agreed, "But the Buffum family has chosen to subdivide it and sell it." He swept his arm across the landscape, "Of course we want to preserve the natural beauty of it, as much as possible anyway."

She laughed in his face, "Oh that's rich. You might be able to sell that load o' manure down in LA, but I know better. You won't be satisfied 'til you've paved everything from here to Frisco."

Cliff gave her his friendliest smile. "Well, there's no stopping progress, but I'm going to save as many of these trees as I can. I'll show you what we're planning to do here." He took a roll of blueprints from the Porsche and spread them out on the tailgate of her truck. "This is the site plan, it shows the property lines and where the building will be." He pointed out the details on the blueprint.

She studied the drawing a moment, then looked toward the oak tree. "Looks like your building is going to be right over there."

"Yes ma'am."

She squinted at him. "Hell, I know I can't stop progress so

I'm not going to try. But that tree, when I was a child we used to play under it, the Hilliard and Buffum kids. Their house was right there," she said, pointing at the foundation, "Oh my, did we have fun here." She kicked at the gravel with a booted toe. "Now the kids are all grown and gone, and the grandkids don't ever come here. Nobody remembers much about this place anymore." She paused another moment, staring at the tree.

"What happened to the farmhouse?" Cliff wanted to know the history of the place.

"Oh, it burned down forty years ago, back in forty-seven. The Buffums built a new house farther up the hill. You can't see it from here. They didn't want to see this place from the new one."

"Why not?" Cliff pushed his sunglasses up on his forehead and studied the woman's weathered face.

"Tom Buffum died in the fire. Things were never the same after that."

He stared at the ruins of the farmhouse and imagined the flames. "Who was Tom Buffum?"

Alice looked off toward the west a moment. "Tom was the youngest of the Buffum boys. He joined the Marines in '43, right after he turned eighteen. He went to fight the Japanese on those islands, I don't remember the names anymore. When he came home, he wasn't right in the head. Had terrible nightmares. One night he took a gallon of gasoline into his bedroom and locked the door. They said he poured it all over the room and struck a match. It was more like an explosion than a fire." She took a deep breath, "I was seventeen when Tom enlisted. He asked me to marry him before he left, right under that old oak tree." She paused a moment, then sighed. "I told him I'd wait for him. But he died before we got married." She nodded toward the tree and said in a quiet voice, "I'd be obliged if you let that one live."

Cliff looked her in the eye. "Miss Hilliard, I promise you, I'll do my best to save that tree." He rolled up the plans and tucked them under his arm.

"Well, I don't put much stock in what you people with fancy sports cars and sunglasses say." She nodded toward the Porsche and cocked an eye at the glasses perched on his head. "If I catch you takin' a chainsaw to that tree, I'll come after you. Don't you forget that." She turned to get into her truck.

"I understand, ma'am. Nobody's going to cut down that tree."

She put the truck in gear and drove away.

Alone again, he glanced at the oak tree and frowned. He hadn't intended to promise not to cut it down, but that's what it sounded like: A promise.

Back in his office at the firm of Larsen Haines, he sketched a new façade for the building that curved behind the tree, the way he had envisioned it. When he was finished, he took it into Bob Larsen's office. Bob was the president of Larsen Haines.

"Evergreen's board is going to love this," Bob said with a sad smile. "Those guys who sit in paneled offices in LA are going to drool over it until the accountant does the math and says they can get ten percent more space in a square building for less money."

"Let's at least present this alternative to them. A concrete box in that beautiful landscape is going to be ugly. Let's use that setting to do something inspiring instead of another tilt-up."

"Hey," Bob retorted, "We do very well with concrete boxes." He pointed a finger at the rendering. "This façade is beautiful, Cliff, but you know curved walls are expensive to build. Plus we'd have to charge them more for the design, and that's not in the budget."

Cliff felt his blood beginning to boil. "Architecture isn't just about money, dammit." This was an argument they'd had before, and one he always lost. He thought of the promise he made to Alice Hilliard and vowed not to give in this time. "All I'm asking is that you present this option to Evergreen."

"Sure, I'll present it," Bob said. "If they sign off on it, great. But if they want a concrete tilt-up out there in Buffum's pasture instead, that's what we're going to design for them."

Cliff knew Bob would fold at the first sign of resistance to the more expensive design. Back in his office, he stared out the window and fumed.

He left the office at five. Friday rush hour traffic in downtown San Luis Obispo was heavy but it thinned out long before he arrived at his house in Avila Beach. When he pulled into the garage, his wife's car was gone. Already in a foul mood over the Evergreen project, he was downright irritated that Janet was working late again. On a Friday night.

Muttering to himself, he grabbed a beer from the fridge and flicked on the TV, scrolling through the channels until he found a football game, a rerun of the Raiders beating the Chiefs. He tried to watch the game but he found himself checking his watch every twenty minutes and growing more irritated with Janet. After an hour, he called her office.

"Majestic Properties, how can I direct your call?"

Cliff knew the perky voice of Helen, the receptionist. Though it was nearly eight on a Friday night, she was still in the office.

"Hi Helen, Cliff Demont. Is Janet still there?"

"No, she is showing property way out in Creston today. A beautiful home on twelve acres, with a vineyard."

"Sounds fabulous. Thanks." *This is the third night this week that she's worked late*, he thought, *I'm getting damn tired of it.*

He was sitting on the deck off the bedroom when Janet arrived home. He'd built it right after they bought the house and it was his favorite place to be. Made of thick redwood planks, it faced southwest, offering a spectacular view of the ocean and the setting sun. To preserve the view he made the railing of glass and later added a hot tub and a stone fire pit. He was staring into the embers of a dying fire when she opened the sliding glass door.

"Sorry I'm late, I got tied up with a buyer at the property," she said while she kicked off her heels.

"Until ten?" His smoldering anger showed in his voice.

"The house is in Creston, an hour away. I'm going to take a shower. I hope you're in a better mood when I get out."

He continued to stare into the fire while she showered. The sky grew overcast, obscuring the gibbous moon.

She came out of the bathroom wearing a thick terrycloth robe, toweling her hair. "Aren't you cold sitting out there?"

He rose and went inside.

Tall and slender, with long, dark hair and luminous green eyes, Janet reminded him of an actress, Jacqueline Bisset.

"What are your plans for tomorrow? Working?" He undressed and climbed into bed.

"I'm meeting a client at ten." She slid under the covers, facing away from him.

"It seems like I have to make an appointment to see you."

"I have a job."

"Yeah, well, tomorrow's Saturday. What about a home life? What about us?" He reached for her under the blanket and she stiffened.

"I don't complain when you work long hours." She moved to the far edge of the bed. "My job is just as demanding as yours."

"Of course it is, but when you started working, we agreed it would be part-time, until we saved enough to open an office of our own. Remember?"

"That was five years ago." She turned to face him. "The truth is, you're never going to open an office."

"That's not true. I've made up my mind, I'm going to quit Larsen Haines as soon as the Evergreen project is finished. It's time for me to go out on my own."

"Remember the dental office you designed three years ago?"

Janet's voice was quiet and cutting. "You were going to hang out your shingle after that project too."

He had created a bold design for Dr. Kelvin, a prominent dentist in San Luis Obispo. Kelvin loved it, but then opted for a less expensive plain stucco building. Cliff had been incensed at the time and threatened to quit, but somehow, he never did.

Janet went on in a disdainful tone, "You're always going to work for Bob Larsen. It's not what you dreamed of but it's good enough for you. I have dreams too. I'm a very good real estate agent and I'm going to make a lot of money. It's what I want to do." She turned off the light and fluffed her pillow. "Goodnight."

He had to admit she was right. Three years back, he swallowed his pride and redesigned the dental office. It was a good building, but it was uninspiring as architecture, and he knew he was better than that. *Sure, it's difficult to sell a client on a bold, imaginative design, but Bob didn't even try,* he thought bitterly. *Bob doesn't care about anything except getting the contract. And my own wife thinks that somewhere along the way I've given up on my dreams.* He lay awake stewing over these thoughts while she slept.

Janet was gone when he awoke. He lay in bed staring at the ceiling while her words came flooding back. They stung last night, but now they aroused anger. He threw the covers off and jumped out of bed. In the kitchen, there was still-warm coffee in the pot and he gulped down a cup. *Damned if I'm going to mope around the house today,* he thought. He rummaged in the closet for surf trunks and a hooded sweatshirt. When he passed the dresser mirror and caught a glimpse of himself, he froze. There were dark circles under his blue eyes. His light brown hair was neatly trimmed but uncombed. He pushed it back on his forehead, noticing that his hairline had receded a bit. The boyish dimples Janet used to tease him about suddenly looked more like creases. He stood back and studied his body in the mirror. It was the first time in a while that he'd taken a good look at himself. The view was of a man on his way to middle age, not the Cliff Demont he perceived himself to be. At thirty-eight he was six feet tall and well built, but there had been a definite migration of muscle from his arms and shoulders to his midriff, and it wasn't muscle anymore. He tore his eyes from the mirror and headed for the garage.

"Fucking Porsche," he muttered a few minutes later as he attached surf racks to its roof. He used to just toss his board in the back of his truck and go. The Porsche had been Janet's idea. She wanted him to drive a status symbol instead of his trusty Ford pickup. Now he had to be careful not to scratch the paint putting on the racks. He tossed a towel and wetsuit in the backseat and strapped his board on top.

He sped south on Highway 101 and took the Orcutt exit to Highway 1 through Lompoc. A few minutes later the coupe was on the winding two-lane road to Jalama. He pulled over when the beach came into view and scanned the ocean below. The sky was clear and a light offshore wind riffled the tops of the waves that rolled in from the southwest. Jalama waves, big and powerful, were not for inexperienced surfers, and he counted only a few guys in the water.

As a kid in Huntington Beach, Cliff used to go sailing with his father on weekends. When he was twelve, Jack Demont was killed in a fiery car crash. His mother sold the boat almost immediately after the funeral, so Cliff turned to surfing.

Nearly every day before school he surfed with his friends. But as he got older, he grew impatient with the hordes at the good surf spots. He got in the habit of waiting for those days when the surf was big and the crowds thinned out. Eventually, he gained a reputation as a big wave rider, and the other kids would sit on the beach and watch him on those rare days when the surf was too big for them.

"Dude, you should enter surf contests!" his buddies would tell him.

"Nah," he'd reply. "I just surf for fun." He figured the competition would ruin the pure pleasure of surfing. Instead, he savored having the big waves mostly to himself. After his father died, he found solace in the ocean, and spent many long afternoons riding waves in solitude. Nowadays he still preferred the finely calculated risk and thrill of riding big surf, and it was worth it to make the long drive to Jalama.

Paddling out, he gasped when the first wave broke over him and sent frigid water inside his wetsuit. He hadn't surfed in three months and had to work hard to get through the white water to the waves, but it felt good to be surfing again. Sitting on his board, he waited for the next set of waves and took off on the first good one. Paddling hard, he dropped down the face and cranked a hard bottom turn, then the wave collapsed and swallowed him in a maelstrom of whitewater. It was Mother Ocean's way of scolding him for being out of shape and neglecting her too long. He came up sputtering and laughing at the same time and turned his board seaward to paddle out again. After that he got better rides with each wave he caught, regaining his balance, timing, and poise on the board. The waves revived his spirit and he forgot about Janet and Bob Larsen, and old Alice Hilliard while he surfed.

A couple of hours later, he rode his last wave to shore. Exhausted, he threw himself down on the sand and lay there letting the sun warm him while, eyes closed, he replayed the best rides of the day in his mind.

A few minutes later, a shadow fell across his face. He opened his eyes and squinted through salt-crusted lashes at the tall, lanky man in a wetsuit standing above him. His face was hidden in the glare of the sun.

"I thought that was you out there," said Jon Hartmann. he

had just come out of the water and beads of it stood out on his wetsuit like shimmering diamonds. "Haven't seen you in a while."

Cliff rose to his feet and picked up his board. "Yeah, been busy at work."

They walked together up the beach discussing the odds of a big swell arriving next week.

"I'm getting back into surfing," Cliff said as he strapped his board to his car. "If that swell shows up I'll be here next Saturday,"

"Want to ride along with me?" Jon drove a Volkswagen van and they used to occasionally cruise along the coast together, searching for good waves. But as Cliff became more involved with work their trips had come to an end.

"That'd be great. I'll buy the coffee and donuts."

"Alright, I'll pick you up at six." Jon waved and headed off toward his van.

Arriving home, Cliff pulled into the driveway and when he opened the garage door, Janet's car was gone. Irritated again, he put his surfboard away, showered, and ambled out to the deck with a drink. Ominous clouds rolled in from the west, blotting out the sunset.

CHAPTER 2

CLIFF WAS IN his office at five o'clock Tuesday afternoon when Kelly, the office manager, poked her head in the doorway.

"Bob called," she said, "He'll be back tomorrow morning." Kelly kept things running smoothly at Larsen Hanes. Besides Bob and Cliff, there was Jerry, the other architect in the firm as well as four draftsmen and the model maker. Each with his own ideas and quirks.

Cliff closed the folder he'd been working on and looked up. "I'll wager he didn't bother to present my curved facade to them."

"I think it's beautiful, but I doubt that he showed it to them." She gave him a sympathetic look. "Sorry."

Cliff rose from the desk. "Yeah, well..." He reached for his coat and grabbed his briefcase.

"Well?" She asked as he ushered her out of the office.

"Nothing." He switched off the light. "We'll see what tomorrow brings. Have a good night." In the parking lot, he sat in his car, staring ahead. The anger he'd been holding back all day took over and his thoughts raced until he was startled by a tap on car's window. There was Kelly, looking concerned.

He started the motor and lowered the window.

"Cliff, are you okay? You look like you're about to have a stroke."

"Yeah, I'm fine. See you tomorrow." He put the Porsche in gear and drove home.

~

Kelly was at her desk when Cliff arrived at work the next day. "Good morning," he said, "Any word from Bob?"

"He'll be in around ten." She smiled as she glanced up from her computer terminal.

When Bob arrived, Cliff followed him into his office. "How'd it go?"

"They signed off on the plans, with some exceptions. We need to get the changes done by Friday. They really liked the work you did," he said as he spread the drawings on the table. "But cost drives the design." It was a phrase Bob loved. "We're increasing the floor plan from forty to fifty thousand square feet. So the front of the building will be pushed out to here." His finger traced a line that had been sketched on the plan. It bisected the tree Cliff had promised Alice Hilliard wouldn't be cut down.

"What about the curved façade? Did you present it?"

"Oh that. They're not buying it. But see this?" He pointed to a squiggly circle on the drawing. "We're putting in a fountain. That'll dress up the approach to the building."

"A fountain? You must be joking. I'm not doing that."

"Can you get started on these changes right away?" Bob hadn't been listening.

"I'm not making those changes, Bob. I'm not doing this again," Cliff said in a quiet voice.

Bob looked up from the plans, "You're not what...?"

"I'm not going to design another ugly cube. I'm leaving. I should have left a long time ago." He started for the door.

Bob stared at him, dumbfounded, "Hey, you can't just leave!"

Cliff ignored him and walked out. Back in his office, he began stuffing his briefcase. His hands shook as he sorted through his desk drawers.

A moment later Bob appeared in his doorway. "You're serious, aren't you? You're throwing away your career over one goddam building?" He shook his head in exasperation.

"That's the problem, Bob. This isn't about one goddam building. It's about settling for cheap solutions and mediocrity. And this isn't a career, it's just a job." He snapped his briefcase shut and started for the door.

Bob stepped aside and followed him toward the lobby, "You think it's easy, huh? Getting a client to sign a contract?" His face had reddened under his country club tan.

Cliff turned and faced him, "I don't know how hard you try, Bob. You don't care what we design as long as we get the contract, but that's not enough for me anymore."

"Not enough for you? You should try selling one of your own designs. You'll find out how hard it is."

"That's exactly what I intend to do," Cliff shot back.

Kelly stared, wide-eyed, as they approached her desk near the front entrance.

"Kelly, it's been wonderful working with you. I'll miss you." Cliff reached out to shake her hand, but she rose from her chair and hugged him instead, tears welling up in her eyes. Turning back to Bob, he said, "I appreciate all you've done for me over the years, but we've both known for a long time this day was coming. Thanks for everything." He turned and went out the door.

"Hey!" Bob followed him outside. "You're not quitting on me, I'm firing you!"

Cliff unlocked his car and tossed his briefcase in.

"Did you hear me? I'm firing your ass!" Bob reached the curb in front of the Porsche. "I'll make sure you never get a contract in this county," he bellowed. "I'll ruin you before you even get started! You won't be able to design a doghouse when I'm through with you!"

Cliff put the car in gear and backed out of the parking space. Through the windshield he saw Bob standing on the curb, his face twisted in anger. In the background, Kelly stared through the plate glass office window at him. He gunned the car out of the parking lot and headed for the Buffum ranch. The Porsche came to a stop under the oak tree and he got out, taking deep breaths of the fresh air. *That was easier than I thought it would be*, he told himself. *I should have left three years ago instead of redoing that stupid dental building.*

Out on the road, Alice Hilliard's truck drove by. He could almost feel her glaring at him as it passed. He jumped in the Porsche and followed the truck to her ranch house. She was unloading bags of feed from the truck when he arrived. The muscles in her skinny arms stood out as she hefted the bags onto a cart.

"Well, look what the cat dragged up the hill," she said when he approached. "What the hell do you want?"

"I want you to know that I did what I could to save that tree, but I'm afraid it's going to be removed."

She let out a bitter laugh. "You didn't have to trouble yourself to come up here and tell me that. I knew you could no more save that tree than fly to the moon. It don't matter anyway. I reckon I'm the only one who gives a damn about it."

"I care. I'm sorry it's going to be removed. I wanted to tell you this personally."

"Bully for you." She turned and lifted another bag from the truck. "Move along now. I got work to do."

Driving back to town, Cliff vowed that when he opened his office, he'd never use the phrase, "Cost drives the design." Or sacrifice environmental and aesthetic values for money. *Of course*, he thought, *that will be hard to do with Bob Larsen there to underbid me on every project.*

Instead of going straight home, he stopped at Borgia's diner, where he usually ate lunch, and grabbed the Tribune on his way in. He slid into a booth near the window and flipped the paper open to the classifieds. With a sluggish economy, there was no shortage of office space available in downtown San Luis Obispo. But he wanted something different, maybe a house on the outskirts of town that he could convert to an office, something Janet would like.

The waitress had just served him coffee and a ham sandwich when Kelly appeared outside the window and motioned that she wanted to talk. Cliff waved her in.

"What are you doing here? I've never seen Bob so furious." Her normally serene demeanor had forsaken her and she nervously flicked a loose strand of hair behind her ear.

"Want half?" he slid the plate with the sandwich toward her.

"No thanks. If you go right back to the office and apologize, I think this mess will blow over," She looked at her watch. "I was driving by and saw your car in the lot. What's gotten into you, Cliff?"

"Did you see the changes Bob wants on Evergreen?"

"I did."

"Surprised?"

"No."

"That's why I quit. I should've left a long time ago."

"Where will you go? What will you do?" She demanded. "You haven't thought this through, Cliff. You should go back and apologize to him." She looked down at her hands. "This is turning into a real fiasco."

"Actually, Janet and I have talked about opening our own office. With her real estate connections and sales talent along with my experience I think we can make it work," he said, hoping he sounded more confident than he felt.

"Well, that sounds like a wonderful idea. I didn't know you

were making plans to leave." She checked her watch again, "I have to get back to work. Good luck with your new business." She picked up her purse and stood, tears welling in her eyes again. "It's going to be awful without you." She walked out of the diner before he could say anything.

Cliff left some bills on the table and headed home. He was not looking forward to telling Janet he'd been fired, but he would have plenty of time this afternoon to figure out the best way to break the news to her.

He pulled into the driveway and waved to Bill, the neighbor across the street who was mowing his lawn. Surprised to see Janet's car in the garage, he called out to her when he entered the house.

"Blam!" the bedroom door slammed. Concerned, he hurried down the hall and opened it. He saw a half-dressed man stumble out the sliding glass door to the deck and caught a glimpse of Janet's backside as she scurried into the bathroom and locked the door. His eyes took in the scene in the bedroom, the rumpled bedclothes, a bottle of wine on the nightstand, a used condom on the floor. On his side of the bed.

"Hey, come back here!" he shouted. He ran out to the deck in time to see the guy disappear around the corner of the house.

He turned and raced through the house and out the front door. The man was struggling to unlock his BMW parked across the street. Cliff sprinted after him and reached the car as the man got in and stuck the key in the ignition. Cliff jerked the door open and grabbed him by the shirt. "Who the fuck are you?" he yelled, grabbing and punching at the same time. Suddenly the car lurched backward as the man got the car started and found reverse. Cliff was caught by the opened door and knocked down, cracking his head on the ground. Tires squealed as the car sped off, missing him by inches.

Cliff lay on the pavement with the acrid smell of burned rubber filling his nostrils. His head throbbed and he touched his fingers to the rising lump behind his left ear. He swayed dizzily as he started to get up.

Bill hurried over and helped him to the curb. "You okay?" he asked. "I saw the whole thing and called 911, the police will be here any min…" he stopped in mid-sentence and stared when Cliff's garage door opened and Janet's Lexus sped off down the street.

"I'm alright," Cliff shook Bill's hand off his arm and struggled to his feet. He was still dizzy, his knee was beginning to swell, and the knuckles of his right hand were scraped and bruised.

A patrol car drove up while Cliff was still taking stock of his bruises. He recognized the cop, officer Dunham, from the donut shop down by the beach.

"Hi Mr. Demont. You okay?" Dunham asked. "What happened here?"

Cliff told him what he remembered of the confrontation.

Bill excitedly told the cop about the car nearly running Cliff over, then added, "That car's been parking in front of my house a coupla times a week for the last month. Owner's a slick-looking fellow. I thought he was one of Janet's real estate associates."

"Wait a minute," Cliff was still foggy, "That car's been parking here for a month?"

"Yep, it kinda irritated me that the guy was visiting your house but always parked in front of mine."

Officer Dunham listened and took notes in his pad. "All right, Mr. Demont. You came home from work and caught your wife in the act with a stranger. You got into a scuffle with him and picked up some bruises." He nodded toward Cliff's skinned knuckles. "Do you want to file a complaint?"

Cliff shook his head, "No."

The officer closed his pad. "Let me give you some advice. Go stay with a friend a few days, until the dust settles. Maybe you can work things out with your wife, maybe not. Whatever you do, don't get tough with her or threaten her. I don't want to have to come back out here. Got it?"

"Sure. Thanks, officer."

After the policeman drove away, a kind of clarity came over Cliff. He realized this moment had been foreshadowed long before today. "This is the end of you and me, Janet," he said bitterly, then went back in the house and packed a couple of suitcases. He tossed them in the backseat of his car, strapped his surfboard onto the roof, and headed back into the house. Janet usually kept their checkbooks in the top drawer of her desk, but they were missing. Cursing, he searched the other drawers but came up empty until his fingers closed on a manila envelope in the bottom drawer. Their emergency cash. "This is a goddamned emergency," he said aloud as he pulled a thin stack of bills from it and stuffed it in his pocket. "A thousand bucks."

In the kitchen, he looked around but didn't see anything he wanted. Moving to the den, he went to the liquor cabinet and retrieved a bottle of whiskey. Hanging on the wall nearby were a couple of photos of him and Janet: Embracing at their wedding, lying on a beach in Cancun, and there was one of her on a horse. She was wearing a cowgirl's hat and looking back toward the camera, eyes half-closed, and faint smile on her lips. A 'come hither' look. He resisted an urge to smash his fist into the photo. Instead, he left. Across the street, Bill was still in his front yard trimming a hedge. In the rearview mirror Cliff could see him standing on his lawn, clippers in hand, staring after him as he drove off.

Traffic noise from Highway 1 penetrated the walls of the Big Rock Motel. Cliff had driven north, looking for the first motel with a vacancy sign, and found this place on the outskirts of Morro Bay. He lay awake on the well-worn mattress staring into the predawn darkness. The events of the day before played over and over in his mind, until he rose from the bed, wincing in pain. His body was sore from being knocked down by the BMW, proof that what happened the day before wasn't just a bad dream. At noon he checked out of the motel and called Kelly from a payphone.

"Where are you?" she demanded. "Your wife called here three times today. Why didn't you tell her you quit?" She took a deep breath, "Also, a policeman came by this morning looking for you. He said he had some questions about a fight. What's going on with you?"

"Things have gotten a little crazy but I can't explain it over the phone. Do you have plans after work?"

"No. Come to my house at 5:30. I collected a box of things from your office for you."

"I hope you got my Rolodex."

"Yes…Uh oh, Bob's coming, I have to go." The receiver went dead in his hand.

It was dark when he arrived at Kelly's house on Alrita Street. When she opened the door she stifled a laugh.

"What's funny?" he asked, instinctively checking his fly.

"Well, if the police are looking for you, you're making it awfully easy for them, driving that Porsche with a surfboard on top. It sticks out like a sore thumb."

Cliff turned and stared at the car. It did look a little ridiculous.

"Why don't you put it in the garage? I don't want them hauling you to jail before you tell me what's going on."

She put a glass of wine in his hand when he came in from the garage. "Alright. What's this about a fight?" She looked at his skinned knuckles while he drank.

He told her about finding Janet with Mr. BMW, how he bruised his knuckles on the man's face, and about her speeding off in her car. "Then I just packed a couple of bags and left. Haven't been back since."

"That's not the story she told me. She said you terrorized her and beat up a business associate of hers in a jealous rage."

"That's a lie! They were in bed when I got home. I chased the guy and landed a couple of punches but I didn't beat him up, and she left before I could say a word to her," Cliff said angrily. "She's been lying to me all along, and she lied to you too. What the hell's up with her?" He stared hard at Kelly as if, being a woman, she could give him an answer.

"I don't know, but I think you need a lawyer," she replied. "Honesty and fairness are the first casualties of a broken marriage. That's what my lawyer told me when I divorced Steve. She's very good. I'll give you her number."

"Great, finding a lawyer is on my to-do list."

He waited while she wrote down the number, then rose to leave. "I'd better get going."

"You don't have anywhere to go, do you?"

"I was thinking of the motel I stayed in last night."

"That sounds too depressing for words. You can stay here, in the spare bedroom for a day or two. You shouldn't be driving anyway. Not when you're emotionally upset."

He stood, "I'm fine…I couldn't impose on you this way."

"Don't be silly. You're staying here tonight and that's final."

Cliff stayed through the weekend, and when Kelly left for work on Monday, he drove into town to meet with her divorce lawyer, Angela Braun.

"Have you considered counseling and reconciliation? Angela asked. "An infidelity doesn't always have to end in divorce."

"File the papers. I want to finish this and get on with my life."

"Very well, I can see you've made up your mind," she said. "It will take about a week for the paperwork, and you'll have to reach a property settlement with Janet. Six months after that the divorce would be final."

"Fine. Let's get it done."

Back at Kelly's house, he groped in his suitcase for his bottle of whiskey and went out to the backyard, grabbing a glass along the way. He settled into a patio chair and watched a hummingbird swoop down to a feeder hanging in a tree. The sun was low and the air was cool. The bourbon warmed his throat as he tried to remember the last time he was in real trouble. He recalled his tour of duty in Vietnam, his platoon taking fire from Vietcong guerillas. He remembered being summoned from his seventh-grade classroom and his mother telling him his father had been killed in a crash on the San Diego Freeway. And then, years later, watching her succumb to breast cancer. He survived those terrifying times, mentally and emotionally battered, but fundamentally intact. Janet's betrayal wasn't as terrifying as being shot at, and it wasn't as heartbreaking as losing his parents. In fact, this sudden freefall was strangely exhilarating. Even now, sitting in Kelly's backyard, he couldn't help assuming that he would come out the other end of this dark tunnel okay. He lifted his glass to his lips.

"I knocked but no one answered," Jon said as he wandered into the back yard.

"How did you find me?" Cliff was surprised that anyone besides Kelly knew where he was.

"I called your office and that secretary with the sexy voice told me." Jon looked around the tidy backyard. "Nice place." He sat in the other patio chair and lifted the bottle of bourbon. "Maker's Mark. I'm glad you're maintaining your standards."

Cliff got another glass from the kitchen and poured him a drink.

"So, what's up with you and Janet?" Jon asked, "I stopped by your house Saturday morning and waited for you. We were supposed to go surfing, remember?"

"I completely forgot. Sorry."

"No problem. The waves weren't that good anyway. When I knocked on your door Janet said you didn't live there anymore. Said she didn't know where you were or how to get in touch with you, so I called your office."

Cliff told him about finding Janet in bed with Mr. BMW.

"Jesus. You lost your job too?"

"Yup."

"And the cops are looking for you?"

"I doubt it."

Jon drained his glass. "You need some money to tide you over until you get things sorted out?"

"Nope, I'm okay for now."

They sat in silence a moment, then Jon spoke. "So, what are you going to do now?"

Cliff poured himself another shot of bourbon before he answered. "I don't know, but I can't stay here any longer."

"Why don't you go down to Wilmington? You can stay on my boat for a while. It's nice and quiet, a good place to plan your next move."

CHAPTER 3

CLIFF DOUBLE-CHECKED THE directions Jon had written on a slip of paper as the Porsche bounced over a set of double railroad tracks in a gritty industrial part of LA harbor. To his right lay a vast, sulfurous oil refinery, its blackened stacks issuing lazy columns of greasy smoke. To his left, a seemingly endless train of boxcars rumbled and squealed slowly by. The road ran straight ahead toward a boatyard, then veered hard right. He followed it and two minutes later passed through the rusted iron gates of the Harbor Haven Marina, coming to a stop near the water's edge. He sat a moment, taking in the sight of a hundred or more pleasure craft moored to weather-beaten floating docks. Some of the boats looked like they'd sailed their last voyage and were patiently waiting to sink at their moorings. Cliff began to wonder if this was such a good idea after all.

Jon emerged from a rickety storage building nearby and waved to him. "It's not exactly Marina Del Rey, but it's a good place to work on the boat," he explained as Cliff followed him down a gangway that swayed under their weight. The boards of the dock itself were rough and splintery. Cliff nodded when Jon said, "Don't go barefoot around here." They passed a dozen boats tied to the dock with frayed, sun-bleached lines. Up close, they looked even more dilapidated than they had from a distance. It was near midday and the morning clouds had burned off, leaving a hazy sky and air fouled by the nearby oil refinery. Above, a yellowed sun bore down on them, causing prickly sweat between Cliff's shoulder blades.

"There's the *Staghound*." Jon pointed toward the far end of the dock.

Cliff squinted at the bright white shape in the distance. As they approached, the sleek lines of the hull came into view. Spotless teak decks, a sleek, low-slung cabin, and polished stainless-steel deck gear made the sixty-four-foot sloop stand out from the other boats like a graceful swan in a flock of sooty terns.

Cliff tilted his head back and sighted up the gleaming aluminum mast. "How tall is it?" he asked.

"Seventy-nine feet from the deck." Jon climbed a wobbly three-step staircase mounted on the dock and stepped aboard the boat. "Come on, I'll show you around."

"Wow, this isn't a boat, it's a yacht!" Cliff exclaimed. He followed Jon around the deck, fascinated as Jon pointed out details of the boat's fittings and construction.

"Let's go below, I'll show you where to stow your gear," Jon said, leading him down the companionway. Sunlight filtered through the hatches, bathing the interior in the warm glow of satin-varnished mahogany. To the left and right of the stairs were a pair of private staterooms.

Jon pointed to the door on the left, "This is my cabin. The other one is Lena's."

"Lena?"

"She's part of the crew for our trip."

"You're going on a trip?" Cliff asked, surprised.

"Yeah, to the South Pacific. We're leaving in January. You can stay here until then if you want."

Just forward of Jon's stateroom was the navigation station with a built-in chart desk and cushioned seat. Single sideband and VHF radios, a radar screen, and a Weatherfax receiver were mounted on shelves over the desk. Above them were repeater displays for wind speed and direction, knotmeter, and depth sounder. Mounted on the adjacent bulkhead was a large panel of toggle switches and meters along with a polished brass barometer and a ship's chronometer. There was also a shelf full of books on navigation, meteorology, and seamanship.

"Navigation instruments are here," Jon said, pulling open a drawer containing parallels and dividers, pencils, and a bronze sextant all perfectly arranged in felt-lined individual recesses. Lifting the lid of the chart table, he said, "Charts are in here."

Forward of the nav station was a big, built-in freezer with drawers above it. Cliff lifted the lid and peeked inside the freezer. It was nearly full. To starboard was a galley that consisted of a sink nearly as big as a washtub, a stainless steel three-burner stove set on gimbals, and a built-in refrigerator. Above the counter were dish lockers and a pantry. It looked well organized and spotlessly clean.

"The galley is Lena's domain. She'll rip your lungs out if you leave a mess here." Jon smiled as he said this but Cliff saw he was serious.

"Got it." He pictured a hard-faced woman fussing in the galley.

Forward of the galley was an L-shaped dinette big enough to seat five. The table was varnished mahogany with a beautifully inlaid compass rose made of lighter wood. Outboard of the dinette was a pilot berth. Across from the dinette, on the port side, was a settee and another pilot berth.

"The starboard berth is Mike's," Jon said. "You can use the port one. Tony usually sleeps there but he won't be back until we're ready to leave."

"They're the crew?"

"Yeah, Mike's the deckhand. Tony's a big wave surfer from Peru. He's kind of a Jack-of-all-trades, and an all-around good guy to have aboard."

Cliff inspected the pilot berth. It was about seven feet long by two feet wide, with a reading lamp, a small shelf for personal items, and a privacy curtain. "Looks snug," he said.

"Well, you want a snug berth when you're at sea. This boat is a passage-maker, not a vacation home." He opened a door forward of the berth. "The head. There's a shower in here, but it's better to use the one by the marina office."

Cliff glanced inside, noting how small it was. "Okay." He was impressed with the quality of the woodwork everywhere he looked. "Did you build this boat, Jon?"

"Not from scratch. It was originally built in New Zealand. There was a fire in the engine room. Damaged the interior and deck but the hull was intact." He laid his hand affectionately on a varnished bulkhead. "I found it propped up in a boatyard in Costa Mesa. The insurance company sold it to me for scrap and I rebuilt it."

"I've never seen anything quite like it. I bet it's really fast."

"Yeah, she was designed for speed. Won a bunch of ocean races before she burned. Now she's just a very fast cruising yacht."

Have you done many long passages in this boat?" Cliff could almost feel the big sloop tugging at her dock lines.

"Yeah, mostly to Latin America, the Caribbean, and the South Pacific, and once to Thailand."

"All the way to Thailand? That must have been an adventure." Cliff was impressed.

"That's one way to put it, my friend." Jon chuckled. He led Cliff farther forward into a kind of workshop with lockers and shelves full of spare parts on the port side, a workbench with a vise, and a plethora of hand tools mounted on a shadow board to starboard. "We call this area the shop."

"Looks like you have enough spare parts to fix anything on this boat." Cliff was impressed with the extensive inventory.

"Yessir. I put a lot of effort into being self-sufficient."

Overhead, Cliff noticed two surfboards in slings attached to the ceiling. There were slings for several more. "Mind if I hang my board up there?"

"Not at all, bring your longboard too, if you want."

Forward of the shop, sails in bags were stored outboard of a central walkway. Along the hull were hooks for ropes and shelves for spare parts. Farther forward was a bulkhead. It was painted white, with an aluminum watertight door built into it. Cliff pulled it open and poked his head into the compartment. It was also lined with shelves and lockers. "Looks like a pantry."

"Yup, we carry provisions for about four months." Jon turned back to the main cabin. "So that's the cook's tour. Let's go grab some lunch, then I gotta head back to Avila."

They walked a quarter-mile to a small waterfront café overlooking the channel and ordered burgers and beer.

When the beers came, Cliff took a long drink and asked about the trip Jon was planning.

"There's not much to it." Jon ran a hand through his sun-bleached hair and swigged his beer. "Every once in a while, I run into someone who wants something delivered to some out-of-the-way place. We're taking some crates to a guy on an island way down south."

"Wouldn't it be easier to ship them than take them by boat?" Cliff was beginning to think there was more to Jon than just a surf bum with a sailboat.

"Well, there are places in the world that UPS doesn't deliver to, and sometimes it's just better to bypass the bureaucracy. Two years ago we took a load of fine art, paintings and sculpture, to a guy who was building a home on a little island called Raivavae, in French Polynesia. He wasn't going to sell them or anything, just wanted nice art in his house. If he'd gone through regular channels the French authorities would have charged a lot more in taxes than it cost for us to sail the stuff down there. But worse than that, he'd be on their radar. They'd hassle him about every little thing."

"Who was the guy?" Cliff asked, intrigued.

"Just a guy who made a lot of money in the stock market. Leveraged buyouts or something."

"Is that legal, what you did?" Cliff wanted to know. "It sounds like smuggling."

"It's coloring outside the lines a bit, but it's not a hanging offense."

"What happens if you get caught?"

"Probably get my wrist slapped. Pay a fine. But the risk is minimal because we're just some guys on a sailboat roaming around the South Pacific looking for good surf, and happened to do a guy a favor. Very low key." Jon smiled.

Cliff pictured Jon spending months cruising on a sailboat in the tropics, as free as a man can be, riding pristine undiscovered waves. "So, how was the surf in Raivavae?"

"Pretty awesome. The island is surrounded by coral reefs. On the south side, there's half a dozen good breaks. Tony, Mike and I had them all to ourselves for six days. Then another guy showed up."

"That's it? Just one other guy?"

"Yeah, I told you it was pretty awesome."

Alone aboard *Staghound* that night, Cliff tried to get comfortable in the narrow bunk. He was still awake at midnight, listening to the rumble of powerful diesel motors approaching. Curious, he went on deck and watched a pair of tugs shepherd an old freighter into a dock at the scrapyard across the narrow channel. Shivering in the damp air, he climbed back into the bunk and tried to sleep, but he couldn't. Since he got fired, and found Janet fucking some jerk in his bed, he had operated with outward calm while inside he seethed. But now, alone in this cold, dark boat the protective heat of anger was no match for the loneliness that wrapped its icy fingers around his shoulders. Still shivering, he pulled the blanket up to his chin, but he couldn't get warm.

His thoughts were stuck on Janet like a boat jammed on a reef. *Deep down,* he thought, *I knew all along that the day would come when she would betray me. I could blame her, but that would be like blaming a rattlesnake for its bite. No, if anyone's to blame, it's me. I should have left her long ago instead of waiting for her to turn on me.*

Unable to stop shivering, Cliff got up and stole a blanket from the other berth. Back under the covers, he eventually warmed enough that his teeth stopped chattering. His thoughts turned to Bob Larsen. Bob's guiding principle was money, and money as a guiding principle might be good for a banker, but not for an architect. *Thinking I could change Bob's priorities was foolish. I should have left the firm as soon as I realized money motivated him far more than the quality of the architecture we produced. Instead, I stayed on. So what does that make me? A loser? A dupe? A failure? Weak?* Cliff stewed over these thoughts until, mercifully, sleep finally came.

An hour later, the seven o'clock steam whistle at the scrapyard blew, signaling the start of its massive machinery. His body sluggish from lack of sleep, Cliff felt for his watch on the shelf above the bunk.

"Shit, I have to be in San Luis by one," he said aloud. He found instant coffee in the galley and boiled water on the stove, careful not to leave a drop on the polished countertop. Though he was rushed, he couldn't help admiring *Staghound's* finely fitted and varnished furniture while he gulped the coffee. He grabbed his towel and trotted up to the marina office and found the showers. Having forgotten his shaving kit, he could only stare at his gaunt, hollow-eyed reflection in the mirror for a moment before hurrying back to the boat. Ten minutes later he was on the road north, arriving at Angela Braun's office just in time for his appointment with her.

"Your wife proposed a settlement, including buying your half of the house," Angela said, shuffling papers on her desk.

"Good, I was sure she'd jump at the chance to buy the place."

"She's already had it appraised and will pay you when the divorce is final, if you accept these figures," Angela paused, "I must say, she didn't waste a minute."

"That's Janet." Cliff checked the numbers and noted the appraisal came in at $500,000 and that after expenses, his share would be $150,000.

"I think the appraisal is on the low side. We can hire our own appraiser and fight for more money. You deserve…"

Cliff held up his hand. "Stop right there. The house is worth six hundred. She knows that as well as I do. I could fight it out with her in court, and let's say after a couple of court appearances and six months of back and forth with her, I get thirty thousand more. It's not worth it to me."

"Are you sure? Thirty thousand is a lot of money."

"Six months of bickering with her over thirty grand? She can have the money. I'm done with her. I never want to see her or have to deal with her ever again. Hell, I'd almost pay thirty grand to never have to see her face again."

"You're upset now, you should take a few days to think it over."

"I've already thought it over. Let's finish this now, today. I'm ready to move on."

"Well, if you're certain…"

"I've never been more certain of anything in my life."

"In that case, we'll prepare the documents right away."

"How much time do you need?" Cliff was already rising from his chair.

"We can have the documents ready by…" She checked her calendar, "Thursday."

"Perfect. See you then." He left the office feeling like a weight had been lifted from his shoulders.

～

Cliff was back in Angela's office that Thursday.

"I've prepared all the documents for you to sign." She pushed a stack of papers across the desk.

When he finished the last signature, Angela gathered up the documents and pressed a button on her desk. A moment later an assistant entered. "Please make copies of these and prepare them for filing with the court."

When the assistant left, she smiled at Cliff and handed him an envelope. "This is your half of the money in your joint savings account."

Cliff opened the envelope and checked the amount. "Looks about right," he said. "I'm surprised she just handed it over."

"I threatened her with prolonged and public litigation if she didn't release the money immediately. It would not serve her career well, or that of her boyfriend, who is married, by the way, to have a messy divorce exposed in the papers."

"Ah, her career." Cliff chuckled as he pocketed the check. "So, what's next?"

"For the moment, our work is done. I expect the final decree around May first." Angela leaned back in her chair. "What are your plans, Cliff?"

"I'm going to collect my belongings from the house. Put them in storage."

Angela, middle-aged and bookish, with ash-blond hair, removed her glasses and studied Cliff's unshaven and haggard face. "You're at loose ends now, I understand that, but will you stay in the area? Still planning to open an office, as you mentioned before?"

"My plans," he paused, "Are in a state of flux right now."

She looked at him quizzically, "Okay. Well, I wish you the best of luck, whatever you do. We'll contact you when we receive the final decree."

On the street, Cliff breathed a deep sigh of relief, glad to be out of Angela's stuffy office. Half an hour later he pulled into the driveway of his house. The curtains were drawn and the place looked dark, as if it was in mourning. He thought he might become sentimental when he saw his former home, but he didn't. He pressed the garage door opener and got out of the car as the door rolled up.

"What the hell?" he said aloud. His clothes lay in a pile in the middle of the garage floor. Beside them were a few boxes of his belongings. It appeared that Janet had tossed the stuff in a pile and left.

"The fucking bitch," he said to himself as he furiously rummaged through his clothes, sorting out what he wanted from the rest. He filled the Porsche to the roof with clothing and stuffed the boxes into the car's tiny trunk. He grabbed his longboard from its rack on the wall and strapped it on his car, thinking enviously of Jon and his crew riding perfect South Pacific waves.

Surveying what was left of his things on the garage floor, he felt as though he had shed his old life, like a cobra sheds its skin, and the fury he felt a few minutes before ebbed. He shut the garage and drove away without a backward glance.

At the public storage place on Higuera Street in San Luis Obispo, the clerk looked out the window at Cliff's overstuffed car.

"Kicked out?" he asked. "Or walked out?"

"I guess you've seen this before," Cliff said.

"You aren't the first person to show up here with a carload of stuff and a sad story." He shoved a rental form across the counter. "All I have right now is a ten-by-twenty. Fifty bucks a month. Pay six months in advance, you get a ten percent discount."

The clerk sounded to Cliff like he had long since lost interest in marital tragedies, which was just fine with him. He signed the form and paid for six months, then dumped his things in unit 171.

Back in his car, he headed north on the freeway. *They'll be putting up construction fencing at the Buffum ranch soon,* he thought. *I want to see the place again before I'm locked out.*

The Porsche came to a stop at his usual spot under the oak. He got out of the car and sat on the crumbling concrete foundation of the burned farmhouse, looking down the hill toward the highway. Surveyor's stakes stood in the tree-dotted landscape like the scouts of an invading army, marking where the tractors would soon tear up the earth and subdue the land under a layer of blacktop and concrete. He sat with his elbows on his knees and, suddenly exhausted, hung his head and stared at the ground.

"You look like hell," a voice behind him said.

Cliff turned to see Alice Hilliard standing there, not ten yards away.

"What are you doing here? Ain't you supposed to be at work?" She came forward, her Stetson low on her forehead against the setting sun.

"I quit the firm, or got fired, take your pick."

"I heard. There was another fella from your outfit here yesterday. Said he was takin' over on account o' you gettin' yourself in trouble with the boss." She squinted at him. "That right?"

"Close enough."

"It was over that tree, wasn't it?" It was a statement, not a question.

Cliff slowly shook his head, "Not exactly. I was fed up with the place anyway." He stood to leave. "Have a good evening."

"Hey." She reached out and caught him by the wrist and he turned around to face her. "I appreciate you tryin' to save that ol' tree." She let go of his arm.

"Sorry it didn't work out the way you and I wanted it to." The sun was touching the horizon. "I should be going now."

"You take care o' yourself, you hear?" she called after him as he reached his car.

Driving south, Cliff reflected on Angela Braun's words: "You're at loose ends now." *Yes,* he thought, *definitely at loose ends. I have no idea what the future will bring. It's strange to suddenly be free of the mundane responsibilities of home and work, but it's also an empty feeling.*

It was near midnight and fog had descended on the harbor when Cliff arrived back in Wilmington. He drove slowly, groping through the gloom until he found the gates of the Harbor Haven marina. Walking down the dock to the *Staghound,* mist clung to his lashes and the stubble on his face. Water had pooled on the canvas dodger over the boat's companionway and dripped down his neck as he fumbled with the lock on the hatch.

Inside the boat, it was cold enough that his breath turned to fog. He undressed and climbed into the pilot berth. *Tomorrow,* he thought, *I will have no place to go and nothing to do. It's as if I'm starting over again. Starting from scratch. Alone.*

After a few minutes of fruitless contemplation he fell into a troubled sleep.

CHAPTER 4

COLD GRAY DAWN came too early. Cliff gave up trying to sleep and clambered out of his bunk. Shivering, he hurriedly dressed in jeans and a sweatshirt.

In the half-light of the galley, he stood at the stove and counted the seconds until the water boiled. He brewed a cup of instant coffee, scalding his lips when he took his first sip of the bitter stuff. Still, it was better than nothing.

The whistle blew at the scrapyard across the channel. He went on deck and watched the loading of the freighter that had arrived the night before. A conveyor belt rose some sixty feet above the dock and cantilevered over the old ship. With a dull roar, the conveyor dropped scrap metal into the ship's hold, sending up a malignant cloud of dirt and rust that drifted on the wind across the channel. Cliff soon learned that this would go on day and night until the ship rode so low in the water that he wondered how it could stay afloat, let alone survive crossing the ocean.

He shoved his hands in his pockets and wandered around the docks and ramshackle streets of the area. The marina was deserted except for a few people who lived aboard their decrepit boats. They kept to themselves and went about their business mostly in silence, like specters in the fog. The streets were dirty and smog-choked, filled with the constant rumble and roar of the ever-present big rigs that clogged the intersections and railroad crossings.

Back aboard the *Staghound*, he slumped on the settee in the main cabin. Boredom was not something he had often felt in his life, but now it weighed on him. He stared emptily at the books on the shelf in the nav station. Curious, he opened one titled 'Celestial Navigation' and was soon immersed in the history of that ancient art. The story of John Harrison's clock, the first accurate shipboard chronometer fascinated him. Harrison's invention enabled navigators to find their longitude at sea, solving a problem that had plagued them since the first ship ventured out of sight of land. The steady ticking of *Staghound*'s chronometer took on new significance to him.

He lifted the sextant from its felt-lined drawer, feeling the heft of the big bronze instrument. He studied the engraved numbers on the arc and worked the index arm. Afternoon turned to evening as he read the book and played with the sextant, forgetting to eat until his growling stomach demanded food.

"There's not much in the way of provisions aboard," Jon had said, "But feel free to rummage through the pantry if you get hungry." Cliff found a can of soup and warmed it on the stove. He was spooning it straight from the pan when he heard a noise on deck and hurried up the companionway to investigate.

"Can I help you?" he asked of a young man who was struggling to heave a large, heavy blue bag onto *Staghound*'s deck.

At the sound of Cliff's voice, he whirled around and glared at him. "Hey! What the hell are you doing on this boat?" he demanded.

"I'm a friend of the owner." Cliff eased himself into the cockpit, ready to defend himself if necessary. "I'm staying aboard a few days."

When the man came aboard, Cliff extended his hand, "Name's Cliff Demont. Are you Mike?"

'Yeah." The stranger hesitated, eyeing him suspiciously.

Cliff nodded toward the bag, "Need a hand with that?"

"There's a lot of homeless people around here. They'll break into a boat and stay until the owner kicks 'em out." He looked Cliff up and down. "I guess you don't look like a squatter."

"No, I'm not a squatter." Cliff gave him a friendly smile.

"Come on, I'll help you with that bag." He moved forward on deck and the man followed.

"What is this thing?" Cliff asked as they dragged it across the deck. "It must weigh a couple hundred pounds."

"New mainsail." Mike slid the foredeck hatch open and they lowered the sail into the boat. "Don't shut the hatch, I have another sail to bring down." Agile as a cat, he jumped to the dock and pushed a large dock cart up the gangway to the parking lot, returning three minutes later with another bag.

"Which one is this?" Cliff asked as he helped lift the second bag onto the boat.

"Number two genoa." The man wiped his hands on his jeans. "Jon didn't tell me anyone was staying aboard." He went down the companionway and forward to the sail locker, where he muscled the two sails into their respective bins. When he returned to the main cabin, Cliff watched Mike's eyes come to rest on his suitcase, lying on the settee next to his bunk.

"What's that?" Mike asked.

"My stuff."

"Jon'll blow a gasket if you scratch the varnish with that thing."

Cliff stared at the gray Samsonite. *Of course!* he thought, *I should have gotten a duffle bag.* "I'll get rid of it tomorrow."

Mike's gaze shifted to the pan of still-warm soup on the stove. He stared at it a moment then abruptly turned and headed up the companionway, muttering to himself.

Cliff followed and watched him go up the gangway at the end of the dock and drive away in a white van. *Guess I got off on the wrong foot with Jon's deckhand,* he thought. He returned to the galley and finished his soup. There was something about Mike that didn't fit the laid-back characters Cliff had imagined Jon's crew to be.

The next morning he bought a couple of duffle bags and transferred his clothes from his suitcases into them, glad it had been Mike instead of Jon who had admonished him.

At noon the sun came out, prompting Cliff to grab his board and head down to Huntington Beach for some waves. The wind was beginning to blow but he didn't care. Surfing Huntington felt like coming home to him. He stayed in the water all afternoon.

Back on the beach, tired from the sun, wind, and waves, he sat on the sand and stared out to sea. A small sailboat passing in the distance, its taut sails catching the afternoon breeze, reminded him of his father's boat.

Jack Demont had kept a twenty-two-foot sailboat in Alamitos Bay. When he was a kid, Cliff used to count the days until he was let out of school for the summer. Then the two of them often sailed across the channel to Catalina Island. It took all day for the little boat to make the trip from Long Beach, and before they were halfway there Jack would turn the helm over to Cliff. "Wake me when we reach Ship Rock," he would say, and disappear into the cabin for a nap.

It was no small thing for a boy to command a sailing vessel, and ten-year-old Cliff reveled in it. The feel of the tiller in his hand meant freedom to him. Even then, he knew that beyond the west end of the island, it was open ocean all the way to Hawaii. On a sailboat, anything was possible.

Watching the little boat in the distance, Cliff thought of his father again. More than anything else, they had shared an abiding love for the sea. Jack once told him that someday, they would go cruising to tropical isles with exotic names like Tahiti, Bora Bora, and Rarotonga.

A careening big rig on the San Diego Freeway had ended Jack Demont's dream and shattered young Cliff's world. His mother, never particularly fond of the boat, sold it immediately after the funeral.

Cliff, bereft of that connection with his father, had buried those boyhood memories of Catalina long ago. Now they surfaced again: His dad's boisterous laugh. The hikes to the peaks above the bay. The other kids that spent summers on the island. A girl with blonde hair and the sweetest smile he'd ever seen, who gave him his first shy kiss. The big full moon hanging over the lights of LA. The feel of his dad's boat as it gathered speed and skimmed over the water.

Along with the memories came a flood of emotions, and there, sitting on the beach, he found himself almost weeping. And just as powerfully, came the answer to the question he'd been asking himself. He knew what he was going to do. He gathered his surfboard and towel and headed back to the *Staghound*. Cliff Demont was not at loose ends anymore.

He left before dawn the next morning, gunned the Porsche over the Vincent Thomas Bridge and took the sweeping turn onto the Harbor Freeway with the needle on the speedometer touching ninety. Rush hour traffic slowed him to a crawl in LA, but it thinned as he topped the Sepulveda Pass, heading north. By eleven o'clock, the morning clouds had burned off. Cliff downshifted and took the Avila Beach exit.

He glanced to the right when he passed the road that led to his hillside home. A fleeting moment of anger came and went as the memory of Janet and her scumbag boyfriend flashed through his mind. For an instant, he was gripped by an urge to drive by his house but he resisted. Fuck that, he told himself, that part of my life is over.

He pulled to a stop in front of Jon's Spanish style house in a quiet neighborhood on the south side of the village. The front yard was enclosed by a high adobe wall with a heavy wrought iron gate that creaked on its hinges when he pushed it open. Inside the wall, the yard was a shady oasis of ficus and pittosporum, bromeliads, and bougainvillea, with a flagstone path leading to a broad portico at the front of the house.

When he rang the bell a young Asian woman answered the door. She told him Jon was in the woodshop and led him in silence through the house to the backyard, which was planted in the same style as the front yard.

"Jon," she called from the door of the woodshop, "Someone's here to see you." She smiled shyly and left when Jon looked up from his workbench at the far end of the shop.

"Cliff!" Jon came forward, wiping his hands on a rag. "Everything okay on the boat?" He was dressed in faded jeans, a baggy paint-stained sweatshirt and sandals, his mop of blond hair held in check by a bandana.

"Yeah, fine," Cliff replied. "I thought I'd drop by and check in with you." He looked around the small but well-equipped workshop. The pleasant smell of freshly cut wood hung in the air, reminding him of his days working as a carpenter while he was in college. "You haven't been around the boat for a while."

"I've been busy, getting ready for our trip," Jon said. "Making boxes." He led Cliff back to his workbench, where a partially completed box sat. It was about thirty inches long by sixteen inches high and wide. The bottom and sides had been glued together with epoxy, and he was in the process of fitting the lid on it.

Cliff studied it, noticing the craftsmanship in the reinforced joints. "This is a helluva box," he said, running a hand along a well-finished edge.

"It's a bit overkill but the truth is, I enjoy the work. I want them to be sturdy and watertight because we never know what we'll run into at sea."

Cliff hesitated a moment, watching him adjust the position of the lid on the crate. "I was wondering, how many people do you usually have in the crew on your voyages?"

"Four or five," Jon replied without looking up.

"I'd like to go with you."

Jon stopped working and stared at Cliff. "Why?"

Cliff told him the story of sailing with his father, and that he died before he could realize his South Pacific dream. "Aside from that, right now I'm as free as I'll ever be."

Jon laughed, "Well, I gotta agree with you there," he said, then continued more seriously, "This trip isn't a vacation, it's business. Besides, I already have a crew."

"How many?" Cliff wanted to know.

"Four."

"But you said you sometimes take five. I could be the fifth," Cliff insisted. "I'll help you build these crates, swab the deck, or whatever else you need done."

Jon picked up a piece of wood and eyed an edge for straightness. "I'll think about it. Right now I have work to do."

Cliff watched a moment longer. "How many do you have to build?"

"Twenty."

"Sounds like a lot of work." He nodded toward a stack of plywood on a table next to a bandsaw. "Those the pieces for the rest of the boxes?"

"Yup, they're all cut to size. I just need to sand the edges before I glue them together." Jon finished fitting the lid and set the assembly on the floor. "First one's done."

Before he looked up, Cliff had found a piece of sandpaper and was working on one of the plywood pieces. Jon watched him a moment, slowly shook his head, then started sanding another piece.

They worked in silence for a quarter-hour and the stack of sanded panels grew quickly. Suddenly Jon tossed his sandpaper aside. "You've never been offshore, have you?"

"Nope. Just sailing with my dad, but he taught me a lot of seamanship because he was sure that someday we'd take that cruise. Said I needed to know what I was doing when we got out there." Cliff finished one piece of plywood and started on another. "I believed him and learned everything I could about sailing. But when he died, my ma sold the boat and I took up surfing instead. I've forgotten a lot of it, I guess."

Jon watched him in silence for a minute. "There's some bar-clamps hanging on the wall over there," he said, pointing toward the far end of the workshop. "We need eight of them to glue a box together."

While Cliff got the clamps, Jon mixed epoxy glue. Together they assembled two crates. Wearing latex gloves, Cliff was wiping off excess glue that had squeezed out of a joint when the Asian woman appeared at the door.

"Lunch is ready," she said and disappeared back to the house.

"Your girlfriend?" Cliff asked as they walked through the backyard to the house.

"Suki? No, she lives in the guesthouse." Jon pointed to a cottage next to the main house. "She looks after the place when I'm traveling."

Suki had set a table for them on the veranda overlooking the backyard, then disappeared again. Poached salmon on a bed of jasmine rice, green salad, and sparkling water.

"I always thought you lived in a bedroom of your parents' house," Cliff said as he savored the fish. "You know, a surf bum with wealthy parents."

"Yeah, I was." Jon squeezed a lime over his salmon. "But then my folks died and left me this place and a small trust fund. Just enough to buy *Staghound*."

"Sorry about your folks. Both died at the same time?"

"Killed in a plane crash in West Africa." Jon buttered a roll and passed the basket to Cliff. "My dad was an engineer-inventor.

Had fifty-seven patents to his name. Most of them weren't commercially valuable, but a few were. He retired at fifty and became a photographer. His specialty was endangered animals in Africa. He photographed lions, elephants, Cape buffalo, and animals that were being poached to extinction in the Sahel. He was popular with the environmentalists, which made him unpopular with hunters and poachers. He and my mom were flying from Bamako to Timbuktu in a Cessna, following some South African poachers when the plane went down. They were never found." Jon poured more water. "No one knows if it was shot down or had an engine failure."

"That's an amazing story," Cliff said. "My dad was killed in a car crash on the San Diego Freeway when I was twelve. My mom died five years ago." Cliff sipped his water. "Cancer."

"And here you are. No job, no woman, no money and no prospects," Jon said. "And you think a boat ride will fix things for you?"

"Not at all. I don't need anything to fix what's wrong with my life," Cliff shot back. They finished lunch and headed back to the workshop. By late afternoon they had assembled all but two of the crates. Cliff swept sawdust and wood shavings from the floor while Jon cleaned sticky epoxy off the tools they'd been using.

"Thanks for your help," he said as Cliff prepared to leave. "But the answer is no. I have a crew for this trip."

"I understand. Mind if I stay aboard a few more days?"

"Not at all. I'll be down there in a week. Maybe we can grab some waves together."

Cliff headed out the front door, "See you in a few days." Driving down the highway toward Wilmington, he was not about to give up on sailing to the South Pacific on *Staghound*. He considered how he would change Jon's mind. *First, I'll buy everything a sailor needs for an ocean voyage, so I'm ready to go if the opportunity arises. Second, I'll learn everything I can about the Staghound. I'm sure there's a lot of work involved in preparing a boat for a long trip. I'll be able to help the next time Jon or Mike shows up. I'll figure out what they need before they need it.* Then another thought struck. *Twenty boxes. Why does he need twenty boxes? What's he going to put in them?*

It was after nine when Cliff arrived back in Wilmington. The damp air created swirling haloes around the yellowish lights above the gangway and docks. In *Staghound's* cabin, he took off his jacket and headed straight for the workshop where there was a shelf lined with books and manuals for the systems and equipment on the boat, all neatly arranged alphabetically. He settled into his bunk with the manual for the Adler refrigeration system. It was near midnight when he finished all the "A's".

In the morning he started on the "B's", pulling the Barient manual from the shelf. He disassembled and lubricated all eight of *Staghound's* Barient deck winches as well as the coffee grinder, an apparatus mounted in the middle of the cockpit that looked like a pair of bicycle pedals mounted on a pedestal. The handles were linked to the two biggest winches, one on each side of the cockpit. When he was finished, his fingers were coated with grease, but he could strip and reassemble a winch in a couple of minutes. Later, he started at the bow of the boat and, working his way aft, studied every fitting and piece of equipment on the sloop's deck. By late afternoon he had the Harken manual out and had memorized the name and purpose of all the Harken blocks, cleats, and other gear that was mounted in the cockpit. The sun was just touching the hills above San Pedro when he stood at *Staghound's* five-foot diameter steering wheel. He ran his hands over its elk-hide-covered rim and for a few seconds, he closed his eyes and imagined *Staghound* with a fair wind on her starboard quarter, bound for some unnamed tropical isle.

When he opened his eyes, a woman was standing on the dock

next to the boat, staring at him. Cliff sprang from the wheel, his face flushed in embarrassment. "Can I help you?" he asked.

The woman stepped aboard and set her backpack on the cockpit seat. "You're Jon's friend, correct?" she said, appraising him with large brown eyes.

"My name is Cliff, I'm staying on the boat temporarily."

"Lena Voss. Jon told me about you."

She was not much more than five feet tall, slim-hipped and athletic. Her face had the smooth skin of a child, but her eyes held an older, more experienced look, making it impossible for him to determine her age.

Jon said she was the ship's cook but she doesn't look like any cook I've ever seen, Cliff thought. "I was checking the steering system," he said, pointing to *Staghound's* wheel.

"I saw," she said, wearing a bemused smile. She started down the companionway.

Cliff followed her, glad he'd managed to keep the galley clean.

She took a clipboard from her pack and started opening lockers above the stove, taking inventory of food and spices.

"Jon told me about your upcoming voyage. It sounds exciting," Cliff said as he watched her work.

"It will be an interesting trip." She spoke perfect English but with a slight accent that he couldn't place. She finished in the galley and moved to the pantry, forward of the workshop.

"Why are you staying on the *Staghound*?" she asked, without looking up from her clipboard.

"Marriage broke up." Cliff didn't want to share the details and changed the subject. "You have an interesting accent. Where are you from, originally?"

"I was born in Chile. I came to America when I was twelve, after the coup."

"The coup?"

"In Chile. My parents sent me here because it was too

dangerous after Pinochet took power in seventy-three," she said while she counted canned goods in a locker.

"Forgive me, I guess I don't know much about Chilean history."

"Not many Americans do. Chile is a small country. It is only interesting to Chileans."

"Do you miss it, your home country?" he asked.

"Certainly. But I cannot go back."

"Really? Why not?"

"My parents are doctors. They emigrated from Spain in 1955 to escape Franco's secret police. They are socialists so, naturally, they moved to the mountains near the Bolivian border, bringing health care to the poor and the natives." She jotted something in her notebook. "When Pinochet took power, the socialists and communists were hunted down. My parents refused to leave the country, but they sent me to live with my aunt in Pasadena. I am an American citizen now."

"What about your parents, are they still in Chile?" Cliff asked.

"Have you heard of the Villa Granada?" Her eyes flashed when she spoke.

"No, it sounds like a resort."

"It is a prison in Santiago, the capital of Chile. A special place for political prisoners." She looked up from the clipboard and stared at him.

"I'm sorry to hear that." He didn't know what else to say. "Are they safe there? Can our government help you get them out?" The words sounded lame, and he regretted them instantly.

"No." A condescending smile crossed her face. "The CIA is General Pinochet's benefactor. He wouldn't last long without American support."

"I should have known that."

"It's one of America's greatest failures," she said bitterly.

"That we support dictators?"

"No, that the American people don't know we support

dictators." She moved back into the main cabin and picked up her coat and backpack. "I'll be back with provisions in a few days. If you're still here, you can help load them on the boat."

Alone in the cabin, Cliff had a vague sense that somehow the world had just shifted on its axis. He climbed into his bunk with the manual for the Raymarine radar system, which he had planned to study. But though he tried, he couldn't concentrate on it. His thoughts kept returning to Lena Voss.

CHAPTER 5

CLIFF CROUCHED AND squeezed his body through the watertight hatch leading into the triangular confines of the chain locker, the forward-most part of the boat. In the semi-darkness, he saw a fat stainless steel pipe jutting two feet down from the deck above. Heavy anchor chain emerged from it, culminating in a briny pile at his feet. Aside from a spare anchor, a couple of coils of rope, and some anti-chafe material, there was nothing else in this compartment except a heavy aroma of salt and seaweed. He backed out and closed the hatch.

Now he was in the sail locker, standing in a central passageway between waist-high sail bins. This is where Mike had stowed the mainsail and #2 jib. He read the tags on other sail bags: Genoa, #3 Jib, #4 Jib, Spinnaker, Stays'l, Storm Jib, Storm Trys'l. On the starboard side of the boat, he checked a bank of lockers above the sail bins. The shelves were full of sail hardware and spare parts. On the port side, a couple of dozen coils of rope hung from large hooks mounted on the hull. Each one had a label above it: Afterguy, Jib sheet, Spinnaker Sheet, and so on.

He reached for one of the spinnaker sheets, a thick hundred-fifty-foot coil of rope with a stainless-steel shackle at the end of it. At his touch, it fell from its hook and slid down behind a sail bin. He had to reach over the mainsail bag to retrieve it. To lift the heavy coil he leaned on a sort of box or compartment that was molded into the side of the hull, semi-concealed behind the line of ropes hanging above it. Curious, he tried to open it but couldn't until he felt along the bottom of it and found a pair of latches. When he released them, the cover opened, revealing a compartment five feet long, a foot-and-a-half high, and eight inches deep. It was only by chance that he stumbled on it because it blended in with the contour of the hull.

He pulled more coils of rope off their hooks so he could get a better view of the compartment. "I'll be damned," he said aloud as he peered into it. "A hidden gun safe."

He reached in and released a carbine from its bracket, an AR15. He cleared the chamber and held it up to the light coming in from the hatch overhead. It was a weapon he knew well, a semi-automatic version of the M16. With its stubby barrel, it felt almost like a toy in his hands. He carefully replaced it and lifted a shotgun from the bracket next to it, a 12-gauge Mossberg pump with an eighteen-inch barrel. He replaced it and pulled a handgun from its plastic holster. It was the same type he carried in Vietnam, a .45 caliber M1911. He hefted the weapon in his hand, recalling an incident when he had used his service pistol in combat. It saved his life when a squad of Vietcong guerillas posing as ARVN military police tried to hijack the truck he was riding in. He put it back and inspected the rest of the contents, finding ammunition, spare magazines and gun cleaning supplies. *A well-stocked armory*, he thought. He closed the cover and re-hung the ropes that concealed it, wondering why Jon had so much firepower on a sailboat.

In the two days since Lena's visit, he had gone over every inch of *Staghound* that didn't require climbing the mast or diving under the hull. One thing that stood out was the meticulous organization of it all, from sails to spare parts, even to the pots and pans in the galley. There seemed to be a place for everything, and everything was in its place. It gave him a powerful insight into the mind of Jon Hartmann. On the surface, he was casual and informal, but the way the boat was organized and maintained revealed a more disciplined person.

Cliff discovered a three-ring binder labeled '*Staghound*' among the books on the shelf in the workshop. When he opened it, he couldn't help murmuring, "Thanks, Jon." The binder was filled with specifications and scale drawings of the boat itself. As an architect, plans and specifications were like milk and cookies to him. He noted that the boat had been designed by one Hermann Friedriksen and built in Auckland in 1974. The scale drawings were foldouts and Cliff spent hours sitting at *Staghound*'s dinette, drinking coffee, and studying the boat's plumbing and electrical systems, structural details, and rigging plans. When he was finished, he knew *Staghound* as well as anyone. That is, he reminded himself, aside from the fact that he'd never actually sailed the boat.

The following morning a cold front arrived. It rained all day and into the next. Cooped up inside the boat, Cliff perused the ship's library. A book on knots caught his eye. In the sail locker, he found a four-foot length of quarter-inch rope, whipping twine, and a rigging knife. Using the book as a guide, he whipped both ends of the rope, then practiced tying various knots: The indispensable bowline, the sheet bend and clove hitch, the rolling hitch and the Prusik knot were ones his father had taught him and they were all in the book. It was almost as if Jack Demont was there again, patiently teaching him as the rain drummed on the deck above. The more he played with the rope the faster his fingers moved until the knots came automatically. When he was sure he could tie any of them blindfolded he stuffed the rope in his pocket and put the book back on the shelf.

When the storm broke, it left brilliant sunshine and blustery winds in its wake. The sound of halyards slapping against masts carried throughout the marina, but there was none of that aboard *Staghound*. No longer surprised at the way Jon kept his boat, Cliff saw that every halyard had long since been secured, and while the other boats in the marina seemed to look more and more tattered with each gust of wind, *Staghound* appeared solid and seaworthy, ready for anything.

He was on deck checking the boat's docklines when a couple of guys appeared, bringing long-handled brushes and cleaning supplies. With a brief nod to him, they set to work hosing and scrubbing the boat's deck and cabin, talking to each other in Spanish, ignoring him.

"How often do you guys wash the boat?" he asked the older one in Spanish.

He peered at Cliff, surprised to be addressed in his native tongue. "Two times a month," he replied. He turned away and sprayed soapsuds off the cabin, then started wiping it down with a chamois while the other guy polished a pair of cowl vents on the foredeck.

Cliff watched and listened for a few minutes, then left them to their work and drove to the marine store.

"Looks like someone's gonna get some real nice Christmas presents," the cashier said as he rang up the foul weather gear, sea boots, knitted watch cap, and a dozen other seafarer's necessities that Cliff piled on the counter.

"What? Oh yes, Christmas." Cliff had forgotten that the holiday was only a few days away.

"We can gift wrap these items for you." The clerk's vest was embroidered with Santa's sleigh being pulled across the sky by a pair of dolphins.

"No thanks." Cliff gathered up the goods and headed out the door.

"Merry Christmas!" The cashier called after him.

Man, I am in no mood for Christmas, Cliff thought as he drove back to *Staghound.* The gaudy decorations that festooned the lampposts and storefronts along the streets annoyed instead of cheered him. Janet had once said that he was like a bear who retreats to his cave when he's wounded, while she was inclined to reach out to friends. *Well, I feel like a bear now. Holed up in a boat while the rest of the world celebrates.*

Back aboard *Staghound*, he packed the sailing gear he bought into a duffle bag, ready for use if the opportunity arose. Night had fallen and he sat alone in the darkened boat. Janet crept into his thoughts again. *Was I too hasty in divorcing her? Could I have found a way to forgive her, rebuild what we once had? Don't be ridiculous,* he scolded himself. *It's okay to grieve over the loss of what I thought we had, but since she was fucking someone else, what we had was really just an illusion. The lesson here is that I should learn the difference between illusion and the real thing.*

His thoughts turned to Kelly. *She's recently divorced. I should have asked her advice: Reach out instead of hole up. I think I'll call her right now.*

He started up the dock toward the payphone outside the marina office but hadn't gone ten feet when he saw Lena Voss walking down the gangway. Two others were behind her, each pushing overloaded dock carts. In the darkness, he couldn't make out what was in the carts.

"You're still here." She wore the same appraising expression he'd seen once before.

"Yup." Somehow, he was at a loss for words.

"Good, you can help us load provisions."

It was obvious to Cliff that she was used to being in command.

Lena introduced Mike and Tony, and the four of them worked for an hour, loading and storing canned and boxed food in *Staghound's* cavernous pantry.

This woman would make a good drill sergeant, he thought as he shoved canned goods into a locker.

When the work was done, they gathered in the main cabin. Lena made notes on her clipboard while Mike, dressed in jeans and a hooded sweatshirt, took inventory of sail repair supplies.

Cliff was impressed by Tony. He had an accent like Lena's, but the similarities ended there. He was well over six feet tall and built like an NFL quarterback. His piercing obsidian eyes and black hair pulled back in a ponytail gave him a sinister look. "Jon mentioned you're from Peru. I've never been there but I've heard there's lots of good surf there." Cliff remarked.

"Yes, big waves." His broad grin revealed perfect teeth. "*Olas grandes!*"

Cliff recalled Jon saying Tony was an all-around good guy to have aboard. *If you need a bodyguard or a bouncer,* he thought, *Tony would be your guy.*

"*Es muy guapo,*" Tony said to Lena in a low voice, "He's quite handsome."

Lena glanced at Cliff and replied in the same language, "He used to be married. I don't think he's your type. Get your things, we have to go."

Cliff overheard them and stifled a smile. *They don't know I speak Spanish*, he thought. *It sounds like Tony's gay.*

Lena slid her clipboard into her knapsack. "Jon will be here in the morning. We are going sailing, to test the new sails."

"Does that mean I should leave the boat?"

"Jon will have the final word, but I don't mind if you sail with us. Testing sails is a lot of work and an extra person would be helpful." She gathered her jacket and hat. Mike and Tony also prepared to leave.

"Well, I'd love to join you. I'll speak to Jon in the morning," Cliff said. *Sounds like Lena is second in command,* he thought. *The others are already climbing off the boat, so they don't have a say in who sails aboard Staghound. I wonder if she really does the cooking.*

❧

"All right, let's get the mainsail bent on and see how it looks before the wind comes up," Jon said to the crew. He had arrived early and didn't object when Cliff asked if he could sail with them today. The others had arrived at nine and immediately set to work.

"First, we're gonna attach the tack and clew to the boom," Mike said as he and Cliff worked the heavy mainsail out of its bag. "We'll shove the battens into their pockets as we hoist."

The jargon was foreign, but it was obvious to Cliff what they were doing. Tony cranked the winch that raised the sail while Mike inserted its luff slides into *Staghound's* mast. It took an hour to get the big sail attached to the mast and boom, the battens secured in their pockets, reefing lines run, and the sail hoisted to the masthead.

"We used Kevlar to reinforce the corners," Mike said, pointing at the gold-hued fabric sewn into the tack, clew, and head of the sail.

"Pretty," Lena said.

Jon started *Staghound's* diesel engine. They cast off the dock-lines and slowly backed out of the slip. Cliff noticed that Jon, who was so laid back and unassuming ashore, was a commanding leader aboard the *Staghound.* He was amused to see the transformation in him.

They motored slowly down the channel toward the open water of LA harbor. Once they were in the main channel a light westerly breeze rose and the boat heeled slightly to port under the big mainsail.

"What do you think?" Jon asked Mike, nodding at the sail.

"A lot more roach than the old one," Mike said, sighting up the back edge of the sail.

"I like the full-length battens," Tony added, his silvered sunglasses glinting in the sun.

Cliff observed them, absorbing what they were saying and how they moved on the boat. Out of the corner of his eye, he noticed Lena studying him. They locked eyes for a second, then she looked up at the sail and added a comment about spreader patches.

"Light air today," Jon said, glancing skyward. "Perfect for what we have to do." He pointed the boat directly into the wind and the crew hoisted the new #2 jib, and *Staghound* came alive as the sails were sheeted home.

Tony stood at the coffee grinder in the middle of the cockpit and spun the handles, trimming the jib in until Mike was satisfied. With the sails perfectly trimmed, *Staghound* gathered speed, heading straight down the channel. They sailed down the harbor toward Long Beach for half an hour, then Jon turned the boat upwind. Tony motioned Cliff over to the coffee grinder. "When I say, 'Grind!' you crank those handles as fast as you can until I tell you to stop."

Mike hooked a bosun's chair to a halyard that Tony had led to a primary winch, which was linked to the coffee grinder.

"Grind," Tony said when Mike secured himself in the chair.

Cliff spun the handles, pulling Mike up the mast. When he reached the lower spreaders Tony said, "Stop."

Like a performer on a trapeze, Mike swung out to the end of the lowest spreader, hooked his leg around a shroud to steady himself and drew a line on the jib with a black marking pen, then pulled himself to the mast and did the same on the mainsail.

"What's he doing?" Cliff asked.

"Marking the sails for spreader patches," Lena said.

"Done!" Mike shouted when he finished marking the sails at the lowest spreader.

"Grind," Tony said. Cliff spun the handles again, raising Mike to the middle spreaders where he marked the sails again.

Puffing hard, Cliff hoisted Mike to the upper spreaders, where he repeated the process.

When he finished marking the sails Tony lowered him back to the deck while Cliff caught his breath.

They sailed all afternoon, and by the time they got back to the dock Cliff's arms were limp with fatigue, his back was sore and he had cracked his shins against the cockpit sides a couple of times.

He was about to sit down in the cockpit when Jon pointed to him and Mike.

"Let's bag the main and jib. They're going back to the loft for spreader patches," Jon said.

"I'll lay out the sausage bag on the dock," Mike said to Cliff. "You and Tony feed it over the lifelines. Jon and I will flake it into the bag. Got it?"

"Sausage?" Cliff asked.

"You'll see." Mike jumped off the boat and spread a blue nylon bag on the dock. Cliff estimated it to be eighteen feet long and three feet wide, with a zipper running nearly its full length.

Tony stood on deck near the mast. "I'll do the luff, you do the leach. Watch me and do exactly as I do."

Cliff followed Tony's actions and within five minutes the mainsail was folded, accordion-style, on top of the bag. Mike and Jon pulled the bag around the sail and zipped it closed, then folded it in quarters lengthwise and tied it into a tight bundle. They bagged the jib the same way.

"Is that how you always bag the sails?" Cliff asked Tony as he watched Mike and Jon load them into dock carts and wheel them up the gangway.

"Every skipper has his own preferences but on *Staghound*, we do it this way." Tony turned toward the cockpit, where Lena had appeared with sandwiches. "Ahh, mi amor!" he exclaimed. "Your cooking is the only reason I sail on this bucket!" He gestured to Cliff, "Come, before Mike gets back and eats them all!"

The sun was touching the hills to the west and a chill wind blew across the channel, but it didn't bother *Staghound*'s hungry crew.

"So, how did you like sailing today, Cliff?" Jon asked, grinning.

"I'm a little wrung out, but it was totally fun!" he exclaimed.

"Yeah, we kinda gave you the business, but you did okay."

"I'd love to go again anytime."

"The sails will be finished next week, right, Mike?"

"Yup," Mike said. He was stuffing a sandwich in his mouth and drinking a beer at the same time. "We can sail again next Saturday."

"Perfect." Jon finished his sandwich and drank the last of his beer. "Hurry up guys, we still have work to do tonight," he said to Tony and Mike. He grabbed his jacket and called to Lena who had disappeared below, "You ready?"

She came up the companionway with her knapsack slung over her shoulder. "Let's go."

After they left, Cliff slumped on the settee. Though he was tired, he felt good. He couldn't remember the last time he had done so much physical work as today. He was impressed with the way the crew worked together. Jon would say something like "Let's tack." and Mike would load the lazy jib sheet onto the winch while Tony assumed his position on the coffee grinder and Lena stood at the mainsail controls. All of this was done without a word spoken until Mike said "Ready." Jon would say "Tacking." There would be a flurry of activity and flapping sails as the boat turned and settled on its new course. Then Mike would say a couple of words to Tony as they dialed in the trim of the jib to perfection while Lena handled the mainsheet. To Cliff, the way they worked together with perfect timing and coordination was beautiful to watch.

The hours he spent studying *Staghound* paid off. When they changed from the #2 jib to the genoa, the jib lead blocks had to be moved aft on their tracks. He knew what to do and moved them before anyone said anything, surprising Jon and Mike. Then when Mike and Tony were sheeting the big headsail in, he ran forward and "skirted" it over the lifelines, before being told what to do. After each tack, jibe, and sail change, he coiled ropes and stowed them keeping the cockpit cleared for the next maneuver. He took his turns on the coffee grinder and tailing in the sheets and halyards. It was fun, but more than that, he had been part of the crew and not a mere passenger. He felt good about that too.

CHAPTER 6

IN THE MARINA'S shower room, Cliff stood under a torrent of deliciously hot water. The blast massaged the muscles of his back and shoulders. *Just what I need after surfing cold winter waves this morning.* He toweled himself, dressed quickly, and checked his watch. In the week since they'd gone sailing aboard *Staghound*, he surfed every day, but he was really just waiting for today and the chance to sail again.

Walking down the gangway, he saw Mike on the dock struggling to lift another bulky sail bag onto *Staghound's* deck.

"Fucking Tony never showed up at the loft," he said when Cliff approached him. "I had to load both of these sails myself."

"I'll give you a hand."

With the sails aboard the boat, they waited in the cockpit for the others to arrive.

"It ain't like Tony to not show up," Mike said.

"Did you try calling him?" Cliff asked.

"Nah, he never answers his phone. Jon's gonna be pissed." He nodded toward the gangway, "Here comes Lena. She ain't gonna be too happy either."

"Have you seen Tony?" Mike asked when she stepped aboard.

"No. Wasn't he going to help you with the sails?" She set her knapsack down and started down the companionway.

"Yeah, but he never showed," Mike said as she disappeared below. He glanced up toward the gangway. "Jon's here."

Lena stuck her head out the companionway and they watched Jon hurry down the gangway with a newspaper in his hand and a grim expression on his face.

"Let's take a walk, Lena." Jon beckoned her to join him on the dock. They headed toward the far end of the marina.

"Wonder what that's all about," Mike said, shading his eyes against the morning sun as he watched them walk away.

"Whatever it is, Lena's upset about it," Cliff said. She had put her face in her hands as Jon held her in a gentle hug.

A few minutes later Jon returned without her.

"What's going on?" Mike asked.

"Tony's dead."

The color left Mike's face. "Dead? What happened?"

Jon took a deep breath. "He was ambushed in his condo." He handed Mike the newspaper and pointed to an item on the front page, below the fold.

"I'd better find Lena," Mike said after he read the article. He gave the paper to Cliff and hurried down the dock in search of her.

The article was titled, "Two Dead in Bizarre Murder Mystery." Cliff read it aloud. "Passersby were horrified when they discovered a man impaled on an eight-foot wrought-iron fence outside a condominium complex in an upscale Pasadena neighborhood. The man had reportedly been thrown from a third-story balcony above. When police entered the condo unit, they discovered another man, identified as Juan Gonzalez, dead from multiple gunshot wounds. Police say Mr. Gonzalez arrived home sometime after midnight and surprised an intruder inside. A struggle ensued and Gonzalez, a large and powerfully built man, threw the intruder over the balcony, but not before he was shot three times in the arm and torso. The assailant was killed instantly when he landed on the spiked top of the fence. Mr. Gonzalez appeared to have tried to administer first aid to himself but was unable to stop the bleeding from a chest wound and was pronounced dead at the scene. No calls to 911 were received. The identity of the assailant is unknown, but a nine-millimeter handgun with a silencer was found in the bushes nearby. Investigators would not release any more details but urge anyone with information about the incident to contact the Pasadena Police Department." Cliff looked up at Jon after he finished reading. "Juan Gonzalez, is that Tony?"

Jon nodded.

"Was he related to Lena?"

"No, but they go back a long time." Jon looked toward Lena, who was standing at the far end of the floating dock.

Cliff followed his gaze and watched her shake off Mike's attempt to put an arm around her. "Do you know what happened?" he asked. "An intruder with a silencer on his gun isn't a burglar."

Jon continued to stare at Lena. "Tony was a man of the world. He did business with dangerous people."

Cliff scanned the article again. "Is Juan his real name?"

"Probably not," Jon took the paper back from Cliff. "Let's just say he had more than one passport."

"Was he doing business with you?"

"No, just giving Lena a hand with a project she's been working on."

Cliff frowned, "Is she in any danger?"

"Probably not."

"Why would someone murder Tony?" Cliff asked.

"Couldn't tell you, even if I knew." Jon glanced at him and back to Lena. "But she's not involved with his business dealings. I'm sure of that."

"Okay. I guess it's none of my business. We still going sailing today?" Cliff had been looking forward to it.

Mike and Lena walked slowly back toward *Staghound*. When they boarded the boat Lena's eyes were still moist.

"You okay?" Jon asked her.

"I'll be alright," she replied. "We have to move quickly now."

Jon started to say something, but she cut him off, "We don't have time to be sentimental. We have to move the boxes." She glared at him when he hesitated. "Now."

This woman's got a lot of grit, Cliff thought as he watched her expression change from grief to a resolute mask.

"We may have to rethink the trip," Jon said.

"No." She looked at the three men. "We've come too far to stop now. The police will investigate Tony's death. We have to get the boxes before they find them."

"Hold on, Lena." Jon put a hand on her arm. "We can stop now. We just take them out to sea and dump them. Mike and I will get them today, okay?" He shot a glance at Mike.

"No," Mike said. "I'm with Lena. Let's put them aboard and get out of here."

"Get below," Jon said, glancing around. "I don't want the whole marina listening to us." In the main cabin, they gathered at the dinette.

Mike spoke first, "Why is he still here?" he asked, jerking a thumb at Cliff.

"You need at least four in the crew, don't you?" Cliff said. "I can take Tony's place,"

Mike snorted in disgust. "We don't need no rookies aboard. All he'd do is get in the way," he said to Jon.

"It'll be harder, but we can sail with three," Jon said. "The question is, is it wise to go forward without Tony?"

"Hell yes, it's wise. All we gotta do is deliver the damn crates, collect the money, and go surfing, just like we planned. Only difference is we split the money three ways instead of four."

Lena had taken off her hat, freeing her long, dark hair. Her tears had been short-lived, though her eyes betrayed her grief. "We mustn't forget why we undertook this mission," she said in a quiet voice. "Abandoning it now would be a betrayal of Tony and the people who are waiting for us."

Jon wavered. "If we go with three crew, you'll have to stand a watch as well as cook. That okay with you?"

"If I stand a watch, you and Mike will have to help with cooking." She looked at both of them and managed a wry smile.

"I don't doubt that the three of you can sail this boat, but a fourth would make it a lot easier," Cliff interrupted. "Isn't that right, Jon?"

"What about operational security, huh?" Mike broke in, pointing an accusatory finger at Cliff. "We don't know this guy. Maybe he knows more about Tony gettin' hit than we do. Or maybe he's working for the government."

Jon smiled. "You're getting a little paranoid there, Mike. I know Cliff. He's a square from San Luis Obispo who lost his job and his old lady. He's not working for anyone." He glanced at Lena. "What do you think?"

"I think you're both terrible cooks," she said, eyeing Cliff while she spoke to Jon. "When we were sailing last week, he seemed to know what to do. He lacks experience but he's eager, and he's a quick study. I think he would be a good deckhand."

"Wait," Mike interjected, "Tell us why you even want to go on this trip," he demanded of Cliff.

Cliff looked each of them in the eye. "You guys are on some kind of mission and now one of your team is down. I don't know what your project is and I don't care. You need a replacement to help sail the boat and I'm volunteering to go. You asked why, I'll tell you. For the first time in my life, I'm free. I want to go for the adventure, to fulfill a dream I've had since I was a kid." He stared directly at Mike, "As for the money, keep it. I'm not interested in the money, just the sailing."

Jon raised his eyebrows toward Mike, "Satisfied?"

"I guess so, but I still say the three of us could do it without him."

"I've tasted your cooking. No, we couldn't." Jon reached out his hand to Cliff. "Welcome aboard." Cliff shook hands with each of them.

"Alright, that's settled," Jon said. "Mike, you and I are going to the warehouse. Lena will get the fresh food and Cliff will top up the water tanks while we're gone. Let's move."

✑

Cliff mixed chlorine dioxide pellets into a bucket of water, enough to keep 240 gallons drinkable for six weeks. When the pellets were dissolved, he poured the mixture into the starboard fill pipe, a fitting on *Staghound*'s deck that fed a water tank below. Then he stuck the hose into it and turned the water on. While he waited for the tank to fill, he pondered the events of the morning. *These people are smugglers*, he told himself. *In my former life, I wouldn't think of associating with their kind. But that was before. I can't explain it, but the guy I used to be doesn't exist anymore. That guy was careful and conservative. He didn't take chances and he didn't really live, dammit! I'm going sailing with these people and if bad things happen, I'll either survive or I won't. Either way, it'll be better than sleepwalking through life.*

His thoughts turned to Lena. *Jon may be the skipper of the boat, but Lena seems to be the kingpin of this operation. It sounds like money is the driver for Mike, and maybe Jon too. But it's clearly something bigger than that for her. She seems deadly serious about this "mission", as she calls it.*

Water spurted out of the tank's vent, telling him it was full. He tightened the cap and moved to the port side of the boat and repeated the operation. With the port and starboard tanks full, *Staghound* carried nearly five hundred gallons of fresh water. He went below and pulled out the duffle bag that held his seafarer's equipment. Mike had hung his foul weather gear on hooks next to his bunk, and Cliff did the same with his own brand-new gear. He arranged his sea boots on the sole, stowed his sea bag in a cubby at the foot of his berth, and shoved his toiletry kit into a smaller cubby just as Mike had done, all neat and organized. After living aboard for the last few weeks he was acutely aware of the benefit of not leaving things lying around, and he made sure all his possessions were put away.

He heard a knock on the hull and went to investigate.

"Give me a hand with these," Lena said, lifting a large bag of onions from an overfilled dock cart. They worked for a couple of hours, loading and storing a variety of fresh fruit, eggs, meat, and vegetables aboard *Staghound*.

"The potatoes will last three months in the reefer," she replied when he asked how long they would keep. "We have to freeze the onions or they'll spoil in a couple of weeks." She packed them, four at a time, in plastic bags and put them in *Staghound's* cavernous freezer. "We'll have fresh eggs for a month, then switch to frozen, which aren't nearly as good."

"What about powdered eggs?" Cliff asked.

"Jon forbids them on his boat."

"Smart man," Cliff said with a chuckle. He was impressed when they finished stowing the food. It all went into *Staghound's* pantry, fridge and freezer so the galley looked as tidy as the day he first stepped aboard.

They carried the used packaging up to the bins near the marina office. On the way back Cliff offered his condolences over Tony's death. "Was he like a big brother to you?"

"More than that, he was my savior," she replied. "And you are an architect. I think of that as a proper, respectable profession. Architects are steady and predictable, no?"

"Yes, I'd say that's part of being an architect." They reached the top of the gangway and paused, looking out over the marina. The water in the channel sparkled in the bright winter sunshine.

"Some would say abandoning a safe and predictable office for the deck of a sailboat a thousand miles at sea seems a bit extreme, don't you agree?" She had turned and looked him in the eyes as she spoke.

"Steady and predictable are what I've been for as long as I can remember. Those are fine qualities but they are not necessarily the road to happiness. I need a change, that's all." He caught himself gazing into her eyes and looked away. "Is that a good enough answer?"

"It sounds like an honest answer." She paused to watch a squadron of pelicans skim just above the water, then bank left to avoid a tugboat coming up the channel. "Will you go back to your profession, and your wife when it's over?"

"Profession yes. Wife no." He looked at her again. "What about you? It seems like this voyage is a delivery trip for Jon and Mike, but you call it a mission. Why?"

She turned her face into the breeze. Her hair blew back, revealing her features in a way he hadn't seen before. "I am in a race against time. My parents have been in Pinochet's gulag for years. They are old and not well. Tony found a way to get them out and help hasten the end of Pinochet's regime at the same time." She looked at him again. "I don't want them to die in prison." Before she could say more, the sound of Jon's Volkswagen van rose and they watched it come to a stop near the top of the gangway, followed by Mike's nondescript van. "They're here," she said as she started toward the Volkswagen. "Come along."

Jon gave her a thumbs-up as they approached. "It went well," he said. "We got all twenty boxes. No signs of trouble."

Mike climbed out of his van and went to open its back doors, but Jon put up a hand.

"Leave them 'til after dark," he said. "Most of the people that live around here will be drunk by then. Nobody'll notice us lugging them down the dock." He nodded toward a man heading down another gangway with a paper bag that held a bottle cradled in his arm and a cigarette dangling from his lips.

"We have the fresh food aboard and the water tanks are full," Cliff said. "What's left to do before we leave?"

"Get fuel, bend on the sails, load the cargo, and install the table."

"Gotta run jack lines too," Mike said. "How about the dinghy?"

"Yeah, we'll stow it on deck like we usually do."

Aboard *Staghound*, they got to work.

"Since you're taking Tony's place, you're on the winch," Mike said as they laid the big mainsail out on deck and shoved the battens into their pockets. It was dark before they had the sail bent on and flaked on the boom.

"Alright," Jon said, "Let's get those crates."

"These things gotta weigh a hundred pounds each," Mike said as he and Cliff loaded a box from the back of his van to a dock cart. "The cart can't handle more than one at a time."

Jon was waiting when they got the cart to the boat. "Easy now, don't scratch the varnish," he said as they maneuvered each gray-painted box down the companionway. He had taken up some of the floorboards in the middle of the main cabin, leaving a space big enough for three boxes abreast and three lengthwise. Without the floorboards in place, they rested on the floor timbers which were set thirty inches apart, matching the length of each box.

"Nice design," Cliff said, admiring how the nine boxes nested perfectly together, three wide and three long.

"Yup, I'm ready for the next nine," Jon said.

When they were finished, eighteen boxes were stacked together and lashed down with webbing straps. They made a block four feet wide by seven feet- six inches long, by thirty-two inches high, in the middle of the main cabin.

"There's two more boxes in my van," Jon said. "Put them in the sail locker, under the sail bags."

With all the boxes aboard, *Staghound*'s crew gathered in the main cabin.

"I'm leaving," Lena said to Jon. "I'll send a message tonight, telling them we'll be there around February fifth instead of the end of the month."

"How long will it take them to acknowledge?" he asked.

Lena picked up her jacket and put on her cap. "Could be a day or a week."

"Tell them to acknowledge by radio, because we're shoving off in twenty-four hours."

Mike grabbed his jacket. "I'll walk up with you," he said to Lena. "I'll be back in the morning and take the boat to the fuel dock first thing," he said to Jon.

After Mike and Lena left, Cliff stared at the boxes. "What's in them?" he asked.

"I'm not going to answer that question," Jon said. "The less you know, the better it'll be for you if something goes wrong." He switched on a red cabin light in the galley. "Want a beer?"

"Why not." Cliff took the offered bottle. "My guess is weaponry."

Jon froze and stared at him. "What makes you say that?"

"The boxes smell like gun oil. It's faint, but it's there."

Jon stared at him another instant, then twisted the cap off his beer. "Well, you didn't hear it from me. The less said about it the better, okay?"

"Got it." The beer felt good on Cliff's throat. "Where, exactly, are we taking them?"

Jon pulled a nautical chart of the Pacific Ocean from the navigation desk. "Ever heard of Robinson Crusoe Island?" he asked as he spread it out on the dinette table.

"I read the book in junior high school."

Jon ran his finger down the chart to a tiny speck off the coast of Chile. "This is where we're going."

"How many miles is it from here?"

"We'll cover a bit less than six thousand getting there. It'll take about thirty-five days, sailing nonstop."

Cliff studied the chart for a moment, puzzled by the name, "Why is it labeled Juan Fernandez on the chart?"

"Juan Fernandez is the name of the island group, which actually consists of three islands," Jon said as he pulled out another chart. "This is a small-scale chart that shows them in detail." He pointed to the easternmost island. "This the main island. It used to be called Isla Mas a Tierra, but a few years ago the Chilean government changed it to Isla Robinson Crusoe. The real Robinson Crusoe was a cat named Alexander Selkirk. Back in 1704 he got into an argument with the captain of the ship he was on, a British privateer called the *Cinque Ports*, and he was put ashore on the island. He spent over four years there, completely alone." Jon took a drink from his beer. "He was picked up by another ship in 1709. When he got back to England, Daniel Defoe wrote a book about his ordeal, except he changed his name from Selkirk to Crusoe. Two hundred and fifty years later the Chileans decided they could attract tourists to the island if they renamed it after the famous fictional Crusoe." He took another sip of beer. "It didn't work."

Cliff studied the chart. "So that's where we're headed?"

"Yup. It's pretty isolated so it's a good place to rendezvous. That's where we'll meet Lena's friends."

"Her friends? Do you know them?" Cliff asked.

"Lena does. They work for the rebel forces trying to overthrow that bastard, Pinochet."

"And you think what we're doing is safe?"

"Yup. We're just going to drop off the crates and collect the money, then we're free to explore the islands. There could be some good point breaks here and here." Jon pointed to the southwest and southeast corners of Crusoe Island. "As far as I can find out, no one's ever surfed them. We might be the first." Jon's blue eyes shone in anticipation of surfing undiscovered waves.

CHAPTER 7

CLIFF EASED THE Porsche into the storage unit and pulled the door shut. He snapped the padlock and walked out to the street where Jon waited in his van.

"All set?" Jon asked. Light rain had begun to fall and he switched on the windshield wipers as Cliff climbed in.

"Yes. My future ex has been forwarding my mail to my lawyer. She'll keep it 'til I get back. So yeah, I am ready to go."

Jon maneuvered the van into heavy San Luis Obispo traffic, its wipers clacking unsteadily. "It's going to be a slow drive back to Wilmington in this weather."

"What time are we shoving off?"

"Probably not until midnight." Jon slouched over the wheel as he drove. His baseball cap was turned backwards and his clothes smelled of wood and varnish. "I didn't finish the table until a couple of hours ago."

Cliff leaned back in the seat and watched the scenery go by. "It'll fit over the crates in the main cabin?"

"That's right. A disguise we've used before."

"You've really thought of all the contingencies," Cliff remarked. "I'm impressed."

"Not all. We sure didn't plan on losing Tony."

It was only yesterday that Cliff learned of Tony's death but it seemed like a week ago. "I hope I can fill the gap his passing left. It seems like a big decision to take on a new crewman at the last minute."

Jon glanced at him before he spoke. "Tony was a great shipmate. He was fearless and a very capable sailor. I'm going to miss having him aboard." He pulled the zipper on his jacket a little higher. "He was also inexperienced in the beginning, kinda like you. But he grew into an excellent sailor."

The van's feeble heater didn't put out enough warmth to keep the windshield from fogging. Jon pulled a rag from under his seat and wiped it clear.

Cliff watched the wipers swing back and forth, smearing the light from oncoming headlights into streaks. "Lena said he was her savior."

Another glance from Jon. "Yeah, he helped her get out of Chile when she was a kid."

Cliff waited for him to say more, but Jon focused on driving instead.

"Do you know why I invited you to join the crew?" Jon suddenly asked.

"No."

"First, I know you've been studying like hell to learn about the boat. You even tore down and lubed the winches, right?"

"How'd you know?" Cliff asked, surprised.

"The marina manager's been keeping an eye on you. You haven't done anything that I didn't know about in twenty-four hours." Jon grinned. "He gave you excellent marks." He downshifted as the van labored up a steep section of the freeway. "Second, I've seen you surf massive waves at Mavericks."

Cliff was a little irked that he had been watched. He let that go but couldn't connect surfing and crewing aboard *Staghound.* "What does surfing Mavericks have to do with this sailing trip?"

"Nothing, except Tony was a big wave rider too."

The rain turned to drizzle when they arrived at the marina. Jon parked near the gangway and they unloaded three large slabs of wood from the van, carrying them down to the boat one by one. At Jon's knock on the hull, Mike appeared in the companionway. "There's more pieces in the van," Jon said. "You guys bring them down while I get started assembling the table."

An hour later, Cliff ran his hand over the varnished mahogany top of the big drop-leaf table. It covered and disguised the stack of crates. With the leaves extended it reached across the boat from the port settee to the starboard. Folded, they left room to pass on both sides.

"It'll fool some people, but if we get boarded by the Navy or Coast Guard, the jig'll be up," Jon said.

While they worked, Lena had emerged from her cabin and made sandwiches and coffee for them.

"You should eat before we get underway," she told them as she passed around the platter.

"Are we leaving tonight?" Cliff asked.

"We ain't foolin' around," Mike said through a mouthful of sandwich. "We've got fuel, the dinghy's lashed down and the jack lines are run. Only thing left to do is finish these sandwiches." He winked at Lena.

She ignored the wink. To Jon, she said, "I got a message through to Villareal. They'll be at the rendezvous on February fifth."

Jon sat at the nav station and flipped half a dozen switches on the electrical panel. Blue-green light from the radar screen illuminated his face.

The idea of actually leaving had been an abstraction for Cliff. A dream that would never come to pass. Now the adrenaline rose in him. On the outside he managed to contain himself, inside he was suddenly a bundle of nerves.

Jon looked at him and grinned. "Better get into your foulies."

Cliff fumbled with the buttons and zippers of his yellow foul weather pants and jacket. His fingers trembled as he worked his feet into new sea boots. Mike, already suited up, headed up to the cockpit and started the diesel engine. The vibration of the motor resonated through the boat, sending another shiver of anticipation down Cliff's spine. He pulled his knitted watch cap on and joined Mike in the cockpit.

"Clear the dock lines," Mike said.

Cliff jumped from the boat to the dock and untied all four lines. Lena stood on deck and took the lines in as he cleared each one. Freed from the dock, *Staghound* floated motionless at first, then began to drift slowly out of her slip. Cliff paused, taking a last look around the rain-soaked marina, then leaped aboard the big sloop.

At the helm, Mike turned the boat into the fairway leading to the channel. "The rain stopped but there's fog ahead," he said. "It's going to be dicey until we clear the breakwater."

Cliff strained his eyes looking forward but all he could see was the dim glow of the red and green running lights on *Staghound*'s bow. Mist collected on his lashes and ran into his eyes, further clouding his vision.

"How do you know which way to go?" Cliff asked.

"Skipper's watching the radar," Mike replied.

Just then, Jon's voice came from below. "You're in the channel now, come to port ninety."

Mike repeated the command and turned the wheel, watching the compass as the boat changed course.

Cliff stood on deck gripping a stanchion in the darkness, tense and ready to jump into action at Mike's command.

"We're in the turning basin now," Mike said. He was calm and relaxed, as if handling the boat in fog was something he did every day. "In a minute we'll be in the main channel."

"Starboard ten degrees," Jon's voice drifted up the companionway. "Steady there."

A minute later a blinking light came into view a hundred feet off the port bow.

"Base of the bridge tower," Mike said. High above, the intermittent loom of lights on the Vincent Thomas Bridge came into view. A minute later they vanished in the gloom.

"You're drifting right, come to port five," Jon said. A moment later he appeared in the companionway and looked around. "I have a ship on the radar. He's a quarter-mile dead ahead, moving at five knots, we'll follow him down the channel and out through the breakwater."

"Roger." Mike adjusted the throttle, matching *Staghound*'s speed to that of the unseen ship ahead. His watch cap was pulled down to his eyebrows and the collar of his jacket rose to his beard. He reminded Cliff of a Viking.

Jon went back to his post at the radar screen.

"We're at the end of the channel, Mike. Turn thirty degrees to port." Jon called out quietly. Five minutes later he spoke again. "Ten degrees to port… Steady there, you're on course for Angel's Gate."

Cliff felt *Staghound*'s bow rise and fall almost imperceptibly as the vessel approached the harbor entrance. The deep baritone note of the foghorn on the Angels Gate lighthouse came across the water and before long he saw the loom of its light brighten the fog every thirty seconds. At first it was ahead, then off the starboard side of the boat. Half a minute later it was slightly aft of them. *Staghound* was outside the harbor and Jon called out a new course of 170 degrees, or south-southeast on the compass.

Cliff leaned over the compass and watched as the boat settled on a course of 170 degrees. "Where are we headed?"

"We're gonna leave the east end of Catalina to starboard,"

Mike said as he pushed the throttle forward. *Staghound* gained speed while Cliff thought about his reply.

"Catalina is to the southwest, so why are we going southeast?"

Mike, more relaxed now that *Staghound* was in open water, chuckled. "Magnetic variation."

"Variation?"

"Yup, the compass points to the magnetic north pole, not the true north pole. In this part of the world, the difference between magnetic north and true north is about thirteen degrees. So if we want to head straight south, we steer a course of 167 degrees on the compass."

While Cliff pondered what Mike said, Lena came up the companionway bearing cups of coffee. Her hair was tucked up into a knitted watch cap and she wore a short jacket and jeans. She looked more like a ski bunny than a sailor to Cliff.

"I spiked the coffee with a shot of rum. Happy new year," she said, handing Cliff and Mike steaming mugs.

"Goodbye eighty-six, hello eighty-seven," Mike said, raising his mug.

Jon joined them. "To the new year, may it be better than the old one," he said, raising his own mug.

With the urgent preparations to set sail, Cliff had lost track of the date. Now he sipped his coffee and looked forward into the darkness. *There's nowhere I'd rather be*, he thought, *than embarking on a mysterious voyage on New Year's Eve.*

For three hours *Staghound* moved over the black water. Though the visibility was no more than a few dozen yards, sounds were amplified by the fog. The dismal foghorn on the lighthouse competed with others coming from unseen ships anchored off the harbor entrance.

"Sounds like they're coming from all directions," Cliff said.

"Yup." Mike's face was barely illuminated by the dim red light in the binnacle. "Without radar, we'd have to anchor and wait."

Another hour passed. Jon emerged on deck and looked around. "We're about six miles from the island," he said.

"Yeah, fog's lifting," Mike said, nodding toward the southwest where a sprinkling of lights had appeared beneath low hanging clouds.

Jon peered into the distance. "Yes, that's Avalon." He rose and stretched. "I'll relieve you at six," he said before going below.

Cliff checked his watch. It was a quarter of four. He'd been awake for twenty-two hours.

"Take the helm." Mike motioned Cliff to stand behind the wheel.

"What course should I steer?" Cliff asked, shaking off his drowsiness.

"One-seventy until we clear the east end of the island. Then we'll head southwest.

It had been calm all night, but now Cliff felt a puff of wind on his cheek, out of the northeast. "Should we hoist the sails?"

Mike, lounging on the cockpit seat, sniffed as if he could smell the wind. "Nah, this ain't the real breeze. Better to keep motoring until after sunup."

An hour later the mountainous east end of Catalina Island was visible, a dark mass off the starboard beam. Mike leaned over and checked the compass. "We can start our turn now, bring her to two hundred."

Another hour passed. The sky toward the southeast had begun to lighten while *Staghound* glided over a calm sea. At six, Jon relieved Cliff at the helm. "Get some rest."

Cliff dropped down the companionway, hung his foul weather gear up, and barely made it into his bunk before he fell asleep.

"Wake up!" Mike jabbed a finger at Cliff's shoulder. "We need you on deck."

Cliff groggily tumbled out of his bunk. Shifting patches of blinding sunlight poured through the cabin windows as he groped for pants and shirt. When he went on deck everything had changed. Under a brilliant sun, deep blue northwesterly swells rolled *Staghound*, causing him to grab for a handrail to steady himself.

Mike grinned, "Haven't quite gotten your sea legs yet, huh."

Cliff focused on the horizon and took a moment to get his bearings. "I guess not." He managed a lopsided grin.

"It's almost noon," Jon said. "The wind's filling in, we're going to make sail."

Looking aft, the dark palisades of Catalina Island stood out in the midday sun. "How far are we from the island," Cliff asked. Despite the sunshine, the cold breeze made him shiver.

"Fifteen miles," Jon said. He pointed to another island off the port beam. "That's San Clemente."

"Take a good look at it," Mike said. "That's the last of the US you'll see for the next three months."

Cliff gazed at the island, a hump of land not more than ten miles away and his pulse quickened at the thought of sailing into unknown adventures.

At the helm, Lena was in command. "Alright, let's get the main up. We're burning fuel." To Cliff, she said, "You're on the winch."

He took his position at the coffee grinder and made sure it was linked to the winch Jon had wrapped the main halyard around. "Ready here," he said.

Mike clipped the halyard to the mainsail and shouted, "Halyard's made!" while Jon uncoiled the mainsheet.

Lena turned the boat into the wind and the crew hoisted the big sail.

Five minutes of work on the coffee grinder left Cliff puffing, but the sail was up and Jon was busy sheeting it home. Cliff glanced back at Lena, who had brought the boat back to its original course. Normally noncommittal, she gave him a brief nod of approval.

Staghound heeled to port under the pressure of the mainsail and gained speed.

"Jib up!" Jon shouted above the growing noise of the wind in the rigging.

Cliff spun the handles of the coffee grinder again and the jib rose up the headstay, snapping and flogging in the growing breeze. When it was up, he let go of the handles and coiled the halyard while Jon trimmed the jib.

Staghound heeled before the wind, gathering more speed. Occasional bursts of spray flew from the bow, sending cold seawater streaming aft along the port gunwale.

Oblivious to the spray, Mike moved around the boat, checking the trim of the sails and making adjustments to the vang, outhaul, and jib lead until even to Cliff's inexperienced eye, the sails were trimmed to perfection.

With a twinge of envy, Cliff watched the easy, confident way Mike handled himself on *Staghound*'s slanted deck. He noticed that Jon moved the same way, keeping his legs slightly bent and his center of gravity low, knowing exactly what to grab, when to pause, and which ropes to pull without hesitation.

He stole a glance aft, where Lena stood at the helm. She glanced from the compass to the bow, then to the telltales on the jib as she steered. Then those smoldering eyes fixed on him. Suddenly uncomfortable sitting there, he rose and made his way across the deck to the mast, doing his best to get there without stumbling. "Need help?" he asked Mike who had coiled a rope and was securing it to the mast.

"Sure, you can stow the other lazy jack." He pointed to a rope that lay on deck. "We won't be using 'em for a while." He left Cliff alone and ambled back to the cockpit.

After a couple of tries, Cliff managed to stow the port lazy jack exactly the way Mike had done the starboard. He imitated Mike's gait and got back to the cockpit without mishap.

"The three of us will take a regular watch and Lena will monitor radios and weather," Jon said. He held up a card for Cliff to see. "I'll post this schedule in the nav station. You might need to refer to it at first," he said. "But in a couple days it'll be instinctive for you. We stand four-hour daytime watches: Six to ten, ten to two, and two to six. At night, three-hour watches: Six to nine, nine to midnight, midnight to three and three to six." He looked at his watch. "It's 1400 hours. Mike will take the first watch, starting now, then you, then me. Got it?" He handed Cliff the card.

Cliff studied it a moment. "We run on twenty-four-hour time?"

Jon nodded. "From now on, as long as we're at sea."

"So, six pm is 1800?"

"Yup. It's your responsibility to be on deck when your watch begins. Set your alarm ten or fifteen minutes early, whatever you need, so you don't turn up late."

"Yeah, it's really bad form to show up late for your watch," Mike said.

Cliff sensed all eyes were on him. "I understand."

Lena spoke up. "I always leave a thermos of coffee in the galley for night watches. If you run out, there's a kettle on the stove. Feel free to make more. One more thing, don't leave dirty dishes in the sink."

Cliff hadn't considered the almost military precision of shipboard life, but it was obvious that it needed to be this way. *There're probably dozens of little rules that I'm not even aware of,* he thought. "I'm sure I'll screw up a bit at first, but you'll only have to tell me once."

"Alright," Jon said. "Our course will take us west, then southward. We'll pass to the west of Clarion Island then head southeast, crossing the equator a hundred miles west of the Galapagos. Then we'll head for Crusoe Island. Today is January first, I expect to arrive there between February fifth and fifteenth." He looked around at the others, "Any questions?" When there were none, he turned and went below, followed by Lena.

Mike stood at the helm as *Staghound*, driven by her powerful sails on a beam reach, surged over the waves.

So begins my first day at sea, Cliff thought. He climbed up to the starboard rail and stood facing forward. From that vantage point, he took in the graceful curve of *Staghound's* sheer, her sails towering above, and the sparkling sunshine on the white-flecked waves. In his mind, it was a picture of supreme beauty and endless possibilities. *Yes,* he thought, *this is why I came on this voyage.*

CHAPTER 8

THE COLD WIND drove Cliff below to rummage through his sea bag
for a warmer jacket. He was putting it on when his eyes seemed
to go out of focus, his face flushed and he was seized by a powerful wave of nausea. He lurched toward the companionway, barely
noticing Lena in the galley. On deck, the fresh air seemed to ease
the nausea, but it didn't last. He lunged for the leeward rail and
vomited. He hung on to the lifeline for ten minutes, feeling like
he had the flu and a hangover at the same time. When he couldn't
vomit anymore, he slumped onto a cockpit seat while Mike
watched in amusement.

"Here." Lena had appeared with a wad of paper towels.

Cliff wiped his mouth and nose. When he finished he croaked
a thank you to her.

"Turn around," she said. She ran her fingers up the back of
his head, lifting the hair from his neck. With her other hand,
she pressed a dot of adhesive tape behind his ear. "You'll feel
better soon."

Cliff touched the patch with his fingers, "What is it?"

"Scopalomine." She took the paper towels from his hand and
tossed them over the side. Without another word, she turned and
went below.

Cliff slouched on the cockpit seat after she left, struggling
with another bout of nausea.

"You're just seasick," Mike said. "C'mere, take the wheel." He beckoned Cliff with a hand.

Cliff slowly shook his head, "I think I'm gonna barf again."

"Nah, c'mon over here and take the wheel. If you stand up, get your eyes on the horizon and quit thinking about yourself, you'll feel better."

Cliff stood unsteadily and made his way over the heaving deck to the helm. "I'll give it a try."

Mike stayed next to Cliff when he took the wheel. "Our course is two-fifty, but don't worry about that, just keep the wind coming over the starboard rail."

Cliff glanced down and saw the lubber line hovering over '250' on the compass, and quickly looked up to the horizon ahead, where the sun was dipping below the horizon. If he felt better, he would have thought it was a beautiful sunset, but now he was just glad to settle his eyes on something stable.

"Anticipate the roll of the boat," Mike said as Cliff labored to keep *Staghound* on course. "When you feel the stern lifting, give her a little helm before she starts to yaw."

Cliff concentrated on the feedback from *Staghound*, feeling a little extra pressure on the wheel when a wave lifted the stern, and a bit more heel as it rose under the hull. He turned the wheel to port a little, then as the wave passed, the pressure eased and he let the wheel come back to straight. *Staghound* sailed a straighter course instead of yawing from port to starboard and back.

Mike sat on a cockpit seat and watched Cliff handle the boat for another ten minutes.

"You're getting the hang of it," he said. "Pretty soon it'll come natural."

Cliff's nausea eased as he concentrated on guiding the big sloop over the waves, glancing at the compass occasionally to be sure he was still on course. A few minutes later, night had fallen and Mike switched on the vessel's running lights, red and green on the bow, and a white light facing aft.

Before the last rays of the sun disappeared, a gibbous moon rose in the east, causing *Staghound*'s hissing wake to shimmer in the moonlight. Cliff checked the knotmeter, 9.5 knots. He did the math in his head. *At this speed, we'll travel twenty-eight miles in the next three hours.*

Mike interrupted his thoughts, "My watch is over. You're on until twenty-one hundred."

"Okay. I'll see you at oh-three-hundred, I think."

"That's right." Mike disappeared below.

Alone on deck, Cliff stood at the helm and focused on the faint line of the horizon. Half an hour later he felt well enough that his mind began to wander. *What if we hit a whale? In this darkness, I'd never see it.* He strained his eyes searching for dark shapes in the water ahead. Instead, a light came into view off the port bow. *A ship! Is it headed at us?* Soon he could make out a pair of white lights up high and a green one farther down. *Okay, the green means I'm seeing his starboard side. If I'm right, he'll cross in front of our bow.* He was tensely watching the lights grow closer with every passing minute when Jon came on deck with a cup of coffee in hand.

"Looks like a container ship," Jon said, casually. "Headed for LA." He turned his gaze to Cliff. "How're you feeling? he asked. "Lena said you had a touch of *mal de mer.*"

"Better. That patch she gave me seems to be working." He jutted his chin toward the oncoming vessel. "I was going to turn to port if that ship got too close."

"Good. Give him plenty of room."

"It seemed to come out of nowhere," Cliff said.

"In clear weather, a ship's lights become visible roughly eight miles away. He's probably doing twenty knots, and we're doing nine, so the closing speed between us is nearly thirty knots."

"Wow, that's only about fifteen minutes from the time we see him until he runs us down."

"Yeah. Keeps you on your toes." Jon pointed to more lights off the port beam. "That looks like a fisherman."

Cliff had been so focused on the ship ahead that he hadn't seen the other lights. He peered at them, mentally preparing to take evasive action.

"He's headed northwest," Jon said. "Probably making twelve knots. He'll pass ahead of us."

They watched in silence as the ship passed by, a mile off *Staghound's* starboard beam. Cliff breathed easier when he could see its bright white stern light receding in the distance.

Jon drained his cup and glanced at his watch. "I'll relieve you in an hour," he said before going below.

Alone again, Cliff turned his attention to the fishing boat. All he could see of it was a green light and a couple of white lights, but it had moved forward, so instead of on the port beam, it was now forty-five degrees off the port bow. Slowly the white shape of its superstructure emerged from the darkness and Cliff heaved a sigh of relief when he realized it would cross *Staghound's* bow, a quarter-mile away. With no other vessels in sight, the tension in his back and shoulders eased and he took a lighter grip on the wheel. The moon rose higher in the sky, and the wind remained steady out of the northwest. *Staghound* heeled before it and reeled off another nine miles before Jon appeared on deck to relieve him.

"The ship's log is on the chart table," he said as he took the helm. "Jot down the average speed and course for your watch before you turn in."

In the dim red glow of the chart table light, Cliff sat and studied the logbook. It was open to a page labeled 'Dead Reckoning Log' and each line was divided into boxes for speed, course, wind, sea state, sky, and barometric pressure along with space for a brief note. The last entry had been Mike's at 1800. Cliff considered the conditions he had experienced on his watch and concluded that they were pretty much the same as what Mike had logged in, so he copied what Mike had noted. Speed: 9.0 knots, Course: 250M, Wind: NW @ 15knots, Sea State: 4, Sky: 0. He checked the barometer on the bulkhead, it read 1020Mb, and he wrote 1020 in the box labeled 'Baro'. When he was finished, he leaned back and reread his notations, then went back up the companionway.

"Seasick again?" Jon asked.

"No." Cliff managed a wry grin. "I'm curious about the log notations. Why do we add new notes at the end of each watch?"

"I navigate by noon sight when we're offshore. But if the sky is overcast and I can't shoot the sun, I can still estimate our position based on the DR log." He waved his arm in a slow arc around the dark horizon and grinned. "No signposts out here, except the sun, moon and stars."

Cliff glanced at the moon, then searched the sky for Polaris, the North Star. "It's awesome that you can find your location anywhere on Earth with just a sextant and a watch."

"Well, it's not quite that simple. But if you're interested, I'll teach you the rudiments of celestial navigation."

"Yeah. I'd like that." Cliff took another look at the stars. "Well, I'd better get some rest. I have the oh-three-hundred watch."

⌁

The sky was brightening in the east when Cliff finished his next watch. He congratulated himself for not dozing off at the helm before Jon relieved him at 0600.

"Any excitement on your watch?" Jon asked as he took the helm.

"Nope. Saw two more ships but they were pretty far off." Cliff stretched and twisted his back, loosening muscles that had grown stiff over the last three hours.

"Okay. Don't forget the logbook before you turn in," Jon said as Cliff headed for the companionway.

Throughout his watch, Cliff had maintained the same course and speed as before, so it took only a minute to fill in the blanks in the log. Two minutes later he was in his bunk. It was a strange sensation hearing the water rushing by only inches from his ear and feeling *Staghound* surging through the waves as he lay under the covers. But before he could think much about it, he was fast asleep.

It seemed like only moments later he was awakened by the aroma of freshly cooked bacon. He thought he was dreaming, but when he looked toward the galley, there was Lena at the stove with Mike standing next to her eating a strip of bacon with his fingers. Lena pushed him out of the galley.

"Go sit down, you're eating all the bacon before I can make the sandwiches."

Mike sat at the dinette licking his fingers. When he noticed Cliff staring at him from his bunk, he said, "She's making BLT's, want one?"

Cliff checked his watch; it was just before noon and he was famished. He looked at Lena, who was standing in the galley, one hand on a hip, gazing at him. "Have enough for two sandwiches?" he asked.

"Of course." She turned back to the stove.

By the time he was dressed, she had finished making the sandwich and he took it out to the cockpit, where the sun was shining brightly and Jon was at the helm.

"Bold of you to eat bacon after being seasick," Jon said with a grin. "You must be feeling a lot better."

"I almost forgot I was sick."

"That's a good sign. Means once you get used to the motion of the boat, you'll be fine." Jon glanced at his watch as he spoke. "You're lucky. Most people would be sick again just smelling that bacon you're eating."

Mike joined them in the cockpit. "I'll take the wheel now." He wiped his hands on his jeans and gripped the wheel.

Jon went below and returned a minute later with the sextant and a notepad. He went forward and sat on the cabin top, bracing himself against the mast.

Cliff watched in fascination as Jon worked the sextant, checking his watch every few seconds. After a couple of minutes, he lowered the instrument and jotted something on a notepad, checking his watch at the same time. He closed the pad and went down to the nav station with Cliff following. At the chart table, he pulled a Nautical Almanac from the shelf and opened it to the page labeled 'January 2, 1987' and ran his finger down a column of numbers. "We need the Sun's declination and Greenwich Hour Angle," he said to Cliff. "Ah, here it is."

Cliff watched in silence as Jon finished his calculations and plotted *Staghound's* position on the chart. "Thirty degrees, forty minutes north by a hundred twenty-two degrees, forty–seven minutes west," he said, gazing at the mark on the chart.

"Yup." Jon grabbed a pair of dividers and stepped off the distance to the coast. "We're south of the US-Mexico border and about 340 miles off the coast of Baja." He closed the book and put the dividers away. "Technically, we're in Mexican territorial waters, but we can bend our course southward and soon we'll be beyond their reach."

"Is that why we came so far west?" Cliff asked.

"Yeah. It's better to keep well clear of Mexico. Their navy is pretty aggressive about vessels traveling in their waters."

"Why? Mexico seems like such a laid-back country."

"American and Japanese commercial fishermen have fished Mexican waters pretty hard, sometimes without permission. The Mexicans don't like foreigners taking what they consider their fish." He handed Cliff a book before he rose from the chart table. "Celestial Navigation for Beginners. Read it."

It was the same book he'd already started reading. "Thanks." He put it on the shelf above his berth and joined the others in the cockpit. Lena, dressed in her usual baggy jeans and sweatshirt, sat in the shelter of the dodger wearing mirrored sunglasses. Jon took the helm while Mike, with a beer in his hand, told Cliff about *Staghound*'s voyage to Thailand.

"It was four years ago. We sailed non-stop from Mexico to the mouth of the Bang Pakong River. That was a helluva trip, man." He looked at Jon. "Mind if I tell him the story?"

Jon shrugged.

"I'd like to hear it," Cliff said. *Staghound* was sailing southwest with the wind coming out of the north, a broad reach. On this point of sail, it was warmer than the day before, when the wind was abeam.

"Well, we anchored off the river mouth after dark. By dawn, we'd taken on six thousand pounds of high-grade pot and were headed south." He took a long drink from his beer and rose from his perch. "Talking makes me thirsty. I need another beer." When he came back from the galley, he brought beers for everyone. "I hate to drink alone."

Lena snorted at that comment but took the beer he offered her.

"So, as I was saying, we sailed down the gulf of Thailand, dodging fishing boats practically every mile of the way. Did you know that gulf is four hundred miles long?"

Cliff shook his head.

"When we finally turned east, around the southern tip of Vietnam, a couple of fishing boats took an interest in us. Pirates operating out of Ca Mau."

"How'd you know they were pirates?" Cliff asked.

"Fishermen don't carry AK47's, and they don't chase sailboats. Luckily, we had a lot of wind and managed to outrun them. We were halfway to Brunei before they finally gave up the chase." Mike took a pull from his beer.

Cliff thought of *Staghound's* hidden gun locker. "Did they shoot at you?"

"Yeah. Scared the bejesus out of us, but they didn't hit anything."

"Did you shoot back?"

"No, all we had at the time was a handgun. They were too far away for a forty-five." Mike took another drink of beer. "We got more firepower now."

"So then what happened?" Cliff asked.

"We blasted up the South China Sea with thirty to forty knots of wind behind us. I don't think this boat's ever gone that fast before or since, right Jon?"

"Probably not," Jon admitted.

"Go on." Cliff prompted Mike.

"We were glad to get out of the South China Sea, but then we caught the tail end of a cyclone between Luzon and Taiwan. Had two days of sixty-knot winds. We were reefed down to nothing but a storm trysail, and still nearly out of control in those steep Luzon Strait waves.

There's a bunch of islands in that strait too. It's a wonder we didn't knock one of 'em clean out of the ocean."

Cliff smiled at Mike's hyperbole but said nothing.

"After that, we were pretty much in open ocean. We kept five hundred miles between us and the nearest land until we got near the west coast. I gotta say, Jon's navigation was dead on. We passed Cape Flattery just after dark and had the hook down in Clallam Bay by midnight. We were unloaded and headed out the Strait of Juan de Fuca before sunrise the next morning."

"And nobody challenged you, Coast Guard, police or Navy?" Cliff asked.

"We had a scare when a Coast Guard cutter approached us off

Tatoosh Island, but Jon got on the radio and convinced them we were just a cruising yacht headed for sunny California."

Jon broke in. "To this day, I don't know why they didn't board us. If they had, it would have been all over because the boat reeked of pot." He and Mike laughed over that narrow escape, even Lena cracked a small smile.

"What happened then?" Cliff asked.

"Nothin'. We spent the next five days coming down the coast and working our asses off scrubbing the boat to get rid of the smell. By the time we got to Catalina, *Staghound* smelled pretty as a rose. Didn't she, Jon?"

"She did. That was the last time we had pot on the boat. After that little adventure, I decided it was safer to move goods out of the States than in."

"Mexico was nice though," Mike said wistfully. "I almost jumped ship in Puerto Vallarta."

"Your problem is that you fall in love in every port," Jon said, laughing. "You're supposed to love 'em and leave 'em, not get yourself all tangled up with them," he said, winking at Lena, who sat impassively behind her sunglasses.

She rose from her perch, saying "I have weather coming at 1500." She went below to switch on the single sideband radio and Weatherfax machine. Half an hour later she called Jon below to discuss the latest weather report.

"How long have you been sailing?" Cliff asked Mike, who took the helm when Jon left.

"Been on the water all my life," Mike replied. "My dad was a fisherman so it sorta came naturally. I grew up on a fishing boat. Loved the ocean, I love fishing too, but not on a commercial boat." Mike's eyes shifted from the bow to the sails, to the compass, and back again. "I got off fishing boats and started sailing when the old man died. Commercial fishing is damned hard work." Mike glanced at Cliff. "Sailing *Staghound* is a friggin' vacation compared to fishing."

Cliff gazed toward the east and pondered Mike's story. *Smuggling, pirates, and cyclones isn't exactly my idea of a vacation,* he thought. He turned back to Mike and asked, "Is that how all your trips go?"

"Oh no. Nowadays we carry a rifle and a shotgun. We can defend ourselves against pirates now, and with the Weatherfax, there's no way we'll get caught in another hurricane." Mike glanced at the compass again. "But mostly, we don't carry drugs or nothin' like that so the danger's pretty minimal."

"Wait a minute," Cliff said, "We have twenty crates of guns aboard. That sounds kind of dangerous to me."

Mike stared at him a moment, then cracked a smile. "Well, if it wasn't for Lena, and Tony, we wouldn't be doin' this."

"How's that?" Cliff wanted to know.

"She's got connections with the rebels down there. She's one of them, if you ask me. Jon's doing her a favor. Normally he'd never touch a deal like this."

Cliff scratched his chin through his stubbly beard. "I don't understand."

"Welcome to the club. I don't either."

"Why are we taking these crates to Chile?"

Mike laughed. "You should've asked these questions before you shipped out with us."

CHAPTER 9

"WEATHERFAX SHOWS A front coming," Jon said when he and Lena came back on deck. He pointed northward where a thin dark line of clouds lay on the horizon. "It'll have plenty of wind in it and I want to shorten sail before it gets here."

Cliff gazed at the line of clouds that seemed to grow darker before his eyes. His muscles instinctively tensed and he pictured his life vest hanging on a hook near his bunk. He watched Mike casually look over his shoulder and assess the clouds, and wished he could be as relaxed.

"Whaddaya think, skipper?" Mike said. "A reefed main and the number three jib?"

"Yeah, it'll be blowing thirty knots in a couple of hours," Jon said as he reached for the jib halyard. To Cliff, he said, "We'll douse and bag the number two, then put up the number three. Go below and get the bag for the number two jib, and put on your safety harness before you come back up."

Cliff raced below and put on his harness, then found the sail bag. Back on deck, the boat was already heeling more under the freshening wind. He made his way to the foredeck and handed Mike the bag. The motion of the boat was more pronounced here. He crouched low and kept one hand on the starboard lifeline.

"We're going head-to-wind, then Jon will lower the halyard," Mike said. "You take the leech and I'll handle the luff. Watch out for the jib sheet when the sail starts flogging." He made a hand signal to Lena at the helm, and *Staghound* turned into the wind.

The jib began to flog and flutter and before Cliff knew it, the jib sheet slapped him in the forehead. It felt like he'd been hit with a pool cue, but he grabbed it and hung on as the halyard was eased and the jib started coming down.

Mike stood at the headstay and pulled the sail down as Cliff wrestled the leech into submission. In a minute the sail was on deck and Mike was tying gaskets around it. Together they worked it into its sausage bag.

"Open the foredeck hatch!" Mike shouted above the rising wind.

Cliff slid the big hatch forward and they fed the bagged sail down below. A wave broke over the deck, soaking him with cold seawater and sending a small torrent down the hatch as well.

Jon dragged the number three jib forward along the deck. Day had turned to dusk and Cliff paused a second to look at the turbulent water from *Staghound's* slippery foredeck. *If I fell overboard right now, they'd never find me.* He double-checked his footing and took the jib sheets Jon handed him.

"Tie these into the clew," Jon said, then hurried back to the cockpit.

Back at the dock in Wilmington, Cliff could tie a bowline blindfolded. Now, with the wind and spray coming over the bow, his fingers were suddenly stiff and clumsy. After what seemed like five minutes, he had the sheets tied into the jib and he shouted "Made!" to Jon who pulled the slack out of them and waved Cliff back to the cockpit.

"You grind and I'll tail the halyard," Jon said. When Cliff was ready, Jon made another hand signal to Mike.

In a couple of minutes, the new jib was up and Mike came back to the cockpit while Jon trimmed the sail as Lena steered the boat back to its original course.

Cliff had broken a sweat while he was grinding the winch, but now his teeth started to chatter as the cold wind blew through his wet clothes. He stayed at the coffee grinder as the mainsail was reefed, hauling the main halyard and reefing line taut. *Staghound*, now under shortened sail and on a broad reach, surged almost calmly among the waves. Cliff briefly relived those moments on the foredeck, heaving eight or ten feet up and down with every wave, the wind blowing his hair into his eyes and spray flying across the deck. It was exciting and scary at the same time. Yet when he glanced at Mike lounging in the cockpit completely unfazed by the experience, a stark revelation hit him. *All the sailing I've ever done was nothing compared to what I just experienced, but to the rest of the crew, it's not even worth a comment!*

"You have the twenty-one hundred watch," Jon said to Cliff, jolting him from his reverie. "Go get warmed up and eat something. It's going to be an interesting night."

Cliff descended the companionway and quickly changed into dry clothes then hurried back on deck.

"You're not due to start your watch for another half hour," Mike said.

"Yeah, I wanted to watch you drive the boat in these rough conditions before I start my watch." Cliff pulled his woolen cap on as he spoke.

"On a dark night, you have only the compass and wind instruments to steer by." Mike nodded toward the dimly lit wind and speed displays that were mounted next to the compass on the binnacle.

Night had fallen and the moon had not risen yet. Cliff peered ahead but all he could see was the dim glow of *Staghound's* running lights in the darkness. Looking aft, he saw only a faint glimmer of the boat's churning wake, and nothing but blackness where the sky should have been.

He leaned over and checked the compass. *Staghound* was

headed southwest. The displays told him the wind was still out of the north, blowing twenty-five knots.

Mike glanced at him. "At first you'll be trying to keep the boat exactly on a compass heading but that's impossible. Just relax and keep the boat roughly on course."

"I understand that. But you can't see anything ahead. How can you be sure you won't run into something?"

Mike chuckled. "Just keep her on course. That's all you have to do."

Cliff stood, "Okay, I'll take the wheel now." He took the helm and emulated the relaxed attitude Mike had shown, steering as much by feel as by the compass.

After a few minutes, Mike went below.

Cliff was surprised at how easily *Staghound* handled under shortened sail. Though the seas had built to ten feet or more and gusts of wind as high as thirty knots whistled through the rigging, the boat responded to the helm the same way his Porsche responded to a twitch of the steering wheel. He spent the rest of his watch playing with the helm and feeling the boat accelerate down the faces of the waves. When he steered it just right, the boat would briefly accelerate to twelve, thirteen, and even fourteen knots. The speed was intoxicating and he felt a strange sense of power guiding the sloop at high speed through the night.

At midnight Jon appeared on deck and, as he always did, checked the sails, the sea, and sky. He glanced at the compass and knotmeter before he spoke. "When I'm lying in my bunk, I can tell by the motion of the boat who's at the helm." He zipped his jacket to his throat and pulled his woolen cap down to his ears. "When Mike drives, the boat feels like a Cadillac barreling down the freeway. Tony was a good driver too, but when he was steering, the boat felt a little more jerky." He put a handle in a winch and tightened the mainsheet a couple of turns.

"What about Lena?" Cliff asked.

"She's good too." Jon paused before he spoke again. "You need more time on the helm, but you're making progress."

"The boat almost seems to tell me what to do."

"That's a good observation. She'll reward you with speed and easy motion if you handle her right."

When Cliff's watch was over, he went below. Lena sat at the nav station reviewing a printout from the Weatherfax with Mike hovering over her.

"Looks like we'll be on this course tomorrow too," Mike was saying to her. He leaned close, studying the page over her shoulder.

She pushed him away with the back of her hand and pulled her collar up. "I think we'll jibe around noon. She had plotted *Staghound*'s position on the flimsy sheet. Now she ran her finger diagonally down the page. "From here south, the wind will be lighter for the next few days."

Mike leaned close again and she leaned away.

"I'm going to bed." She left the paper on the desk and disappeared into her cabin.

Mike's gaze followed her until the cabin door shut behind her.

Cliff stripped off his foul weather gear and climbed into his berth, where he concentrated on the sound and feel of *Staghound* until he fell asleep.

The alarm on Cliff's watch chirped at 0545. He dressed quickly and grabbed a cup of coffee on his way up to the cockpit. The sun was still below the horizon, but its rays illuminated the broken clouds to the east in hues of blue, gold, and pink. The wind had eased a bit and so had the sea.

"There's a ship over there." Mike, who was at the helm pointed westward. The low-slung vessel was barely visible in the distance.

"What is it?" Cliff asked.

"Can't tell yet. Could be Coast Guard." Mike held binoculars to his eyes. "We won't bother Jon unless it starts coming toward us." He lowered the glasses. "Alright, you're on watch."

Cliff took the helm, checking *Staghound*'s course and speed. Sometime during the night the wind had veered and now *Staghound* was sailing nearly dead downwind, with the boom way out to leeward and the jib bellying out so far that it occasionally collapsed, only to snap taut with a bang when the wind caught it.

Staghound rolled a bit under the northerly wind. Cliff discovered that if he steered ten degrees to starboard, a course of one-ninety degrees instead of due south, the boat rode more steadily and the jib didn't collapse as often. *It's not the course Mike was steering,* he thought, *but I'm driving now and this seems better to me. If it's not right, he'll tell me.* But the sun burst over the horizon and *Staghound* continued southwest for another two hours and no one came up to correct him.

At 0800 Lena came on deck. She was bundled in a jacket and wool hat and cradled a cup of coffee in both hands. Just then a school of flying fish darted out of the water around *Staghound*'s bow, their wings glistening in the morning sun. They were the first Cliff had ever seen. More astonishing to him was the unabashed smile on Lena's face as she watched them soar across the wave-tops. That was also a first.

A moment later her face resumed its stoic countenance. "I'm making Mexican omelets for breakfast. Want one?"

He paused, picturing her as a rebel instead of *Staghound*'s cook. *I can't imagine her as a gun-toting guerilla fighter. But a spy? She's mysterious and inscrutable. Yeah, she could easily be a spy.*

"Cliff," she repeated. "Omelet, yes or no?"

"Oh yeah, that sounds great."

Staghound's crew had established a routine during daylight hours. At noon Jon would bring out his sextant and take a sun sight, then plot *Staghound*'s daily position on the chart. Later, when the Weatherfax machine spit out the latest forecast, they would discuss the weather and decide whether to change sails or which heading to steer. Afternoons, they often lounged in the cockpit chatting or reading.

Cliff had read the book on celestial navigation and started doing the calculations necessary to convert the readings from the sextant to latitude and longitude, essentially duplicating the math Jon did. After a few days, he asked if he could try taking a noon sight.

Jon stared at him a moment. "Sure, go ahead."

At noon the next day, Cliff took the sextant on deck and brought the Sun down to the horizon, swinging the instrument the way he'd seen Jon do it until the Sun's lower limb just touched the horizon when it was at its zenith. Twenty minutes later he had worked out their latitude and longitude and plotted *Staghound's* position on the chart.

"Looks good," Jon said after he checked Cliff's calculations.

"Great, I'll do the noon sights from now on if you'd like." Cliff toyed with the pencil while Jon considered his proposal.

"It's drudgery to me," Jon said. "I'll check your work for a few days. Just to back you up."

From then on, Cliff did the daily navigation, with Jon checking his results.

Ten days into the voyage Cliff plotted *Staghound's* position and looked up from the chart. "Nine degrees north by one hundred four degrees west. That puts us thirteen hundred miles from home," he said.

Jon leaned over the chart table and put a finger on the chart. "And seven hundred miles southwest of the Gulf of Tehuantepec. Right where we want to be at this point in the voyage."

"Tehuantepec. Isn't that where hurricanes form?" Cliff asked.

"Yup. There used to be some really good waves around Salina

Cruz. We surfed a bunch of point breaks there back in the seventies. But that's all over now."

Cliff studied the chart where Jon had pointed to. The jagged Mexican coast faced southward and he imagined hurricane-driven waves pounding the shoreline. "Why do you say it's over now?"

"Too crowded. Every break in North America is over-surfed. In a few years, there won't be any un-surfed waves left on the planet." Jon disappeared into his cabin, leaving Cliff to marvel at the chart. Doing the navigation gave him a new perspective on the world. It was no longer made of just hills and freeways, beaches, and valleys. He was acutely aware that *Staghound* was traveling on the surface of a giant sphere, like an ant on a classroom globe. He thought of Magellan and Drake, Columbus and Cook, who did exactly what he was doing, using the sun to find their way around the globe.

"You're staring at the chart like you're in a trance." Lena had come out of her cabin and was gazing at him. "Are you?"

"What? No, I was just thinking," he replied self-consciously. He put the chart away.

She eyed him quizzically. "Are you homesick?"

"Oh no. Far from it. I'm quite enjoying where I am."

"Well, you'll have to enjoy being somewhere else for now. I have a Weatherfax coming in five minutes."

She took the seat Cliff vacated and switched on the single sideband radio, tuning it to receive weather information. It was wired to the Weatherfax machine which converted radio signals into a weather map, then printed it the same way the fax machine in his office did. While he watched, Lena plotted *Staghound*'s position on the printout.

"Looks like fine weather for another day or two. After that, the wind will veer to east-northeast and bring lots of squalls.

❧

The days grew hot as the sloop pressed farther south and her crew switched from foul weather gear to shorts and T-shirts. As Lena predicted, the northerly wind coming over *Staghound*'s transom gradually shifted more easterly, and the sloop sailed on a beam reach under a mainsail and jib, reeling off an average of one hundred seventy miles from noon to noon each day. This was easy sailing and Cliff often joined the others in the cockpit in the afternoons. Mike, the ship's bartender, served a cold drink, usually gin and tonic before dinner, which Lena prepared, often with fish Mike caught that day. Those meals were usually served in the cockpit under a glorious sunset.

On January 20th, three weeks into the voyage, the steady wind that had carried *Staghound* for over three thousand miles began to falter. By mid-afternoon, it was no more than a zephyr. Without wind, the temperature in the cabin soared. Cliff took refuge from the heat on the foredeck, in the shade of the jib. He was reading one of Jon's books on ocean meteorology when Lena emerged on deck and found a bit of shade nearby. "Too hot in your cabin?" he asked.

"Yes." She sat against the mast, opened a novel, and went back to ignoring him as she usually did. She was wearing a bathing suit, floppy sun hat, and dark glasses. To Cliff, she looked like a Hollywood starlet. Better than a Hollywood starlet.

He tried to focus on his book, reading the same line he'd read before she arrived, "Known to sailors around the world as the 'Doldrums' or 'Horse Latitudes', the Inter-Tropical Convergence Zone is a belt around the earth extending approximately five degrees north." But that was futile. He'd never seen Lena in anything but baggy jeans and shirts or jackets and it took all his willpower to keep his eyes on the page in front of him.

"You've been reading Jon's books like you're studying for an exam," Lena said, interrupting his train of thought.

"It's fascinating to read about the weather and see it at the same time." He closed the book and looked southward toward a cloudbank that ran from east to west as far as he could see.

She followed his gaze. "So, does the book say what those clouds are about? Is it a storm?"

"I think it's the doldrums, where the trade winds from the northern and southern hemispheres meet."

"The doldrums? Are you becoming a weather expert too?" she asked with an amused smile.

"I'm afraid I'm still a novice at weather," he replied. "There is a lot to learn. Back home I didn't think much about the weather except when it affected me. Out here, the weather dictates everything we do."

"Especially the doldrums. Both on land and sea." She peered at him through her mirrored sunglasses. "Weren't you in the doldrums when you moved aboard this boat?"

Cliff hesitated, puzzled for a moment. "Ah, a different kind of doldrums." He always seemed to be slow on the uptake with her. He felt his face redden. "I wouldn't call it the doldrums. More like adrift. How about you? Have you been in the doldrums lately?"

She ignored his question and returned to the weather. "Those clouds are a sign that we're getting close to the equator. Soon we'll cross the line and enter the southern hemisphere. We'll be halfway to Crusoe."

Cliff studied her for a moment as she lounged against the mast. "You like it out here, don't you?"

"I do. I love the pristine beauty of the sea and sky. It's so peaceful."

"Is that why you're here? I mean, you could have hired someone to deliver the crates, right?"

She lifted her sunglasses and stared at him for a moment. "Wrong." She lowered the glasses and stood. "This mission is too important to entrust to anyone else."

Cliff watched as she made her way back to the cockpit, not

sure if he had offended her somehow. He tried to concentrate on his book but thought of Lena instead. He still knew nothing about her except that she was the prime mover behind this delivery trip. She had deftly turned the conversation in other directions the few times he had inquired about her personally.

∾

Wearing only a pair of trunks, Cliff took a noon sight and headed down to the nav station. A bead of sweat ran down his forehead as he worked the calculations. He caught it with a thumb before it dripped onto the desk. When he was sure the math was correct, he plotted *Staghound*'s position on the chart with a tiny "x", adding the date in his precise hand: January 20th, 1987.

Jon came down the companionway. "Where are we?"

"Zero degrees, sixteen minutes north, by ninety-nine degrees west," Cliff replied. "Sixteen miles from the Equator."

Jon glanced at the knotmeter display on the bulkhead. "We're averaging about three knots, so we'll cross the Line before sunset." He lifted his cap and wiped sweat from his brow. "It's too hot to sleep in my cabin. Guess I'll go back on deck."

In the afternoon, under a blazing equatorial sun, Jon suddenly tossed aside the novel he'd been reading. "Mike, rig up the target," he said before disappearing down the companionway.

"Oh boy," Mike said as he rummaged in the lazarette for a man-overboard pole. "Target practice!" About eight feet long, the man-overboard pole was designed to float upright, its tip riding about six feet above the water. Mike tied the end of a hundred-foot length of light line to it and secured the other end to a stanchion on *Staghound*'s stern.

A moment later Jon reappeared on deck with the AR-15 carbine Cliff had discovered the month before, along with a couple of boxes of ammunition. "Ever seen one of these?" he asked Cliff as he held up the weapon.

Cliff took it, checked the safety lever and released the 20-round magazine. He pulled back the charging handle and deftly caught the round that flew out of the breach. "It's the semi-automatic version of the M16."

"You served in the military?" Jon asked.

"Drafted in '68." Cliff handed the weapon back to Jon.

"Go to Vietnam?"

"Yup."

Lena came on deck with a stack of paper plates. "Targets," she said, handing one to Mike.

"What'd you do over there?" Mike asked Cliff.

"My job," Cliff replied.

"I missed out," Mike said. "Too young. Did you see much action?"

"Some." Cliff had put the war behind him.

"Kill any gooks over there?" Mike asked.

"He doesn't want to talk about it, Mike." Lena spoke up when Cliff didn't answer the question.

Cliff grabbed the top of the pole. "You slide the plate on top, like this?" He punctured the plate in two places and slid it onto the pole.

"Yeah, then I lower it over the stern." Mike eased the pole with the plate on it into the water and let out the line that tethered it. "It'll drift a hundred feet back, then we can shoot."

The pole, weighted at the bottom with a float a couple of feet up, bobbed in the waves, making the plate at the top dance back and forth five or six feet above the water.

With Staghound barely moving, it was a couple of minutes before there was a hundred feet between it and the pole..

Jon took up a kneeling position on the stern and braced himself against the backstay. At a hundred feet the paper plate wavered and twisted on the pole. One second it looked like a white circle, the next it was nearly invisible when it turned edge-on.

Cliff watched him take aim and fire. In the middle of the ocean, with nothing to reflect off of, the sharp report of the rifle sounded strange to him. More like a firecracker than a gun.

Lena put binoculars to her eyes. "Miss," she said.

Jon fired again.

"Miss!"

He fired three more times and got one hit, then handed the weapon to Mike, who fired five times and scored no hits. He handed the gun to Cliff. "You get five rounds."

Cliff took the same position Jon had and let his body relax while he timed the movements of the paper plate, left to right and back. The pistol grip of the weapon felt exactly like the M16 he once carried. A flood of memories came back to him, but he put them out of his mind and squeezed the trigger.

"Hit," Lena said, peering through the binoculars.

Cliff fired four more times and scored two more hits. He thumbed the safety and turned to Lena. "Are you going to shoot?"

"Of course." She took the weapon and knelt, resting her left arm on her knee the same way Cliff had done. Taking her time, she fired five rounds, scoring two hits. When she was finished, she ejected the empty magazine, engaged the safety, and checked the chamber before handing the rifle to Jon.

Cliff was impressed by the expert way she handled the gun. "Where did you get your training?" he asked.

As usual, she ignored the question. Instead, she said to Jon, "Let's practice with the pistol too."

Jon left and returned a moment later with the .45 Cliff had seen in *Staghound*'s hidden armory. He handed Lena the gun and picked up the binoculars.

Mike reeled in the target and put a fresh plate on it.

When all was ready, Lena stood on the stern deck and, gripping the pistol in the two-handed police firing position, put two of her allotted seven rounds into the plate.

"Damn good shooting, Lena. Two out of seven at a moving target from a moving platform," Jon said.

Mike shot next and managed to put one round into the plate.

Jon shot after Mike and scored two hits. He reloaded and handed the gun to Cliff, who obliterated the plate, scoring six hits.

"Jesus," Mike said when Jon called out Cliff's score. "Where'd you learn to shoot a pistol like that?"

"In the army."

"Really? Were you an MP or something?" Jon asked.

"Nope, but I carried one of these in Vietnam so I got pretty good with it," Cliff replied.

Later in the afternoon, there was still no more than a breath of wind and the boat drifted along, making little headway. Jon trailed a thick rope over the transom and dove into the water and, hanging onto the rope, dragged behind the boat for a few minutes. The sea temperature hovered around eighty-six degrees, a refreshing fifteen degrees cooler than the temperature in the cabin. Soon everyone took turns dragging in the water. Around five, Cliff estimated that *Staghound* had finally crossed the equator.

Jon and Mike looked at each other, "Well, I think it's time," Jon said.

"Time for what?" Cliff asked.

"Your initiation," Jon said.

Before he could respond, Jon and Mike grabbed him and tied his hands behind his back.

"What the hell…" Cliff struggled against them for a moment but it was useless.

"Relax," Jon said. "Every sailor who crosses the Line must be initiated."

Lena stepped up and blindfolded him. "Take him to the foredeck".

They dragged him forward and forced him to his knees.

Cliff felt the late afternoon sun on his shoulders and *Staghound* rolling slowly in the calm sea. A restraining hand was on his shoulder, but he took Jon's words to heart and waited for whatever came next. A moment later his hands were untied and the blindfold was removed. He looked up to see Jon standing in front of him, wearing a crown on his head and a cape over his shoulders. Cliff was taking in this sight when, from behind, Lena dumped a bucket of seawater over his head making him sputter and gasp.

"Clifton Demont, you are ordered to stand trial for your crimes and transgressions against King Neptune and his domain!" Jon bellowed. "Now, how do you plead?"

Cliff looked around and saw the crew solemnly gazing at him. He started to speak but was cut short.

"Silence!" Jon bellowed while another bucket of seawater was dumped on him. "The charges against you are serious! You have wandered over King Neptune's waves without paying homage, you Pollywog! You have even had the balls to cross His Line, the Equator, Pollywog, without so much as asking His permission! Now you must pay for your crimes!"

Lena had changed into a bikini, cape, and tiara. She held a pitcher full of a brown liquid. "My special concoction of Neptune's finest," she said. "Made especially for this kind of ceremony." She poured a glass of it and said, "Drink this, your punishment will go better if you have been properly anesthetized." Cliff eyed the vile looking stuff in the glass and hesitated.

"Too slow!" She cried. Mike held his head back and she poured half the pitcher down his throat and over his head. It tasted of brandy and rum, gin and vodka, with a twist of coconut. She pointed to the glass in his hand, "Now drink!"

Cliff took a swallow.

Mike guffawed, "That's not a drink, that's a sip!"

"This Pollywog is weak!" Lena said, "He needs another tot of Neptune's grog!"

Mike pulled his head back again and Lena poured the rest of the pitcher over his face. "Now drink!" she commanded again.

Cliff drank half the glass. The alcohol burned his throat and stung his eyes.

"That's better," Jon said. "Now, Queen Lena, you can pour the ceremonial toast.

"Your chalice, my lord." She poured red wine into a cup and handed it to him, then poured wine for the rest of the crew and herself.

Jon raised his cup and said, "To Neptune! May he keep us safe while we pass through his domain!" They all tossed back their drinks, and Jon said, "Alright, back to the business at hand. Now, Pollywog, how do you plead?"

"Guilty as charged!" Cliff shouted, laughing.

"Splendid! Now for the punishment. By the power vested in me by the King of All The Oceans I hereby declare that Cliff Demont shall be suffered to endure ten lashes, he must kiss the belly of the queen, and then he shall be tossed into the sea! Lena, the cat o' nine tails, please."

She produced a makeshift whip made of braided twine.

Jon said, "Queenie, I get queasy at the sight of blood, so you'll have to do the honors."

"With pleasure!"

Mike interjected, "All this crime and punishment makes me thirsty, how about another round first?"

"Excellent idea," Lena said and poured another round for the others.

"Would you like another glass too, Cliff?" she asked.

"I'll be braver if I'm fortified with another shot of your...I mean Neptune's finest."

She poured him a shot while the others waited, then she shouted, "To Neptune!" and drank. "Now let's get on with the punishment." She stepped forward and administered the lashes with surprising vigor, causing Cliff to wince in pain as the whip left marks on his back. When she finished, she stood in front of him, and Jon said, "Now you must kiss the belly of the queen!" and pushed Cliff's head into Lena's belly. It was a sensation he found himself enjoying mightily, but he was instantly pulled away by Mike and Jon and dragged to the starboard gunwale.

"Do you have anything to say for yourself before the final punishment?" Jon asked.

"God save the Queen!" Cliff shouted as they tossed him overboard. The cool water refreshed his sunburned skin and washed Lena's concoction from his hair and beard. He turned on his back and floated while *Staghound's* crew lined the rail and applauded. He rolled over and dove deep, swimming toward the front of the boat. Brightly striped pilot fish swam alongside the bow, paying no attention to him as he swam past and turned to swim back along the port side of the boat, toward the stern. He grabbed the rope that trailed behind and pulled himself back aboard. By then the rest of the crew were gathered in the cockpit.

"Kneel!" they shouted in unison. Then Jon said in a stentorian voice, "By the power vested in me by King Neptune himself, I now pronounce you a true Shellback, and you shall never bear the stigma of the name 'Pollywog' again!" Another round of Lena's grog was served and they toasted King Neptune and all the ships at sea.

With the ceremony over, the crew congratulated Cliff on his graduation to Shellback. Moments later, a whisper of a breeze arose and *Staghound* slowly began to move again.

PART II

CHAPTER 10

IN THE OUTSKIRTS of Antofagasta, a dusty industrial city on the northern coast of Chile, Yori Santos Lobos sat at a desk in a dingy second-floor office of a slaughterhouse. A large plate-glass window offered an expansive view of the floor below. If he wanted to, he could watch the workers in bloody aprons manhandle freshly butchered sides of beef hanging from meat hooks on a conveyor line. The high-pitched wail of industrial bone saws and the stench of death nearly made him gag, but he was determined to appear nonchalant while he counted the money. Two hundred thousand US dollars, twenty packets of hundred-dollar bills. They made a tidy stack that fit nicely in his small canvas valise. He zipped it shut and hefted it in his left hand. It would be easy enough to handle.

"It's all here," he said in Spanish to the man seated behind the desk. He rose from his chair, anxious to get outside.

"Sit down," the man said. "I want to tell you about our enterprise here." He waved a hand toward the window.

"Thanks, Mr. Machado, but I have a long drive ahead of me. I should be…"

"Sit down," Machado interrupted. It was an order.

"Okay. I guess I have a couple of minutes." Yori sat again. He glanced out the doorway to a waiting room, where a couple of thugs lounged on a broken-down sofa, watching a soccer match between Chile and Bolivia on a black-and-white TV.

"We handle cattle here, but sometimes we find it necessary to spice the beef with, shall we say, more interesting meat." Machado's expressionless eyes looked as dead as the eyes of the reeking cattle downstairs. "It's an efficient operation. An animal is brought in through a chute so tight it can barely move. He gets shot in the head, not to kill, only to stun." A slow grin spread across Machado's face, revealing yellowed teeth. "He is hung by his hind hooves on the conveyor line, with his head hanging down. Then his throat is slit and his heart pumps the blood out of his body as he dies." The smile disappeared and Machado leaned forward, his eyes boring into Yori's. "We can handle any kind of animal this way, even a man. You get the picture?"

Yori's hand instinctively went for the pistol tucked in his waistband, but he checked himself. "I've been in a slaughterhouse before," he lied.

Machado leaned back. "You will deliver the goods to our warehouse in Coquimbo on February 15th. You will be paid when all the goods are accounted for."

Yori rose again from the chair. "Don't worry, I'll be there." He held out his hand to shake on the deal.

Machado ignored the hand. "I am not worried," he said. "The woman and the boy will be our guests until you return with the goods." His gaze remained fixed on Yori like a python eyeing its next meal.

Yori's eyes focused on the spot where Machado's brows came together on his sweaty forehead. *That's where I'd like to put a bullet*, he thought. Instead, he adopted his most reasonable tone. "That wasn't part of the deal."

"Oh but that is the deal, my friend. Surely you did not expect us to give you this much money without collateral. Look down there," he pointed through the window toward a line of bloody cattle parts hanging from meat hooks.

Yori didn't look, the smell told him all he needed to know.

"You see, this little office is the loan department," the man's reptilian eyes remained fixed on Yori. "Down there is where we handle delinquent loans. Understand?"

If you want her, take her…and the kid too. Instead of saying what he thought, Yori lied. "Please. I'll do anything to be sure they are safe."

"You bring back the goods, you'll see them again. You fail," Machado's eyes went toward the window. "We add something extra to the *hamburguesa* we sell to the *Supermercados*."

Yori stole another glance at the two *sicarios* in the other room. He could take out Machado, but not all three of them. He picked up the valise and left. Out on the street, he paused to light a cigarette and walked toward his car. He thought of the two hundred thousand American dollars in his valise and smiled.

Yori climbed into his beat-up old Volkswagen and slowly made his way through the clogged streets of dusty Antofagasta. He was in no hurry. If Machado really wanted Maria and the kid, his men would be there soon. It wouldn't do for Yori to arrive home while they were in the process of kidnapping them.

He made it to the rundown neighborhood where he lived in thirty minutes, driving slowly past the flat-roofed cinderblock house he shared with Maria and her seven-year-old boy, Enrique. There was no sign of Machado's men, but the front door was ajar. Inside the house, everything looked normal, with the obvious exception of Maria and Enrique, who were probably bound and gagged in the trunk of a car, en route to a Parga safe house. Machado worked for Vicente Parga, whose enterprises included cocaine, human trafficking, murder, extortion, politics, and other loathsome pursuits. His empire, based in northern Chile, included various front companies, even a certain slaughterhouse in Antofagasta.

The phone in the kitchen was ringing when he entered the house. There was silence on the other end when he picked it up.

He waited, saying nothing into the mouthpiece, and was about to hang up when a harsh voice spoke. "Yori!"

"What?"

"We have the girl and her snot-nosed kid."

"Good. Make sure Enrique gets to school on time. Education is important to a growing boy. By the way, he likes hamburgers for dinner."

"Listen, wiseass, bring us the fucking guns or both of them are going to be hamburger. Got it?"

Yori hung up. *They're your problem now, asshole,* he thought.

In the bedroom, he filled a duffle bag with clothes, then pushed the bed to one side and lifted a floor panel, revealing a compartment about two feet wide and four feet long that he had dug into the ground beneath. In it was a canvas rifle case and an ammo box. He unzipped the case and inspected his AK47. He had stolen it from a Chilean Army garrison a few years back, when government troops were swarming the country searching for communists and anti-government guerillas after General Pinochet took over. They had confiscated thousands of them from captured insurgents.

Yori opened the ammo box. In it were ten loaded thirty-round magazines for the rifle and five boxes of bullets and a spare magazine for the Walther PPK he kept tucked in his waistband. *This ought to be enough firepower for this operation,* he thought as he set the floor panel in place and pushed the bed back where it belonged.

In the kitchen, he dialed a number in Coquimbo. While the phone rang, his eyes wandered around the kitchen and he noticed a pot of *cazuela* simmering on the stove. *They must have snatched her in a hurry.* He turned off the flame and was shoveling spoonfuls of steaming stew into his mouth when a man finally answered.

"Juan, you bastard," Yori said in Spanish. "I'll be in Coquimbo in the morning. If the boat isn't ready to go, I'm going to shoot you."

"Hey, take it easy, man. Everything's ready. We can leave when you get here."

"What about food? We need enough for three weeks. And whiskey, and cigarettes."

"*Si, si,* we got everything, man. Plenty of Marlboro's too." Juan's voice carried the rasp of a chain smoker.

"Okay, I'm leaving now. I'll pick you up at six." He took another mouthful of stew and hurried out the door to his car. He carefully slid the valise under the driver's seat and slipped his trusty Walther in a door pocket, ready for instant use if necessary. The car sputtered to life and he jammed it into gear.

Yori drove down the rutted street to a gas station on Avenida Argentina where he filled the tank and bought a bottle of *Pisco Capel.* Coquimbo was twelve hours south of Antofagasta on Highway 5, so he would have to drive all night. He settled his lanky body into the driver's seat and twisted the cork out of the bottle of *Pisco.* He took a long pull for luck and drove onto the road, lighting a Marlboro at the same time. Since Pinochet took over, there were shortages of all kinds in Chile, but American cigarettes were always plentiful, and for that, the General could have Yori's vote in the next election, if there ever was one.

Yori was born in a shack in the hills above Valparaiso. His father was a house painter until he fell from a scaffold while painting the third story of a mansion in Vina Del Mar. After that, his vertebrae shattered, he was bound to a wheelchair. He was in pain for the rest of his life, which, mercifully, did not last long. He was dead before Yori's ninth birthday.

Yori's mother went to work in the hotel district, making the beds and cleaning the toilets of wealthy vacationers from Santiago. Every day she and her son walked a kilometer down the steep cobblestone street to the bus stop and caught the number 23 that took them to the beach where high-rise hotels lined the broad Avenida San Martin. After school, Yori played on the sand with the other ragged kids while she mopped floors and made beds. When he was a little older, he watched the hustlers and whores work their trades around the casino by the Rio Marga Marga.

Eventually, he was recruited by Manuel Silva, a small-time criminal who ran a gang of juvenile pickpockets along the beach from Marga Marga to the far end of Avenida San Martin. At the end of each day he picked up his young thieves in his car and they would hand over whatever they stole. Silva, whose beady eyes and pointed snout reminded Yori of a rat, paid each of them ten or twenty pesos a day, except the kid who brought in the least amount of goods, who got nothing. That was Silva's incentive program.

By the time he was fifteen Yori was a top producer for Silva, but he could barely buy a pack of cigarettes with what he was paid. One day he took a bus to Concón, a tourist area about ten kilometers north of Vina Del Mar, well beyond Silva's turf.

He worked the boulevard along the Playa Amarilla and raked in over three hundred pesos. After that day he still worked for Silva, but often rode the bus to Concón afterward. One evening he picked the pocket of an American tourist on Avenida San Fabian and darted into a nearby alley. After withdrawing the cash he tossed the stolen wallet into a trash can. He was still counting the money when a searing pain ripped across his face. He staggered and fell among the clattering trash cans still clutching the money in one hand and probing a flap of skin from his face with the other. He felt the money snatched from his hand and looked up to see Silva's face inches from his own.

"Get out of Concón, and stay out of Vina. Next time I see you I'll kill you!" he hissed. He wiped the blood from his knife on Yori's shirt and walked quickly into the street, stuffing the money into his pocket as he went.

Yori was left with a livid scar that ran from his left ear, down his cheek to his throat. When his face was healed, he packed a suitcase, kissed his mother goodbye, and caught a northbound bus. He got off in Antofagasta, about thirteen hundred kilometers north of Vina del Mar. Wedged between the cold Pacific Ocean and the Atacama Desert, Antofagasta was the kind of city that tourists avoided like the plague. Lacking any skills except thievery, Yori nearly starved until he found work as a mule, delivering liquid cocaine disguised as cooking oil from the mountains to Antofagasta. There, it was loaded onto boats and shipped to Valparaiso to be processed into powdered form and sold on the streets. He spent four years traveling the drug routes from the mountains to Antofagasta. If working for Silva was his apprenticeship, four years on the cocaine trails made him a journeyman in the arts of smuggling, assault, and murder, all essential skills of that trade.

Not long after arriving in *Anto*, as the locals called it, he met Maria, a singer in a waterfront nightclub. A few months later she moved in. To him, she was little more than a housekeeper and a fuck, and her brat a nuisance. She often complained that he treated her like a maid and constantly threatened to leave him, which he encouraged her to do. So, to spite him, she stayed.

Tall, attractive, and skilled in bed, Yori figured she'd be taken by one of Parga's men long before she faced a meat grinder, and he didn't waste a second worrying about her, or the kid.

His business situation was complicated. Cocaine came from Bolivia and Peru via clandestine trails from high in the Andes to transfer points in Arica and Antofagasta. The trails in northern Chile were loosely controlled by the Parga gang. There was also *the Movimiento de Izquierda Revolucionaria*. MIR was a leftist guerilla group that had been fighting an insurgency against the Pinochet regime for years. It operated from strongholds in the southern mountains and financed its operations in part by selling cocaine to smugglers in Chile's port cities, who exported it to the US and Europe. Their goods traveled the same routes from the mountains that Parga used. Sometimes there was cooperation between Parga and MIR and sometimes they clashed.

Yori also dealt with the national police, the Carabineros. He worked in the spaces between these three groups. He carried drugs down the mountains for Parga, and sometimes for MIR. He did favors for the Carabineros, providing drugs, bribes, or women, whatever the situation called for. And he sold information to all three. The Parga gang took in far more money than they could launder, and cash accumulated in storerooms and safe houses, including the slaughterhouse in Antofagasta.

Yori knew he couldn't continue working between these three dangerous groups much longer. He felt like a minnow swimming with sharks: Eventually, he would be eaten by one or the other. When he learned that MIR was having a shipment of guns delivered on an American sailboat, he saw his chance. He would snatch the guns before the guys from MIR could get them.

Yori's MIR informant said they planned to exchange 200,000 US dollars for the shipment. He proposed to his Parga boss, whom he knew only as *El Halcon* that he intercept the sailboat and deliver the goods to him instead of to MIR. All he needed was the $200,000 to give to the Americans. Nearly a month passed before *El Halcon* approved his idea, and Yori fretted that the delivery would be made to MIR before he could intercept it, especially since his MIR informant relayed to him that the American boat would arrive around February 5th instead of early March.

"Yori," *El Halcon* had said to him, "I like you. You've got brass balls to come to me with this proposition. Sometimes I think maybe I'll kill you and go get those guns myself, but I don't like boats, so it's better you go." They were riding in a car in Antofagasta. Yori sat in the front seat with *El Halcon* behind him.

He tried not to imagine *El Halcon* putting a pistol to the back of his head and pulling the trigger. He kept his voice calm, though his knees were shaking. "It would be a serious blow to those communist MIR bastards, *Jefe*. Besides, with that much firepower, no one can stop us from taking whatever we want, from Arica to Valparaiso."

"You think big, Yori, I like that. Go see my man at the packing house." *El Halcon* patted him on the shoulder. "When you deliver the guns, I'll give you twenty thousand dollars and a promotion. Of course, if you fuck up, I'll kill you."

The Volkswagen labored up the twisty highway out of Antofagasta. At La Negra, the road straightened and Yori steeled himself for the mind-numbing monotony of driving across the Atacama Desert at night. For the next two hundred kilometers, the road was a straight line punctuated by a few gentle curves. With a landscape as bleak as any on Earth, some parts of the Atacama Desert went years without a drop of rain. NASA found it so similar to the surface of Mars that they brought their Mars landers there for testing.

Yori didn't think about Mars or NASA scientists. Instead, he turned the car's puny heater to maximum and chain-smoked. Every half-hour he fortified himself with a pull from his bottle of *Pisco*. By midnight the little car had traversed the desert and was dropping down winding sections of road toward sea level near the town of Barquito. He found an open gas station where he filled the tank and bought a cup of coffee, then got back on the road. The coffee and the winding coast road helped to keep him awake.

At Caldera, the road turned inland and the Volkswagen climbed slowly into the mountains of Chile's coastal range. Yori zipped his jacket up and lit another Marlboro. The moon had set and the car's feeble headlights did little to illuminate the road ahead. Soon he was falling asleep at the wheel. Fighting to stay awake by rolling down the window and sticking his face into the frigid air as he drove, he managed to make it another hundred kilometers to Vallenar. There he stopped at a roadside diner and downed more coffee. He wished he had some cocaine to keep himself awake the last hundred kilometers to Coquimbo and chastised himself for not thinking of getting some on his way out of *Anto*. Instead, he managed to stay awake by sheer force of will, and by five-thirty he was rolling into the port city of Coquimbo. He pulled to a stop in front of the seedy apartment building where Juan lived and leaned on the horn.

Juan, dressed in fishermen's dungarees and carrying extra clothes in a dirty backpack, hurried out of the predawn shadows and climbed in. He was built like a pugilist, with long arms, thick shoulders, and the black eyes of a sadist. The son of generations of fishermen, Juan knew the sea as well as he knew the land, and the predators that dwelt in both places. He was good with a knife and knew how to handle a fishing boat too.

They drove through the town, past the *futbol* stadium to the harbor, where a fleet of fishing boats lay moored just off the wharf. It was a sad sight. Most of them had been idle for years, with owners who could no longer afford to maintain them. Once painted in bright colors, now they wore streaks of rust and guano, a flotilla of derelicts.

The local fishermen were hit hard after Pinochet took power and assigned fishing rights to his cronies. Before then, a commercial boat could work anywhere along Chile's 6,400-kilometer coastline. Now hundreds of independent seiners from Puerto Montt to Arica were idle, rotting at their moorings. But one boat, the twenty-four-meter *Tortuga Negra*, had a wisp of smoke coming from its stack and a chubby crewman standing on the aft deck squinting at them in the early morning light. Juan waved and the man clambered into a rowboat that was tied alongside and began to row toward them.

While they waited for the rowboat, Yori eyed the rundown vessel's peeling paint and rust-streaked superstructure. It did not fill him with confidence. Built in the 1950s, the *Tortuga Negra* had once been a proud member of Chile's fishing fleet, but after Pinochet took power the vessel was converted to a workboat and traveled among the islands of Chile's Patagonian Archipelagoes, bringing supplies to remote villages. With its fish hold converted to a machine shop, her crew could repair the bent shafts, busted propellers and worn-out engines that the natives brought down to the harbor wherever she anchored. Suspected of smuggling contraband, her owner had been arrested and disappeared into Pinochet's prison system, leaving the vessel to be repossessed by the bank.

Yori had traveled to Coquimbo the month before and looked at a dozen boats rusting at their anchors in the harbor. Considering the *Tortuga Negra* the best of a bad lot, he bought her on the spot, paying the bank three million Chilean Pesos out of his own pocket, the equivalent of five thousand US dollars.

When the rowboat arrived at the dock Antonio, the overweight oarsman, took Yori's bag and rifle case, but Yori clutched the valise and carefully clambered into the boat.

"I quit working at the jail, boss," Antonio said when Yori asked. He had been a cook at the city jail since he was laid off from a fishing boat.

"Good. You're our chef on this trip," Yori said.

"Yeah, I'll cook," Antonio said as he rubbed his fat belly with both hands. "But let me buy the meat. The stuff they called beef at the jail came all the way from Antofagasta. I don't know what kind of cattle they have up there, but some of it didn't look like any beef I ever saw."

Yori felt his throat constrict. "No! No Antofagasta meat!" he said more vehemently than necessary.

Aboard the *Tortuga Negra*, Yori took the valise upstairs to the captain's stateroom, just aft of the bridge, and shoved it under the bunk along with his rifle. After driving all night he longed to lay down and sleep, but first, he had to make sure the boat was ready to make the voyage.

While Yori was in Antofagasta, Juan was able to get the workboat's massive diesel engine running. He led Yori on a tour of the engine room, a dark cave filled with machinery and metal catwalks, eager to show him his handiwork. "This boat is in rough shape, boss, but the engine is perfect!" he said with pride.

"Just make sure it runs," Yori said, as Juan bustled around the motor. Later they stared at the balky auxiliary motor that powered the vessel's electrical generator. Juan had been able to get the two-cylinder diesel to start, but it leaked oil.

"Can we get by without it?" Yori asked. He detested having oil on his hands and looked around for a rag to wipe them with. "Don't you have any clean rags on this tub?"

"Here." Juan handed him a rag that was slightly less oily than his hands. "I'd have to rebuild the motor to fix the leak." The motor was mounted on steel beds next to the main engine and powered the generator with a pulley and a big V-belt. "Without the generator, there's no power for lights, pumps, or anything."

"So, what do you suggest?" Yori was lost when it came to mechanical things.

"Buy lots of oil," Juan replied.

Exasperated, Yori pulled a wad of Pesos from his pocket and counted out a thousand. "Get enough to last a month," he said, handing Juan the money. "Show me the fish hold."

Juan led him aft, across a passageway and through a door to the hold. It had been converted to a crude machine shop and was cluttered with a mill, a lathe, drill press, and other machine tools. Above a long, metal workbench on the port side, shelves and storage lockers were full of hand tools and machinery parts. Bits of worn out and rusty engine parts, pulleys, and shafts overfilled buckets and crates strewn around the floor. More crates of junk were piled along the starboard side of the hold. An electric motor the size of a watermelon lay on a workbench. "What's that?" Yori jabbed a finger at it.

"An air compressor motor."

Juan sure knows his way around machinery, Yori thought, feeling a twinge of envy. "Looks like the bearings are shot," he said, trying to show Juan that he knew something about motors too. They moved aft past the cluttered workbench to a stairwell, which led up to the aft deck. Yori examined a metal seining skiff that was lashed across the stern, a leftover from the *Tortuga Negra's* previous life as a purse seiner. "Does this thing run?" he asked. "We're going to need it when we get to Crusoe."

"Oh yes," Juan replied. "Antonio and I drove it around the harbor yesterday."

"Then everything is ready?" Yori asked.

"I just need to get the oil," Juan replied.

"Good. Go get it now." Exhausted, Yori climbed the stairs to his cabin where he flopped on the bunk and tried to sleep. Instead, he lay awake, staring at the ceiling. Step one of his plan had gone like clockwork. Of course, Maria and the brat would disagree, but Yori had always considered them expendable. Step two of his plan was to beat Captain Villareal to the rendezvous with the American boat. He rolled over and went to sleep.

He awoke before dawn and went down to the galley. Juan and Antonio were already up and eating a breakfast of toast and coffee. Yori poured a cup for himself and joined them at the dinette. "Did you get the oil?" he asked Juan.

"Three cases, boss." Juan poured himself another cup of steaming black coffee. "It will last at least a month."

"And you're sure you know the way to Isla Crusoe?" Yori asked him.

"I've been there many times," he replied.

A calendar was taped to the bulkhead next to the refrigerator. Below a photo of a swimsuit model, the month of January 1987 was displayed. Yori lifted that page and put a finger on Tuesday, February 3rd. "We need to be at Isla Crusoe before this date. How long will it take to get there?"

Juan put down his coffee and scratched his head. "Well, it's 250 miles to San Antonio. That will take two days. From there it's 360 miles west to Crusoe. That will take another two or three days."

"So, five- or six-days total?"

"Maybe," Juan said. "Probably more, because we gotta wait for good weather."

Antonio folded a slice of toast in half, shoved it in his mouth and washed it down with a slurp of coffee. When he finished swallowing, he dragged a hand across his crumb-laden lips. "This boat is old, *Capitan*, she doesn't like rough weather anymore."

Yori stared at his crew, exasperated again. "I don't give a fuck about the weather. Today is January 22nd. We're going to be there on the second." He dumped the last of his coffee in the sink and started for the bridge. "Start the engine, we leave in half an hour."

CHAPTER 11

AFTER CROSSING THE equator, *Staghound* continued southward in easy winds and gentle waves, passing 150 miles west of the Galapagos Islands. In this deserted part of the ocean they saw no vessels of any kind. It was as if *Staghound* had sailed into a world of her own. *A lonely ship on an empty sea,* Cliff thought as he scanned the unbroken horizon with binoculars. Even the ever-present sea birds seemed to have vanished.

The Weatherfax machine stopped receiving reports. Jon said it was because they were too far south to get a signal, so they relied on the old methods of forecasting, using their eyes and the barometer, which was beginning to fall.

On January 23rd, high clouds drifted overhead and a halo appeared around the sun, sure signs of bad weather coming. By midafternoon, the wind had shifted toward the east and built to about twenty knots. The crew triple-reefed the mainsail and hoisted the storm jib.

"Bear off to a course of south-southwest," Jon called to Mike, who was at the helm.

After nightfall, the wind increased to over thirty knots accompanied by heavy rain that was blown almost horizontal. Mike, dressed in foul weather gear, added a diver's mask to protect his eyes from the blowing rain and salt spray that was whipped off the tops of the waves. *Staghound* ran all night with the seas on her port beam. Often a wave would break over the rail, sending an explosion of spray over the boat, drenching the helmsman and filling the cockpit with cold seawater.

Down in the cabin, Cliff helped Jon check lashings on the crates, relieved that they didn't budge when the boat heeled over in the powerful gusts. In the galley, the stove swung on its gimbals but Lena, ever the reliable cook, made hot meals and kept a pot of coffee going for the crew as they came and went on their watches.

Later, when Cliff came below from his watch on deck, the skin on his face burned from the constant onslaught of wind and salt spray. He slowly stripped off his foulies, hanging on to the cabin's handholds while he did so. He wedged himself into his bunk but sleep was impossible as *Staghound* lurched and slammed through the raging seas. He watched Mike and Lena sitting at the dinette, legs braced against the table supports, talking. He couldn't make out what they were saying because of the shrieking wind and the roar of the ocean, but it was strange to see them engaged in casual conversation in the midst of the storm. After a few minutes, Lena stood and, timing her movements perfectly with a lull in the waves, darted into her stateroom. Mike remained at the dinette, staring at the space where Lena had just been, as if she had left a luminous wake behind when she disappeared. Cliff turned over in his bunk, closed his eyes, and tried to sleep as *Staghound* careened over the wild swells.

For four days, *Staghound* labored southward under gloomy skies and strong winds that varied between east and southeast. Nights were dark, with scudding clouds and ominous white-capped waves big enough to heel *Staghound* thirty degrees or more when they slammed into her port beam. There were no more afternoons of friendly banter in the cockpit. Instead, the crew encased themselves in foul weather gear whenever they were on deck. They took to their bunks when they came off watch, tired out by the constant struggle to keep the boat on course as they stood their watches, day and night.

On January 27th, there was a break in the clouds. The wind had eased a bit too, though the seas remained mountainous. Half an hour before noon Cliff grabbed the sextant and made his way over the pitching deck to his perch at the base of the mast. To him, the view was magnificent and terrifying at the same time. One moment *Staghound* rode the crest of a wave and his view was of endless whitecaps as far as he could see. The next moment she was in a trough between waves as high as the spreaders with gray scudding clouds racing overhead. He put the sextant to his eye and peered through the scope, but the huge waves made it hard to steady the instrument and bring the sun down to the heaving horizon. He jockeyed around the mast in hopes of finding a suitable position to take a sight. The sun reached its zenith and hung there as if stopped at ninety degrees above the horizon. *That's not the way it's supposed to work*, he told himself. *It's supposed to start descending within seconds after its zenith. I must be doing something wrong.* Eventually, he gave up, jotted down the time, and headed down to the nav station. He struggled with the calculations until Jon joined him.

"I'm having trouble solving for our position," Cliff said. "I couldn't even get a good fix on the sun."

"I'm not surprised," Jon said with a chuckle. "You've never sailed under the sun before."

"What? That doesn't make sense."

"Sure it does," Jon pointed to an "x" on the chart. "This is our position based on my dead reckoning, roughly 19 degrees south." He opened the nautical almanac and found January 27th. "The Sun moves from 23°-27' south on the winter solstice, to the equator by March 20th, headed north." He looked at Cliff. "You follow me?"

"Right, March 20ᵗʰ is the vernal equinox." Suddenly he understood. He checked the Sun's declination for January 27ᵗʰ. "The Sun is at 18°-44' south. Until today we were always north of it, but now we're almost directly under it. Tomorrow we'll be south of it."

"You got it." Jon smiled. "When the sun is exactly ninety degrees above your horizon, it seems to just hang there and you can't get an accurate time of its zenith." He chuckled again. "But you confirmed that my dead reckoning has been pretty damned accurate after four days without a noon sight." He left Cliff and disappeared into his cabin.

Using a pair of dividers, Cliff measured the distance to Robinson Crusoe Island. *1,250 miles distant. At this rate, we'll be there in eight days.* He checked the calendar on the bulkhead and put a pencil mark on February 4ᵗʰ.

᷍

Cliff's noon sight on February 3ʳᵈ put *Staghound* at 33°-30' south by 82°-30' west. He sat at the chart table thinking of Los Angeles, which was at the same latitude, but in the northern hemisphere. February 3ʳᵈ was the deepest part of winter there. Aboard *Staghound*, it was the height of summer. His thoughts drifted to his former home in Avila Beach, where at that moment it was probably cold and foggy.

"You look lost." Lena had come out of her cabin. She seemed to have a knack for catching him daydreaming.

"No, just thinking of home." He tapped the chart with his pencil and changed the subject. "We're about 180 miles from Crusoe."

"If your navigation is correct," she said.

"Yeah, there's that."

She leaned over the desk and studied the chart a moment. It

was the large-scale chart he'd been using since they left Wilmington and showed Crusoe as nothing more than a speck.

"Plot our position on the small-scale chart. It'll be more useful." Cliff searched in the desk for the detailed chart of the Juan Fernandez Islands. When he laid it out on the table, he was surprised to find that there was another island to the west of Crusoe, which wasn't on the large-scale chart. When he plotted *Staghound's* position, it appeared to be just eighty miles ahead of *Staghound*. "Isla Alejandro Selkirk," he said. "The big chart doesn't show it at all."

"That's right," Lena said. "It will be in sight before dark. We're stopping there." She turned and knocked on Jon's cabin door.

"A change of plans?" Cliff asked when Jon appeared.

"Yeah" Jon studied the chart and put a finger on the east side of Selkirk Island. "We're going to anchor here." He glanced at his watch, "We'll have the hook down by midnight."

"Why are we stopping there instead of Crusoe?"

Lena spoke. "That's the rendezvous point."

"I thought we're going here." Cliff jabbed a finger at Crusoe Island on the chart.

"Selkirk is better," Jon said. "It's completely deserted."

"Captain Villareal suggested it, just before we left," Lena remarked.

"Why didn't you tell me that before?" Cliff demanded.

"Security precaution," Jon replied. "It's nothing personal. You didn't need to know this until now."

Cliff stared at both of them. "What about Mike?"

"He doesn't care. All he cares about is sailing and surfing...and his share." Jon put on a reassuring smile. "It's for our safety that we keep a tight lid on information about what we're doing. You've heard the old saying, 'Loose lips sink ships', right?"

Cliff continued to stare at them doubtfully. One part of him understood that secrecy was vital to their plans, but he was also disappointed that they didn't trust him.

As if reading his mind, Lena said, "It's not that we don't trust you. We must keep everything secret until the mission is accomplished. If you needed to know where we're going before now, we would have told you."

"See," Jon said, "If the wrong people figure out where we're going, we might have an unpleasant surprise waiting for us when we arrive. So, yeah, we use a little misinformation about where we're going and what we're doing."

"I guess I can understand that," Cliff said. "But we're almost to this Selkirk Island, and I want to know the details."

"Fair enough, we'll anchor on the east side of the island and wait for a fishing boat, the *Peregrino,* Captain Villareal's boat," Lena said. "We'll make the transfer and be on our way in no more than six hours."

"Who is Captain Villareal?"

"He works for MIR, the group I told you about," Lena replied.

"And he's going to use the weapons to storm the prison where your parents are? That sounds a little crazy."

"No. He's paying us for the weapons. I'll use my share to buy their freedom." Lena wore a determined expression. "The Pinochet government is totally corrupt. You can buy anything or anyone with American dollars."

Cliff couldn't quite imagine her making a deal with a prison warden. "How are you going to manage that?"

"That's my business." She paused a second. "You'll be home and back with your wife by then."

Cliff let that comment go. "Alright. We are where we are. What's my role in this transfer?"

"You don't have to do anything except help get the boxes off the boat," Jon said.

"Then what?"

"We go wherever we want. Hell, I bet Selkirk has some waves. We might be the first people ever to surf them. That would be awesome! If it doesn't, we'll head for Easter Island. We can be there in seven or eight days. From there we can cruise eastern Polynesia before we head home."

Jon's enthusiasm was contagious. Cliff imagined warm water and an infinity of crystal blue waves breaking on beaches lined with coconut palms and no footprints. "Yeah, that sounds interesting, but what about Crusoe?"

"We might go there yet, depending on what Villareal says about the situation there."

⋘

A crescent moon hung overhead as *Staghound* glided quietly a mile off the north shore of Selkirk Island. Mike eased the mainsheet, taking advantage of the light northerly breeze. Cliff stood at the helm while Jon and Lena took turns with the binoculars, scanning the high cliffs and rugged shoreline of the island.

"What's your heading now?" Jon asked Cliff, holding binoculars to his eyes.

"Due east," Cliff replied, glancing at the compass.

"Okay, we'll go around that point off the starboard bow and head south. The anchorage should be three miles past it."

They all scoured the island with their eyes, seeing nothing but dark, forbidding cliffs as the sloop turned southward along the eastern shore of the island.

Lena held the binoculars now. "I see a couple of buildings ahead. That's the place."

"Okay," Jon said. "Let's douse sails and start the engine."

With the sails down, *Staghound* motored slowly closer to shore. Now they could see two buildings on a rocky beach.

"Anchor's ready!" Mike shouted from the bow.

Jon glanced at Lena, who nodded as she stared at the bleak shoreline. "Okay, lower away," he said to Mike.

Twenty minutes later *Staghound* lay at anchor a hundred yards off the beach, her bow pointed into the breeze. No lights or signs of life appeared on the shore. The others, accustomed to making landfall in strange places went below, but Cliff stayed on deck, He went up to the foredeck and sat with his back against the dinghy. The sight and smell of land tantalized his senses and he imagined what it must have been like for Columbus and Magellan when they discovered a distant island. He lay down on the foredeck and gazed up at the strange, scattered constellations of the southern hemisphere as the moon disappeared behind a high peak on the island. The light wind coming over the bow was cool. He had just zipped his jacket and pulled his black watch cap down to his ears when he heard someone approaching. Lena had come on deck and stood near the mast, not more than ten feet from where Cliff lay. In the dark, and hidden behind the dinghy, Cliff was sure she hadn't seen him.

"What is it?" he heard her say in a low voice.

The other voice was Mike's. "We've been out here for over a month. Tomorrow let's ditch those guys and get it on."

"You called me out here to ask me to sleep with you?"

"No. I'm tellin' you we could have some fun without Cliff and Jon around. I know you want it as bad as I do."

There was a pause. Cliff froze, not daring to breathe. This wasn't a conversation he wanted to overhear.

Lena spoke, "Mike, we've been over this before. I like you, but I'm not sleeping with you or anyone else on this boat."

"No one needs to know. We could all go ashore in the morning, then you and I could slip back to the boat without them. You could say you don't feel well. We could fool around and then I'll take the dinghy back ashore. Those guys wouldn't even know."

Lena laughed softly. "Wouldn't know? How long do you think

it would take for Jon or Cliff to figure out we're sleeping together, an hour? Surely no more than a day."

Mike didn't respond.

"Look, Mike, I'm not interested, okay? If you pester me again, *you're* going to be the one who doesn't feel well," she said, her voice moving away.

Cliff held his breath, waiting for Mike to leave. After a minute, he shuffled aft toward the companionway and Cliff breathed again. He stayed on deck another hour before returning to his bunk. In the cabin, he glanced over at Mike's berth and saw that he was in it.

With perfect timing, Jon gunned the dinghy's outboard motor and the inflatable boat rode a wave far up the bouldered beach. Mike and Cliff jumped out and held it steady while the wave receded. Jon and Lena clambered out of the little boat and the four of them hauled it farther up the seaweed-covered beach. The pungent smell of decaying seaweed hung in the air and they were swarmed by thousands of kelp flies.

"Come on! Let's go before they eat us alive," Jon said. Waving hands in front of their faces to keep the pesky insects from crawling up their nostrils and into their ears, they scrambled out of the zone of flies toward the building they'd seen the night before. Cliff entered and squinted up at the roof. Daylight shone through in a dozen places. Inside, there were a couple of old wooden fishing skiffs propped up on sagging sawhorses. Worn out fishing gear and old nets lay in piles behind the skiffs. Along one wall was a rough workbench with a few rusty hand tools lying on it, as if the workers had knocked off for the day and never came back.

Finding nothing of interest in the boathouse, they headed inland toward other buildings, which were arranged on the banks of a dry wash that ran down the middle of the abandoned village.

"Looks like this is where fishermen live during the season," Mike said. They surveyed a dilapidated shack that contained several cots with moldy mattresses, a few chairs and other furniture. "Hey," he said, picking up an old magazine, "A Playboy!" He flipped through the water-stained pages searching for the centerfold, then tossed the magazine aside when he discovered it had been torn out.

They moved on to another shack with its door ajar. Mike pushed on it and peered inside. "Well looky here, boys. A pool table."

The building was a sort of dirt-floored community center with a few chairs and benches, and a makeshift bookshelf with a hundred or more paperbacks, all in Spanish. The centerpiece of the place was the old pool table. Its green baize surface was worn and faded, and the leather around the pockets was cracked and missing in some places. On the wall was a rack of cues and a complete set of billiard balls, even a couple of chalks. The balls were chipped and half of the cues were missing tips.

Mike racked the balls and selected a cue. "Eight-ball. Buck a game," he said to Jon. Within minutes they were deeply engrossed in their game and barely acknowledged Cliff when he left.

"See you guys on the beach at sundown," Cliff said.

"Yeah, okay," Jon responded without looking up. "Five ball in the corner pocket."

Leaving the settlement behind, Cliff followed the trail inland a quarter mile. It ended at a crude dam made of mortar and stones with a mossy pond behind it. Trees and ferns overhung its banks. After a month of seeing nothing but sea and sky, the deep greens of the vegetation dazzled his eyes. He reached out and touched the rough bark of a tree, his mind spinning back to the Buffum ranch, Alice Hilliard, and the oak she had wanted him to save. He paused, giving thanks that there were still places where men hadn't wreaked their will on nature. After a moment he gave the tree a final pat and moved on. To the left of the pond, he discovered a rocky footpath leading toward the ridge high above. From *Staghound's* deck, he had seen a trail along that ridge and figured this path would intersect it so he could hike down to the beach that way instead of heading back the way he came. It was a strenuous climb and he estimated he'd gained five hundred feet of elevation when he reached the ridge. In the ravine, the air was still, but on the ridge, a gentle breeze blew out of the north. The view was something he might have dreamed of when his father spoke of south sea voyages. The sea stretched infinitely to the east. To the north and south, he saw nothing but mountains and sky. Below, *Staghound* rode gracefully to her anchor in the placid waters of the bay. Cliff noticed there were no roads on the island. *I'll probably never be so far from civilization again.* Inspired, he turned west, toward higher country.

The walking was easier on the ridge but the trail was no less steep. Cliff was puffing when he topped a small rise and stopped to catch his breath. Looking back, he saw that he had covered roughly half a mile in distance and gained another five hundred feet of elevation. Ahead, the trail continued up the ridge and disappeared behind a grassy outcrop. He sat on a rock and took off his shoe to examine a blister that had started on his foot. He was rubbing the painful spot when he looked up and saw Lena coming down the trail.

"Are you okay?" she asked.

"Yeah, just a little blister on my foot," he replied, embarrassed that she found him this way.

"Let me see," she knelt and examined his foot. "You shouldn't be up here without proper shoes," she scolded. "Sit still." She poured water from her canteen onto a cloth and washed the area around the blister. "I have moleskins." She dug into her knapsack and retrieved a tiny medical kit. She applied the moleskin and covered it with a small bandage. "There," she said, patting his foot. "No sign of gangrene, so you'll survive."

Cliff found his voice, "What are you doing way up here?"

"The same as you, hiking," she replied. "Only I came better prepared."

They sat in the shade of a stunted tree and Lena produced a plastic container with sliced apples, nuts, hard cheese, and salami. "These are the last of the fresh apples, so enjoy them."

Cliff took a bite of the apple and gazed seaward. A spark of light caught his eye. It disappeared, came back, and disappeared again. He stared another moment and it reappeared, the sun's reflection on a windshield.

"There's a boat coming."

CHAPTER 12

IN THE PILOTHOUSE of the *Tortuga Negra* Yori watched Juan go through the procedure to start the engine. After a couple of sputtering coughs, the stack emitted a belch of black smoke and the old diesel came to life. Leaving the transmission in neutral, Juan pushed the throttle forward and the engine revved to an uneven rumble.

"She's good." He grinned at Yori.

"You drive." Yori stepped to the pilothouse door and flicked a cigarette butt into the water, then nodded to Antonio who waited on the foredeck for a signal to release the mooring line.

The old boat slowly gathered way while people on the nearby wharf stared at the unlikely sight of a boat from the moribund Coquimbo fishing fleet heading out to sea.

Back in the pilothouse, he watched Juan handle the spoked steering wheel, guiding the boat past the ancient stone fort that guarded the port. Beyond it lay the open sea.

The boat rolled and heaved as its high bow pushed into the oncoming waves, sending spray across the corroded steel deck. Their course was southward along the coast to the fishing port of San Antonio, where Yori knew the *Peregrino* was anchored, waiting for the order to depart for its rendezvous with the American boat, the *Staghound*.

Tortuga Negra waddled down the coast with Yori and Juan

taking turns at the helm while Antonio kept the engine running and cooked the meals. Bucking a northbound current, they made slow progress and after twenty-four hours the boat was little more than halfway to San Antonio. It was near midnight the following day when *Tortuga Negra* made her way into its tiny harbor. At Yori's command, her rust-eaten anchor splashed into the murky water. With the boat secure in the anchorage, the tension headache that had dogged him since they left Coquimbo eased. During the nearly two days at sea, he figured he'd gotten about six hours of sleep.

Alone in his cabin, he undressed and washed his face at a small metal sink mounted to a bulkhead. As he dried it, he looked in the grimy mirror above the sink. His dark eyes were deep-set and he had a long, Roman nose. His beard was thin and wispy and his thick hair hung down over his brow and ears. He ran a finger along the scar on his face. Maria used to joke that he had once been handsome, but with that scar, he would never be a movie star.

He lit a Marlboro and, on impulse, crouched down and groped under the bunk for the valise. Not satisfied to just feel for the money in it, he pulled it out. The stacks of hundred-dollar bills were all there. Reassured, he zipped up the bag and shoved it back under the bunk. *I won't breathe easy until this operation is over*, he thought. He lay down on the bed and put his pistol under the pillow. From where he lay, he could reach the light switch, his bottle of whiskey, and his glass. He took a small metal ashtray from the table and, lying on his back, set it on his chest and smoked in the dark, reaching for his glass occasionally and letting the warmth of the Jack Daniels soothe his tobacco-parched throat.

He thought about old Captain Villareal and the money he would be carrying to pay for the American guns. His mind wrestled with the idea of killing Villareal and taking that money too. But he knew the Captain was wily, and his heavily armed crew were loyal to MIR. *Too risky*, he thought.

His thoughts turned to the Americans. He had to admire the idea of using a sailboat to smuggle guns, a perfect disguise for a gunrunner. A sailboat was benign, a softer target than the *Peregrino* and its crew of fucking communist zealots.

He thought about the money again. *If El Halcon finds out I kept the money, I'm a dead man. With Juan and Antonio, it will be only a matter of time before one of them tells someone. I can't risk that, so they will have to go, before we get back to Coquimbo.*

That left Maria. *Let's say we pick up where we left off. She's not stupid, she would quickly figure out where the money came from. Then no matter where we go, she could pick up the phone and call El Halcon, and I'd be a dead man. I can't have a woman with that much leverage over me. Fuck that. I'm going to Buenos Aires, get fake papers and disappear. That's the only way I'll survive.*

He drained his glass and poured another.

The next morning Juan pointed out a nondescript looking vessel among a fleet of aging fishing boats anchored nearby. "The *Peregrino*," he said.

Yori picked up a pair of binoculars and examined it carefully. It was a fishing boat slightly smaller than the *Tortuga Negra*. But it was a real fishing boat equipped with the mast, boom and nets of a purse seiner instead of the *Tortuga Negra's* added-on deckhouse. He counted three men on the aft deck hauling a skiff up the transom, and two more in the pilothouse. He put the binoculars down and thought for a moment. "I want you to take the rowboat to that beach over there," he said to Juan, pointing to a deserted spot on the shore. "Bring back a couple of buckets of sand."

"Why do we need sand?"

"You're going to dump it into *Peregrino's* fuel tanks tonight."

"Ah, I see! The sand will clog their fuel filters."

"As long as the boat is at anchor, a few kilos of sand will sit on the bottom of each tank and the engine will run fine. But when they get out of the harbor, the rolling of the boat will stir up the sand and it won't take long for it to start clogging those filters." Yori allowed himself a brief smile and lit a cigarette.

That night, after 0200, Yori watched Juan and Antonio row silently across the harbor to the *Peregrino*. Juan climbed up the side of the fishing boat with a bucket of sand while Antonio waited in the rowboat. With binoculars, he could clearly see Juan work the cap off the starboard fuel fill and dump sand down the fill pipe, then move to the port side and repeat the process. He then sneaked forward along the bulwark and seemed to freeze.

What the fuck are you doing? Yori thought. He held his breath, suspecting Juan had been noticed, but after half a minute Juan moved aft and slipped over the side of the fishing boat, landing softly in the dinghy.

"How'd it go?" Yori asked when they were back aboard the Tortuga Negra.

"Perfect. Two kilos of sand in each tank."

"I saw you go forward, that was risky. What were you doing?"

"I pissed in their water tank." Juan grinned. Mischief came naturally to him.

"You pissed in their water?" Yori asked, incredulous.

"I told him not to do it," Antonio said, his chubby face wore a worried expression.

Yori couldn't help smiling, then they all broke into laughter.

"The great *Capitan Villareal* will be drinking my piss in his morning coffee," Juan said, setting off another round of guffaws.

They waited seven long days in San Antonio. During that time, Yori was nervous and irritable. He stayed in his cabin or the pilothouse listening to weather reports and chatter on the VHF radio while the crew kept out of his way, playing cards and listening to music in the galley. At dawn on February 1st, Juan knocked on Yori's cabin door.

"What?" Yori demanded irritably. He'd been asleep.

"The *Peregrino,* she is getting underway," Juan said.

"Quick! Get the engine started." Yori rushed to the porthole in his cabin, anxiously watching the other boat begin to move toward the harbor mouth while he dressed. "Hurry, dammit. I don't want to let those bastards get out of sight."

Twenty minutes later Juan stood at the helm as the *Tortuga Negra* cleared the breakwater with the *Peregrino* a couple of miles ahead. Coming south from Coquimbo, they had punched directly into the waves. Now they were headed west and the waves washed up the port side of *Tortuga Negra's* rusted black hull. The boat rolled ten, fifteen degrees to starboard and then fifteen degrees to port as each wave struck and passed under the keel. The *Peregrino* rolled the same way.

"Steer ten degrees to the south of the *Peregrino,*" Yori growled to Juan. "I don't want Villareal to suspect we're following him." He switched on the radar and waited impatiently for the machine to warm up. The *Tortuga Negra* trembled every few seconds as her propeller bit into the ocean, making him wonder if it might fall off its shaft before long. A minute later he forgot about that as the radar screen began to glow. He stared at it until he saw the blip of the other boat appear, two miles off the starboard bow.

The *Tortuga Negra* rolled sickeningly and Yori had to steady himself as his stomach sent a disconcerting alarm to his brain. Juan and Antonio were inured to rough weather but Yori was unaccustomed to the gyrations of a fishing boat in a cross-sea. Suddenly he lurched out the door of the bridge and vomited over the side. He wiped his mouth on his sleeve and stared down at the waves. *A week of this shit,* he thought bleakly, *I hope I can make it.* A few minutes later he recovered enough to stagger back into the pilothouse, fighting down waves of nausea while he searched for

Peregrino on the radar screen. "Hey Juan, did you change course?" he asked.

"No. Still the same, boss."

"Take a look at the radar. Looks like *Peregrino's* stopped," he pointed to the blip that was now on the far right edge of the screen. He took the helm while Juan studied the radar.

"Yeah, their filters are clogged," Juan said gleefully. "They're dead in the water."

Yori tried to smile but he was still gripped by nausea. "Okay, good work. Point this tub toward Crusoe," he said.

Neither Juan nor Yori was a trained navigator so they used the same method Chilean fishermen used in the old days. Crusoe lay almost exactly due west of San Antonio. But they must cross the Humboldt Current, which flows northward at the rate of about one mile per hour. To compensate for that, Juan steered a course of 265 degrees. "Don't worry," he said to Yori. "We'll be there in two days."

Yori waited until Juan turned the wheel and the *Tortuga Negra* settled on the new course before he opened the door to his cabin. "Call me if anything changes," he said and stumbled in. He washed his mouth with water from the basin and flopped onto the bunk.

⁓

Six hours later, Yori relieved Juan at the helm. "Where is the *Peregrino*?" he asked as he took the wheel.

"They disappeared off the radar about two hours ago," Juan said. "As far as I could tell, they were still dead in the water and calling for help on the radio."

"Excellent," Yori said. "One less thing to worry about. How far are we from Crusoe?" He estimated that they had traveled about eighty nautical miles since leaving port.

"Maybe three hundred miles," Juan replied. "We'll be there at dawn the day after tomorrow, boss." He glanced at Yori. "Antonio is staying in the engine room babying the generator motor. He'll give it a liter of oil every twelve hours."

Yori had forgotten about that motor. "Okay, keep him at it. And get some rest. I want you back up here in four hours"

Alone on the bridge, Yori stared at the endless waves rolling from south to north, pushed by a steady southerly wind. An hour later it was dark except for the dim red bulb in the compass binnacle and the bluish glow of the radar screen. Peering through the windshield, he saw a waning crescent moon hanging low in the sky ahead. Its reflection lay on the waves like a silvery path while stars peeked through the scattered clouds. For a moment he was struck by the beauty of the sea at night.

An hour later the moon sank below the horizon and the clouds closed in, blotting out the stars. *If this old rust-bucket sprang a leak and sank*, Yori thought, *no one would even know where to look for us.* He gripped the wheel harder and focused on the compass.

Time passed slowly while the *Tortuga Negra* made its way westward. During the night Juan had stood a watch, and at dawn Yori relieved him. Now, slouched in the helmsman's chair with one hand on the wheel, Yori struggled to keep his eyes open as he counted the minutes until Juan would come up and relieve him. When he finally arrived, Yori found his cheery "Good afternoon" annoying. He said nothing in reply, locking himself in his cabin and taking a pull from his bottle of whiskey before falling asleep on his unmade bunk.

The following afternoon, a small dark bump appeared on the horizon. Yori strained his eyes looking at it through binoculars, but couldn't make out whether it was the island or a ship in the distance. It was getting dark and whatever it was soon disappeared in the gloom. Four hours later he was awakened by Juan pounding on his cabin door.

"I see it! The island is there on the port bow," he said excitedly.

Rubbing sleep from his eyes, Yori picked up a pair of binoculars and leaned against the railing outside the pilothouse. He scanned the horizon ahead and couldn't see anything at first, but then he spotted a tiny, intermittent pinpoint of light, barely visible in the distance.

"You sure that light is Isla Crusoe?" Yori asked.

"There's no other lights out here, boss. I'm sure it's Crusoe." Juan replied with a grin. At dawn, the *Tortuga Negra* was skirting along the northeast coast of the island. Yori stood in the frigid wind on the narrow landing outside the pilothouse, scanning the island with binoculars. Sea birds soared above while hundreds of sea lions sunned themselves on the narrow gravel beaches at the base of the cliffs. There was no sign of human life along the shore or up the narrow valleys that punctuated the bluffs. For a panicky moment, he feared that they had missed Crusoe and found some uninhabited island instead.

His nerves stretched taut, he darted into the pilothouse to check the chart again.

"Steer closer to shore," he snapped at Juan. "I don't want to miss the harbor."

"We can't see it from here, the village is around that point," Juan said confidently, pointing at a dismal black outcropping of rocks off the port bow.

A few minutes later *Tortuga Negra* rounded the point and a small village came into view, nestled in the southwest corner of the cove ahead. Yori saw a few buildings along the shore, and maybe twenty houses on the hillside above a wide gravel beach. In the cove, half a dozen fishing boats tugged at their anchors and a few skiffs lay beached near the jetty. A couple of fishermen in a launch worked a net in the middle of the cove. They glanced at the *Tortuga Negra* for a moment but didn't pay any attention to the old workboat.

"San Juan Bautista," Juan said nodding toward the village.

Wind funneled down the valley, whipping up whitecaps on the water.

Yori felt a twinge of accomplishment. Not that they'd made it to Crusoe, but that he wasn't seasick. "Alright, which way to Selkirk from here?"

"We go around that point, then steer 265 degrees," Juan replied, pointing toward a high bluff about three miles ahead.

"How far is it again?" Yori spread a chart on the desk and found a speck labeled *Isla Mas a Fuera* that lay almost exactly due west of Crusoe.

"About a hundred miles." Juan glanced over at Yori. "I hope that sailboat is there because, boss, that is a lonely fucking island." Juan slowly shook his head. He was standing at the helm and turned the wheel a couple of spokes to port and then back, keeping the *Tortuga Negra* on course.

"Yeah? That's exactly what we need for this caper." Yori stood behind him, leaning against the chart table. He drew a pack of cigarettes from his shirt pocket. Holding a match to his cigarette, his eye drifted to the back of Juan's head, where the braid of his pigtail began. He imagined putting the muzzle of his Walther there and pulling the trigger. Mentally going through the motions. He'd do it quickly, before Juan could react.

Juan spoke, and the vision of the murder Yori was planning vanished. "The fishing's good there. Maybe I'll catch us a tuna or dorado after we finish with the Americans. That would be fun."

Yori took a drag on his cigarette and exhaled a plume of smoke. "Yeah, that would be fun."

When the Tortuga Negra cleared the northwest point of Isla Crusoe, the southerly waves, which had been blocked by the island rolled the boat as much as before. Yori hated the rolling and feared another bout of seasickness, but it didn't come. *A hundred miles, ten hours of rolling. I can handle it.*

"Know why the government changed the name of that island to Selkirk?" Juan suddenly asked.

"No."

"Tourism! Can you believe it? They thought by changing the name from *Mas a Fuera* to fucking Selkirk, tourists would show up there." Juan snorted. "Who the fuck would want to go four hundred miles out to that fucking rock on vacation? Nobody! There's no fucking hotels, no bars, no cars and no bitches. The government is fucking crazy!"

"That was before Pinochet's time, wasn't it?" Yori asked.

"Yeah, but that doesn't mean Pinochet isn't crazy too. Look what he did to the fishermen!"

"Okay, I'm going to get some sleep." Yori knew when Juan got going about the government there was no shutting him up. He checked his watch. "Call me in three hours."

Leaving Juan, Yori stepped into his cabin and locked the door. He pulled the Walther from under the pillow on his bunk and made sure it was loaded, then reached for his AK47. He snapped a loaded magazine into the receiver and propped it behind the door, ready for instant use. Next, he removed a flag from his bag. It was the venerable blue, white and yellow of the *"Patria Vieja"*, the Old Fatherland. It had been Chile's national flag when it declared its independence from Spain back in 1810. After Pinochet took power, the MIR adopted it as their own. His MIR informant told him the Americans were expecting to rendezvous with a boat flying the *Patria Vieja*.

CHAPTER 13

IT WAS MIDNIGHT when the strange vessel arrived in the bay at Selkirk Island. *Staghound's* crew gathered in the cockpit, eyeing the new arrival, which dropped anchor a hundred-fifty yards from the sloop.

"It don't look like any fishing boat I ever seen," Mike said, binoculars in hand.

Jon took the binoculars and studied the vessel. "It has the look of a purse seiner, with a big seining skiff on the stern, but there's a deckhouse where the fish hold should be."

As the boat swung to her anchor, the name, crudely painted near its prow, came into view.

"*Tortuga Negra*," Jon read.

"Okay," Lena said. "It's not our contact. It's probably a fishing boat, or maybe a lobster boat."

"Nah, I think that old rustbucket came out here to die," Mike said with a chuckle. "She don't look like she's got any more miles left in her."

"Hang on, they put a dinghy in the water," Jon said, peering through the glasses. "Two guys got aboard it, and they're headed this way."

As the little boat got closer, Cliff didn't need binoculars to see the two men in the dinghy, which looked more like a rowboat to him. The one sitting in the stern was tall and slender. The other one, manning the oars was shorter, his pigtail clearly visible in the moonlight.

"*Hola!*" the tall one said when the dinghy came alongside. He stood in the stern and gripped *Staghound's* starboard gunwale. "*Americano,*" he said, pointing a finger at them and wearing a disarming grin. "*Yo Chileno!*" he pointed the finger at his own chest.

"Look at the scar on that guy's face," Mike muttered. *Staghound's* cockpit light was just bright enough to reveal an ugly dark line running down the left side of the man's narrow face.

Lena stepped forward and they spoke in Spanish.

"What are they saying," Jon asked Cliff out of the side of his mouth.

"He's a friend of Captain Villareal…something about engine trouble," Cliff replied. "Lena's being coy. Says she doesn't know what he's talking about."

Lena turned to Jon. "His name is Yori. He said the *Peregrino* broke down in San Antonio and Villareal sent him instead. I told him we're surfers looking for waves. But I don't think he's buying that story."

"Can you reach Villareal on the radio?" Jon asked. "Check Scarface's bona fides?"

"I can try." Lena turned back to Yori, whose expression darkened as she spoke. He let go of the gunwale and ordered the oarsman to take him back to the *Tortuga Negra*, saying something to Lena in harsher terms as they left.

"He says he's not playing games," Lena said, not taking her eyes off the rowboat. "He said there's a storm coming." She looked at Jon. "He'll be back at sunup."

Mike spoke, "The barometer is falling. He's right about the weather."

"The wind's shifted already," Cliff said. "Two hours ago it was coming from the north, now it's northeast."

"I'll try to raise Villareal." Lena headed below, followed by Mike.

"So, what now?" Cliff asked Jon, who lingered a moment on deck.

Jon ran a hand over his bearded face. "We wait for an answer from Villareal. If she can't reach him, we'll have to make a decision." He gazed at the workboat, whose lights were being turned off, one by one until only its white anchor light shone.

Cliff stayed on deck after Jon went below. Until now he had given little thought to how the transaction would go down when Lena's friends arrived. *Suppose this boat is her contact. Transferring the crates could be a challenge if the bay gets choppy.* Just then a gust of wind, stronger than before, whistled in *Staghound's* rigging. He pulled his collar up and watched high clouds drift across the starlit sky.

The night passed with Cliff dozing in the cockpit. Every hour or so he roused himself enough to check on the *Tortuga Negra*. The wind shifted from northeast to east, and the two vessels swung to their anchors in unison, offering Cliff a changing view of the dilapidated old boat. When the sky began to lighten in the east, he could make out more details. The *Tortuga Negra* appeared to be about eighty feet long, with a black hull and white superstructure. The steel hull was dented and battered, as if it had been through a war. On the losing side. Its grimy pilot house rose high above the foredeck with stairs leading up to it on both sides of the boat. The deckhouse stretched aft some thirty feet, leaving enough room for a boom crane and twenty feet of open deck in the stern. The transom incorporated a wide ramp where the seine skiff was lashed down. Cliff estimated the skiff to be twenty feet long. High sided and boxy, it looked capable of carrying a heavy load, like crates full of weapons.

As the morning grew brighter Cliff stared at the old boat through binoculars. Rusted oil drums, old coils of wire rope and unidentifiable bits of machinery were strewn about the *Tortuga Negra's* deck, most of it streaked with rust, or guano. Already a quartet of gulls had landed on its stubby mast, claiming the perch as their own. A flag flying from the mast seemed strangely out of place because it looked new, not the faded, tattered remnant he would have expected on such an old boat. Just then the pilothouse door opened and Yori appeared. *What did Jon call him? Scarface. He looks more like an assassin than a fishing boat captain.* Through the binoculars, Cliff watched him gaze at *Staghound* while he lit a cigarette, then descend the stairs to the main deck and disappear inside the deckhouse. A minute later he emerged with two other men. One was the pigtailed guy and the other was tall and heavy-set. Cliff watched Yori and Pigtail climb down a pocket ladder built into the side of the *Tortuga Negra's* hull and scramble into the rowboat. The oars glinted rhythmically in the sun as Pigtail rowed the boat toward *Staghound.*

Cliff dropped down the companionway. "Company's coming," he said to Jon, who was sitting at the chart table.

"Jeez," Jon said when he came on deck and studied the Tortuga Negra through binoculars. "That thing looks like a floating junkyard." He shifted his gaze to the approaching rowboat. "Lena," he called down the companionway. "Any luck with Villareal?"

"No. He's not responding on any of our designated channels. Either his radio is down or he's not aboard the *Peregrino*," she said when she came on deck. She suddenly grabbed the binoculars from Jon and peered at the flag flying from the old boat's mast. "Blue over white and yellow," she said. "The Patria Vieja. That's the flag Villareal was supposed to fly."

"Good morning," Yori said in Spanish when the rowboat reached the *Staghound.* "I trust you slept well?"

Cliff translated the gist of Yori's words under his breath for Jon.

"*Si.*" Lena replied in Spanish

"Good, may I come aboard? We have much to discuss and

very little time." He pointed toward an ominous-looking cloud-bank that had already blotted out the morning sun. "The storm is coming. We cannot stay here when it arrives."

"He wants to come aboard and talk," Lena said to Jon. "He knows why we're here. It's no use playing dumb with him."

Jon paused a moment, stroking his beard. "Alright, bring him aboard."

On deck, Yori looked around *Staghound*'s well-appointed cockpit. "Your yacht is very beautiful. May I look around?"

"No," Lena stepped between him and the companionway. "What did you want to talk about?"

"You know," came Yori's terse reply. When Lena hesitated, he leaned closer to her. "Quit wasting time. I know who you are and why you're here. If you don't believe what I'm saying come to my boat and I will provide you with proof."

His Spanish was clipped and rapid-fire, different from the Mexican Spanish Cliff had learned from his mother, but it wasn't hard to understand.

Lena turned to Jon. "I'm going with him to his boat. He says he has proof that he was sent by Villareal."

"Not without me. Tell him we'll come in our own dinghy. In fifteen minutes."

Cliff had noticed the oarsman bailing water out of the old wooden rowboat while he waited for Yori. *I wouldn't set foot in that thing either.*

"*Bueno*, but don't make me wait too long." Yori climbed into the rowboat and set off toward the fishing boat. The little boat yawed and heaved in the rapidly building waves.

"Mike, you'll have to stay here and make sure the boat's ready to leave on short notice," Jon said before he and Lena climbed down the boarding ladder to *Staghound*'s inflatable dinghy. "Cliff, you come with us and keep an eye on the dinghy while we meet with Scarface."

When they arrived alongside the old fishing boat, Jon and Lena managed to negotiate the pocket ladder built into *Tortuga Negra's* hull near the stern while Cliff passed the dinghy's painter around a massive cleat on the boat's bulwark.

"Welcome aboard," Yori said. "Come to my cabin." He motioned them forward to the boat's pilothouse.

Left alone, Cliff watched two of Yori's crew struggle to launch the big seining skiff. When it finally slid into the water it bucked and bounced off the fishing boat, putting more dents in its already battered aluminum hull.

Five minutes later Jon came hurrying down the ladder. "Let's go."

Cliff hesitated before untying the painter. "Where's Lena?"

"She's staying here until we get the crates transferred." Jon started the outboard and pointed the dinghy toward the *Staghound*. "We confirmed Yori's bona fides, so the deal is on."

"Really?"

"Yeah…He showed us the money." Jon gunned the outboard.

Cliff hung on to his cap, saying nothing as the little boat sped back to the sloop.

"Get some fenders out on the port side. I don't want that piece o' shit skiff banging against the hull," Jon said to Mike as he climbed aboard the sailboat. "We'll stage the crates in the cockpit. I think that skiff can handle at least ten of them at a time." He grinned at Mike. "We'll be outa here before the storm hits."

The big seine skiff plodded across the gap between the two boats at five knots, with the pigtailed oarsman at the helm and the heavyset crewman in the bow.

"Watch out!" Mike shouted as the clumsy skiff banged into *Staghound's* hull. "Toss me your painter. Oh hell, these guys don't speak English." He leaped into the skiff and threw its painter to Cliff then turned to the helmsman, pointing a finger at his chest.

"I'm Mike, you got it?" He jabbed his finger into his chest again. "Mike!"

Pigtail pointed to himself. "Juan!", and then at his crewman, "Antonio!"

"Okay, Juan, let's get these boxes loaded."

Juan stared at Mike in confusion.

Cliff spoke to him in Spanish, explaining how they would move the crates from *Staghound* to the skiff.

"*Bueno*" Juan said, and barked orders at Antonio.

It was nearly noon when the first squall struck, bringing pelting rain with the gusty east wind. Cliff stood on *Tortuga Negra's* wet deck, trying to keep the tenth crate from slipping overboard as they muscled it from the skiff to the fishing boat. *We should've put handles on these crates. I'll remember that the next time I get involved in a crazy gunrunning scheme.* He glanced over at *Staghound*. In the strong wind, her anchor rode was stretched taut and her stern had swung around so it was pointing directly at the island's bouldered beach.

With the crate safely aboard, he made his way forward and up the stairs to the pilothouse. He opened the door and poked his head inside. Yori, Jon, and Lena sat at a small dinette with stacks of bills arranged on the table. "The tenth crate is aboard."

Jon nodded to Yori, who slid several stacks of bills across the table.

Lena stuffed them into a waterproof bag. "That's half the money for half the crates," she said, glancing at Jon.

"Okay," Jon said to Cliff. "Bring the rest of them."

Back on the *Tortuga Negra's* aft deck, Cliff waited as a large wave passed under the fishing boat. Alongside, the seine skiff rose nearly to deck level on the swell and he jumped, landing in the middle of the ungainly craft. Antonio cast off the painter and the taciturn Juan put its diesel motor in gear and pointed the bow toward *Staghound*.

The weather had worsened in the last half hour. Rain swept across the bay in slanted sheets. Several inches of it had accumulated in the skiff and sloshed into Cliff's shoes. He shielded his eyes from the rain and braced himself in the bow of the lurching skiff as Juan guided it toward *Staghound*. The wind sent waves crashing on the beach, not a hundred yards from where *Staghound* tugged at her anchor. Looking back toward the *Tortuga Negra*, he saw the old boat rolling heavily in the churning waves.

"Hey. We gotta get out of here," Mike shouted over the gusts when Cliff climbed aboard *Staghound*. "I rigged the number four jib ready to hoist, ran the sheets, overhauled the halyards, and brought the anchor up as short as I dare. If you guys don't get back here soon, I'm afraid we'll drag right onto the beach," he shouted.

Cliff glanced shoreward and calculated that if *Staghound* dragged her anchor forty yards, she'd be in the surf line.

Mike jerked his head toward the fishing boat. "Tell those guys we can't stay here much longer."

"Come on then, help me put the boxes in the skiff," Cliff said. He hurried below and grabbed his foul weather jacket before he started hefting crates up the companionway.

"I'm gonna start the engine and take some strain off the anchor, otherwise it might break loose and this boat'll be on the beach in about a minute," Mike said when the crates were loaded onto the skiff. "You'd better do the same thing on the *Tortuga*,"

"Okay, I'll tell Yori!" Cliff yelled. He pulled the hood of his jacket up and pushed the skiff away from the sloop. Juan gunned the motor and the skiff bounced and bobbed back to the fishing boat.

They repeated the precarious process of transferring the boxes to *Tortuga Negra's* deck. When all were aboard, Cliff headed to the pilothouse. "We're done loading," he said.

With that announcement, Yori smiled and pushed the rest of the bills across the table.

"Now, a little celebration." He rose and brought a bottle and four small glasses to the table while Lena stashed the money in her waterproof bag.

Yori pulled the cork from the bottle with a flourish. "A drink to seal the deal."

Lena glanced at Jon, then double-checked the seal on the waterproof bag. "Okay."

Yori beckoned Cliff to join them.

"No thanks." He swept his eyes around the pilothouse. Rain pelted the windows and wind whistled in the rigging. "The storm's getting worse. We should leave now." His gaze settled on Yori. "You should too." He had switched to Spanish.

Yori raised his glass and said, "To General Pinochet. May he rot in hell!" He smiled and downed the drink in a single gulp.

The others did the same and stood.

"Let's go," Cliff said from the doorway.

Yori followed them down the stairs to the aft deck where Juan and Antonio, dressed in oilskins, had finished stowing the crates in the aft deckhouse.

Jon shook Yori's hand and climbed down to *Staghound*'s dinghy, which was banging against the rough steel of the *Tortuga Negra*'s hull.

Lena started to follow Jon. Before she stepped over the bulwark to climb down to the dinghy, Juan reached out and pulled her back.

"Let go of me!" She broke free of him, but Yori had pulled a pistol from his jacket and stepped between her and the *Tortuga Negra*'s boarding ladder.

"Give me the bag and you can go."

"Get out of my way!" She rushed toward the ladder, but Juan roughly pulled her back.

Cliff froze when he saw the gun in Yori's hand, but when Juan shoved Lena he reacted. "Hey!" He jumped to her defense, taking a swing at Juan, who dodged the punch. Off-balance on the slippery deck, Cliff staggered and fell against the bulwark. Before he could gather himself, Juan delivered a kick to his head and he sprawled face down. His left ear felt like it had exploded.

Juan, grinning now, kicked him again, driving his foot into Cliff's ribs.

"Take the bag," Yori said to Juan.

"No!" Lena tried to hold on to it, but Juan easily overpowered her. He snatched the bag from her grasp and gave it to Yori.

Jon's head appeared above the bulwark, "What's going on?"

Yori turned and fired, missing him by inches as Jon fell back into the dinghy. He stepped to the Tortuga Negra's bulwark and pointed the gun down at Jon. *"No te muevas!"*

The wind was blowing harder now, sending the rain almost horizontally across the fishing boat's deck. Cliff slowly raised his head. The ringing in his ears was beginning to ease and he started to think again. It occurred to him that the dinghy could easily be swamped in the rough seas. They could drown just trying to get back to the *Staghound*. Still, it was reassuring when he heard its outboard motor start.

Soaking wet in the rain, Lena's thin jacket clung to her, revealing the contours of her body, distracting the men. She stood and confronted Yori, who smiled at her audacity.

"You're going to keep the money. What about the guns?" She moved closer to him.

"Don't worry, they'll be well taken care of." Yori grinned.

"You're not taking them to MIR?" she asked.

"Of course not."

"They'll hunt you down," she said. "Wherever you try to hide, they'll find you."

"Let me tell you something, *chica*. You've been out of Chile too long. You don't know what's going on anymore. MIR is dead, they just don't know it yet. The old leaders are in their graves or rotting in prison, and no one wants to take their place because *el Movimiento* has been completely infiltrated. They can't fart without Pinochet knowing who did it." He waved the gun toward the dinghy. "Go back to America and forget about Chile. You might have a future there, but in Chile, Pinochet owns the future."

"What about you?" Lena asked. "You've given up on the future?"

"What future? You mean hauling cocaine down the mountains on my back? Shaking down tourists in Vina del Mar? That's not a future," he shouted over the howling wind. He raised the waterproof bag and shook it at her. "This is a future!" He pointed the gun at Cliff. "You! Get in the dinghy. Be thankful you're alive, and don't ever come back to Chile."

Cliff slowly got to his feet.

"You still haven't answered my question," Lena said. "Who gets the guns?"

"*El Halcon.* He has the money to buy them and the balls to use them."

"Never heard of him," Lena said.

"You might know him by his given name, Vicente Parga."

"Parga is a drug lord. You work for him now?"

"No. I made a deal with him." Yori smiled.

"You think you can double-cross him?" She gave him a disdainful smirk. "You're a fool! If Parga doesn't get you, MIR will."

The smile disappeared from Yori's face. "In Chile, you have to hedge your bets if you want to get ahead. Pinochet is a shithead, but who would MIR replace him with? Another shithead, only he'd be a communist shithead. At least Parga is honest. He just wants the guns." He hefted the bag and smiled again. "Either way, I'll be long gone before anyone finds out."

"Why don't you just kill us now?" She moved closer to him.

"Well, I might, but...Hey!"

With lightning speed, Lena snatched the bag. Yori made a grab for her and missed, but Juan tripped her. She landed with a thud on the rain-swept deck. He bent over her and pulled the bag from her grasp. "Like snatching a purse from an old lady," he said, tossing it to Yori.

Cliff lunged and pulled Juan off her, they staggered and fell to the deck. While they wrestled, Yori tried in vain to aim his pistol to shoot Cliff without hitting Juan.

Gathering herself, Lena leaped on Yori's back, both hands going for his eyes. She scratched and gouged, but Yori got his free hand on her and flung her off. Somehow the bag he'd been holding went with her.

Sitting on the deck, she held up the bag for Yori to see, then side-armed it overboard, glaring at him as the bag sailed on the wind.

"Why did you do that?" he screamed at her. The gun in his hand fired accidentally as he yelled. He lurched toward the fishing boat's bulwark, looking to see where the bag fell.

"Holy shit!" he screamed. He raised his pistol and fired until the hammer came down on an empty chamber as the roar of Jon's outboard came over the sound of the wind.

"The bastard has my money!" Yori screamed again. He kicked Lena, then turned on Cliff, smashing him across the face with the empty pistol.

Cliff saw a brief twinkling of stars, then everything faded to gray. Stunned and semi-conscious, he felt his arms being jerked behind his back and his wrists bound. His feet were tied and he was dumped in the same cluttered workshop where the crates had been stored. The muzzle of Yori's pistol had caught him just above his right eye and now it was swollen almost shut. Blood ran down his face and into his beard, leaving a metallic taste on his lips.

Moments later, a new sound entered his brain: The low

rumble of *Tortuga Negra's* main engine. He could feel its vibration coming through the dirty floor he was laying on. Suddenly he jerked his head up, more awake. *Lena!* He tried to sit up, but it was impossible because his hands and feet were bound. *Okay. Relax. Breathe. Think it through.* He rolled onto his stomach and pulled his knees up to his chest. From there he was able to raise himself to a kneeling position. With his one good eye, he searched the workshop for a knife, a blade…Anything to cut the rope from his wrists. Mechanic's tools hung on a pegboard above the workbench. Higher up was a hacksaw. Still on his knees, he maneuvered his body so his back was against the workbench. Gasping for breath he worked his feet under him until he could stand with his back to the bench. He craned his neck around, searching for the hacksaw. *Damn! I'll never be able to reach it.* Looking around, his eye fell on a grinding wheel bolted to the workbench a few feet away. He inched his body along the bench until he could stand with his back to the grinder. Now his fingers fumbled for the switch. *What are the odds that it'll turn on?* He was thinking this when his thumb found the switch and its electric motor came to life. The spinning abrasive wheel singed the skin around his wrists, but it took less than a minute for it to cut through the rope enough to free his hands. He reached for the hacksaw and feverishly worked on the rope around his ankles. Strand by strand, the blade cut through the rope until it parted and he was free.

CHAPTER 14

CLIFF STUMBLED TO the door and opened it a crack. It faced aft, and he saw Juan and Antonio struggling to winch the seine skiff up the stern ramp. Juan shouted something to Antonio, who slipped and slid on the wet, sloping stern where the skiff appeared to be stuck partway up the ramp. Cliff looked to his right and saw *Staghound*, still anchored 150 yards off *Tortuga Negra's* port side. There was a lull in the rain, but the wind was blowing harder than ever. Dark clouds shrouded the island's high bluffs and blotted out the sun, which would be setting soon.

The engine is running and they're bringing the skiff aboard. Yori probably decided he can't risk staying here any longer. Cliff glanced back toward Juan, whose attention was still on the seine skiff and the hapless Antonio. *I'm getting' off this boat!* He stripped off his clothes, took a deep breath, and dashed from the doorway. He sprinted to the port bulwark and dove over the side. The cold water made him gasp and stung the cut above his eye, but he came up swimming as hard as he could. Riding big surf taught him to swim in rough water, and that experience paid off now. The waves pushed him toward shore, forcing him to swim at an angle to them. Expecting Yori to start shooting any minute, he swam furiously. *If Staghound leaves before I get to them I'll be like Alexander Selkirk, stranded on a deserted island.* His throat burned and eyes stung, and his arms felt like they were on fire as he redoubled his effort, determined not to be left behind. He slowly closed the distance to *Staghound* and grabbed for the boarding ladder that hung over the port gunwale, gasping for breath as waves washed over him.

"Gimme your hand!" It was Jon reaching an outstretched arm to him from above. Cliff climbed the ladder far enough that Jon and Mike could pull him aboard. He flopped into the cockpit like a landed fish, gasping and shivering. Jon helped him down the companionway and draped a blanket over him.

"Here, drink this." Jon held a cup of black coffee in front of him. "What happened to your eye?"

Cliff reached up and touched the gash above his eye. The cold saltwater had eased the swelling and he could see as well as ever. "Just a little bump," he said. "Where's Lena?"

"Still on the *Tortuga*. Here are some clothes. What happened over there?"

Cliff took a gulp of coffee. "Lena threw the money overboard. After that, the lights went out. By the time I got my wits about me. The engine was running and they were pulling that big skiff aboard. I thought they were leaving, so I jumped overboard."

"Yori's not leaving without the money. He's running his engine to take the strain off his anchor. Otherwise, he'd drag and end up on the beach." Jon nodded toward the cockpit. "Mike's up there doing the same thing. When this storm blows out, I'll give Yori the money in exchange for Lena."

"You have it, the money?"

"Yeah." Jon grinned. "I was standing in the dinghy waiting for you and her to come down the ladder. Then I saw the bag come sailing over the side and just reached out and one-handed it. Without thinking, I gunned the motor. I heard Yori shooting but I kept the throttle wide open. He missed me but hit the dinghy. It sank from under me when I got back here." He paused, "So yeah, we have the money and Yori has Lena."

The rain returned, so hard it roared as it pelted *Staghound*'s deck. The wind moaned in the rigging, and darkness had fallen. *Staghound* leaned under the pressure of a gust.

"How long do you reckon this storm will last?" Cliff asked.

Jon went to the barometer on the bulkhead and tapped its glass face. "This thing hasn't budged since it dropped. I'd say we're in for another twenty-four hours of this."

"So it'll be another day before you can exchange the money for Lena?"

Jon looked down. "It's too dangerous to put a dinghy in the water in these conditions."

"You said the dinghy sank."

"We have a backup. It's a little roll-up inflatable. But if we launched it now it would blow away in this wind."

"What if Yori decides to leave, take Lena with him?"

Jon pointed at the bag of money on the dinette table. "He won't leave without that."

Cliff rose and looked out a window at the *Tortuga Negra*. He could see it rolling and plunging in the stormy waves. "His anchor chain could let go any minute. What then?" Cliff stared at Jon. "What if our chain lets go?"

Jon sat down and rested his forehead in his hands. "It's not going to let go. All we have to do is wait 'til this storm blows out. Everything is going to be okay."

Cliff gazed at him a second longer, then went forward to the sail locker, where wetsuits were stored, and grabbed the one he used for surfing.

"What are you doing?" Jon asked.

Cliff pulled the suit up to his waist and shoved his arms into the sleeves before he spoke. "I'm going to get her."

"You're going to swim over to the *Tortuga*? Are you insane? It's impossible in these conditions!" Jon exclaimed.

Cliff zipped the suit up to his neck and pulled a bootie onto his foot. "I'm going." He pulled the other bootie on and rummaged among the wetsuits until he found a hood.

Jon grabbed his arm. "I can't let you do it. It's too dangerous."

Cliff pulled away. "It's not too dangerous. I just swam it, remember?" He pulled the black neoprene hood over his head. "Besides, I'm going to paddle." He looked up at the surfboards hanging overhead and pulled his big-wave board down from its straps. Surfers called this type of board a "Gun". It was eleven feet long, over three inches thick, and built for speed.

Take a look out there," Jon said. "It's blowing harder now. I can't let you go." He grabbed at the surfboard, but Cliff jerked it away and started aft. The unwieldy board bounced off bulkheads and furniture as *Staghound* lurched and yawed in the waves.

"What the fuck?" Mike stared in amazement as the longboard came out the companionway followed by Cliff. The wind caught it and nearly knocked him over as he maneuvered it to the gunwale.

"He wants to rescue Lena." Jon had followed Cliff up the companionway.

Mike looked at Cliff and let out a laugh. "You look like a friggin' walrus, with that beard sticking out of your hood." He turned to Jon. "He's not serious, is he?"

"I tried to talk him out of it." Spray flew across the cockpit, plastering Jon's hair to his face.

"Dude, you ain't gonna make it." Mike nudged the throttle as a wave slammed into the sloop, jerking the anchor chain taut. "We're about ready to get blown out of here. If I wasn't manning the throttle we'd already be on the beach." He nodded toward the *Tortuga Negra*. "Same for them."

Cliff stared at the old boat. There was a light in the pilothouse, where he was sure Yori or Juan was working the throttle. Otherwise, the boat was dark, except for a faint flicker of light coming from the deckhouse farther aft. It flashed slowly three times, then three quick flashes, repeating that sequence over again. "You see that light going on and off?" he asked Mike.

"Yeah." Mike glanced at the light. "So what?"

Jon picked up a pair of binoculars and watched the light flicker another moment. "It's Morse code... SOS."

"Does Lena know Morse code?" Cliff asked, not taking his eyes from the flashing light.

"She had to learn it to get her HAM radio license."

"Then she's signaling us." Cliff grabbed the tether that was attached to the surfboard and cinched it around his ankle. The waves had grown dangerously high. They passed under the two vessels almost simultaneously. Seconds later they crashed against the rocky beach. The boom of the pounding surf could be heard over the shrieking wind.

"Listen to me!" Jon said. "We can't stay here anchored on a lee shore any longer. Neither can they." He grabbed Cliff by the shoulder. "We can motor around to the leeward side of the island and wait until this storm blows out, then we can work something out with Yori. Give him back the money if necessary."

"The odds of you making it over there are slim," Mike said, shaking his head. "The odds of you actually rescuing her are slim to none." He waved an arm at the streaming whitecaps. "And the odds of the two of you making it back here before this tub washes up on the beach are fuckin' zero at best." He looked at Jon. "We have to get out of here now, before we all end up dead."

Jon looked at Cliff. "Yori won't leave without the money, or he'd be gone by now."

"We're not leaving without her." Cliff glared at them.

"Of course not. But it's too dangerous to go on some half-baked rescue mission in these conditions."

"Dude, we can't stay here any longer!" Mike yelled. "The anchor's gonna break loose any fuckin' minute."

"Give me half an hour. If I'm not back by then, save yourselves." Cliff checked the leash on the board.

Jon gave in. "We'll wait as long as we can."

"How the hell are you going to rescue her?" Mike persisted. "Those guys have guns."

Cliff hadn't considered that. "I'll think of something."

"Wait," Jon disappeared down the companionway and returned with a dive knife in a plastic sheath. "Take my knife." He strapped to Cliff's thigh.

"Make sure the boat's ready to leave the minute we get back." Cliff lifted the board and prepared to jump.

"Good luck!" Jon shouted as Cliff plunged into the turbulent water and started paddling. He locked his gaze on the dimly flashing SOS coming from the *Tortuga Negra* each time the board rode up the crest of a wave. Down in the troughs, he was blind. Wind-torn whitecaps blasted him as he paddled, but the big board handled the waves well and he made the crossing to the fishing boat in ten minutes.

If Yori saw me coming, he thought, *he'll be waiting for me when I step on deck*. He slid off the surfboard and secured it to the bottom rung of the boarding ladder by its leash. When he let it go, the leash went taut and the board bobbed and bounced against the rough hull of the *Tortuga Negra*.

He reached down and felt for the dive knife strapped to his leg. The sheath was there but the knife was gone. *Damn! It must have slipped out while I was paddling*. He grabbed hold of the ladder and started climbing. When he reached the top, he cautiously raised his head high enough to see over the bulwark. He was on the port side of the *Tortuga Negra*, near the stern. To his left, a walkway led forward alongside the deckhouse toward the stairs leading up to the pilothouse. Directly in front of him, the big metal skiff was haphazardly lashed on deck, with its stern hanging over the *Tortuga Negra's* transom. There was no sign of the crew.

Cliff climbed over the bulwark and made his way forward, stopping at an open passageway that led down a couple of stairs, across the boat, and up matching stairs on the other side that opened to the starboard deck. Dim light came from an open door halfway across the passageway. He could feel the vibration of the boat's diesel engine in the soles of his feet and even with the wind, the smell of diesel emanated from the passageway. *The engine room. Yori is probably in the pilothouse, so it's Antonio or Juan down there.* He crept down the stairs. To his left, forward of the passageway, *Tortuga Negra's* massive diesel engine rumbled on its beds. Beyond it, ten feet from where he stood, Antonio sat on a stool, his back to the doorway. He was pouring oil from a can into the auxiliary motor, a cigarette dangling from the corner of his mouth.

To Cliff's right was another door that led aft to the machine shop. He entered the pitch-dark space and groped blindly on the workbench for something to use as a weapon. The first thing his fingers closed on was a bundle of zip ties, big ones. He stepped back into the passageway and zipped two of them together, making a hoop out of them. He stuck a dozen more in his bootie.

Antonio was still in the engine room, his back to Cliff.

Cliff quietly approached and dropped the zip tie hoop over his head, jerking it taut around his neck.

Antonio's hands flew up, frantically grabbing at his throat. Cliff jerked him backward off his stool, then flipped him onto his belly and sat on his back, holding him down.

Antonio's fat neck twisted and his eyes swiveled back in his head while Cliff grabbed his hands and cinched them with a zip tie. Speaking Spanish, he said in a soothing tone, "Relax Antonio, I'm not going to kill you."

Antonio struggled to throw Cliff off, but it took only half a minute for the fight to leave him. The veins in his neck bulged and he made a last writhing attempt to free himself. After that he lay still, his mouth working like a fish out of water.

Cliff spoke into his ear. "Listen to me," he said, "You're going to be alright if you do what I say. Nod your head if you understand."

His eyes wide with terror and his breath coming in tremulous wheezes, Antonio stared at Cliff and nodded.

"Good," Cliff said. "I don't want to kill you but I will if I have to. Understand?"

Another terrified nod.

"I'm going to ask you some questions, if you give me good answers, you live. If you don't," Cliff reached for the zip ties around his neck and made as if to pull them tighter.

Antonio squeezed his eyes shut in terror and nodded desperately.

"Okay, we have a deal then," Cliff said, "Where's the woman?"

Antonio lifted his chin and looked up.

Cliff pointed toward the ceiling, "Up there, in the deckhouse?"

Antonio nodded.

"And Yori?"

Antonio croaked and his eyes went upward again.

"In the deckhouse? Is he with the woman?" Cliff asked.

Another terrified nod and strangled croak. Tears had started from the corners of Antonio's eyes.

"Is he armed? Does he have a gun?"

Antonio nodded again, his breath rasping through his constricted windpipe.

"Okay. Where's Juan?"

Antonio pointed forward with his chin.

"In the pilothouse?"

Another nod.

Cliff considered the situation. *If Yori was with Lena, how could she be sending out an SOS?* He looked down at Antonio, whose attention was completely devoted to inhaling enough air to stay alive.

"If you're lying, I'm going to come back and kill you," Cliff said to him.

Antonio's eyes widened again and he croaked something unintelligible that Cliff assumed was an assurance that he was telling the truth.

He pulled more zip ties from his bootie and secured the fat man's ankles. "Do you have a gun?" he asked.

Antonio shook his head.

Cliff patted Antonio's pockets and found only cigarettes and a lighter. *That figures.* He looked around the cluttered engine room and picked up a pipe wrench. *This'll have to do.*

Hefting the wrench like a club, he stepped into the passageway and crept back up to the deck. The wind was as strong as ever, but the rain seemed to be easing again. *Staghound*, now a hundred yards away, reared and tugged at her anchor in the darkness. He saw Mike at the helm and Jon in the cockpit with binoculars to his eyes, trained on the *Tortuga Negra*.

Cliff turned his attention to the portholes. There were three and the signals had come from the middle one. He moved forward, pressing his body against the deckhouse, expecting Juan to pop out of a shadow anytime. It was only two steps to another dark passageway that led across the boat, and two more to the first porthole. He crouched and moved to the second one and waited for the SOS.

A few seconds passed without any flashes. Doubts began to flutter in his mind, then he saw the curtain behind the porthole pulled back three times in quick succession, then slowly, three more times. He realized that there was a light on in the stateroom, and the flashes were only the curtain being pulled back. With each movement of the curtain, he caught a glimpse of the hand that moved it. Lena's. He tapped lightly on the glass porthole and got no response, just the rhythmic opening and closing of the curtain. He rapped harder, with a knuckle and the curtain stopped. He cupped a hand around his eyes and put his face to the glass, peering straight into the window, then jerked his face away, startled.

What the hell was that? he asked himself, his heart thumping. He had expected to see Lena. Instead, he was confronted by a pair of big dark eyes in a white mask staring back at him, inches from his own face. It was surrounded by a frightful mass of Halloween hair, streaked black and white. The entire image was backlit, like a scene in a horror film.

Seconds later he heard frantic tapping on the porthole and dared to look again. This time he realized the person in the white mask was Lena. She wasn't wearing a mask; her face and hair were covered in white powder. She put two fingers to her eyes then pointed them into the room. When Cliff nodded that he understood she wanted him to look, she pulled the curtain back and stood aside. Cliff peered in and saw Yori lying motionless on the floor. "Jesus," he muttered, "She killed him."

Lena motioned him around the back and he made his way back to the passageway and entered. Halfway across the boat was a hallway leading forward. There were doors on both sides. He turned the knob on the first door on his left and pushed. It was an empty stateroom, barren and dank. Cliff moved forward and put his ear to the next door, but heard nothing. He reached for the knob, but it opened before he touched it. Light spilled into the passageway and he looked around the door, trying to understand what he was seeing. It looked like a blizzard had hit the room. The air was thick with choking white powder. Yori lay on the floor, his face and hair covered in white except for a splotch of red where his nose should be. Cliff's eyes moved to Lena, standing next to the rumpled bed. Her face wore a similar coat of white, except her mouth, which looked like a bloody smear. Her hair was wild and suffused with white, and she was wearing a bedsheet as if she was going to a toga party. A spent fire extinguisher lay on the bed, its nozzle caked with white, powdery retardant.

Lena said nothing, just threw her arms around Cliff's neck and clung to him.

"Are you okay? Can you talk?" he asked when she pulled away.

She nodded and wiped a trickle of blood from her bruised mouth. "He tried to rape me," she whispered. "He took my clothes."

"Where? Where'd he take them?"

She shook her head. "I don't know."

Cliff glanced around the stateroom. The walls were bare and the only furniture aside from the bed was an empty footlocker. "Okay, stay here, I'm going to find your clothes." He opened the door and looked up and down the passageway, no sign of Juan. Directly across from him was another door. He cautiously pushed it open. Another stateroom. Inside was an unmade bunk and a footlocker. Foul weather gear hung on a hook above a pair of sea boots. On a shelf above the bed was a stack of girly magazines and a carton of cigarettes. A cheap metal ashtray, overflowing with butts, rested on the floor by the bed. Next to it lay a sodden clump of clothing. Lena's.

"My shoes?" Lena asked when Cliff handed her the wet clothes.

"Didn't see them. Hurry, put these on. We're leaving." He knelt and placed two fingers on Yori's throat while she dressed. There was a pulse. He patted the unconscious man's pockets, hoping to find a gun, but came up empty.

When he rose, Lena was dressed. "Ready?" he asked.

She nodded and he led her out of the stateroom. When they reached the door leading outside, he paused. Visibility was better with less rain, and *Staghound*'s sleek profile stood out in the distance. With no sign of Juan or Antonio on deck, Cliff led Lena to the ladder at the stern.

"Where's the dinghy?" Lena asked.

"I came on a surfboard. We're going to paddle back to the boat." Cliff leaned over the bulwark to make sure the board was still there. "We have to get in the water. I'm going to put you on the board. Just hang on and I'll paddle you home."

Lena looked at the wind-driven waves, topped with whitecaps, churning and tumbling toward the rocky shore. "I don't know," she said, "Why didn't you bring the dinghy?"

"The dinghy's dead," Cliff replied, "We have to go now, we can talk about the dinghy later."

Lena took a step back, looking around with frightened eyes. "No…"

Before she could say another word, Cliff lifted her and threw her overboard, then dove in after her. When he surfaced Lena had grabbed the boarding ladder and started to climb back aboard the fishing boat. He pulled her off the ladder and floated with her, saying, "Lena, look at me."

Her eyes had taken on a glazed, terrified look and he realized she was going into shock. "Lena, I'm going to take you home to *Staghound*, you'll be safe there," he said. "Do you understand?"

She nodded, shivering.

Cliff pulled the surfboard to him with the leash and pushed her on top of it. "Just stay on the board and you'll be fine." He freed the leash from the boarding ladder, slid his body partway onto the board and placed her ankles over his shoulders. He was half-submerged, but his arms were free to paddle and his legs free to kick. With the weight of two people on it, the board was sluggish and hard to handle. Lena gagged and sputtered when waves washed over them and nearly capsized the board. He struggled to keep them moving forward, paddling as hard as he could. His arms ached and he strained to keep his head above the water. Every few seconds the board rose on a wave and he caught a glimpse of *Staghound*. Lena's body had gone limp and he couldn't tell if she was breathing, but she managed to cling to the board as he paddled. After what seemed like an hour, they had crossed the gap between the two boats. A few more strokes and they were within arm's length of the boarding ladder.

Cliff slid off the board, took Lena in one arm and grabbed the ladder with the other. Her head lolled against his shoulder and she clung feebly to him as waves surged around them.

Jon's head appeared above them.

"Get the sling," Cliff shouted between gasps. "I don't think she can climb the ladder."

"Roger. I'll be back in a sec."

While he waited, Cliff noticed the surfboard floating away. Caught by wind and waves, it quickly drifted into the surf line and disappeared.

"Here's the sling." Jon lowered the device down to Cliff.

"Okay, Lena," Cliff said, gently prying her arms from around his neck. "I'm going to put this on you." He placed the sling over her head and pulled it down to her chest, where he cinched it tight. "Jon's going to pull you aboard now." He watched as Jon pulled her up, then climbed aboard *Staghound* himself.

"Take the helm," Mike said as soon as Cliff was on deck. "I'm going forward to raise the anchor. We're getting' outa here."

Still panting, Cliff took his place at the helm. The rain, now a wind-driven mist, was illuminated by moonlight shining through a fleeting break in the clouds. He glanced over at the *Tortuga Negra*. It was dark except for the light in the pilothouse.

"Wait half a minute, then give 'er full gas," Mike said. "Head straight into the wind until the anchor breaks out, then turn downwind and take us around that point." Mike waved his arm toward the northeast point of the island.

"Got it!" Cliff eyed the oncoming waves as Mike raced toward the bow. He slowly counted to thirty, then pushed the throttle lever as far as it would go. *Staghound's* motor roared, its propeller sending water gushing aft under the transom. The big sloop slowly gathered speed. Suddenly it slowed, the bow sagged downward for an instant before it rose again and the boat accelerated. *That was the anchor breaking out,* he thought. *It must have been buried mighty deep.* He spun the helm to port and for a moment the waves were on her starboard beam. A big one struck, sending a torrent of water across the deck, filling the cockpit. Cliff kept the helm hard over to port and seconds later the waves were on the starboard quarter, lifting the stern and sending *Staghound* rushing forward. The knotmeter climbed from five to ten, to fourteen knots as the boat surged down the faces of the waves.

Mike returned to the cockpit. "Anchor's secured." He peered aft at the receding pinpoint of light that was the *Tortuga Negra*. "They're gonna be out of sight in another five minutes."

Cliff wanted to look in that direction, but the dark mass of Selkirk Island was looming on the port bow. Waves crashing on the point sent whitewater skyward only to be whipped away by the wind.

Mike crouched in the cockpit, gauging the bearing to the point, and when it was off the port quarter he said, "Bring her to a course of two-seventy."

With the wind and waves now on the port beam, and no sails up, Cliff had to fight to keep the boat on course. Then, almost as if a switch had been thrown, the waves calmed and the wind eased to nothing more than a brisk breeze.

Jon came up the companionway and looked around. "We're in the lee of the island," he said, "Hoist the sails." He took the helm and Cliff scrambled to the halyards.

"I already tied in the third reef," Mike said as he untied the gaskets securing the mainsail to the boom. "Grind away!"

Cliff spun the handles on the coffee grinder and the mainsail rose about 45 feet and stopped at the third reef. Mike, at the mast, jumped the jib halyard, raising the small number four jib. When it was nearly hoisted Cliff took over and winched it the last few feet.

While he worked Mike raced aft and trimmed the mainsail, and when the jib luff was taut, he trimmed it too.

Sweat had broken out inside Cliff's wetsuit and he was huffing from the exertion of hoisting sails. He leaned on the coffee grinder and looked behind *Staghound* for the *Tortuga Negra*. When he didn't see it, he slumped on the cockpit seat and heaved a sigh of relief.

Jon had followed his gaze. "It was still anchored, facing southeast when we rounded the point."

Cliff ran a hand over his salt-crusted face. "How's Lena doing?"

"A little banged up but nothing's broken. I gave her a sedative and put her in her bunk."

Jon's attention was taken by a gust of wind as the big sloop emerged from the lee of the island. With thirty knots of wind and a following sea, the boat could maintain a speed of fourteen knots or more. Jon checked the compass and pointed the boat northnorthwest, broad reaching on starboard tack. He looked back at Cliff. "Lena tell you what happened to her?"

Cliff's recollections of the day were a jumbled mess, but the sight of her, battered and wearing only a bedsheet was burned into his memory. "She said Yori tried to rape her."

"She told him she'd do whatever he wanted if he would bring her a bottle Pisco. He left to get a bottle and when he came back, she was waiting with a fire extinguisher. She stuck the nozzle in his face and pulled the trigger. When the thing was empty, he was on the floor choking on the stuff. Said she smashed his face in with the extinguisher." Jon stifled a chuckle. "You saw him, right?"

"Yeah, his face was bloody, but he was alive." Cliff searched the dark horizon behind them. The black bluffs of the island were receding in the distance and there was no sign of the *Tortuga Negra*. Still, he had a sense of foreboding. "I have a hunch we haven't seen the last of them."

CHAPTER 15

CLIFF WENT BELOW and climbed into his bunk. His head barely hit the pillow before he was asleep. Sometime later he woke to the sound of voices, of feet on deck, the clatter of winches and the slap of flailing sheets. He opened his eyes and saw shafts of sunlight streaming through the overhead hatches. He struggled out of his bunk, aching muscles complaining as he stood. *Staghound* was heeled twenty degrees to port and from the sound of the water rushing by, she was moving fast. He rubbed his eyes and dressed in jeans, sweatshirt, and jacket, for it was cold in the cabin. On deck, he found Jon and Mike trimming sails.

They both stared at him, then Jon said, "How are you feeling?"

"A little banged up."

"You've got a black eye and a fat ear," Mike said.

Cliff gingerly felt his ear, which was sore to the touch. He ran his fingers to his brow and found that it was swollen and sticky. "Juan kicked me a coupla times," he said, working his arms and shoulders. He looked eastward, where a brilliant morning sun shone through broken clouds. "Where are we?"

Jon, at the helm, answered. I figure we're about eighty miles northwest of Selkirk."

Cliff looked up at the sails. "You shook the reefs out of the mainsail." He glanced forward and saw the number two genoa instead of the number four. "And changed jibs."

Mike rose from where he was sitting and said, "We're out of the storm now. We'll have good weather for the next few days." He drank the last of the coffee in his cup and started below. "We should get back on our regular watch schedule. That means it's Cliff's watch now. I'm going to hit the rack."

"You stood my watch for me last night. Thanks."

Mike, at the companionway, glanced back at Cliff. "Yeah, you were pretty wrung out."

Jon remained at the helm. "I made coffee. You look like you could use some."

"Good idea." Cliff rose stiffly, feeling like every muscle in his body had been pummeled. "How is Lena?"

"Lena's resilient. Give her a few days and she'll be her old self." Jon's eyes found Cliff's and held them. "That was damn brave, what you did last night. You probably saved her life."

Cliff paused a moment. "I'm just glad she's back," he said before heading below for the coffee.

Back on deck, he relieved Jon and stood his watch while the others slept. The sea had eased from mountainous waves to long swells that *Staghound* rode easily. Storm clouds had given way to bright, sunny skies and a brisk wind.

Mike appeared at half-past eleven and took the helm. "Skipper wants a noon sight."

The feel of the sextant in his hands was somehow reassuring as Cliff took his perch near the mast. He raised the instrument to his eye and tracked the sun as it climbed to its zenith and jotted down its altitude and the date and time. It was strange to think that he first laid eyes on the *Tortuga Negra* less than forty hours ago and it was only February 6th. He felt as if he'd lived a long time in those forty hours.

At the chart table, he worked the math and plotted their position at 32°-10' south by 82°-21' west. Using dividers, he stepped off the distance to Selkirk Island: 125 nautical miles. He put the small-scale chart away and plotted the position on the large-scale chart. When he was finished, he leaned back, surveying the distance to go before they reached the equator. He recalled his initiation ceremony when they crossed it coming south, especially the part when he kissed the belly of the queen. He must have closed his eyes because he didn't see Lena emerge from her cabin and jumped when he heard her voice.

"Where are we?" she asked.

"Here." He pointed to the mark on the chart.

She leaned over his shoulder to see, while Cliff studied the bruises on her face: Two black eyes, a swollen lip, and a dark mark on her neck, as if she had been choked.

She shifted her gaze to him, then brushed the hair away from the cut above his eye to examine it more closely. "Stay there." She left him and returned a minute later with a first aid kit. "You need stitches, but a butterfly bandage will have to do." She washed the wound with disinfectant and skillfully applied the bandage. When she finished, she turned his head to the side. "No sign of bleeding from your ear. That's good. Do you have a headache?"

"No."

"Nausea?"

"No."

"Lightheadedness, dizziness?"

"No."

"Do you know what day it is?"

"Yes. Do you?"

She stopped. "Saturday?"

"Friday."

They stared at each other, then she spoke. "I was checking to see if you had a concussion."

"So was I." Cliff grinned at her.

She reached out and tousled his hair, then briefly hugged his head to her chest. A second later she was briskly putting the medical kit together while Cliff stared at her.

᎒

That night Cliff was back at the helm. The Southern Cross was high above, and the southeast wind had backed to east. *Staghound* was still headed northwest, broad-reaching under a full main and number two jib, with enough wind to keep her moving at nine knots when Jon hurried on deck.

"Bring her up to due north," Jon said. He winched the jib in tighter and trimmed the mainsail as Cliff changed course.

"What's up?" he asked. With the wind abeam, it felt stronger and the boat heeled before it.

"Lena spotted a blip on the radar. We're altering course to keep clear of it." Jon nervously coiled the mainsheet while he spoke.

Cliff scanned the horizon ahead. The night was clear and visibility was at least ten miles. Any ship that might pose a hazard would be clearly visible. He looked astern and saw nothing but an unbroken horizon. "Looks to me like we're all alone out here."

"It just popped up on the screen, about twenty miles behind us." Jon put binoculars to his eyes and gazed astern.

Cliff's throat tightened. "The *Tortuga*?"

"Could be a ship or a fishing boat. But if it follows us, we should assume it's the *Tortuga* until we're sure it's not." Jon lowered the binoculars and checked the knotmeter. "It'll take a while to tell if that blip is following us." He glanced up at the sails. "In the meantime, we'll keep going as fast as we can."

"Can we outrun them?" Cliff followed Jon's eyes to the knotmeter.

"A fishing boat like that can run at a top speed of around fourteen knots and has a range of up to three thousand miles at cruising speed. But it's like a car, the faster they go, the shorter their range. If we can't outrun them, we might be able to outlast them."

"And if we can't?"

"Yori will kill us." Lena had emerged into the cockpit.

They both stared at her. Even in the darkness, her blackened eyes were visible, reminding Cliff of a terrified raccoon. "I smashed him in the face with a fire extinguisher." She pointed a finger at Cliff. "You hog-tied his crewman. He won't let that go unpunished."

Her words hung in the air while fear slipped icy fingers down Cliff's spine.

Mike joined them in the cockpit. "We just gave him a zillion guns. How are we gonna defend ourselves against that?"

"I doubt that they know how to use them," said Cliff. "Let's not scare ourselves yet."

"Yori has a Kalashnikov, an AK47," Lena said. "He showed it to us when we were counting the money in the pilothouse."

There was another tense pause. Cliff checked the knotmeter then said what the others were thinking. "The wind's getting lighter."

Jon reached over and started the engine, pushing the throttle up to 3,600 RPMs. At that speed, the engine emitted a muffled roar and *Staghound* gained a little speed.

"How long can we run at thirty-six hundred?" Cliff wanted to know.

"Watch the temperature gauge," Jon replied. "If it goes over one-ninety-five we'll have to throttle back." *Staghound* steadied at 10.5 knots with the temperature gauge settling at 180 degrees. He turned to go below. "There's nothing else we can do so I'm going to try and get some rest."

"Me too." Mike followed him down the companionway.

At the helm, Cliff's eyes darted from the knotmeter to the sails and back again as he coaxed as much speed as possible from the boat.

Lena moved to the starboard coaming and turned her face to

the wind. Her hair was like a dark mane blowing in the breeze. "I want to thank you," she said without looking at him. "For rescuing me."

"No thanks are necessary." He watched her a moment, remembering the fight on the *Tortuga Negra's* stern deck. "Did you intend to throw the money to Jon?"

She turned to face him. Her eyes were luminous despite the raccoon look. "No. That was pure luck."

"Why did you do it?"

"It was an impulse, nothing more."

Cliff shook his head slowly. "I don't know if you're crazy or brilliant, but I admire your courage."

"I was thinking the same thing about you." She approached and took his face in her hands, staring into his eyes for an instant, then examining the bandage over his brow. "I'll change that in the morning." She went below.

Alone, Cliff contended with the thought that Yori was somewhere behind them, closing the distance with each passing minute. He checked *Staghound's* speed again and concentrated on steering the boat as fast as it would go. A cold knot formed in the pit of his stomach.

Two hours later he came off watch and found Lena and Mike huddled at the radar screen. She looked up when he approached. "He's following us."

The knot in his stomach tightened. "I was wondering, does Yori have a stronger radar than us?" Cliff studied the blip on the screen as he spoke.

"Probably. A commercial boat in the States usually carries a fifty-mile unit. They use it to spot other fishing boats and stuff like that." Mike tapped the screen in front of him. "I'm sure he got underway long before we were fifty miles from the island. I bet he never lost sight of us."

"What's our fastest point of sail?" Cliff asked.

"If we had more wind, we could hoist a spinnaker and average fifteen knots or better." Mike shifted his gaze to the instrument repeaters on the bulkhead. "We only have about twelve knots of wind now, so we make our best speed beam reaching." He pointed to the knotmeter. "If we weren't running the engine too, we'd only be doing about nine knots."

Cliff did the math in his head. "So, if he's twenty miles behind us and going five knots faster, he'll catch us in four hours. We have to be ready when that happens." He hurried on deck where he found Jon looking grim.

"What if Yori rams us? That big steel hull would rip right through this boat, wouldn't it?"

Jon kept a tight grip on the wheel and nodded. "Yup. But we're more maneuverable. He can't ram us as long as we're moving."

Cliff visualized the *Tortuga Negra* bearing down on *Staghound* from astern, then spinning the wheel hard over at the last second. *Staghound* could easily turn ninety degrees before the fishing boat could turn twenty. "Okay, I get that."

"When we were being chased by pirates in the South China Sea, we built a barricade around the aft end of the cockpit out of anchors, chain, toolboxes and stuff." Jon cast an involuntary glance astern. "Fortunately they gave up the chase before we had to use it."

Cliff tried to envision a barricade around the cockpit. *It probably won't be very effective, but it'll be better than nothing.* "I'll get started on it now."

Two hours later he and Mike had built a rough shelter around the cockpit with a crude firing position facing aft. It was made of everything they could find aboard that might stop a bullet, including anchors, chain, toolboxes, sail bags, even coils of rope.

In the cabin, Lena had arranged their weapons on the dinette table. "We have three magazines and two hundred rounds for the AR," she said, handing him a loaded magazine and the carbine.

Besides ammunition, she had arranged a dozen distress flares and a machete on the table, along with the pistol. She picked up the flare gun. "This is a twenty-five millimeter."

"Have you shot it before?" Cliff asked.

"I have. It takes two hands, but I can manage it."

"What about the .45?"

"Two boxes of bullets," she replied.

"We also have two boxes of shotgun shells," Mike said, loading the twelve-gauge as he spoke.

Cliff took the AR-15 to the stern and crouched behind the barricade. He swiveled the barrel of the weapon left and right, checking the view. "I have about a thirty-degree field of fire so you'll have to keep our stern pointed at him," he said to Jon, who was still at the helm.

Jon crouched next to him. "You tell me which way to steer and I can do it from here." His hand was on the wheel at the "eight o'clock" position.

The barricade extended forward along the sides of the cockpit, with space to fire from on each side. Cliff moved to the starboard firing position, then the port, checking fields of fire. "These aren't as good as the aft position," he said to Jon, who was watching him from the helm.

"I'll keep our stern to them as much as I can," Jon said in a tight voice, his face betraying more tension than fear.

Lena came on deck, followed by Mike. They all searched the sea astern.

"I've been thinking about how we'll defend ourselves, if it comes to that," Cliff said. "I'll handle the carbine and Jon will steer. Mike, you'll handle the sails and keep us moving as fast as possible. Lena will stay below and keep us supplied with ammunition."

"I made a firing position at the foredeck hatch," Mike said. "Check it out." He led Cliff below to the sail locker where there was a ladder leading up to the hatch. "If those guys get within shotgun range, I can slide the hatch open and fire from here.

Cliff climbed the ladder and checked the view from the hatchway. "Looks good," he said before climbing down. "But remember, your first responsibility is to keep us moving as fast as we can go."

"Yeah, don't worry about that." Mike's eyes glittered with excitement. "If I get a shot, I'm taking it. I'm not afraid of those motherfuckers."

"Okay, go for the helmsman first." Cliff laid a hand on Mike's shoulder to calm him. "Take your time, breathe, and make your shots count."

Mike grinned nervously. "I'm looking forward to putting a load of double aught buckshot in that bastard Yori."

"What's the effective range of that shot?"

"Fifty to a hundred yards." Mike grinned again and hefted the shotgun. "This is our close-in defensive weapon."

Back on deck, the sky was beginning to lighten in the east, promising a sunny day. With the dawn came more wind, and *Staghound* accelerated. Still assisted by the engine, her speed hovered around eleven knots.

Despite Staghound's improved speed, the *Tortuga Negra* was faster, and came into view before noon. At first, it was a speck, only visible through binoculars. Later, the binoculars revealed the menacing black hull and foaming white bow wave of the pursuing vessel. More wind brought more speed to *Staghound*, lengthening the chase. But slowly, inexorably, the distance between the two boats diminished. By midafternoon Cliff could make out the dark windows in its pilothouse.

Mike came on deck and scanned the cloudless sky. "The barometer's up. We're probably going to lose this wind soon." He turned his baseball cap backwards and gazed up at the sails, checking their trim. "You know, without wind, that jib won't help us much, speed-wise. And it'll actually make it harder for us to maneuver."

"I was wondering about that," Cliff said. "What do you recommend?"

"If they get close enough to shoot at us, we should drop it, and lash it on deck. With just the mainsail up, we can focus on them instead of wrestling with the jib every time we want to change course." Mike stared at the now plainly visible *Tortuga Negra*, gauging the distance between them. "How close will he be before he starts shooting?"

"Five or six hundred yards, maybe a little more."

"Well, he's still at least a mile back. At this speed, it'll be dark before we're in range."

Cliff checked the knotmeter. "I hope you're right. Moonrise won't be until around midnight, so it will be real dark for a while."

Mike glanced at Cliff. "We should wear our wetsuits. We'll be harder to see."

Jon came on deck and studied the engine gauges. "Temperature is a little warm." He tapped the glass front of the fuel gauge. "We used a lot of fuel, running at full throttle all day. We can afford to do this another couple of days, but not much more." He turned his gaze westward, where the setting sun was swallowing the breeze. He picked up the binoculars and studied the Tortuga Negra. "Yori is on the bridge, looking at us through binoculars. He'll be the shooter, I'm sure of that."

"What about the others?" Cliff asked.

"Juan will be at the helm. He's the real sailor of that bunch. He'll be plenty busy steering that tub once we start maneuvering."

"Antonio?"

"He didn't strike me as anything but a mechanic. My guess is he'll stay down in the engine room, where it's safer."

"I agree. Yori is the key. But he's likely to be hard to spot in the dark. We know they need to have someone at the helm and we know he'll be right in the middle of the pilothouse. That's where I'm going to focus, unless I get a shot at Yori." Cliff's grip had tightened on the wheel as he spoke. He noticed that and tried to relax and breathe more deeply. *One way or another, this is going to be over before dawn,* he told himself. He looked westward, where the last rays of the sun set off a green flash. *A good omen, I hope.*

Just then the jib began to luff. The sound of the flapping sail drew their attention.

"We might as well take it down now," Mike said, "There's hardly any wind left."

With the jib down and the mainsail sheeted in tight, Cliff could turn any direction without the need for Mike to tend the sails.

Mike went below and returned five minutes later wearing a black wetsuit. He took the helm while Cliff went below and pulled his own wetsuit on. When he came back on deck, it was dark. Though the temperature was dropping, sweat was soon trickling down his back inside the suit.

Whang! They all dove for cover at the sound of a bullet ricocheting off *Staghound's* aluminum boom, followed by the flat report of Yori's AK47.

Cliff's throat was suddenly dry and his fingers trembled. He grabbed the AR-15 and crawled to the aft end of the cockpit. Peering through the makeshift gun slit, he couldn't see where Yori fired from, but he saw a dim light through the windows of the pilothouse. He aimed and fired at the center pane, where he knew the helmsman would be, but the *Tortuga Negra* didn't waver.

The sound of Yori's rifle came across the water three times in rapid succession, but his bullets missed the sailboat..

Jon, crouching next to Cliff, whispered, "Which way should I go?"

Cliff's heart was thumping so hard it was hard for him to answer, let alone steady the carbine. He swallowed and said, "Hold this course." He waited until his pounding heart had eased, took aim, and fired another round at the pilothouse. His ears started ringing when he fired.

"You hit the windshield." Lena was standing in the companionway, binoculars to her eyes. "I saw a tiny flash almost dead-center."

The *Tortuga Negra* continued straight at *Staghound*'s transom. With the darkness of a moonless night, the bioluminescence of her wake seemed almost bright. Cliff watched it rise and fall as the fishing boat pushed through the waves. He estimated the distance between the two boats at less than three hundred yards. "I'm going to fire again," he said to Jon. "Be ready to turn left thirty degrees."

"Roger."

Cliff aimed for the pilothouse and waited until *Staghound* was poised on top of a wave. It was there that her motion was steady long enough for him to aim and fire. He squeezed the trigger three times. "Turn now."

Jon spun the wheel and steadied the boat on its new course while Cliff watched for a reaction aboard the *Tortuga Negra*. Ten seconds passed before it turned to follow, but it didn't slow down at all.

"We're not exactly scaring them off," he said. He aimed and fired five more rounds at the pilothouse, squinting to see if he'd done any damage. "I can't tell where my shots are going."

Lena spoke from the companionway. "Tell me when you're going to fire and I'll spot for you." Her head was just visible over the companionway sill.

Yori opened fire. A dozen rounds flew, some hitting the transom, others missing.

"He switched to automatic!" Cliff said. *I must have scared him with my last shots.*

"I saw muzzle flashes from down low. He's firing from the foredeck, not the pilothouse." Lena spoke in a calm voice, as if she was describing a bowling match.

She's done this before, Cliff thought as he prepared to fire.

"I'm going for the pilothouse again," he said, resting his cheek on the carbine's stock. He sighted the windows and waited until *Staghound* paused at the top of a wave, then fired.

"Looks like you hit the windshield again," Lena said calmly.

"Wait, something's changing. Yes, he's turning to port and there's definitely a hole in his windshield."

Yori began firing, a couple of rounds every few seconds. Cliff stayed low until there was a pause in the firing. He guessed Yori was reloading and rose just enough to see through the gap in the boat's rudimentary armor.

"Okay, he's turning back toward us," Lena reported.

"I'm going to fire again. Ready?"

"Ready."

Cliff fired three rounds.

"Hit, hit." Lena crouched low again. "The hole in the windshield is bigger now. Your last shot could have gone through it."

"Jon, does Yori have an autopilot? Am I shooting at ghosts in the pilothouse?"

"He has one." In the dim glow of the engine gauges, Jon's face was tense. "But somebody still has to steer when we turn."

Mike crowded Lena in the companionway. "Hey, I have the portable spotlight. You guys close your eyes and I'll shine it on them."

"Yori will shoot at it, so don't leave it on more than a couple of seconds," Cliff said.

"Okay. I'll count to three, then hit the switch. One. Two. Three!"

Cliff squeezed his eyes shut but the brilliant light still penetrated his eyelids.

Mike switched off the light just before Yori sent a dozen rounds rattling and ricocheting off *Staghound's* barricade.

"I saw Juan in the pilothouse. He put his hand over his face when the light hit him. Yori's down by the anchor windlass on the foredeck." Mike scrambled down the companionway.

"Good job, Mike! If Juan's steering, he's not shooting." Jon gave him a thumbs up.

"Yeah, but they're a lot closer now," Mike shouted up from the cabin.

Yori fired another dozen rounds. With a sound like a hammer hitting steel, a bullet slammed into the hydraulic backstay adjuster, severing a high-pressure hose and sending a fine mist of hydraulic oil spraying into the cockpit. With a couple of feet of slack in the backstay, it flopped around loosely. Coated with oil, the cockpit was suddenly as slick as an ice-skating rink.

"It's okay," Jon said. "We can manage with a loose backstay."

Cliff slipped and slid, struggling to brace his feet on the steering pedestal so he could fire from a stable position, but every movement of *Staghound* caused him to slip enough to affect his aim. He finally braced himself well enough and was about to aim and fire when a shrill alarm went off. BEEP-BEEP-BEEP-BEEP…

"The engine!" Jon shouted above the noise. "It's overheating! We have to shut it down."

"NO!" Cliff yelled. "We can't stop now. He turned and pounded a fist on the alarm but it kept going…BEEP-BEEP-BEEP.

Jon grabbed his shoulder. "I'm going to shut the engine down. If I don't it's going to seize up. We're fucked either way!"

Cliff watched him switch the engine off. The sudden silence after the constant noise of the motor rang in his ears until he heard the throbbing diesel of the *Tortuga Negra* approaching from astern. He spun around and aimed at the fishing boat, exchanging fire with Yori.

"What happened? What's going on?" Mike was shouting from the companionway.

Cliff's hands shook as he tried to reload, the magazine clattering against the receiver until he slammed it home. "The engine over-heated. Jon shut it down," he shouted.

"But what's wrong with Jon?" Mike's voice broke and his eyes were saucer-like.

Cliff turned to Jon, who sat motionless next to him. He reached out a hand to shake him and Jon slumped over. Cliff drew his hand back in horror. It was warm and slick, covered in blood. "He's hit!"

"NO!" Lena screamed, she lunged toward Jon but suddenly froze, staring straight aft as the Tortuga Negra's bow loomed over Staghound's stern and rammed the sailboat.

The sound of steel ripping and crushing fiberglass was like a slow-motion car wreck. The impact knocked Cliff off balance and he slipped on the slurry of blood and oil that had spread across the cockpit floor. He went down on his back. From there he had a perfect view of the black prow of the fishing boat jammed into Staghound, and Yori crouched behind its high bulwark, reloading his rifle.

Cliff struggled off the floor. His wetsuit was now coated with blood and oil, so he slithered over the starboard cockpit coaming as Yori opened fire again. Bullets slammed into the cockpit where he'd been two seconds before. Yori sprayed the deck and cabin top, shattering hardware, sending shrapnel in every direction and severing the main halyard. The big sail slid down the mast, blanketing the deck under eight hundred square feet of heavy sailcloth. Caught under the sail, Cliff lay face-down on the deck. He heard two shotgun blasts. *Mike's shooting from the foredeck hatch.* His shots were followed by another volley from Yori and a single muf-fled scream. Then the shooting stopped. Cliff lay still, his breath ragged and his blood pounding in his ears. Somehow, he had lost the carbine.

The Tortuga Negra's diesel roared as it backed away from the sailboat. When there was a hundred feet between the two boats it came forward, accelerating at full throttle until it crashed into *Staghound's* stern again.

"Hey boss, we knocked a hole in the stern. She won't last long now," Juan's guttural Spanish came from the pilothouse. For a minute, all Cliff could hear was the Tortuga Negra's idling diesel, then Juan again. "I see two dead guys on the deck. The other guy must have gone overboard when the sail fell down."

"What about the girl?" Yori yelled up to Juan from the foredeck of the fishing boat.

"She's probably dead inside the cabin. Too bad. She was a spicy little *chiquita*. We could have fucked her all the way back to the mainland." Juan cackled.

"Shut up and bring us alongside. I want that money."

Still face down under the sail, Cliff considered his options. *Stay here and get shot or take my chances with the sharks.* His hand found a loose rope, perhaps a reefing line. Using it to break his fall, he slid over the side.

CHAPTER 16

WITH LITTLE BREEZE and no sails up, *Staghound* wallowed in the gentle swells while Cliff floated in the water, one hand still hanging onto the rope. He couldn't see the *Tortuga Negra* from where he was, but he could make out the sound of Yori's voice yelling over the noise of the fishing boat's idling engine.

Thanks to the wetsuit, he wasn't too cold. Random thoughts flitted through his brain as he floated on his back, gazing up at the stars. *I've got blood all over me, what are the chances of a shark being in the neighborhood? What are the odds of Yori finding the money before Staghound sinks? Shouldn't my life be passing before my eyes now? How the hell am I going to get home, even if I do live through this?* He looked around in the darkness and nearly chuckled out loud. The idea that he'd live to see the next sunrise seemed preposterous. A series of images came to him. Images of Lena. He pictured her lounging on deck in her bikini. He saw her hiking on Selkirk Island. He remembered the feel of her in his arms aboard the *Tortuga Negra*. His mind rebelled at the thought of her lying dead in *Staghound's* cabin. Instead, he imagined her still alive. He thought of the terror she must be feeling now, with Yori preparing to take revenge on her. *They'll rape and torture her. When they're done, they'll toss her overboard.* A cold, murderous resolve rose in him and he forgot about his own predicament. *I'm not going to let that slimeball lay hands on her.*

He let go of the rope and swam to *Staghound*'s stern. A gaping hole in the transom caught his eye but he kept going. The *Tortuga Negra* had sidled up to the port side of the sailboat and Yori attached a rope to *Staghound*'s mooring cleat about halfway between the bow and stern. The sailboat was close enough to the fishing boat to step from one to the other.

"*Traeme una linterna!*" Yori called to Juan. "Bring me a flashlight!"

Cliff swam around the stern of the fishing boat to the boarding ladder on its port side, the same ladder he had climbed before. Once on the boat's deck, he crept forward past the passageway to the engine room. Three steps more and he was at the porthole Lena had flashed the SOS from. He continued forward to the stairs leading up to the pilothouse. He heard Yori shouting to Juan again.

"Come on, dammit. Where's that flashlight?" Yori called.

"Found it, boss. Here."

"Don't throw it, you idiot! Bring it to me."

Cliff climbed the portside stairs to the pilothouse as Juan descended on the starboard side. Cliff pulled the door open and entered the darkened bridge. Shattered glass covered the floor and he was glad he wore booties with his wetsuit. He kept his head down but peeked through the blown-out center window and saw Juan cross the deck to where Yori stood. Cliff watched them talk for a moment, then Juan started back to the pilothouse. Cliff searched for a weapon but didn't see a gun or a knife, not even something he could use as a club. Juan was halfway up the stairs when Cliff's eye fell on the VHF radio next to the steering wheel. He ripped the microphone out of it and hid in a corner as Juan reached the top of the stairs. When he entered the pilothouse Cliff stepped behind him and wrapped the microphone cord around his neck, jerking it tight. Juan's eyes bulged and his arms flailed as Cliff pulled him down to the floor. It was over in three minutes.

When Cliff felt him go limp, he gave the cord a final jerk and left it tied tightly around his neck.

"Juan! Juan! What the hell are you doing up there?" Yori had been shouting while Juan was busy dying. "This fucking flashlight doesn't work!"

Cliff hunched below the level of the shattered windshield and cautiously peered over the bottom of it. Yori was still on deck angrily fiddling with the flashlight, whose beam was flickering. He had traded the AK47 for a handgun, a better weapon for the close quarters of a boat's cabin.

"Juan, goddammit, I want the big one!" Yori shouted. He tossed the faulty flashlight aside and started toward the stairs.

Cliff frantically searched for another weapon but couldn't find anything. Even the furniture was bolted to the floor. Yori bounded up the stairs and when he pulled open the door Cliff punched him full in the face with his right fist, catching Yori off guard. The blow drove him backward on the landing outside the pilothouse and he lost his grip on the pistol in his hand. For a split second, they both watched it fall, bouncing off the bulwark and splashing into the water. Cliff's next punch sent Yori tumbling down the stairs, cracking his head on the steel deck below. He sprang up like a cat, but the fight had gone out of him. Instead, he turned and fled with Cliff in pursuit. He ducked into the passageway that led to the engine room door and pulled it shut behind him, latching it from the inside just before Cliff caught up to him.

Cliff grabbed the handle on the steel door and tried to open it but Yori resisted. Cliff stopped pulling long enough to look around the dimly lit passageway for another way into the engine room. He was going to finish this fight now…One way or another. Instead of a different way in, he noticed the heavy steel hasp that was welded to the door jamb. Hanging next to it on a short length of chain was the padlock used to lock the engine room when the crew wasn't aboard. He flipped the hasp over the bail that was welded to the door and snapped the lock on it. Opposite from the engine room was the machine shop. He peered into the dark and cluttered area and spotted the gun crates that they had transferred from *Staghound*. He stumbled toward them, barking his shin on a box of rusty engine parts as he went.

Jon's craftsmanship in making the crates worked against Cliff now. He would have to find a screwdriver and remove over a dozen screws to open one of them. Just then he heard a loud bang. It was Yori pounding on the engine room door.

If he's trying to get out through that door, there's probably no other way out. He's trapped in there! Cliff's mind raced. He forgot about opening the crates and focused on making sure Yori stayed trapped. He lifted a crate, took it to the passageway, and set it on the floor in front of the engine room door. He saw the hasp on the door strain when Antonio, who had been in the engine room when Yori rushed in, threw his weight against it.

"Harder! You gotta hit it harder!" Yori encouraged Antonio.

Cliff had forgotten about him. Apparently, he'd taken refuge in the engine room when the shooting started. Now he was trapped along with Yori.

Cliff hurried back to the stack of crates and brought another one to the passageway, setting it on the floor next to the first one. Side by side, they were nearly as wide as the passageway. He brought two more crates and placed them on top of the first two. The sturdy boxes would prevent the door from opening more than a couple of inches.

Out of breath, Cliff strained to lift another crate onto the stack, and then another while Yori furiously pounded on the door. Now the passageway in front of the door was completely blocked by the crates.

"*Voy a matarte!*" Yori screamed through the door. "I'll kill you!"

"You're trapped, Yori. You're gonna die in there!" Cliff shouted in Spanish as he double-checked the stack of crates.

"I'm gonna kill you so fucking dead, you fucking gringo!" Yori screeched.

Still out of breath, Cliff went to the box of parts he'd stumbled over before and found a heavy steel bar about two feet long with gear teeth machined into one end of it. *This'll work,* he thought. He took it with him up to the pilothouse.

Stepping over Juan's lifeless body, he moved to the radar mounted on the dash panel and took aim at the screen. It exploded in a crystalline cloud of shattered glass. Another swing of his club obliterated the compass. His next blow tore the VHF radio from its mount and sent it skittering across the floor. The single-side-band radio went next. After that, he went for the boat's gauges and meters. Suddenly the motor died. In the silence, he stood in the middle of the pilothouse and listened. Yori and Antonio were desperately pounding on the engine room door, which could be heard even in the pilothouse. Yori's muffled screams of anger seemed to have gained a note of anguish.

Satisfied, Cliff resumed his assault. He attacked the engine control levers until they broke away from their mounts. He blasted the ship's chronometer and barometer off the wall, smashed the overhead lights, and battered the main electrical panel until sparks flew from it. When there was nothing left to break, he went down the stairs to the deck and untied the rope that held *Staghound* against the *Tortuga Negra*. A crescent moon was just rising in the east as he stepped aboard the sailboat.

Cliff made his way aft and felt a lump rise in his throat when he saw Jon's body lying on the cockpit floor. He went down the companionway, expecting to find Lena's body. As he reached the bottom of the stairs, the blade of her machete flashed in front of his eyes and stopped a millimeter from his throat.

"It's you," she gasped, "I almost killed you." Her terrified eyes melted into tears. She dropped the machete and fainted. She would have collapsed to the floor if he hadn't caught her. He eased her unconscious body down onto a settee in the main cabin. "Everything's going to be okay," he whispered to her. "We're going home now."

The machete at his throat was the closest he'd come to being killed. For a moment he was bewildered by the crazy thought that she'd nearly killed him, and yet he was overwhelmed with relief that she was still alive. His head swam and he stumbled to the dinette to keep from falling. It took a moment to gather himself, and when his eyes could focus again, they focused on Lena, who was beginning to stir. He helped her sit up. "You okay?" he asked.

She slumped back down. "I'm so tired…"

"Okay, get some rest." He pulled a blanket and pillow from his berth above and covered her, then went back on deck.

Moonlight in the cloudless sky illuminated the carnage in *Staghound*'s blood-streaked cockpit. Cliff had to move Jon's lifeless body to get to the engine controls. Slipping on the oil-covered floor, he could barely manage to lift Jon onto a cockpit seat. He looked over at the *Tortuga Negra,* which was now drifting a hundred feet away. No lights showed on it, and though he strained to listen, no sound came from it either. He pressed the starter and *Staghound*'s engine came to life. Cliff put it in gear and the boat began to move. He got to the helm and pointed the boat northward. A wave of relief ran through him at the thought that they were finally free of the *Tortuga Negra.* He was still staring back at the fishing boat when the engine overheat alarm sounded. *Staghound* hadn't gone five hundred yards.

Cliff frantically shut off the engine. With the mainsail draped over the deck he knew it was useless to try and hoist it. His only option was the jib. *I've got to get it up before those guys break out of the engine room!* He hurried forward, slipping and stumbling on the oil-slicked deck to where Mike's body lay sprawled, his head shattered by one of Yori's bullets. One look told him Mike had been killed instantly. He went below and retrieved a sail bag and zipped Mike's body into it, wrapping it tightly with gaskets. It was impossible to carry, so he dragged it, his oily feet slipping on the deck, to the cockpit. Blood oozed through the nylon fabric of the bag onto his hands as he laid it on the seat opposite Jon's body. *Christ! I can't go on with blood everywhere, but I've got to keep us moving.* He wiped his hands on his wetsuit and went back to the foredeck to release the jib from its lashings, then made his way aft and hoisted it while the boat drifted aimlessly. What little wind there was, blew from the southeast and he sheeted in the jib, then turned the boat north again. Slowly, *Staghound* began to move.

With the boat settled on its course, Cliff pulled a bucket, soap, rags, and a deck brush from the lazarette and quickly scrubbed the cockpit floor, sluicing it with seawater until he could move around the cockpit without slipping too much. He took a rag and splashed soapy water on himself and got the blood and oil off his hands and wetsuit. While he worked, his mind wrestled with what to do with the bodies in the cockpit. *We're at least five hundred miles from the nearest land, and the nearest help. I need to bury them at sea, but I don't know the first thing about burial at sea. But we surely can't keep them in the cockpit. We have to do it! I'll get a noon sight so I can at least record where they're buried.* Thoughts like these raced and ricocheted through his tortured mind. He struggled with his emotions, nearly cracking at one point and bawling out loud. He hung his head, gulping air, struggling to get a grip on himself. *I'll get on the radio,* he told himself. *Put out a mayday call. There must be ships nearby.* He went down to the nav station and flicked on the light. He was stunned at the amount of damage Yori had done to *Staghound*. Fragments of blasted wood, glass, and metal covered the floor and counters. Moonlight shone through dozens of bullet holes in the cabin. He switched on the VHF radio to channel 16, the international distress frequency, and spoke into the microphone, "Mayday, Mayday. This is the sailing yacht *Staghound*." He repeated it a dozen times and heard no reply except hissing static. He tried the single sideband radio and got the same result.

He switched off the radios. In the quiet of the cabin, he heard the faint sound of water sloshing beneath the floor. Lifting a floorboard, he was alarmed to find nearly a foot of water in the bilge. Jon had always prided himself on *Staghound*'s dry bilges. Cliff's mind froze for a second before it registered that the hole in the transom must be letting in a lot of water. He lurched to the breaker panel by the nav station and reached for the bilge pump switch but stopped himself with his hand in midair. *The engine's dead. Without it, we can't charge the batteries. If I drain the batteries with the bilge pumps, I might not be able to start the engine to recharge them.*

He wracked his brain trying to remember what he had read about the engine before they set sail. The owner's manual was in the workshop. He hurried forward and rummaged through the books on the shelf until he found it, then feverishly scanned the "Troubleshooting" index. Flipping through the dog-eared pages he found the section on overheating. *Okay, I got it. First, check the raw water strainer, then the water pump, then the heat exchanger.* The sound of sloshing water seemed to grow louder every minute.

Cliff crouched in *Staghound*'s cramped engine room and found the strainer. It was clear. Next, he moved to the water pump and removed the cover. *Aha! A broken impeller.* Jubilant, he quickly replaced it with a new one from the boat's vast store of spare parts, silently thanking Jon for his meticulous outfitting of the boat.

On his way to the cockpit, he grabbed another sail bag. He started the motor, then carefully slipped the bag over Jon's body, securing it the same as he did with Mike. When he was finished, he looked up to see what had become of the *Tortuga Negra*. It was half a mile astern, still dark and dead in the water.

The engine temperature gauge settled at 180 degrees and Cliff pushed the throttle forward, bringing *Staghound*'s speed up to nine knots, then set the autopilot before he switched on the bilge pump. The wind was still light, blowing out of the east, causing the jib to luff a little. He was going to sheet it in, get the mainsail properly stowed on the boom, and assess the damage to the stern, but while he sat at the wheel gathering his thoughts for these tasks, exhaustion overtook him and he slumped down, chin on his chest and fell asleep.

When he woke, the sun was above the horizon, its rays burning his retinas when he opened his eyes. In broad daylight, he saw dozens of bullet holes in the cockpit, the damaged deck gear, the bloodstains... and the two bodies. He twisted around and gazed astern, searching for the *Tortuga Negra*, but the sea was empty in all directions. He wondered what the smell was that assaulted his senses, then realized it was his own body giving off a dank odor of sweat, blood, and oil. He stripped off his wetsuit and sluiced himself with bucket after bucket of cool seawater.

A sudden puff of wind blew the mainsail across the deck. It needed to be flaked on the boom before any more wind came, so he went below and dressed in shorts and a shirt, then checked on Lena, who was still asleep on the settee in the main cabin. He checked the bilge and was relieved to see that the water was lower than it had been before. *There are a dozen things I need to do that are urgent, but at least for now, the bilge pump is doing its job.*

Back on deck, it took an hour to flake the heavy mainsail on the boom and secure it while the boat continued northward over the placid sea. He couldn't avoid stealing occasional glances at the two corpses in the cockpit. *Rigor mortis is going to set in soon, if it hasn't already.* He grappled with that morbid idea while he worked, dreading the thought of dropping those bodies into the ocean. *But what else can I do? What would I want them to do if I was the one in a sail bag?* That question solved his dilemma. He took a deep breath and made ready to bury them.

He strapped dive weights around each body and went below to wake Lena. *She needs to be a part of this.*

"Mike didn't make it, did he?" she asked in a shaky whisper when she woke. She didn't look good to him; her eyes were red and her face was pale and drawn.

"No, he didn't. Neither did Jon."

"I know." She lowered her head and sobbed.

Cliff gave her a gentle hug, but she pushed him away. "I am to blame for this…this stupid, tragic folly."

"No. Yori is," Cliff spoke firmly. "You shouldn't blame yourself. Mike and Jon knew the risks. I did too. We took a chance and it cost two lives. But it's not your fault."

She hung her head and wept.

He gripped her shoulders and looked her in the eyes. "You still have to free your parents, right?"

She looked up at him through tears. "Yes, of course."

"If you do that, Jon and Mike's sacrifice will not be in vain."

"Yes. You're right." She used the heels of her hands to wipe the tears from her cheeks.

"We have to let them go, today. Do you think you can handle that?"

She stared at him, then gave a small nod. "I'll try."

On deck, the reality of what he was about to do weighed on Cliff. "Was Mike religious? he asked Lena. "Do you know anything about his family?"

She could barely look at the corpse, wrapped in its blue nylon sail bag. "He was not religious." She looked across the sea to the horizon. "Nor was Jon." She turned her gaze to Cliff. "Neither of them has any living relatives that I know of. Mike once told me he was the last in the Lundin line."

"Lundin?" Cliff asked.

"His name is Michael James Lundin."

Cliff drew a deep breath. "Alright. Do you want to say goodbye to him?"

Lena moved to the corpse and laid a hand on its shoulder

and spoke in a halting voice, "Mike, you were fun, and funny, an incredible sailor, and I'm sorry I couldn't love you the way you wanted me to. But I did love you very much. You...you..." Unable to continue, she turned away, burying her face in her hands, her shoulders heaving.

Cliff lifted the stiffening body and maneuvered it to the stern. "So long, buddy. I'll always remember you." He carefully slid the body down the transom and let it go. He watched it sink in the crystal-clear water, leaving nothing but a thin stream of bubbles. In a few seconds, it disappeared into the depths.

He turned back to Lena, whose face was frozen in a mask of grief. "We have to let Jon go too."

She nodded.

Cliff could see she was trembling, her hands at her throat. He hesitated a moment, but there was no getting around the fact that he had to do it. He lifted the body and moved it to the stern.

"His name is Johannes Oliver Hartmann," Lena whispered.

"Okay. Do you want to say a few words?"

Speechless, she gave a tiny shake of her head.

Cliff let the body slide partway down the transom. "Johannes Oliver Hartmann. I know the sea is what you loved more than anything in life. You're free now, in Mother Ocean's arms, where you've always wanted to be." He lowered the body as far as he could, then let it slip from his grasp. It glided beneath *Staghound*'s wake for a second then slanted into the deep blue ocean. Cliff watched until he couldn't see it anymore. When he turned around Lena was gone.

CHAPTER 17

CLIFF HAD SLOWED the boat before he eased Mike and Jon's bodies overboard. Now he pushed the throttle forward and set the autopilot on a course of due north. With a light midmorning breeze and only the jib up, he wanted to keep *Staghound* moving as fast as possible. He wouldn't rest easy until he was sure he was well beyond Yori's reach.

He scanned the horizon astern with binoculars. When he was certain the fishing boat was not in sight, he went below to check on Lena. He knocked on her cabin door and when there was no answer, he opened it a crack. She was curled up on her bed, crying softly. He closed the door, thinking it best to let her grieve.

He couldn't recall the last time he'd eaten, but he was as hungry as he'd ever been. In the galley, he found a loaf of bread and canned tuna. He made a sandwich and wolfed it down while he mentally sorted through all the things that needed urgent attention. Still chewing the last bite of his sandwich, he leaned over the stern and examined the damage the *Tortuga Negra* had wrought. Its steel bow had driven two feet into *Staghound*'s stern. Cliff had once seen the mangled fiberglass body of a Corvette that had been rear-ended. The damage looked similar. It extended four feet up from the bottom of the transom and was roughly three feet wide at the top, narrower at the bottom. Jagged strands of needle-like fiberglass lined the perimeter of the deep gash. Cliff opened a lazarette hatch and lowered himself down into the semi-darkness of *Staghound's* stern. The hydraulic autopilot motor whined as it made small steering adjustments. He crouched near the massive rudder post and peered aft. Daylight shone through a two-inch-wide vertical gap in the transom exactly in the center of the wider dent the fishing boat had pushed into the stern. This was where the *Tortuga Negra's* bow had broken completely through *Staghound's* skin. Below the transom, the gap extended forward a foot into the hull itself. He watched a wave rise under the stern and send a couple of gallons of seawater gushing into the boat through that gap. Twenty seconds later another wave rose and sent in another gush of water. It flowed forward through a limber hole in the ring frame just aft of the rudder post and disappeared. Cliff knew it would collect in the bilge sump, which was built into the top of the keel. When the water in the sump reached a certain level, the bilge pump would turn on automatically and pump it overboard.

He counted three dozen bullet holes scattered across the transom. A couple of bullets had torn through the antenna tuner that was wired to the backstay. *Now I know why the single sideband radio won't work,* Cliff thought while another surge of water came through the gap in the hull. He hurried up through the hatch, his brain formulating a plan to repair the gash in the hull.

The sun was high in the cloudless sky, reminding him that he had to get a noon sight. He grabbed the sextant and perched near the base of the mast. A few minutes later he got a good fix on the sun and went below to work out their position, marking the chart at 25°-35'S by 84°-05'W. He also marked a pair of "X's" where he estimated he said goodbye to Jon and Mike, writing their names and the date, February 8, 1987, next to them. He knew he should be grieving for them but his mind kept going back to the damaged transom. *I'll grieve after I fix that hole in the stern.*

On his way back on deck, Cliff stopped and knocked lightly on Lena's cabin door…Nothing. He opened it and saw her sleeping.

That's probably the best thing for her, he thought, *considering all she's been through.* He closed the door and hurried on deck.

The wind had picked up while he was below and now the jib bellied out solidly under it, and Cliff turned off the motor. Without the engine noise, the only sounds came from the breeze in the rigging and the gentle hiss of *Staghound's* wake. Cliff would have enjoyed it, but his eyes fell on the blackening bloodstains and debris in the cockpit, reminding him of the horror of yesterday's battle. *Christ! Was it only yesterday?*

With only the jib up, *Staghound* slowed from nine knots to five. Cliff watched the tiny beginnings of whitecaps forming on the waves. Were they a harbinger of more wind to come? *More wind means bigger swells. Bigger swells mean more water in the boat. There's not a minute to lose!* He hurried below to muster the tools and materials he needed to start the repairs.

An electric drill, jigsaw, router, sander, and planer were all in *Staghound's* tool inventory but they were useless without 110-volt electricity. They were intended to be used when the boat was in a marina with shore-power available. He'd have to use hand tools for the repairs. He found a hand-powered drill and an assortment of saws. He didn't worry about nuts and bolts and screws because *Staghound* had drawers full of them, all neatly sorted in separate compartments. The same could be said for caulking compounds.

With all of these materials at hand, he was confident he could fashion a patch for the damaged hull. While he rummaged among the tools, the sound of the bilge pump turning on and off was both reassuring and frightening at the same time. It was doing its job, but it was turning on far too often and running too long before it shut off.

Using plywood from the fake table Jon had made to cover the gun crates, he cut out a piece big enough to cover the hole in the hull, a rough trapezoid two feet long and tapering from two feet wide at one end, to a foot wide at the other. It wasn't perfectly symmetrical and the edges were splintery, but it would work.

He hurried back into the stern of the boat with the patch. He had to crouch low to reach the point where the transom intersected the hull. Kneeling, his knees awash in incoming water, he leaned forward and set it over the hole. He had to cut away the jagged edges of the hole and recut the wood a couple of times but when he was finished, the patch on the inside of the hull was screwed in place with plenty of caulk to seal the water out. He was soaked and his knees were raw but he was satisfied with that part of the repair. Now he had to put a patch on the outside of the transom.

Emerging from the lazarette, he searched the horizon to the south, half expecting to see the menacing black hull of the *Tortuga Negra* in the distance. But all he saw was an empty ocean whose waves were larger than before, each one bearing its own foaming whitecap. The earlier breeze had turned into a southeasterly wind powerful enough to push *Staghound* at seven knots and more, though she carried only a jib. In his mind's eye, Cliff saw each wave send another gush of water into the boat. He was about to go below but stopped short when he saw Lena emerge from the companionway. The bruises on her face had begun to heal. The blackened skin around her eyes was puffy and tinged slightly yellowish. Whether the swelling was from bruises or crying, he couldn't tell. Her hair was whipped across her face by the wind as she stared at him.

"You doing okay?" he asked.

She looked down at the bloodstained cockpit seat where Jon's body had lain, then toward the setting sun before she spoke. "I'll be alright." She brushed the hair from her face. "The *Tortuga Negra?*"

Cliff pointed an arm astern. "Somewhere back there. I don't think they're following us anymore."

She looked doubtful. "Why?"

"I locked Yori in the engine room and tore up the pilothouse. It will take him a while to get underway again. I knocked out his radar too."

The grimness of her expression eased a little. "He can't follow us then."

"Probably not. We've come a hundred miles in the last twelve hours."

She sat on the edge of the cockpit seat, staring at nothing.

"I need to fix the hole in the transom," Cliff said. "Before the weather gets any rougher."

She rose to go below. "I'll find something for us to eat."

Cliff watched her disappear down the companionway. She moved slowly, like an older person. The sun was sinking below the horizon and *Staghound* surged on a wave, reminding him that there was much work to do before he could rest.

❧

It was near midnight, but the moon hadn't risen yet so it was pitch dark. Cliff switched on *Staghound*'s running lights. The stern light, which had escaped the attack undamaged, gave off enough light for him to work on the transom. He had cut a piece of plywood like the one he made for the bottom, only this one would cover the lower four feet of the transom. He wanted to check the fit before he screwed it in place. To do that he had to lean far over the transom and hold onto it with his fingers. While he was deciding where he would put the screws a wave rushed up the stern and snatched it from him like a bully taking candy from a baby. He got one fleeting glimpse of it before it disappeared into the night. He stared at *Staghound*'s foaming wake, cursing himself for not tying a safety line to the wood. Disgusted, he crawled back from the transom and sat in the cockpit to regroup. Before he knew it, he was nodding off. He zipped his jacket and settled into a corner of the cockpit. *I'll rest a few minutes, then try again.*

It seemed like he'd barely closed his eyes when he was roused by the sound of *Staghound*'s motor starting.

"The batteries are low," Lena said. "They need to be charged."

She was wearing a jacket and knitted watch cap, standing at the helm. "Between the autopilot, refrigeration, and the bilge pump, they go down fast." She had switched off the autopilot and was steering the boat by hand.

Cliff groaned as he sat up. His neck was stiff from sleeping in an awkward position. There was the faintest glimmer of light in the east. He licked his cracked lips and squinted at her.

"Go get some rest," she said. "I've got the helm for a while."

"No. I have to fix that hole in the transom." He stood and stretched his sore back muscles.

She glanced eastward. "The sun won't be up for half an hour and there's coffee on the stove." She turned the wheel a bit as *Staghound* heeled in a gust of wind. "You look like you could use some."

"Yeah, coffee sounds good." Cliff went below and returned with two steaming cups. "How do you feel?" he asked as he handed her one.

"Better." She sipped her coffee. "How bad is the damage to the stern?"

"The *Tortuga* knocked a pretty big hole in it. I managed to patch the bottom part of it, but there's still a lot of work to do on the transom." He pointed to the lazarette hatch. "If you want to see the bottom patch, you'll have to climb down there."

"I'll wait until after daylight. How are you going to fix the transom?"

"Put a piece of plywood over the hole. It only has to last a few days, until we reach land." He was already mentally screwing the patch in place. This time he'd tie a rope to it before he slid it down the transom.

"What land?" Lena asked.

"According to the chart, Callao, Peru is the nearest sizeable port where we can put in, repair the boat, and report the deaths of

Jon and Mike to the State Department. I'm sure there's a consulate there. We could..."

"No," Lena interrupted. "We're not going to Peru."

Cliff paused. "Surely you don't want to go to someplace in Chile, do you?"

"We're not going to Chile either. We're going back to the States." She gave him that steady gaze he'd seen before, eyes as hard as marbles.

Cliff stared at her, incredulous. "Do you know how many miles we are from the States?"

"Around four thousand?"

"More like five, considering winds and currents." His patience gave out. "This boat has a big-ass hole in the stern, a zillion bullet holes, no radios, and...and look at the mast!" he sputtered. "The backstay's shot to hell, so's the main halyard. How in the hell are we going to make all the way to the States?" he demanded.

"I'm very confident that you'll get us there," she said calmly.

"Me?" Cliff was beginning to think she might be hallucinating. "Are you sure you're okay? Because you're talking crazy now."

She continued her steadfast gaze at him. "Have you heard of the Napoleonic Code?"

"WHAT?" he exploded, "Napoleonic...Now you really are talking crazy. What the hell does Napoleon have to do with us being stuck on a sinking boat in the middle of the ocean?"

The first golden rays of the sun brightened the eastern horizon, illuminating the undersides of the scattered clouds. She turned her face toward the sunrise, a faint smile on her lips. "I love the first moment of a new day," she said, then the smile disappeared. "Every country that lies between us and the States has laws based on the Napoleonic Code. You are, for all practical purposes, guilty until proven innocent." She waved her hand around the cockpit. "The authorities will take one look at this boat and assume we've been involved in a drug deal that went bad. Wherever we go, from Peru to Mexico, they'll put us in jail while they investigate. On top of that, to them, the only thing worse than smuggling drugs is smuggling weapons. If they connect us to Yori or MIR, you'll be an old man before you're released and I'll be sent straight back to Chile, in handcuffs."

"Well, I'm no expert, but I know this boat is in no condition to spend a month sailing back to California. Remember the storms we sailed through coming down here?"

"How long do you want to stay in a Peruvian jail?"

"How far do you think we'll get in this leaky boat?" Cliff shot back, amazed that she wasn't terrified of *Staghound* sinking under them.

"When you came aboard, you knew nothing about bluewater sailing. But you learned all you could about the sea and this boat. You stood your watches and you did everything that was asked of you. Within a week you were taking noon sights. When we met up with Yori, we all looked to you for leadership, even Jon did, who never looked to anyone for anything. You were the one who rescued me, and you were the one who survived and finally stopped the *Tortuga Negra*. It was you who always seemed to know what to do, but more importantly, you did it. You didn't ask for help. You just did what had to be done." Her eyes flicked from the jib to the compass and back to him. "I haven't the slightest doubt that you will patch the holes, mend the sails, and do whatever it takes to sail this boat wherever you want to go."

Cliff looked around the cockpit. Bullet holes riddled the deck, shattered pieces of deck hardware lay where they landed after they were blasted by Yori's AK47. The makeshift barricade was still in place, also battered by bullets. Blood had soaked into the grain of the teak-covered cockpit seats. "First, I don't know that we can even keep this boat afloat. Second, I'm not an experienced sailor, like Jon. Third, we didn't attack anyone. We were only defending ourselves."

"That won't matter to the Peruvians or the Mexicans."

Cliff paused. "Alright, let's say we do somehow manage to stay afloat and make it back to the States. The police there will draw the same conclusions."

The sun was above the horizon now. Lena pulled sunglasses from a pocket and put them on. "In America, you're innocent until proven guilty…Big difference." Anyway, we have a month to think about it."

It wasn't the first time Cliff had gazed at her and thought she could be a spy, a secret agent. With that cool demeanor and the sunglasses, she certainly looked the part. "Who are you, really?" he demanded.

"I'm exactly who you think I am." She turned her attention to the sails. "I think the wind is getting lighter."

"That's just it, I don't know who you are. As far as I know, you could be working for the CIA." He wasn't joking, but she smiled anyway.

"Well, we're stuck on this boat five thousand miles from home. You're just going to have to trust me." The morning sun reflected off her mirrored glasses as she spoke.

Cliff remained silent. *Yeah, we're stuck on this boat until we sink or get captured…Or figure a way out of this mess.*

"I see you're thinking," she said. "Is it to be California or Peru?"

He stared at her again, long and hard. "It's death by sinking on one hand, Peruvian prison on the other. I guess I'll take my chances with death by sinking."

"Oh, I'm sure we're not going to sink." She beckoned him to the helm. "If you'll take the wheel, I'll go make some breakfast, then you can fix that hole in the transom."

At the helm, Cliff gazed bleakly ahead. *Now I know the true meaning of being caught between the devil and the deep blue sea.* His gaze drifted to the damaged deck gear and bullet-riddled cabin, then to the fiberglass canister mounted on deck near the mast. It had three bullet holes in a neat diagonal line across the back of it, rendering the life raft it contained useless. He looked up the mast.

He was wondering what it would take to rig a new main halyard when the aroma of frying bacon wafted out of the companionway, followed by Lena. Her bruises were visible in the bright sunshine, but the way she moved told him that she was recovering.

"I set a place for you," she said as she took the helm.

Below, he found a plate of bacon, eggs, hash browns, toast, and coffee on the dinette table. While he ate, he thought of Jon, who had an easygoing confidence in everything he did. *What would he do now? He'd choose the deep blue sea over the devil, that's for sure. And he'd go about each task of repairing the boat and getting on with the voyage with the same easy confidence he had always shown.*

Maybe it was the inspiring memory of Jon, or maybe it was that he'd just had his first decent meal in days, but Cliff felt better, more confident. He finished his coffee and headed to the workshop where he started on the transom patch.

❦

Lena leaned over the transom to inspect the patch Cliff had just finished screwing down over the hole. He was in a bosun's chair, suspended just above the water, smoothing out the caulking compound that oozed out around the edges of it.

"It looks good enough," she said.

Cliff hauled himself back on deck. The sun was low in the west, marking the end of a long day of repair work. "I want to be sure." He opened the lazarette and dropped down into the stern of the boat. Where water had gushed in before, it was nearly dry. He had filled the intersection of hull and transom with thick beads of caulking, backed by pieces of wood that were screwed in place.

"Well?" she asked from above.

"Looks watertight." He climbed out of the lazarette and closed the hatch. "We should keep an eye on it, though."

"Okay, get some sleep. I'll call you at nine." She would take the first night watch, from six to nine, then they would alternate every three hours until six in the morning.

When he came on watch, the wind had eased to a light breeze. *Staghound* slowed to five knots under a moonless sky. In these conditions, it took little effort to steer the boat and Cliff found it hard to stay awake until a light appeared on the horizon astern. He watched anxiously as it gained on them, knowing that even if he started the engine and ran at full throttle, the other vessel could catch up if it wanted to.

At midnight Lena joined him. "What is it?" she asked, staring at the light, which was now no more than a mile astern.

"It's not the *Tortuga*." He held binoculars to his eyes. "Too big, and it's heading northwest, not following us."

Lena took over and Cliff went below and climbed into his bunk. A strange kind of exhaustion came over him. He was tired, yet he couldn't sleep. His thoughts stumbled from one thing to another. *Will the patch on the stern hold when, not if, we run into a storm? What if Yori really is following us? This time he won't stop shooting until he's sure we're dead. What about my navigation? I used to rely on Jon to check it, now I must rely only on myself. What if we get dismasted? What if the steering system breaks? What if the engine won't start? What if Lena falls overboard while I'm down here sleeping? What if I fall overboard?*

He rose from his bunk and glanced out the companionway. Lena was at the helm, her face barely illuminated in the red glow of the compass light, her hand steady on the wheel. A strange, involuntary thought crept into his mind as he gazed at her: *I love her.* A second later he shook his head and rebuked himself for having such a thought. *Don't be stupid,* he told himself, *she'd probably slap your face if she knew what you were thinking.* Still, he was reassured that she hadn't somehow fallen overboard and felt sheepish that he had even looked. *I gotta quit worrying and just get on with this voyage,* he told himself as he climbed back into his bunk. *That's what Jon would do. And keep my mind off Lena. You heard what she said to Mike back at Selkirk: She's not interested in anyone on this boat.*

⁓

At noon, Cliff got a sun sight and plotted *Staghound's* position at 23°-31'S by 84°-53'W. With dividers, he stepped off the distance to the equator, just over 1,730 miles. They had traveled 150 miles northward in the last twenty-four hours. *At this speed, it'll take at least twelve days until we cross the Line.* He put away the sextant and went up on deck.

"Ready?" he asked Lena.

"All set." She climbed into the bosun's chair and he winched her up the mast on a jib halyard, where she reeved the spare main halyard through the masthead sheave. Two hours later they were ready to hoist the mainsail.

She turned the boat into the wind as he spun cranks on the coffee grinder. The mainsail rose slowly, flapping in the breeze until he was able to sheet it home as Lena put the boat back on its northward course. With mainsail and jib drawing, *Staghound* heeled before the breeze and her speed rose to eight knots.

Cliff checked the backstay. He had replaced the hydraulic adjuster with a jury-rigged block and tackle system and winched it as tight as he dared. It was holding now, but he knew the real test would come when it got windier.

Lena swept the deck of debris and together they dismantled the barricade around the cockpit.

"*Staghound* is looking more like her old self than a floating wreck," she said, wiping sweat from her brow. They had crossed the Tropic of Capricorn and the day had been warm. "You have the six o'clock watch." She went below, leaving Cliff alone on deck.

CHAPTER 18

CLIFF SETTLED AT the helm as *Staghound* continued northward. The wind was light and the sea calm. He had kept a watchful eye on the southern horizon all day and now, just at sunset, he looked again. *We're over 600 miles from Selkirk. We must be well beyond the Tortuga's range by now.* He breathed a sigh of relief. It was a good feeling that lasted all of five minutes.

Lena stuck her head out the companionway. "Are you sure that patch is holding? Because the bilge pump keeps running."

"I'll check it." She took the helm while he grabbed the flashlight that was kept in a cubby near the helm and climbed down into the stern through the lazarette. The flashlight's beam reflected off a tiny stream of water coming in where he had repaired the transom. Relieved, he went back to the cockpit. "It's leaking a little. I'll fix it in the morning, when there's more light."

"Okay." Lena looked doubtful. "If you're sure."

Cliff felt a twinge of irritation with her. *She's getting worked up over a trickle of water.* "Yeah, it'll be fine."

But it wasn't fine. He tried to think of other things but that trickle nagged at him until, exasperated, he set the autopilot and went below to check for himself. When he shone the flashlight into the dark bilge sump, he was stunned by the amount of water in it. He watched the bilge pump automatically switch on when there were six inches of water in the sump and switch off when the level dropped to an inch. He checked his watch and waited, counting five minutes until the pump switched on again, estimating the amount of water that accumulated in that time was about five gallons. *A gallon a minute!*

He hurried back to the stern and searched around his repair job and confirmed that the amount of water coming in was nowhere near a gallon a minute. He moved forward and checked the rudder stock. With each surge of the boat, it moved laterally a fraction of an inch, allowing a small geyser of water to flow in through the lower bearing and over the rudder tube, maybe a cupful at a time. That water ran down the tube and joined the rivulet coming from the transom. With each little spurt of water, his gut tightened. *I don't know how to fix this.* Still, combined with the water coming in from the transom, it wasn't nearly a gallon a minute. *There has to be another leak somewhere.*

He crawled forward, following the rivulet until he reached the shaft log, where the propeller shaft passed into a bronze fitting and through the hull. He didn't know how that fitting worked but he remembered Jon calling it a 'stuffing box'. There was a steady dribble of water coming from it that joined the rivulet flowing forward toward the bilge sump. His gut tightened some more. *I don't know how to fix that either.*

He shone the light farther forward, past hoses and filters, into the engine room, but didn't see any other leaks.

"Ouch!" He banged his head on the hatch rim as he hurried out of the lazarette and stumbled down the companionway.

"What's going on?" Lena had emerged from her cabin and confronted him at the bottom of the stairs.

"We're taking on water through the rudder and propeller shaft. Maybe from somewhere else too." He rubbed the knot that was forming on his forehead. "We hit the bottom when we were leaving the island, the boat might be more damaged than we thought."

Lena's eyes widened, "Are we sinking?"

"No, but we'll be in trouble if the bilge pump stops working."

"I'll start the engine. The batteries must be getting low with the pump running so much."

If that pump fails, I want all the parts and tools I need for it handy. He searched among *Staghound*'s parts bins until he found a complete repair kit for it. Reassured of that detail, he was ready to take on the stuffing box leak.

"Cliff!" Came Lena's cry. "Cliff!"

When he came on deck, he knew instantly why she was calling him. The wind had turned into a blustery tempest, blowing the whitecaps off the turbulent waves.

"It just piped up," she shouted over the rising wind. "We have to reef!"

Staghound heeled thirty degrees, surging over the waves at twelve knots or more. Cliff looked up at the billowing jib and gulped. Hoisting and dousing it was easy when three men did the work. Now he would have to douse it himself. "Can you handle the boat while I take down the jib?"

"Yes. I'll point us into the wind and hold it there until you get it down." She looked around at the turbulent seas. "Hurry!"

Cliff uncoiled the jib halyard and laid it out so it would run free, then grabbed some sail ties. "Use the engine to keep us head-to-wind," he shouted.

Lena nodded, her face tense in the glow of the binnacle light. "I'm turning now!"

Staghound slowly came into the wind, the jib luffing and flogging so hard its sheets tore through their blocks and flew wildly in the wind.

He released the halyard and ran forward, dodging the flailing jibs sheets as he went. In the darkness, he felt the bow heave and plunge while blinding spray blew across the slippery deck. He tried to hang on to the bow pulpit with one hand and pull the jib down the headstay with the other, but the wind was too strong. He let go of the pulpit and grabbed the luff with both hands, pulling down with all his might. A wave broke over the bow and nearly knocked him overboard, but he hung on and managed to pull the sail down a couple of feet. He worked this way for ten minutes, hauling it down foot by foot until he could reach the head of the sail and finally secure the luff. Much of the sail was awash over the side and it took all his strength to gather it in and lash it down. With the job done, he made his way aft and slumped in the cockpit, his chest heaving and his breath coming in gasps as Lena turned the boat northward again.

"I think we just hit the southeast trade wind," she said, glancing at the instruments. "It was gusting to thirty knots when I called you, it's down to twenty-two now."

Cliff looked up at the dark sky, barely able to discern the dark clouds that scurried westward. "I guess that's good news," he said between breaths, "I thought we were heading into a storm."

"We'll probably have these conditions until we reach the equator. Let's finish the night under just the mainsail and think about hoisting the jib in the morning."

"Good idea, it will be easier to work on the boat if it's not heeled thirty degrees." He went below and checked the bilge sump again. Watching it fill and empty as it had before, he calculated the magnitude of the problem. *The pump runs thirty seconds every five minutes, maybe a bit more. That amounts to about three hours per day. How long will it last before it breaks down? Jon would know.* He checked his watch and sighed wearily. *Time to relieve Lena.*

"Did you make any progress on the leaks?" she asked when he appeared on deck.

"No, but we're okay for now. The pump is keeping up with them." He looked up at the mainsail and trimmed the sheet in. "The wind's backed around. It's almost due east now." He took the helm and Lena went below.

Thus began a period when the hours and days ran together.

The southeast trades blew a steady ten to twenty knots and combined with the southerly swells to push *Staghound* northward an average of 165 miles per day. During this period Cliff and Lena alternated three- or four-hour watches, never getting more than three hours of sleep at a time, and it led to the kind of sleep deprivation that made their bodies sluggish and their minds slow. They saw little of each other except in passing. When he was on watch she was in her cabin, and when she relieved him, he wanted nothing more than to climb into his bunk. Each had their duties and chores: He fixed little things that broke along the way while she cooked the meals. And though the weather was fine and the meals she cooked were good, he was too busy or too tired to enjoy the days or savor the meals.

Somewhere during that time, when he was looking for something else, Cliff discovered a box of flax packing material in the workshop. On the back of it were instructions for repacking the stuffing box. He nearly jumped for joy when he realized how easy it was to adjust the packing nut and stop that leak.

"That's wonderful," Lena had said when he rushed on deck to tell her. "Now if you can stop the leak in the rudder, we might have enough fuel to make it home."

"So far, I haven't figured out a solution for that one." He had already made a couple of fruitless attempts to stop that leak. "I guess we should consider ourselves lucky that hitting the bottom didn't break the rudder off completely."

"Being rammed by the *Tortuga* didn't help either. It knocked me off my feet and sounded like the boat was breaking apart." Standing at the helm, she slowly shook her head as she recalled the moment. "I thought I was going to die right then."

Cliff remembered floating in the water that night, thinking the same thing. *Was it terror?* He asked himself as he relived that night. *No. It was more like peace. I just accepted that my time had come.* For a moment he imagined his own death. He felt the slippery nylon sail bag being pulled over his head, the pressure of the dive weights cinched snugly around his waist. The coolness of the water as he slipped down *Staghound*'s transom and splashed into the sea. The light fading to ever deeper blue until it turned black. Down into the depths of Mother Ocean. Peace.

Lena's voice shook him out of his reverie. "It's almost twelve. Are you going to take a noon sight today?"

"Oh yeah, I almost forgot." He blinked in the bright sunshine and checked his watch before he went below for the sextant.

Half an hour later he marked an 'x' at 1°-05' S by 96°-00' W on the chart, noting the date: 2/18/87. The thermometer on the bulkhead read 88 degrees, but it felt warmer. A drop of sweat ran down his temple and disappeared in his beard. "We're about sixty miles from the equator," he said when he relieved Lena at the helm.

"How far from home?"

"Roughly twenty-four hundred miles along the rhumb line."

"And we're averaging 165 miles a day?"

"Yup. It works out to about fifteen days of sailing, not counting what we lose in the doldrums and the extra distance we sail due to weather and currents."

"So twenty days is more realistic." She looked northward, where massive cumulonimbus clouds rose high in the sky. "If the weather cooperates."

Cliff followed her gaze. Lightning flickered among the clouds, beneath them scattered dark columns of rain fell. *And we don't sink.*

It was dusk when *Staghound* met the line of squalls. To Cliff, the warm, humid air felt like it was charged with electricity and he saw furious whitecaps racing under a fast-approaching squall. Sensing there wasn't a minute to lose, he set the autopilot and shouted for Lena who was in her cabin. "Hurry, we have to douse the jib!"

He overhauled the jib halyard and released it. The sail began an easy descent down the headstay but he knew the wind would jump to twenty or thirty knots in a couple of minutes. He raced forward and gathered in the big sail and was still lashing it down when the wind struck. Pelted by torrential rains, he barely got it secured before it blew overboard.

He was making his way aft when the wind suddenly shifted and the mainsail slammed across the boat in an accidental jibe. The loose mainsheet caught Lena and slammed her into the cockpit coaming. When he reached her, she was slumped on a seat holding her ribs.

"The jib sheet went in the water," she gasped, grimacing in pain. "I went to pull it in."

Steered by the autopilot, *Staghound* was careening along under the mainsail, which Cliff had put a single reef in the day before, against the chance they would be hit by vicious squalls at the equator. It had taken half an hour when he did it, and that was in ten knots of wind. Now the sail was plastered against the starboard running backstay.

The worst of the squall passed quickly, leaving stagnant wind and light rain in its wake.

Lena looked up at the fouled mainsail and said, "I'll be alright. Go fix the sail."

The running backstays had to be reset whenever *Staghound* tacked or jibed. It was a simple job and Mike had always done it, releasing the working "runner" before the boat tacked and trimming the lazy runner afterward. But on this accidental jibe, it had not been done. Cliff tightened the port runner and eased the starboard one. Sighting up the mainsail he noticed an odd kink in the top batten.

Lena also looked up. "The batten's broken," she said, grunting as she spoke. "I think I broke some ribs too."

Cliff helped her down the companionway stairs and into her

cabin. She gingerly sat on her bed, using his arm for support. Her breathing shallow, she lay back in the bed.

"Where does it hurt?" he asked.

"Here." She pointed to her right side.

Cliff gently pulled her shirt up. "There's a lot of bruising here. Can you turn on your side?"

"No," she grunted, her face twisted in agony.

"Okay, I'm going to feel your ribcage, maybe I can tell what's broken."

She winced as he touched her.

"I feel lumps, swelling, on four ribs. They're probably fractured." He pulled down her shirt. "I can wrap them if you want."

"No. It's better not to."

"Alright. Either way, you're going to be out of commission for a while."

Lena closed her eyes, fighting the pain. "There's Vicodin in the medical kit," she said between shallow breaths. "Get me one."

∽

The rising sun sent blinding rays across the water, marking the start of the third day since Lena was injured. Cliff had taken to catnapping in the cockpit instead of sleeping below, since he was essentially single-handing *Staghound* now. He sat up and worked his shoulders to relieve the stiffness that came from sleeping on the hard seat. He ran his tongue over his teeth, feeling scummy and sweaty. He longed for the luxury of three hours of uninterrupted sleep instead of the twenty-minute respites he'd been getting lately.

The wind, never more than a flukey breeze all night, had dropped to almost nothing now, and the boat wallowed as a rain squall bore down on it. Seeing no whitecaps under the squall, he knew this wouldn't be a windy one. He went below for soap and shampoo. The rain fell in torrents when it arrived. Cliff stripped off his clothes and stood naked on the foredeck, scrubbing and soaping himself. When it passed, he slipped on his trunks and, still dripping wet, returned to the cockpit feeling refreshed and rejuvenated.

The aroma of coffee wafted out of the companionway. This surprised him because Lena hadn't left her cabin in the last three days, leaving the cooking to him. He peered down the companionway and saw her in the galley. It was the first time he'd seen her on her feet.

"How are you feeling?" he asked.

"Well enough to want coffee instead of another Vicodin." She moved stiffly. "I would hand you a cup of coffee but it hurts too much to raise my arm."

He went below and took the mug she offered. Her eyes seemed bigger, softer than before. He attributed that to the Vicodin. "A rain squall passed over us a few minutes ago, but now the sky looks clear to the north. I think we're heading out of the doldrums."

She held her mug in both hands, gazing at him over the rim as she sipped. "Three days to get through the doldrums, that sounds about right."

"I'm going to leave a reef in the mainsail and hoist the number three jib." He took a drink of coffee and looked out a cabin window. "We're probably going to be close reaching, so it could be a rougher ride." He glanced toward her ribs.

"I'm not ready to stand a watch yet." She attempted a deep breath and winced. "But I can take over some of the cooking duties."

"Tired of my cooking?" he chuckled. "Me too." He finished his coffee and rinsed the mug in the sink. "I'd better get that headsail changed before the wind comes up."

⚓

The wind shifted to east-northeast, starting as a light breeze that soon built to a steady fifteen-knot northeast trade wind. On a beam reach, *Staghound* made good progress northward. Dolphins played under her bow and the air grew crisper at night. Cliff maintained his routine of manning the boat and getting sleep in short snatches when he could, while Lena recuperated below. Since he stopped the leaks in the stuffing box and transom, the bilge pump ran at ten-minute intervals instead of five. On the fourth day after they reached the trades, Lena ventured out to the cockpit.

"It's getting easier," she said to Cliff, who watched from behind the wheel. "I'm tired of being stuck in my cabin, I'd like to take a turn at the helm."

Cliff thought of his bunk, which he hadn't slept in for a week, and checked his watch. "Sounds good. I've been steering a course of 300 degrees. I'll relieve you at 2100."

His bunk felt positively luxurious, and he was asleep as soon as his head hit the pillow. Suddenly Yori's ugly scar-faced grin leered at him in a dream. He felt a cord wrapped around his neck like a garrote. He struggled mightily but his hands were bound, his airway cut off. The blue nylon sailbag was jerked roughly over his head. He heard Juan's cackling laughter as the weights were lashed to his body and he was dragged to the edge of the Tortuga Negra's transom. He screamed *I'm not dead! I'M NOT DEAD!* over and over until Juan shoved his terrified body over the stern *I can't breathe!* he screamed as he sank into the blackness. His own screams woke him. Wide awake now, he tumbled out of the bunk and lurched toward the galley for a drink of water. Shaken, he ran a hand over his sweating face and stared into the darkness.

"You were screaming." Lena was at the companionway, staring down at him.

He squeezed his eyes shut and shook his head, trying to shake off the nightmare, then looked back at her. "I'm okay. Just had a bad dream."

She continued to gaze at him until he said, "I'm okay. Really."

He checked his watch. "It's time for me to relieve you anyway." He dressed and joined her on deck.

"Do you want to talk about it?" she asked.

"Talk about what?" His eyes involuntarily went toward the horizon over *Staghound*'s transom.

"What you were dreaming."

"No." He checked the compass and the trim of the sails. Overhead, the stars were bright and the friendly constellation of Orion was high in the sky. "Go get some rest, I'll call you at midnight."

⊷

Staghound continued northwest under sunny skies and fair winds. Each day the humid tropical air grew cooler, and each day the sun's zenith was a little lower in the southern sky, while Polaris rose steadily higher each night. On March 1st, Cliff marked the chart at 13°N by 114°W. A week later *Staghound* crossed the Tropic of Cancer 600 miles west of the Baja Peninsula. Day by day the wind shifted from east-northeast to north-northeast and then north, forcing Cliff to sheet the sails in tighter and tighter until *Staghound* was driving hard to weather. Under these conditions, spray often found its way into the cockpit and he wore foul weather gear when he went on deck.

Lena recovered a bit more each day. She didn't grind winches but she had less and less difficulty moving around the boat. One day she raised her shirt and showed Cliff that her black and blue bruises were fading. "I'm breathing better too."

On March 9th, *Staghound* was at 29° north latitude, still heading northwest. Cliff joined Lena in the cockpit and eyed the compass. "I think we can tack. If my navigation is correct, LA is on a bearing of 52 degrees magnetic." He pointed his arm in that direction, almost directly abeam.

"How far?" Lena asked. Recently, she wore a knitted watch cap with her foul weather gear. Today she added gloves.

"Roughly 750 miles."

"Shall we do it now?"

"Yup."

They had been on starboard tack so long, the jib sheets had grown stiff and salt-encrusted. Cliff freed them up, overhauling the port sheet so it would run free and loading the starboard sheet on its winch.

"I'll release the starboard runner," Lena said.

Cliff had replaced the batten in the mainsail right after it broke, a laborious task that she couldn't help with because of her injury. He remarked at the time that he would never let that happen again. He looked around, checking that everything was ready. The mainsail traveler was centered and the sheet eased a few inches. "Alright, let's do it."

Lena eased the running backstay then quickly turned the wheel. As *Staghound* came head-to-wind Cliff released the port jib sheet and winched in the starboard sheet as the boat settled on its new course. Within a few minutes, the jib was sheeted home, the portside running backstay set and the mainsail trimmed. Cliff was standing in the cockpit coiling lines when Lena spoke.

"We can't go to LA."

He considered his response while he finished coiling the running backstay tail. "Is this another misinformation ploy, like the one about Crusoe Island instead of Selkirk?"

"No. It's just that we have to stop in Catalina first, in Cat Harbor."

He hung the coiled rope on its winch and stared at her. "Why?"

"The money. We can't have it aboard when Customs inspects the boat. There's no customs office on the island."

"You just stuff it in a bag and take it ashore?"

"Yes"

"What if we get stopped before we get to Catalina?"

"We've never been stopped before."

Cliff looked skyward before he spoke again. A jet was flying 40,000 feet above them, leaving a long white contrail behind. It was the first he'd seen in a long time. "Alright, let's say we go to Cat Harbor. What then?"

"We'll do what we've always done."

"Which was?"

"We would arrive after midnight, when the few people around there were asleep. I would slip over the stern with my pack before Jon got the anchor down and swim ashore.

It sounded like something out of a spy novel to him, but he said. "Okay, so you swim ashore in the middle of the night. Where do you go?"

"I change into hiking clothes and walk to Avalon. It's about twenty-four miles."

He gazed at her, and slowly shook his head. "When I was a kid, I sailed over to Catalina with my pop every summer, so I'm familiar with it. There are bison, wild pigs, even rattlesnakes on that island. Are you telling me you hiked from Cat Harbor all the way to Avalon by yourself? In the middle of the night?"

"I once lived on Catalina. At the Isthmus. I've hiked all over the island. I know the dangers and I don't need a map to get to Avalon."

"You seem to have answers for everything." Cliff shook his head again. "So what do you do in Avalon?"

"I take the five o'clock ferry to San Pedro and call my aunt to come and pick me up." She casually removed her sunglasses and wiped spray from them as she spoke. To him, she looked inscrutable with them on, and beautiful with them off.

"What about Jon, does he stay in Cat Harbor?"

"For a day or two, then they take the boat back to her slip in

Wilmington." She gave him a brief smile. "Of course, you'll have to do that this time."

Cliff nearly burst out laughing before he realized she was serious. "You want me to take this boat back to Wilmington, alone?"

"No. That's what Jon did, but I don't know what is best now. I was hoping you would have some ideas." She raised her sunglasses and looked at him. "Do you?"

"Me?" Cliff said, taken aback. "No."

"Well, we have a few days to think about it." She glanced at her watch. "You're on watch now. We can talk about this later." She moved from behind the wheel and headed below without another word.

Alone at the helm, Cliff pondered Lena's words. Until now, he had little confidence that *Staghound* wouldn't sink under them, and he devoted his attention to keeping that from happening. He'd given little thought to what they would do when they made landfall. Now he imagined bringing *Staghound* into Cat harbor in the middle of the night. Not an easy task in the dark. As for taking the boat to its home slip in Wilmington, the idea of doing it alone was preposterous. *Besides*, he thought, *I can't anchor in Cat Harbor without reporting the deaths of Jon and Mike. Once I do that, I'm pretty sure I won't be taking this boat anywhere."*

At midnight, Lena relieved him. Too tired to pick up the conversation where they left off. He climbed into his bunk and fell into a troubled sleep.

CHAPTER 19

It was a small, unfamiliar noise that woke him. A creaking sound on the starboard side of the boat. It seemed to come with each swell that passed under *Staghound* as she sailed on port tack, heeled twenty degrees and making good progress toward the California coast. The automatic bilge pump started. It ran for half a minute and stopped, as it had been doing every ten minutes for days. Cliff concentrated on the creaking, trying to decipher what was making that sound. A wave bigger than normal rose under the boat and the creak was accompanied by a small cracking sound that drew him out of his bunk. *Something's up. I've never heard this boat make sounds like that before.*

In the main cabin, he moved to the starboard side of the boat and waited. This time the sound came from under his feet. He lifted a floorboard just in time to see the bilge pump start up again. It had been only three or four minutes at most since it shut off. *Water's coming in faster than before.* He checked the rivulet that had been coming in from the stern. It was the same meager trickle it had been since he tightened the stuffing box. *It's gotta be coming from somewhere else. But where?* He lifted more floorboards, from the companionway to the mast, but aside from the trickle, the bilges were dry. *Staghound* lifted over another wave and with the floorboards open, the creaking and cracking sounds were louder... And the bilge sump was already half full again.

As he stared down at the water swirling in the sump, a frightening thought occurred to him. *The water is coming in around the keel bolts. Staghound's* fifteen-thousand-pound keel was attached to the bottom of the hull by a double row of stainless-steel bolts secured by large nuts in the bilge sump. When the bilge pump emptied the sump, the nuts were exposed, but they were submerged as the sump filled. He watched the sump fill up faster than the trickle of water from the stern flowed into it. He cursed himself for not thinking of this before. With his confidence in them shaken, he wondered if the bolts might break. If they did, the keel would fall off and *Staghound* would instantly capsize. Sweat broke out on his temples as he watched the water. *If the keel falls off, it's over.* More creaking, cracking sounds broke into his thoughts. He crouched down on the slanting floor and put his hand on one of the floor timbers. Spaced about three feet apart, they were transverse structural beams, like ribs, that supported the floor of the boat and gave the hull its strength and seaworthiness. He stuck his head beneath the floor and sighted along the main beam as another wave lifted *Staghound.* As it did, he noticed a hairline crack open on the starboard side where the beam was attached to the hull. As the wave passed, the boat groaned, almost like an animal in mortal pain. The floor timber was slowly coming loose from the hull.

Cliff moved forward and checked the next timber, spotting another hairline crack open and close. He moved to the third timber forward, waited for a wave to pass under the boat, and saw another crack appear. The creaking and groaning came from the timbers lifting the floor a fraction of an inch, putting strain on the boat's beautifully varnished mahogany bulkheads. *Staghound* was slowly tearing herself apart.

Cliff noticed there were no cracks on the port side, only the starboard. *If the boat is heeling to starboard,* he reasoned, *the keel would tend to pull down on the port side of the timbers and push up on the starboard side. If the boat's not heeling at all, the keel wouldn't be pushing the starboard ends of the timbers up.* Now he knew what to do.

On deck, the sun was low in the west, almost directly behind *Staghound.* The northwest wind blew a steady fifteen knots. Lena sat at the helm in foul weather gear and watch cap. Only a little spray came aboard. It was the cold wind that forced her to bundle up. Cliff eased the mainsheet until the sail was luffing slightly, he did the same to the jib. *Staghound* slowed while her mast stood nearly vertical instead of heeled twenty degrees.

"What are you doing?" Lena asked. Her jacket was zipped up to her chin, its hood snug over her watch cap.

"Hold your course, I'll be back in a few minutes," Cliff replied. He hurried below and crouched at the bilge sump, listening for the creaking sound as a wave passed under the hull. It was there, but muted. He waited and watched the crack in the floor timber as another wave passed under the hull. If it opened at all, it was so slight that he couldn't see it. He stayed there and watched the bilge sump fill. With the boat sailing almost upright instead of heeled, it seemed to fill more slowly. The bilge pump started, emptied the sump, and shut off. According to his watch, it was five minutes before it started again.

"What's going on?" Lena asked when he came back out to the cockpit. In the fading light, her questioning eyes were large and luminous.

"When we hit the bottom back at Selkirk, I think it did more damage than we thought." He'd forgotten to put on a jacket and the cold wind bit through his shirt. He shivered before he went on. "There's water coming in at the keel. That leak has been there all this time, but I didn't know it."

Lena's hands tightened on the wheel. "The pump has been managing it so far. What's changed?"

"I found some structural damage. Some of the floor timbers have separated from the hull on the starboard side. The ones right around the keel. As long as we were on starboard tack, everything was fine. The noise didn't start until we tacked. There's something different about being on port tack."

Lena's face remained impassive. "What kind of noise?"

"I heard some creaking and cracking. The boat is flexing because it's not structurally sound anymore." He paused, his eyes fixed on the setting sun. "I asked myself what Jon would do in this situation."

"And?"

"I don't know, but I'm freezing." He went below and put on his foul weather gear, then crouched and listened for the creaking sounds. They were still there, but not as bad. He checked the cracks in the floor timbers. They weren't opening as much as before. He zipped his jacket and went back on deck.

"You're scaring me," Lena said. The sun had dropped below the horizon and the wind was colder. A few strands of her hair had escaped from her cap and blew across her face.

"I'm scared too. I don't know much about boat construction, but I don't think we can repair the damage out here."

Lena nodded toward the mainsail. "It's luffing. Are you going to trim it in?"

"When the sails were trimmed in and we were heeled twenty degrees the boat was making lots of noise, now that the sails are eased, they aren't putting so much stress on the boat. Maybe we can make it to Catalina before things get worse."

"Worse?" Her eyes flicked to the compass before they fixed on him.

Cliff decided not to tell her of his fear that the keel could fall off. "We're seven hundred miles from home. If we baby things along, and don't run into any bad weather, we'll probably make it into port." He tried to sound confident.

Lena checked the knotmeter. "We're still doing seven knots. At this speed, we'll be there in four days, no?"

Cliff had noticed before that when Lena was worried, her almost unnoticeable accent came out. "That sounds about right. What do you think the weather will do?"

Lena looked skyward, where the first twinkling stars had already appeared. "Without a radio to get forecasts, it's hard to say. But the barometer is holding steady. I think we'll have weather like this until we get within a hundred miles of the coast. Then as we get closer, the weather will be more under the influence of the land. It could be very light all the way to Catalina."

Cliff hadn't expected such a detailed prediction from her. "How do you know all this?"

"I've been here before. Jon liked to plot our approach to Catalina so we passed ten or fifteen miles south of San Nicolas Island. Then we would head straight for Cat Harbor." She changed her grip on the wheel. "He always timed it so we arrived after midnight." She glanced at the sail again. "Are you going to trim it or shall we luff all the way to Catalina?"

Cliff followed her glance. The top third of the mainsail was pressed against the spreaders. He rose and trimmed it in just enough so it wasn't touching them. He glanced at his watch. "It's almost 1800, I'll take over now."

Lena rose stiffly from her perch and relinquished the helm. She moved to the middle of the cockpit and raised her arms to shoulder height, then twisted left and right, gently working the muscles of her ribcage.

"Feeling better?" he asked.

"Yes." She rotated her shoulders, then bent and touched her toes. Even in frumpy foul weather gear, her movements had a feline grace.

She disappeared below, leaving Cliff to worry about the boat coming apart beneath his feet. A tiny blinking light passed silently overhead. *An airliner headed for LA,* he thought as he watched it fade from sight. An hour later Lena came back on deck with a pillow and blanket.

"Do you mind if I stay up here?" she asked. "I can't sleep with the noise the boat is making." She sat in the corner of the cockpit, under the protection of the dodger. With her knees drawn up and the blanket tucked around her, she fixed her gaze on Cliff. "Tell me about your wife."

Cliff had been thinking of broken floor timbers and calculating the odds of *Staghound* making landfall before it sank. The question jarred him. He stared at her a moment before he answered. "I put her behind me four months ago."

"Do you miss her?"

"No." He glanced at the compass as he spoke. "Why do you ask?"

"You will be home soon."

"Not home to her."

"To someone else?"

"No one." He noticed a light off the port bow. The first he'd seen in several days. "There's a ship," he said, jutting his chin in its direction.

She said nothing, keeping her eyes on him.

He changed the subject. "How will you get your parents out of prison? Can you just pay off the warden or *comandante*, whoever the prison boss is?"

"Yes. The Pinochet regime is rotting from the inside. Everyone in the government takes *la coima*, especially police and jailers."

"*La coima*? Is that Chilean for *la mordida*? A bribe?"

The ship was closer now. It would pass a mile or two off *Staghound*'s port side. Lena rose and glanced at it before she replied. "Yes. Tony was going to come with me to Santiago, but now I will go alone."

"That sounds dangerous." Not for the first time, Cliff was amazed by her cavalier mention of venturing into dangerous situations.

"Not so much. I have many brothers and sisters in the Movement."

"Tony seemed like the perfect bodyguard…or mercenary. Will you be able to find someone like him to help you?"

"There's no one like him."

"Who was he to you, really?"

"He rescued me from the Villa Granada and brought me to America."

"Was he in the Movement too? MIR is what you call it, right?"

"Yes, the *Movemiento Izquierda Revolucionaria*." The moon had risen above the horizon, its reflection on the sea a shimmering silver path stretching ahead of *Staghound*.

"How did you meet him?"

"He was from Colombia but lived in Peru, for the surfing. He was a big wave rider. When his father and brother were killed by the Medellin cartel, he went back to his hometown to avenge them. He joined FARC because they were against the cartel as well as the government. They also had contacts with MIR. FARC is a communist organization and clothed their corruption in communist drivel, as he called it, and he was quickly disillusioned by them." She stopped speaking and looked around at the rising moon.

"And then what happened?" Cliff prompted her.

"He was recruited by the CIA because he knew about the cartels and FARC, and he was fearless. They made him a US citizen as payment for something he did for them. He wouldn't say what it was. Anyway, he realized the Americans were just as corrupt as everyone else, but they had endless resources. They sent him to Chile to help Pinochet with his counterinsurgency but he mostly misdirected their attacks instead of helping. When he was wounded in the northern mountains he was brought to our clinic. My father saved his life. Tony saw that Papa didn't care which side the people who came to him fought for, only saving lives.

During his convalescence, they became very close, Papa and Tony. When Pinochet's troops burned down the clinic, Tony escaped but we were taken to Santiago and wound up in the Villa Granada. A few months later he rescued me. He was going to rescue my parents too. But the CNI, Pinochet's secret police learned that it was Tony who got me out, so we had to flee. That's how I came to America when I was twelve. I lived with my aunt in Pasadena. Am I boring you?"

"Not at all. I'm fascinated. How do guns fit into the story?" Cliff watched her eyes as she spoke.

"Tony had connections everywhere and allegiance to no one. He knew MIR was desperate for weapons to fight Pinochet, a cause that was dear to both of our hearts. He also knew the US has thousands of surplus weapons from the Vietnam War. He took the guns from a depot in California and concocted the plan to sell them to MIR and use the proceeds to buy my parents' freedom. As I said, the end is in sight for Pinochet and everything is for sale, including his prisoners."

"That was selfless of Tony."

"He wanted my parents freed as much as I do. In America, he was a big brother to me. He protected me and made sure I was able to finish high school and go to college. When I connected him to Jon we suddenly had the means to rescue my parents."

"Do you know who killed him?"

"No, but he had enemies. Even Pinochet put a bounty on his head." Lena fell into contemplative silence. A few minutes later she pulled the blanket up to her chin and closed her eyes.

Cliff watched her sleep from the corner of his eye as he steered *Staghound* eastward. *What was the word Jon had once used to describe her? Resilient. She is certainly that,* he thought. *And beautiful too.*

❦

The next day Cliff sat with his back against the mast and raised the sextant to his eye. There were clouds in the sky but he managed to get a good noon sight and went below to plot *Staghound*'s position on the chart: 29°-54'N by 129°-02'W, noting the date too: March 10th, 1987. Using dividers, he measured the distance to Catalina Island: 580 nautical miles on a bearing of 53 degrees. *We covered 180 miles in the last twenty-four hours. Pretty good, considering that it feels like we're just idling along. At this rate, we'll fetch Catalina in three days.* Throughout the night *Staghound* had creaked and groaned, causing him to check under the floorboards every few hours. Now he checked again. The hairline cracks in the floor timbers that opened and closed before, didn't close anymore, they remained open. With every mile, *Staghound* was getting weaker.

Back on deck, Cliff checked the sails while Lena steered. It had become a kind of race. If they pushed the boat harder, they would reach port sooner. But pushing harder meant more stress on the failing hull. If they didn't push the boat, it would take longer to reach the safety of the island. The longer they were at sea, the greater the chance of meeting bad weather.

Staghound labored under the strain of sailing when she should be in drydock. It showed in the sagging headstay and the play in the leeward shrouds that wasn't there before. It showed in the way the cabin floor bulged upward where the floor timbers had broken, and the way the bilge pump had to work harder to keep up with the leaking around the keel bolts. And it showed in the way *Staghound* groaned every time it went over a swell.

Another day and night passed with the steady northwest wind. Lena, uneasy with the noises *Staghound* made, refused to sleep below, choosing instead to curl up on a cockpit seat with her blanket and pillow.

"Will you go back to your work as an architect?" She asked. The wind had eased in the afternoon and she traded foul weather gear for a jacket.

It was just after sunset and in the twilight, her eyes were dark, inquisitive pools. Cliff glanced at the compass before he looked at her. "Yes."

"I think you must be a very good one."

"I got fired from my firm. Maybe I'm not as good as you think."

"Or maybe you were too good for them. It happens, you know."

He allowed himself a brief chuckle. "Well, either way. I'm not going back to that outfit."

"You will open your own firm?"

"That is my plan." He didn't actually have a plan, just some vague ideas about opening a small office and practicing his profession on his own terms, but they weren't formed well enough to discuss. He gazed ahead in silence. When he looked back at her a few minutes later, she had fallen asleep.

The following morning the sun rose just off *Staghound*'s starboard bow. Through the night, the barometer had been rising and it now stood at 1022 millibars. The wind dwindled with the rising barometer. *Staghound* glided over a smooth sea with just enough breeze to keep her moving at six knots. At noon, Cliff plotted her position, measuring the distance left to go at 270 miles. A container ship, headed southwest, passed a couple of miles off *Staghound*'s port side, the word "Matson" emblazoned on its hull. In the afternoon, another ship headed in the same direction passed.

"We are getting close to home," Lena said as a jet appeared high overhead, its white contrail pointing like an arrow toward Los Angeles. In the afternoon she took a pair of steaks from the freezer and thawed them in the sunshine.

Cliff had long since given up on fishing and was grateful that there was still meat in the freezer. It was a mystery to him that Mike could catch fish almost at will. He, on the other hand, rigged a trolling line with a cedar plug, exactly as he'd seen Mike do many times, but almost always came up empty.

At noon the following day, March 13th, Cliff plotted *Staghound*'s position at 32°-55'N by 121°-01'W. "If my navigation is correct, we're about 130 miles from Catalina," he said when he came on deck.

At the helm, Lena scanned the horizon ahead. "So we will sight San Nicolas Island tonight?"

"I hope so."

The sea remained calm, its surface ruffled by the light wind that had backed to west-northwest. A pod of dolphins approached from the south to glide just beneath *Staghound*'s bow. At sunset, a dark spot appeared on the horizon off the port bow.

Cliff had been tense all afternoon, watching for a sign of the island, but it was Lena who pointed it out to him. His face must have betrayed his relief at sighting the island, because she smiled at his expression.

"Congratulations, Captain. Jon would be proud of you." She left the wheel and came forward to hug him while he was still processing the fact that he had just navigated across five thousand miles of ocean. His head swam as she held him, but a second later she returned to the helm. It took him a moment to gather his wits and search again for the island on the horizon, but it had disappeared in the darkness, like an apparition. Lena was again her usual self, and everything was the same as it was before. Except it wasn't. Something had changed, but he couldn't quite put his finger on it.

Four hours later the island loomed larger, only a few miles off the port bow and clearly visible in the moonlight. The binoculars were equipped with an internal compass and Cliff took bearings, first on the west end of the island, then on the east. He went below and plotted those bearing lines on the chart. Where they intersected was where *Staghound* lay, nearly becalmed.

He was sitting at the chart table, measuring the distance to the island when Lena joined him, casually laying a hand on his shoulder as she peered at the chart with him. He tapped the "x" on the chart with his pencil. "This is where we are," he said, "Twelve miles off San Nicolas, sixty miles from Catalina."

Lena leaned closer. He became aware of her breast pressed against his back. Her hand left his shoulder and pulled his face toward hers. The next instant their mouths were locked together. He rose from the seat, lifting her with him as she tore at his shirt. Somehow, they made it to her cabin and fell together on the bed. She gasped when he entered her and clung to him like a waif in a maelstrom as they convulsed in a crashing climax.

They lay together in silence until their breathing returned to normal. Lena rose on one elbow and stroked his face. "I've fallen in love with you," she whispered. She leaned over and kissed his face and neck.

If he'd been able to, he might have counted a hundred kisses. When she stopped, he pulled her closer as she caressed his chest.

"I didn't want to," she continued, "I resisted as long as I could. It was inconvenient...no, it was impossible. But I should have known you would do the impossible. You're good at that, you know, doing the impossible."

His hand slid down her side, past her bruised ribs and settled at the base of her spine. He marveled at the silky smoothness of her skin. "I don't know what you mean. I'm just a guy who..."

She put a finger to his lips. "You are not 'just a guy'. Without you, I would be dead now. Without you, we couldn't have accomplished the mission, and without you even if I survived, I would have been in despair." She rose and left the cabin.

Cliff stared at the ceiling. *Despair. That's what I'll feel when she's gone.*

Lena returned with a bottle and two glasses. He held them while she poured wine.

"I've been thinking," she said. "When we get close enough to the island, we can scuttle the boat, swim ashore, and hike into

Avalon. From there, we catch the ferry to San Pedro and we'll be safe." She took a sip of wine and watched his face.

"You mean run?" He swirled the wine in his glass and sipped. "Where would we go? What about your parents?"

"You could come with me to Chile. We'll bring them back to the States and start over. Together."

The wind had died completely and *Staghound* drifted. The only sound was the occasional slatting of the sails punctuated by the bilge pump running every five minutes.

"Well, it won't take much to sink the boat, but the rest of your plan, I don't think it will work."

"Why?" she asked. She flicked on a tiny red nightlight above the bed and stared into his eyes. "We have money, we'll have freedom if we do it right."

Cliff considered his words carefully. If he said the wrong thing, she might disappear, or dismiss him as a coward. In the end, he chose to lay his cards on the table. "You take the money and go get your folks out of prison. I'll go ashore and report the deaths of Mike and John."

"But they could put you in jail. You might be blamed for their deaths. They could find out about the guns, and Yori, and all the rest." She squeezed his hand.

"That's true."

"But why," she pleaded. "Why would you just turn yourself in?"

"Because I'm not running. I'm not going to spend the rest of my life looking over my shoulder, worrying that any knock on my door might be the police." He took another drink of wine. "I'll keep your name out of it. I'll lie for you if necessary, but I'm not running." He reached out and touched her cheek. In the semi-darkness, he saw a tear fall. He was sure he'd just killed whatever might have been between them.

She remained silent for a full minute. "That's another reason why I love you," she whispered. She reached for his hand and pulled it to her lips, kissing it.

He put his glass down and gently took hers from her hand, pulling her close. They lay back on the bed, her head on his shoulder as she cried.

"I'm sorry," she said through her tears. "It was a stupid idea, and of course I knew you would refuse." She wiped her cheek with a corner of the bedsheet and sniffed. "It was selfish of me to want to run away with you. It was only because now that I've found you, I never want to be without you. Ever." She reached up and turned off the light.

In pitch blackness now, they relied on touch and taste. Her lips explored, finding his nipples then moving farther south until she took him in her mouth, sending him into a velvet world where he surrendered to the dictates of her tongue. She rose up and straddled him, settling on him like a cowgirl on her favorite mount. Her waist was so narrow his hands almost completely encircled it and he held her tightly while she moved. She pulled his hands up to her breasts and pressed his fingers to her nipples while she rode like a huntress on her steed. Just when he thought he might explode in her she grabbed the handhold above and lifted herself higher and higher until he feared she was leaving. He started to pull her back down but she resisted. For a long tremulous second she paused, like a ballerina en pointe, then plunged herself down onto him and galloped at a furious pace, panting harder and harder until she shuddered, cried out, and collapsed onto his chest.

Cliff held her tight, feeling her breath hot on his neck and her heart pounding against his ribs. They stayed that way until her breathing eased, then he turned them both over so he was on top and began to move. She wrapped her arms around him and moaned with every thrust until he let go, his own breath now coming in ragged gasps.

CHAPTER 20

CLIFF AWOKE IN predawn darkness. *Staghound* lay becalmed and seemed to be utterly motionless on the sea. Neither the slatting of a sail nor the clatter of a block disturbed the silence. Lena slept with her head nestled on his shoulder and her arm across his chest. The warmth of her body against his comforted him. He glanced at her face and bent his head to plant a gentle kiss on her forehead. It dawned on him that his whole life had been a peculiar journey to her. A destination he could never have fathomed until now. His heart swelled with an emotion that was beyond any he had ever felt before. If he had tried to express it in words, he would have failed. For the first time in his life, Cliff Demont had fallen truly, deeply in love. Everything that came before in his life had been nothing but prelude to this. He kissed her again and she stirred. He kissed her once more and, eyes still closed, she turned her face toward his and kissed him back. He held her tightly and gave in to the ineffable pleasure of holding Lena Voss in his arms.

"I know," she said when he told her of his epiphany. "I've loved you for a while now, but I couldn't say so. Not with Jon and Mike aboard. After they were gone, I thought of telling you but I didn't know if you were still in love with your wife. If you were, I would have kept my feelings to myself. You don't know how happy it made me when you said you put her behind you." She kissed his neck. "I knew you loved me when you came back for me on the *Tortuga*. That was love." She smiled. "Do you remember that morning when a squall passed over us and you took a shower on the foredeck? I watched you scrub this beautiful body." She ran her hand over his chest and up to his face. "And I knew you were my destiny."

They talked for another hour as *Staghound* floated silently. Speaking in little more than whispers.

"Tell me about Jon. How did you meet him?" he asked.

She kissed his cheek before she replied. "I was doing research at the science center on Catalina and waiting tables at the only bar in the village. He used to anchor *Staghound* at the Isthmus, sometimes for weeks at a time. He and Mike were regulars at the bar. They and their friends were not terribly reputable but they were fun. Handsome men with a beautiful boat. The women flocked to them. Mike fell in love with a different one every week, but Jon was different, more reserved. It took all summer for him to approach me. Before long I gave up my studies and became *Staghound*'s cook. We sailed to Mexico, Hawaii, the Caribbean, the South Pacific. He told me about smuggling drugs from Thailand, but that was over before I met him."

"So, what did you do on these trips?"

"Surfing. He said Mexico had gotten too crowded, same with Costa Rica. He became obsessed with the idea of being the first to surf the last untouched waves in the world, so we went to more remote places. Bocas Del Toro, San Andres, Providencia, Grand Cayman. Farther east, we discovered that all the good waves in the Antilles had already been surfed. He studied charts of the South Pacific, and a month later we went back through the Canal and headed for the Marquesas, the Tuamotus, and the rest of Polynesia. Nothing pleased him more than finding an island or atoll with perfect waves and no footprints in the sand." She played her fingers through the hair on Cliff's chest while she spoke.

"Were you his girlfriend through all this?"

"No. It's not that I didn't love him, I did for a while. But he was not meant to be with one woman. I can't blame him. Wherever we went, beautiful girls seemed to materialize from nowhere. At first, I was outraged, but the minute I looked away, another little blonde would be climbing on him. After a while, I gave up." She chuckled. "I truly believe he was a reluctant playboy, but it was like trying to stop the tide from coming in."

Cliff stroked her hair while she talked. Her husky whisper was like honey to his ears. "Were you smuggling then?"

"At first I was too naïve to see what he was doing. We'd anchor somewhere and he would take a package or envelope from some hiding place in the boat and give it to someone ashore, passing it off as a gift for a friend. When I became suspicious, he confessed that he did discreet deliveries for people. Wealthy people who preferred to have their Chinese Tael bars, or diamonds, or art, or sometimes laundered money, delivered from one country to another privately. I wanted no part of that and refused to sail with him anymore."

They lay in silence for a moment. Lena reached up and stroked his beard. "The sea has revealed you," she whispered.

"Revealed me?" Cliff didn't understand.

"Yes, the same way Michelangelo revealed David. He found a lump of marble and began with his hammer and chisel. When he was finished, there stood David. He was always there in that stone. Michelangelo revealed him." She pushed his hair out of his eyes. "The sea did the same to you. When you came aboard this boat, you were lumpish, a little pudgy and ill-defined. But like Michelangelo, the sea chiseled you, revealing this beautiful man, Cliff Demont. It revealed your character, your courage, and your resourcefulness," she added. "In your quiet way, you took over *Staghound*, not by challenging anyone, but by becoming very good at everything you did." She rested her hand on his chest. "While you were taking over *Staghound*, you took me over too. I couldn't help falling in love with you."

Again, he was overcome, besotted, with love for her. He compared Lena to Janet for a moment. Janet, self-absorbed, ambitious, and vain, had never spoken of him in such terms. She was more concerned with what he wore, what he drove, and the size of their bank account. He said nothing, but simply reveled in the knowledge that, more than anyone ever in his life, the beautiful and courageous Lena Voss, after all they had been through together, saw him for exactly who he was. And loved him. He tucked that thought into a special place in his mind, so he could savor it again and again.

"So how did you get involved in gunrunning?" He asked, changing the subject.

"I'm not involved the way you imply. This is a one-time operation to get money to free my parents. I have no desire to be a smuggler or gunrunner and I'm sure I'll never do this again." She sat up. "Listen."

Cliff cocked his ears. "I don't hear anything."

Lena put a finger to her lips. "Shhh. There's a boat coming."

Cliff rose from the bed and stuck his head out the companionway. Now he heard it. The faint drone of a motorboat. He saw a light off the starboard bow and grabbed the binoculars. He watched it for half a minute before he lowered the glasses. "Its bearing is changing, it will cross our bow."

Lena took the binoculars and studied the approaching vessel. "There is a pier on the eastern tip of San Nicolas," she said, lowering the glasses. "It could be a supply boat for the island, or a naval patrol boat. I'm going to make some coffee."

Cliff watched the boat came closer, the noise of its engines growing louder every minute.

Lena stayed below and handed him a cup of coffee as the boat crossed *Staghound*'s bow, a hundred yards away. "We're out of regular coffee, this is instant," she said. "If you see anyone on that boat give him a wave as if you're out here on vacation."

Cliff casually raised his cup to a crewman standing in a doorway of the other vessel's pilothouse. He waved an arm and went back inside. "There was a guy on the bridge," Cliff said without taking his eyes off the other vessel.

"Is he holding his course?"

"Yes, it looks like he's headed straight for the east end of the island." Cliff looked down at Lena, who remained below. "You don't want to be seen."

"Right. There will be questions when you report to the authorities. They must not suspect that anyone but you is aboard this boat."

"Got it."

Lena disappeared again.

The sun was above the horizon now. In the daylight, Cliff studied the dark hump of San Nicolas. A white line of surf was visible along the base of its rugged bluffs. He was glad they had not drifted closer to the island overnight. It looked barren and uninviting.

Lena came on deck lugging a pillowcase stuffed with clothes and other personal items. "We have to sink this." She lowered it to the cockpit floor. "There's one more."

"What are they?" Cliff asked when she brought the second pillowcase up.

"My belongings. I don't need them anymore and I don't want any evidence that I've been on this boat. I moved your things into my cabin."

Cliff shook his head in amazement. "You really could be a spy."

She ignored the comment and disappeared below again, bringing a couple of sail ties and a pair of heavy bronze fittings from the workshop when she returned. She put a fitting in each case to be sure it would sink, then tied them tightly shut with the sail ties and dropped them overboard. "The only thing I have left is my backpack, the money, and my wetsuit."

As the sun rose higher, a hint of a breeze stirred the mainsail. Ahead, ripples on the water told Cliff that *Staghound* would soon be on the move again. By midafternoon she was traveling at hull speed and Catalina lay only thirty miles ahead. At dusk the high peaks of the west end of the island were visible.

The moon would not rise until after midnight but the silhouette of the island was starkly revealed by the loom of the lights of Los Angeles, twenty-five miles farther on. It was late evening when the wind began to falter and *Staghound* slowed to six knots, then five, then four. By midnight she was ghosting along with Catalina's rugged shoreline a mile off her port beam.

Lena stood next to Cliff at the helm, an arm around his waist. She pointed to a low spot on the island. "There's the Isthmus. When that light bears due north, we can turn." She pointed her arm toward the light on Cat Head. "We leave it to port."

"Okay, it's time to douse the sails." Cliff left her at the helm and went forward to prepare the halyards.

When he was ready, Lena turned *Staghound* into the breeze and Cliff lowered the jib and lashed it down on deck. Next, he set the lazyjacks and lowered the mainsail as Lena started the engine. By the time he had the mainsail secured on the boom, *Staghound* was approaching the mouth of Cat Harbor. A few minutes later he went forward to the bow and released the chain hook that held the anchor secure. "The anchor is ready to go," he said when he returned to the cockpit.

"I know this harbor," Lena said, "I'll guide you in."

Cliff took the helm and she went and stood by the mast, pointing her arm left or right as *Staghound* slowly entered the harbor. Earlier he had been preoccupied with the sails and preparing the anchor. Now he grew tense as the final moments of the voyage approached. He throttled the engine back to idle and *Staghound* slowed to three knots. Dead ahead, a couple of lights were visible ashore, but the land on both sides of the rapidly narrowing bay was dark.

Lena pointed toward the right and Cliff turned the boat a few degrees as they passed a low point of land. Now he saw the anchor lights of a couple of boats near the narrow head of the bay.

She came aft and said, "Hold this course. In a couple of minutes, you will see a beach on your starboard side. Head in close there." She hugged him tightly, whispering, "I love you." Then she hurried below.

Cliff watched for the beach as *Staghound* groped slowly forward. To his right, the color of the low-lying land began to change. *Yes, there's the beach!* He shifted the engine to neutral and *Staghound* coasted.

Lena came on deck wearing her wetsuit and a black bathing cap, carrying her backpack wrapped in a black plastic trash bag. She blew some air into the bag and tied it tightly closed.

In the darkness, the beach looked perilously close. Cliff expected *Staghound* to touch the bottom at any moment.

She handed him a small slip of paper. "Call this number at noon on Wednesday, April first. Call from a payphone. If I don't answer, call at noon the next day. If I don't answer after three days, it's because I'm on my way to Chile. If anyone but me answers, don't say a word, just hang up."

He held the paper up to the faint red light in the binnacle. "Is this your aunt's number?"

"No. It's a payphone in Pasadena." She peered into the darkness. "There." she pointed to a dark spot on the beach. "That is where I will land. Take us in closer."

Cliff steered to starboard until *Staghound* was no more than a hundred feet from the water's edge, moving parallel to the beach at two knots. "How long will you be gone?"

She hefted her pack. "I don't know. But when my parents are

free and safe, I will come back and find you. From that moment on, wherever you go in this world, I will go. Your destiny will be my destiny. My heart is yours. Forever." She gave him a final hug, then slipped into the water with her backpack.

"Wait!" he called. But she was already swimming toward shore.

Cliff nearly shouted for her to come back but he managed to contain himself. He watched her reach the water's edge and scramble up the beach like a commando on a secret mission. A moment later she was lost in the darkness. He rushed to the rail hoping for a last glimpse of her, but she had disappeared. He grabbed binoculars and searched for her, but still no luck. "She's gone," he said aloud. "She's gone."

Staghound had coasted to a halt when he turned his attention back to the boat. He pushed the throttle forward and the boat began to move away from the shore. When he was a hundred yards from the beach he ran forward and released the clutch on the anchor windlass, paying out two hundred feet of rode. The boat drifted forward until the anchor took hold. Slowly, it turned into the scant breeze, her head brought around by the drag of the anchor and chain. When the boat was facing the direction it had come from, Cliff put the engine in reverse and backed down until the anchor bit into the bottom and brought *Staghound* to a halt. He shut the engine off and searched the beach where Lena had landed, but there was no sign of her.

The moon rose above the horizon, a slim crescent. Cliff looked around the bay, getting his bearings. He spotted a small wooden pier a quarter-mile farther up the bay. He had been there many times before, when he was a boy, and knew it well. Without waiting another minute, he pulled the valise that held the tiny inflatable backup dinghy from *Staghound*'s cavernous starboard cockpit locker. He watched the hillside above where Lena had landed while he pumped air into the dinghy, hoping that he might catch a glimpse of her in the moonlight, but saw nothing of her.

Alright, she's gone, he told himself. *Quit thinking about her and get on with the next step of the plan.*

When the dinghy was inflated, he fitted its oars in place and eased it into the water, tying its painter to a port side stanchion. Below, he stuffed a change of clothes along with *Staghound's* logbook and the navigation chart into his sea bag. He checked his watch. *Three AM. I'll wait another half hour. She'll be well up the trail by then.* In the galley, he brewed a cup of instant coffee to pass the time. In his mind, he went over what he would say in the harbor patrol office, reminding himself to leave Lena out of it. At three-thirty, he rinsed his cup and left it to dry in the sink.

When he left on the voyage back in January, he packed a thousand dollars in his bag. He rummaged for it now, and for his wallet, which he had not carried since the day they set sail. Now he slipped both items into his pockets. He gathered Jon and Mike's passports, took one more look around the cabin, heaved a deep sigh, and went up the companionway ladder.

He dropped his bag into the dinghy and climbed down after it. Pulling on its tiny oars, he thought again of his boyhood, when he had rowed all over Cat Harbor in his father's dinghy, which was about the same size as the one he was rowing now. The moon had risen higher and reflected off the wavelets that pattered against the dinghy's rubber sides as he rowed. He gazed at *Staghound*, whose wounds were not visible. Only the graceful sweep of her sheer stood out in the moonlight.

Cliff tied the dinghy to the little dock and climbed onto land for the first time in over a month. Intoxicating land smells of sage, eucalyptus, and dirt came to him on the gentle breeze. The sound of gravel crunching under his feet reminded him of home. When he crested a small rise in the road, the lights of Los Angeles came into view, twenty-five miles across the channel. The sight of all those lights made him hesitate. To his right stood an old clapboard building. In front of it lay a dirt road that he knew led toward the town of Avalon, twenty miles away.

There's still time, he told himself. *I don't have to report Jon and Mike. I could take that road instead and catch up with Lena at the ferry landing. We could start over, like she said.* He looked around. There was no one in sight. Straight ahead, the little village of Two Harbors was still and dark, except for a few scattered lights. The brightest one was down at the foot of the pier, at the Harbor Patrol office. *No one besides us even knows Jon and Mike are dead. I could run. I could make it to Avalon and take her in my arms again, and never let go.* He looked down the hill toward the beckoning light at the Harbor Patrol office, then back toward Cat Harbor, where he could just make out the distant shape of *Staghound,* anchored in the bay. *I didn't sign on for this kind of trouble. I'm not a gunrunner. I just wanted to sail to the South Pacific.* He looked around once more, then started walking toward Avalon. *I'm going to find her. We'll get on that ferry and leave all this shit behind.*

The road was rocky and he was wearing sandals. A rock got stuck between his foot and sandal. *Ouch!* He shook it free and kept walking. The road got steeper and, after being on the boat so long, he was soon winded. He stopped to catch his breath. He could still see Staghound, it looked beautiful in the moonlight *My fingerprints are all over that boat. What if they dust it when they investigate why it was abandoned? Who would do that, the FBI? They'll know I was on that boat and look for me. Is that what I want, to be on the run? Is that who I am? Who knows what they'll accuse me of? Murder? Smuggling? Wouldn't it be better to face all that now, instead of after they catch me?* He took another step up the hill and stopped. *Stop kidding yourself, you know you're not going to run. You're going to face this now.*

≾

The clock on the wall read 6:00am when Cliff pushed the door open. A Sheriff's deputy sitting at a desk looked up from his newspaper when he entered.

"Good morning. My name is Cliff Demont. I just arrived from the South Pacific on a sailboat and I want to report the deaths of my two friends." Cliff put his bag on the floor and looked the officer in the eye.

The officer lowered his paper and stared at Cliff as if a Martian had just spoken to him. "You wanna what?"

"I want to report the deaths of two people, my friends."

Middle-aged, with graying hair under his cap and a deeply suntanned face, deputy sheriff Jake Eldon slowly picked up a pad and pencil while he appraised Cliff's wild hair and beard. "You know it's illegal to make false statements to an officer, right?"

"Yeah. Is there someone else I should report to, because I just sailed five thousand miles, I'm tired, hungry and I need to file a report about my two friends."

"You came to the right place, but if you're joking…"

"This is no joke," Cliff interrupted.

"Alright then, what happened."

"My name is Cliff Demont. D-E-M-O-N-T. I set sail back in January with my two friends, Jon Hartmann and Mike Lundin. We were headed to the South Pacific on a surf trip. You know, looking for good waves."

"Spelling on those names?"

Cliff spelled the names and laid three passports on the desk, which the officer studied in silence.

"Okay, go on."

"We were attacked by people on a fishing boat off the coast of South America, and my two friends were shot and killed. I had to sail back home alone. I just arrived a couple of hours ago."

The interview went on for an hour, then officer Eldon tossed his pencil on the desk and leaned back. "That's a helluva story,

Cliff. I guess we'd better go take a look at that boat of yours." He picked up a handheld radio from his desk and fingered the mike button. "21, 21 this is Eldon."

A metallic voice responded, "Morning Jake, what can I do ya for?"

"Hey Bill, where'r you at?"

"Just got to the landing, what's up?"

"You see a sailboat anchored out by Ballast Point?"

"Sure do, a big one. She musta come in late last night."

"Okay, wait for me at the landing. I want to take a run out and have a look at it." He clipped the radio to his belt and ushered Cliff out the door.

Deputy Eldon's pickup truck wore a thick coat of island dust and a Sheriff's badge emblazoned on each door. He drove slowly along the gravel road to the landing where Bill and the twenty-five-foot Harbor Patrol launch waited. Dawn was breaking as the three men motored out to the *Staghound*. Seeing the boat from a distance, in daylight, Cliff was struck by its weathered and worn appearance, which he hadn't noticed when he was aboard it.

The launch ranged down the sloop's starboard side, then rounded the stern. "What's that plywood on the transom for?" Eldon asked.

"It's a patch. We were rammed by the other boat. It knocked a hole in the stern."

"You put it on?"

"Yes."

Eldon motioned to Bill, "Let's see the other side of the boat."

All three men stared as the launch moved forward along *Staghound*'s port side. "Those what I think they are?" Eldon asked.

"Bullet holes."

"Uh-huh." Eldon lifted his cap and scratched his head. "I'm going to declare this a crime scene, at least until we get to the bottom of what's going on here. Now, Mr. Demont, I'm gonna search you. Do you have any weapons, knives, needles, anything that might hurt me in your pockets?"

"Nope." Cliff rested his hands on the launch's windshield while the deputy frisked him. "Anybody on board now?"

"No."

"Weapons, drugs, any other contraband?"

"No."

The deputy glanced at Bill. "Before long there's gonna be a dozen looky-loos poking around here. Keep 'em away, and get 22 out here to back you up." He turned back to Cliff. "Is there anything you want to tell me before I go aboard?"

"No."

"Bring 'er alongside, Bill."

Cliff's heart started thumping when Eldon climbed aboard *Staghound*, but he kept his face immobile. *Relax,* he told himself, *I'll find out soon enough if I should have sunk the boat...like Lena suggested.* He waited in silence while Eldon disappeared down the companionway and Bill called for backup on the radio.

After a few minutes, Eldon reappeared and climbed back onto the launch. He nodded toward the dock and Bill cast off. Ten minutes later they were back in the office.

Eldon pointed to a chair against the wall. "Sit there, Cliff."

Cliff picked up his bag and sat while Eldon went into his office and closed the door. The big round clock on the wall said 6:57. His stomach started growling at 7:00. He couldn't remember the last meal he ate.

At 7:30 a young woman entered the office, smiled at him, and went around the reception desk to a coffeemaker on a shelf. Cliff watched her bustle around the machine, the first woman he had seen, aside from Lena, in almost four months. She was big where Lena was slim, buxom where Lena was petite. *I have to stop thinking about her,* he scolded himself.

A few minutes later Eldon came out of his office. "I couldn't read the name on the transom of your boat because that patch covered most of it. But it's the *Staghound*, isn't it?"

Cliff didn't like the way he said it, but he recalled Lena mentioning that Jon came to Two Harbors often, so of course Deputy Eldon would eventually recognize the boat. He swallowed before he spoke, "That's correct, the *Staghound*."

CHAPTER 21

"*STAGHOUND*" THE WORD hung in the air. Eldon froze, gazing at Cliff as if he had turned over a rock and found a scorpion under it.

Cliff shifted in his chair. "Is something wrong?"

Eldon's eye fell on the bag at Cliff's feet. "Is that yours?"

"Yes." Cliff reached for it.

"Leave it," Eldon commanded. "Mind if I take a look at it?"

"No. It's just a change of clothes."

Eldon unzipped the bag and rummaged through the items in it. He glanced at the chart and the logbook. "From the *Staghound*?" he asked.

"Yeah. I thought it would be helpful to show you where we went, where we were attacked, and where I buried my friends."

Eldon thumbed through the logbook. "Okay, sit tight." He went back into his office.

Cliff fidgeted in his chair another fifteen minutes. He heard Eldon's voice on the phone but couldn't make out what he was saying except for the word, "*Staghound*" a couple of times.

The door opened and Eldon beckoned him into his office. "Got a few more questions for you. Come in and take a seat." The chart was spread out on his desk and he laid a finger on it where Cliff had noted the burial of Jon and Mike. "I see you buried your friends here. But you went all the way down here." He pointed to the speck labeled 'Juan Fernandez'. "And according to the log-book, you stayed at Selkirk Island a couple of days, is that right?"

"Yes." Cliff leaned forward for a better view of the chart.

"What did you do there?" Eldon's eyes bored into his own.

"We were looking for waves but didn't find any." Cliff leaned back in his chair. "A storm came up. There's no harbor there, so we left."

"I see." Eldon frowned. He picked up the driver's license he had taken from Cliff's wallet and studied it before he looked back at Cliff. "Alright, here's where we stand. I talked to the sheriff's office in Avalon. They're running your record now and will fax it over here. Sheriff McCoy will be here in half an hour." He came around and perched on the corner of his desk. "Look," he said, "Nobody at the station has ever heard of Selkirk Island and you don't have any witnesses to corroborate your story. Now, Sheriff McCoy is a no-nonsense kind of sheriff and he's going to dig into you until he gets to the truth. So, is there anything you want to tell me now, before he gets here?"

Cliff glanced out the window and saw that the beachfront snack bar had just opened. He nodded toward it and said, "I'd like to wander over there and get some breakfast."

Eldon stared at him a second, then raised his voice so the receptionist could hear. "Rose, would you please run over and get a breakfast burrito for Mr. Demont? Put it on my tab."

She looked in the doorway. "Chicken or chorizo?"

"Chicken is fine," Cliff replied.

He had just finished the burrito when the sheriff arrived, accompanied by another deputy. A big man with steel-gray brush-cut hair and a pistol on his hip, Sheriff McCoy had the face of a man who was quick to anger. He gave Cliff a long, hostile look when he entered the station. "Clifford Demont your real name?"

Cliff rose from his chair, "That's right."

"Sit down and stay there until I tell you to get up."

Cliff returned the sheriff's gaze, then slowly sat.

"Your boat was in Puget Sound four years ago. The DEA says they just missed catching you with a load of drugs there." The sheriff stood with hands on hips and a scowl on his face. "Well, your drug-running days are over."

"It's not my boat and I'm not a drug runner. I…"

"Stop right there," McCoy interrupted. "You can tell your story to the DEA." He nodded to his deputy. "Take him into custody."

Cliff stood and the deputy snapped handcuffs on his wrists.

"What do you want to charge him with?" Eldon asked. "We have to Mirandize him."

"We're not charging him, just holding him until the DEA boys get here." McCoy glanced at his watch, "Which should be any minute now. Did you type up your report?"

"Haven't had time to," Eldon replied.

McCoy's scowl deepened. "I want it on my desk by noon."

The receptionist spoke up. "They faxed Mr. Demont's record over. It's on your desk, Jake."

Eldon retrieved it and the sheriff impatiently grabbed the flimsy pages from his hand.

"This can't be right," he snapped after studying the report for half a minute. "You sure you gave them the right ID? This report is for some yahoo from San Luis Obispo!" he almost shouted. "Jesus H. Christ, I have to do everything myself." He shoved the printout back at Eldon. "Alright, put him in the car."

The deputy motioned Cliff out to the Sheriff's Ford Explorer. McCoy's booming voice carried out to the car.

"Goddammit Jake, you know how the feds are. They're gonna be on me like bees on a hobo if we don't have our act together when they get here. Now, get that report done. Pronto!" He burst out of the office and got in the car, slamming the door. "Let's go."

The deputy gunned the car up the winding gravel road toward Avalon. Despite the handcuffs, Cliff enjoyed the ride. The crisp

March air was crystal clear and the view was spectacular. To his left, the sea sparkled in the sunlight, and across the channel, the green hills of Palos Verdes stood out sharply against the backdrop of Los Angeles. In the far distance, Mount Baldy wore a white cap of snow. Recent rains had left the road muddy and rutted in places, and they passed several ponds and small reservoirs along the way that appeared to be full. At one of them, a lone bison stood knee-deep in coffee-colored water, its shaggy beard dripping as it chewed its cud.

It was near noon when the vehicle passed the turn-off to Catalina's tiny airport. *I'll wager she didn't take a plane because airlines require ID,* Cliff surmised. A quarter mile farther, a group of hikers lolled on the ground in the shade of some trees, taking a break from hiking the Trans-Catalina Trail. Cliff searched for Lena among them but was disappointed.

Just past the airport, the road changed from gravel to pavement and the deputy sped up from fifteen to twenty-five miles-per-hour, but had to slow again for a crew that was repairing a wash-out in the road. Just beyond them, a single hiker strode purposefully on the adjacent trail. *Lena!* Cliff's heart leaped as they locked eyes for a split second.

"We're gettin' some damn good lookers on the trail this year," the driver said. The first words spoken on the drive.

"Keep your eyes on the road," the sheriff growled.

Cliff twisted around in his seat hoping for another glimpse of her, but she had already disappeared behind a curve in the road.

After descending a series of steep switchbacks, the Explorer entered the town of Avalon and pulled into the lot at the sheriff's station.

"Sit there," McCoy pointed to a chair in the reception area. The receptionist was a middle-aged woman with hair pulled back into a severe bun. She looked inquiringly at the sheriff.

"No need to process him in. The DEA will be here soon to

take him off our hands." He gave her Cliff's driver's license and said, "Run this, and make sure you get the numbers right. And call Jake Eldon and tell him to hurry up that report. If I don't stay on him, he'll dawdle that thing all afternoon."

Cliff watched the sheriff go into his office and hang his hat on a hook by the door. From his chair, he could see the receptionist typing at her computer terminal. A two-way radio on her desk squawked with chatter from the harbor patrolmen in the bay. A printer began spitting out pages. When it stopped, she took the printout in to the sheriff.

"Max," the sheriff called from his office, "Bring Mr. Demont in here."

The deputy dropped the newspaper he was reading and escorted Cliff into the sheriff's office.

"You can release him," McCoy said as he gave Cliff an appraising look.

Cliff worked his arms and rubbed his sore wrists.

"Sit down." McCoy motioned toward a chair in front of his desk. "Close the door on your way out," he said to the deputy.

The receptionist entered. "Here's Jake's report. He just faxed it over."

The sheriff scanned the report then looked up at Cliff. "You married?"

"Getting a divorce. That's why I sailed aboard the *Staghound*. Needed a change."

"Uh-huh. Occupation?"

"Architect."

"Ever been arrested?"

"Nope."

McCoy jabbed his finger at a page lying on his desk. "Your rap sheet shows your last address was in Avila Beach. You got a speeding ticket two years ago and a report of a domestic disturbance back in November. That right?"

"I bought a new car, a Porsche, two years back," Cliff said.

"That explains the speeding ticket."

"In November I discovered my wife with another man. There was a scuffle and my neighbor called the police."

McCoy laid the papers on his desk and leaned forward, looking Cliff in the eye. "Did you murder two people on that boat?"

"No. Someone else did. I don't know how I didn't get killed along with them."

The sheriff held Cliff's gaze. "Alright," he said after what seemed like half a minute. "I ran the Lancaster department before I transferred here. Handled seven or eight murder cases every year. I know murderers and you're not cut out for that line of work."

"Thank you."

The sheriff shuffled through Deputy Eldon's report until he found copies of half a dozen photos and spread them out on the desk. They were pictures of Staghound, showing its stern, cockpit, and port side, all pocked with bullet holes. "This report says your boat was hit at least seventy times. What happened?"

Cliff described how the *Tortuga Negra* chased the *Staghound*, rammed it, and then came alongside, and how he went overboard at one point.

"How'd you get back aboard?" the sheriff asked.

"I don't recall, everything was happening so fast. All I know for sure is that the shooting stopped and somehow, I was back aboard. Jon was lying in the cockpit and Mike was on the foredeck. Both had been shot by then." Cliff stopped and heaved a sigh.

"And then what happened?"

"Everything was quiet and we were drifting apart. I got the engine started and headed north as fast as the boat would go."

"What about the other boat?"

"It just sat there, dead in the water. By sunup, it was out of sight behind me." Cliff paused. "That's the last time I saw it."

McCoy stared at Cliff, as if trying to determine if he was telling the truth. After a moment he picked up the report and scanned it again. "That sounds plausible, given these photos. I guess it is a wonder you're still alive." He laid the report on the desk and rubbed his face with both hands before he spoke. "I just got a call from the DEA. They haven't found any evidence of drugs on that boat. They bring dogs and usually find the stuff in five minutes." He gave his head a shake. "Every time a drug boat fetches up on my island, I get a federal posse coming over and creating a huge damn ruckus. So it's a relief to me that they didn't find anything."

"Then I'm free to go?"

"No. Crimes outside of territorial waters are federal jurisdiction, not mine. We already notified the FBI. They'll be here soon. They're the ones who'll decide whether to turn you loose or bind you over for charges." McCoy raised his voice, "Max!" then looked back at Cliff. "The main thing is, you're not my problem, thank heavens."

The deputy opened the door. "Yes sir."

"Put Mr. Demont in the cell." To Cliff, he said, "You'll stay there until the feds get here and decide what to do with you."

"No, I want to talk to a lawyer," Cliff said. "I'm not staying in a jail cell."

The sheriff scowled. "You haven't been charged with anything, so you don't need a damn lawyer. Not yet, anyway. Go sit in the cell for an hour or two. I'll let you out when the feds get here."

The cell was a big, windowless room with a security door, a couple of cots along the wall, and a toilet behind a chest-high partition. Along two walls were benches and in the middle of the room were two tables with chairs, all bolted to the floor. Cliff was exhausted but he avoided the cots, not wanting to fall asleep in the cell. He passed the time pacing the room, impatiently second-guessing his decision to turn himself in and wondering about Lena. *She's probably in Avalon by now. She might even be outside on the street, waiting for me.* He gave his head a shake. *Stop thinking about her!*

An hour later the door opened and the deputy escorted him to a small conference room, where three men sat with Sheriff McCoy at a walnut conference table. They rose and each studied Cliff as he entered the room.

"Hello Cliff, I'm Special Agent Ed Blake. This is Special Agent Frank Pincelli and Agent Jack Dean from the DEA." The FBI men were tall and slender. They wore sportcoats and narrow ties, close-cropped hair, and each had tucked his aviator-style sunglasses into a pocket. The DEA agent was heavyset and wore a windbreaker with DEA stenciled on it. Blake motioned to a chair. "Sit down. You must be exhausted from your ordeal."

Cliff took the chair.

Blake talked while Pincelli set up a tape recorder on the table, spoke a few words into it then pointed its microphone toward Cliff. The DEA agent had a notebook in front of him but said nothing.

"How are you feeling?" Blake asked.

"Well enough, under the circumstances," Cliff replied, massaging his sore wrists.

McCoy rose from the table. "I'm going to excuse myself now. I'll be in my office."

"Thanks for your help, sheriff." Blake looked at Cliff, assessing his haggard face. "If you feel up to it, we'd like to ask you some questions."

"I'll be glad to answer them if I can."

"Good. Then let's get started. I don't think this will take too long." Blake waved toward a coffee urn. "Coffee?"

"Sure."

Pincelli poured some into a Styrofoam cup and passed it across the table.

Blake took the lead, asking questions about Cliff's background and life in San Luis Obispo while Pincelli took notes. The DEA agent sat silently at the far end of the table, jotting in his notebook occasionally.

After an hour of questioning, Blake said, "You had a nice life, Cliff. Wife, home, good job, money in the bank and, from the looks of it, a bright future. Why would you suddenly throw all that away and go off on a sailing trip? Something there's no record of you having any interest in before."

"I had a falling out with my boss and quit. I went home early that day and found my wife in bed with a stranger." Talking about those events made Cliff's blood rise.

"So you just left?"

"I needed to change my life, I thought the trip would be a good way to take stock of things and chart a new future."

"On a sailboat?"

"When I was a kid, I sailed quite a lot with my dad. He used to dream of going on a cruise to the South Pacific. But he died before he got the chance to go. You could say this was a chance to fulfill my dad's dream as well as sort out my own life."

"I see." Blake paused a moment, "How did you meet Johannes Hartmann and Michael James Lundin?"

It was strange hearing Jon and Mike's formal names. "I met Jon four or five years ago, we surfed the same breaks. Sometimes we'd drive down to Jalama or Rincon together for waves, or up to Mavericks when it was big. Mike, I met him aboard *Staghound*. He was also a surfer and was the deckhand on the boat."

"And the purpose of this trip was?" Blake asked.

"Surfing. Jon liked to travel and discover places that hadn't been ridden before. He mentioned some islands off the coast of South America. Said he wanted to check them out and be the first to surf them. It sounded like a once-in-a-lifetime adventure, so I asked to go along."

Blake unfolded *Staghound's* navigation chart and spread it on the table. "Tell us about this chart, Cliff."

"This is our track to and from Selkirk Island. We started from Wilmington and each day we would take a noon sight and plot our position on the chart."

The DEA agent, Dean, spoke, "According to this, you sailed directly to Selkirk Island. Did you stop in, say, Mexico or Costa Rica?" He had narrow-set eyes and a beaked nose, a look Cliff had always associated with the Gestapo.

"We went straight to Selkirk," Cliff traced Staghound's track with a finger from north to south. "No detours."

"Those marks don't mean anything. You could have made them up."

"But we didn't. Anyway, don't you have spies and informants in all the ports where drugs are shipped? Wouldn't you know if a big American sailboat like the *Staghound* showed up in one of those places? If I was the DEA that's what I'd do."

Dean's expression grew hostile. "Yeah, you better hope your boat doesn't turn up on the list."

Blake interrupted, "Jack, would you give us a minute with Mr. Demont?"

Dean hesitated, his glare still fixed on Cliff, "Yeah, I need a smoke anyway."

"He's an excellent agent," Blake said when the door closed behind Dean. "It's impossible to say how many lives he's saved by putting traffickers away."

"That's wonderful, but we had nothing to do with drugs on this trip."

"Well, I'm inclined to believe you. Jack's team didn't find any evidence of drugs on the boat and he's a little frustrated. He was hot on Hartmann's trail four years ago and just missed bagging him in Seattle. After that Hartmann's trail went cold. It's rare that a smuggler just stops. They're usually picked up by us or get themselves killed."

"For what it's worth," Cliff said, "I never saw any drugs on the boat."

"Well, that begs the question."

"What question?"

Blake nodded to agent Pincelli, who squared the notepad in front of him.

"The DEA watched Hartmann for a couple of years after the Seattle fiasco. He moved his boat from LA to Mexico and Costa Rica, then through the Canal and back. Then to French Polynesia and back. All without a whiff of drugs. The question is why would he go to all these places? What was he doing? We thought you might be able to shed some light on that." Pincelli raised his eyebrows while Cliff paused.

"If it wasn't for surfing, I honestly have no idea. I'd see him around Avila Beach where I live, or used to live, then he would disappear. I didn't keep track, but it seemed like he'd be gone for a few months then show up again as if he'd taken a weekend off. I recall asking him once or twice where he'd been and he would just say sailing and surfing," Cliff paused. "To me, he seemed like just a guy with a bit of a wanderlust, and simply loved being on his boat."

"What about money? Did he talk about it?" Blake asked.

"Not much. He once told me his parents left him some. As far as I know, he never had a real job."

Blake studied the chart again, pointing a finger at a notation near the equator. "The handwriting here is different from earlier notations."

"Yeah, that's my handwriting. Jon taught me how to use a sextant and I started doing the navigation." Cliff pointed to other notations farther south on the chart.

Agent Pincelli left the room and came back a few minutes later with a sheaf of papers. "Field office reports."

Blake took the flimsy fax sheets, thumbing through them until he found the one he wanted, studied it a moment then looked up at Cliff. "There have been no missing person reports filed for your companions." He searched through more of the pages until he found pictures of the two sailors and laid them on the table. "Are these Hartmann and Lundin?

They had the grainy look of photos taken through a telephoto lens, but they clearly showed Jon and Mike's faces.

"Yeah, that's them," Cliff pushed the photos toward the agent. "Recognize this?"

"It's a picture of Jon's house in Avila Beach," He recognized the ivied wall and gated entrance to the house.

"Someone was living there until a couple of weeks ago, a woman. Could you identify her?"

"I was there only once. I saw his housekeeper, an Asian woman, but only for a few minutes. I doubt that I'd recognize her."

Blake read from a field report. "The place is locked up. Neighbors report that the woman disappeared at least two weeks ago." He stared at Cliff. "Why would she do that?"

Cliff turned up his palms, "I couldn't even speculate."

Just then there was a knock on the door. A DEA agent stuck his head into the room. "We finished processing the boat."

Blake glanced at his watch. "Alright Cliff, would you excuse us for a few minutes? You can wait in the hall."

The receptionist was behind her desk, busily tapping at her keyboard. Cliff leaned on the counter and watched her a minute. "I'm starving," he said. "Is there food service here?"

"We provide meals for inmates at five," she said without looking up.

The big round clock on the wall read 4:15. Cliff glanced at it and said, "Okay. I guess I can wait."

A few minutes later the DEA agent came out of the conference room followed by the other one, agent Dean. "You can go in now," he said before heading for the front door.

Agents Blake and Pincelli were talking fishing when Cliff entered the room. Blake turned to him, "Did you catch many on your voyage?" he asked.

"Mike was the real fisherman. I didn't count how many he caught but we had a lot of fresh fish. After he was gone I caught only a few."

"Yeah, I don't have much of a knack for fishing either." Blake opened a file on his desk. "Now, about drugs."

Cliff's gut tightened. He didn't know why, since he had never used them. "Okay."

"The DEA agents found nothing illegal on your boat. Agent Dean has already lost interest in you."

"I'm glad to hear that." Cliff's gut eased.

"As to Hartmann and Lundin, we'll follow up on the information you provided. We will notify the Coast Guard, Interpol, and the PDI in Chile to be on the lookout for the..." Blake thumbed through his notes. "Ah, here it is. The *Tortuga Negra* fishing boat."

"How did you do it?" Pincelli suddenly asked, fixing Cliff in a piercing gaze.

"Do what?"

"Bury those men."

Cliff's heart skipped a beat and he felt himself flush. "It was the hardest thing I've ever had to do." He stared down at his hands on the table. "I wrapped them in sail bags, cinched a dive belt around their waists so they would sink, and lowered them over the stern." He shuddered as he relived those moments. "There was nothing else I could do. I mean, the radios were dead, we were five hundred miles from land and, well, I couldn't keep them aboard." He looked up at the two agents and repeated the words, "There was nothing else I could do."

"Okay. We get that," Blake said, not unsympathetically. "Then, instead of heading for the nearest land, you sailed all the way back here. Why?"

"Your first assumption was that I was involved in drug smuggling. It was the logical conclusion, especially since people were killed, right?"

"True," Blake said.

"If I would have gone to Chile or Peru, or anywhere but the US, I would be rotting in jail right now, don't you think?"

"Without a doubt," Blake agreed.

"That's why I was determined to get back to the States."

"It must have been hard, sailing that boat alone," Pincelli said. "How did you manage it? Did you have enough food and water? I mean, it's dangerous out there. Yet you made it back here all alone unscathed. Amazing."

"I wouldn't say unscathed." Cliff looked each of them in the eye. "I didn't plan for this and wasn't prepared for what happened. I don't know why I survived and the others didn't, but I assure you, I'm more amazed than you that I'm sitting here now."

Blake closed the file folder and slipped it into his briefcase. "We have several leads to chase down before we can put this case to bed. At this point, it seems that neither Hartmann nor Lundin had any living relatives, but we'll do a search to be sure." He gave Cliff his business card. "I want you to keep me apprised of your whereabouts. I'll want to talk to you as this investigation moves forward, and I'd appreciate a call if you think of anything that might help us tie up the loose ends." He rose from the table and snapped his briefcase shut. Pincelli did the same.

They shook hands and left Cliff sitting in the conference room. He heard them speak to the sheriff in the reception area for a moment before they left the station. Cliff remained seated, coming to grips with the fact that he would not be held by the FBI. "Unscathed." he breathed the word aloud, closing his eyes as he spoke.

The door opened and the sheriff motioned to him. "Alright Demont, you can go." He handed him a manila envelope and his bag. The envelope contained his wallet, money, passport, and watch. He nodded toward a ferry schedule in the wall. "The next boat leaves at noon tomorrow. I want you on it."

Cliff was at the door when the sheriff spoke again. "Get a room. If we catch you sleeping on the beach, you'll be right back here. Understand?"

It was dark outside. A couple of vacationers hurried past him on the street, bundled against the cold wind. Cliff searched the shadows, hoping one would reveal a petite brunette with a backpack. Disappointed, he headed down the street and checked into the first hotel he came to.

⚘

After a good night's sleep and a hot shower, Cliff had eaten a hearty breakfast and found a barber. At noon, he was the first passenger aboard the Express. He stood on the upper deck and took in the view of Avalon Harbor. Gulls swooped and soared above the pleasure craft bobbing at their moorings. Morning clouds had burned off and the hills surrounding the harbor were lush and green. A young couple came up the stairs for a few minutes but were quickly driven below by the brisk wind. Cliff turned to face it as the ferry backed away from the dock and pointed its bow toward the mainland. Clearing the breakwater, it accelerated to twenty knots. The wind whipped through his freshly trimmed hair and beard as the boat sped toward the mainland.

CHAPTER 22

In San Pedro, Cliff glanced around the ferry terminal on the off chance that Lena might be there. *If she's not here,* he thought, *then that's it. She's gone.* Though his head was sure she wasn't, his heart refused to give up hope until he boarded a bus to downtown LA.

An hour later it pulled into Union Station's vast parking lot. The noise and dirt of the city assaulted his senses as he made his way into the beautiful old railroad station, but inside he was briefly transported back to his days as a college student. He had studied the works of famed architect John Parkinson and considered this building one of his masterpieces. Its forty-foot-high arched windows, polished travertine walls and wood-beamed ceilings combined Spanish Mission and Art Deco design. It had inspired him back then. Now he felt a sudden resurgence of that passion, but there was no time to linger. He hurried to the counter and bought a one-way ticket to San Luis Obispo.

From his seat on the train, he watched miles of ugly urban sprawl slide past the window as the sun sank toward the smoggy horizon. It was night when the train reached the coast and rolled past Rincon Beach. Cliff stared out the window, but instead of the ocean, he saw his own reflection in the glass; A solitary man with longish hair and features abraded by wind and sun. He scarcely recognized the bearded face and haunted eyes.

The train reached San Luis Obispo at midnight. Outside the

station, he hailed a taxi. "Motel on Higuera and Marsh," he said from the backseat of the cab, "The one by the freeway."

In his room, he lay awake for hours despite the exhaustion that had seeped deeply into his bones over the last two months. When he finally fell asleep it was fitful, tormented by nightmares of blood and death. Visions of Yori's hideous face and Juan lying dead in the *Tortuga Negra* woke him. Sweating, he bolted upright in bed and stared vacantly in the dark, disoriented by the strange walls of his room. Near dawn, the nightmares relented and he slept all day and into the following evening.

The next morning, he showered and put on the last clean pair of jeans and shirt in his bag. He'd saved them for this day. Zipped in an inner pocket of the bag was a pair of keys, one would open his storage unit, another would start his car. He pulled the door to his room shut and headed down the street. *The walk will do me good*, he thought. Half an hour later he arrived at the self-storage yard where he had left his possessions.

In the unit, Cliff found boxes opened, clothes strewn about, and his car rifled through. He pulled the overhead door shut and went to the office to complain to the manager.

So you're Clifford Demont," the man behind the counter said, eyeing him suspiciously. "The FBI tossed your unit."

"Really? Did they have a warrant?"

"No, they politely asked if they could take a peek inside," the man replied sarcastically.

"Thanks for the heads up, I'll be checking out in a few days."

"Yeah, that would be good."

As Cliff opened the door to leave, he thought he heard the man mutter "Fuckin' doper" under his breath. He had an urge to turn around and punch the guy, but instead, he closed the door behind him. Back in the storage unit, he packed a suitcase with clean clothes and tossed it in the backseat of the Porsche, which started on the third try.

Later that morning, in Angela Braun's office, she showed him a clipping from the previous day's Tribune. The headline read "Mystery Yacht Has Avila Beach Connection." The article told of the *Staghound*, a sixty-four-foot sailboat owned by Johannes Hartmann of Avila Beach arriving at Catalina Island in the dead of night with one Clifford Demont, also of Avila Beach, at the helm. The story said that Demont had told a harrowing tale of piracy and murder on the high seas and quoted the local sheriff saying the *Staghound* had a history of smuggling drugs. It included a photo of DEA agents climbing aboard the boat in Cat Harbor and closed by noting that Hartmann and another crewman were missing and presumed dead.

"It seems that you're the talk of the town, Cliff," Angela said, her blue eyes fixed on his. "Is that story true?"

"We were attacked, two people died and I had to sail the boat home. All that is true. But the way it's written makes it sound like we were smuggling drugs. We never had any drugs on the boat. None." Cliff leaned forward, looking Angela in the eye. "The DEA searched the boat and I was questioned by the FBI. If they had suspected me of anything illegal, I wouldn't be here, I'd be in jail."

"Did you know the FBI paid me a visit as well?"

"I'm not surprised."

"You shouldn't be. They probably interviewed your former employer and your wife too."

Cliff sat in silence while the implications of the FBI questioning people in town sank in.

"You're going to have to deal with some unfortunate attention from the press, for a while at least. But on a happier note, your wife has been forwarding your mail to my office," Angela pushed a couple of rubber-banded bundles across her desk.

"Speaking of Janet, how is the divorce going?"

"The final decree will be issued in mid-May. Her attorney

informed me that they are prepared to pay you off whenever we execute a quitclaim deed to the property."

"That means she was able to refinance it."

"Well, I believe she found the money privately."

"Like from a friend, maybe a boyfriend?"

"Does that bother you?"

"No. I was just curious." Cliff replied. "How do we go about closing the deal."

"I'll notify them that you are in town and prepared to sign the papers. They will place the funds in an escrow account and when the deed is filed, they will be released to you."

"Write it up and I'll sign it whenever you're ready."

"Very well." Angela opened a folder on her desk. "The exact amount due is $151,201.33. I will have the deed prepared tomorrow afternoon and you can expect to have the funds wired to your bank on Thursday or Friday. Is that acceptable to you?"

Cliff left the lawyer's office and drove slowly back to his motel. *It's weird,* he thought, *People think I'm a drug smuggler. I guess as long as the FBI thinks the voyage was about drugs, I'm safe because there weren't any on the boat. Neither Jon, Mike nor Lena ever mentioned using drugs on the whole trip. Funny, I never even thought to ask about that.* He checked the date on his watch. *Twelve long days until I can call her.*

Back in his room, he had just pulled the rubber band off a bundle of mail when sharp rapping on the door startled him.

When he opened it, the motel manager was there, wearing a hostile sneer. "Checkout time is noon. I want you out of here by then." He pointed to the watch on his wrist. "That's fifteen minutes from now." He peered around Cliff, trying to see inside the room as he spoke.

"Why?"

"You know why." The manager turned and started walking away. "If you're not gone by noon, I'm calling the cops."

Cliff packed his things and put his suitcase in the car. Now he truly had no place to go. Driving down the street he had the paranoid feeling that he was being watched. He fumbled in the glove box for an old pair of sunglasses and put them on before he drove past his old office. Bob Larsen's Mercedes was not in its usual spot, but Kelly's little Toyota was there. Cliff made a U-turn and parked across the street. Somehow, the building looked smaller than he remembered it. The hedges around the front needed a trim, too. It was once a place where his dreams burned brightly, but now it was just a drab little office building, inert and uninspiring.

He started the car and drove away. He would have gone to Borgia's, the diner where he used to eat lunch, but he would surely be recognized there. He preferred the anonymity of a truck stop on the south side of town. He found a corner booth in the bustling café and opened the newspaper he had bought on the way in. He planned to search the classifieds for an apartment but a photo in the lower half of the front page caught his eye. It was of him. He was dressed in a coat and tie and wearing a hardhat at a construction site. Beneath the photo was an article describing how Clifford Demont, who had once been a rising star at the prestigious architectural firm of Larsen Haines, was involved in a sordid drug scheme that resulted in the killing of two other drug dealers. It also included a quote from Janet: "He kept his drug use from me throughout our whole marriage. I never learned of his problem until the FBI knocked on my door." Cliff flushed with anger as he read the story. "This is fiction!" he said aloud. He looked up to find the waitress standing there with a pot in her hand.

"Coffee?"

He quickly folded the paper, hiding the photo. "Sure, and a burger." When she left, he stared at the paper again. *I should call that reporter and set him straight,* he thought angrily as he turned to the classifieds. *But first I must find a place to live.*

Cliff never did call the reporter, deciding it was better to let it go than attract more attention. Thankfully, no more stories about him appeared in the paper.

He rented a dumpy apartment in a four-plex on the west side. It was old, the faucets dripped and the yard was overgrown, but it was the only place he could find on short notice. He was grateful that the owner paid no attention to the newspaper stories about him.

"I've been in trouble a time or two myself," he said when Cliff acknowledged he was the man in the stories. "Pay your rent on time and we'll get along fine."

On the morning of April first, Cliff moved the last of his possessions from the storage unit. At noon he found a payphone and dialed the number Lena had given him the night she swam ashore in Catalina. It rang a dozen times before he hung up. He tried again at 12:05 and got the same result. After a third and fourth try, he gave up and walked home.

He spent the next few days looking for work. None of the three architectural firms in town would even talk to him, but a friend of his at one of them, Rich Donica, had worked construction with him while they were both in college. "There's a new housing tract going up in Baywood Park," he said. "They need carpenters."

"I'll think about it."

The next morning, Cliff was driving down High Street when he spotted a Ford F100 pickup truck in a used car lot and turned into the driveway.

A salesman lounging in front of the building looked up, surprised at the sight of the Porsche. He flicked his cigarette into a planter box and sauntered over.

"How much for the truck?" Cliff asked, nodding toward the Ford.

"Nineteen ninety-nine." The salesman checked his clip-on tie as he spoke. "That there is a '74 short-bed V8 with a stick shift. They don't make 'em like that anymore."

"What'll you give me for this car?"

"Are you joking?" The salesman asked, dumbfounded.

"Nope."

Thirty minutes later the salesman stood beaming at the Porsche while Cliff started the truck. Its exhaust had a low-pitched rumble that pleased him. He found first gear and drove the truck off the lot without a backward glance at the Porsche. He touched his shirt pocket where he had tucked a $10,000.00 check the dealer had given him and smiled. *I liked the Porsche, but I'm a truck guy at heart.*

At noon he set a stack of quarters on the shelf in a phone booth and dialed Lena again. An old woman standing at a nearby bus stop flinched when he slammed the receiver down on the hook after he tried a third time and got no answer. She hurried toward the bus that stopped for her, casting a fearful glance back at him as she stepped aboard.

Cliff watched the bus pull away from the curb. *My nerves are shot. I need to get a grip on things, get hold of myself and move on. And I gotta let go of Lena.* He squared his shoulders and headed home.

❧

A week later he still didn't have any furniture in the living room of his apartment, and he still ate his meals standing at the sink in the kitchen, but he did have a telephone installed. It rang for the first time that morning while he was making coffee. It was the foreman at the construction site in Baywood Park. "You the guy who put in an application last week?"

"I am."

"It says here your last job was an architect."

"That's right. But there are no openings for architects in this town. I'm looking for work as a carpenter."

"You ever swung a hammer before?"

"Every summer for four years. While I was in college."

The foreman snorted, "That ain't much in the way of experience, but right now we're behind schedule and I need framers."

"I'll be glad to help," Cliff said.

"You got tools?"

"I know what I need. I'll have everything by tomorrow."

"Alright, go on over to the office at seven and get signed up. You'll be in Phelps's crew. He'll show you what to do."

The next morning Cliff packed his new lunchbox, loaded his new tools and belt into the truck, and drove out to Baywood Park.

April turned to May, then June as the houses went up. They were simple three-bedroom, two-bath units built on concrete slabs. Cliff's four-man crew could frame one in a week. He enjoyed the job, the smell of freshly cut lumber, and the pleasure of working outdoors. But after a few weeks it had become routine, leaving him time to think about other things as he worked.

Money was not a problem because true to her word, Janet had paid him for his share of their house. On top of that, the proceeds from the sale of the Porsche plus the money he had in the bank before he sailed aboard *Staghound* gave him enough capital to open an office. But an upstart company with a reputed drug smuggler as the chief architect wouldn't stand a chance against the three architectural firms already established in San Luis Obispo. Especially with Bob Larsen itching to undermine him at every opportunity. Cliff stewed over this and considered relocating to another city where he could get a fresh start, but in his mind that would be like surrendering or admitting guilt. *Fuck that!* He told himself fiercely. *No one's gonna run me out of my hometown!*

In the evenings when he was alone, Lena stole into his thoughts. Did she play him for a sucker and run off with the money? He didn't care about the money but the thought that she had played him cut like a knife. He gave up calling her, convinced that he didn't really matter to her anyway. Still, there were moments when he would see a woman with long, dark hair crossing a street or heading into a store and his heart would leap, only to be disappointed when he realized it wasn't her.

On a Sunday in July, the Tribune carried an article headlined "Mystery Yacht Sinks". *Staghound* had been towed to the impound dock in LA Harbor where it had sat unattended while the DEA and FBI, no longer interested in Cliff or the boat, moved on to other things. It eventually settled to the bottom, with only its mast sticking out of the water at an awkward angle. The authorities blamed a faulty bilge pump for the sinking of the unclaimed sailboat. The accompanying photo showed her anchored in Cat Harbor. In the background, Cliff recognized the beach where Lena swam ashore.

The story brought back memories of the voyage: Mike's broad grin as he held up a fish he had caught. Jon's steely gaze as *Staghound* sailed southward with a fair wind and a following sea. Most of all, it brought back visions of Lena's big brown eyes, her perfect smile, and her wild abandon when they were finally together. Cliff was left with a melancholy that he couldn't shake, a hole in his heart that refused to heal.

Frustrated and morose, he threw down the paper and climbed into his truck, driving aimlessly until he found himself on the winding road to Jalama. He pulled to a stop when the beach came into view. In the distance, a couple of surfers sat on their boards waiting patiently for a wave. He thought of his own board, which the sheriff had refused to let him retrieve off the *Staghound. It's time to put the past behind me,* he thought as he started the truck's engine. *I'm going to buy a new board and get back out there.*

Instead of going home, he drove north through San Luis Obispo, stopping at a deli for a sandwich and a six-pack. It was hot enough to make him sweat when he turned his un-air-conditioned truck off the highway at Buffum Ranch Road and pulled over at a wide spot near the old driveway to the Buffum house. The trees had been cleared and the remains of the burned house removed. In the distance, the flat sides of a tilt-up building replaced them, baking in the hot sun. Waves of heat radiated from the concrete apron in front of the building. Fifty yards to the left, the felled trees had been bulldozed into an enormous pile. Graders, dozers, trenchers, and other heavy equipment stood silently nearby.

Cliff leaned on the fender of his truck, finishing his sandwich and beer while he surveyed the scene before him. Down the hill, toward the highway, the ground had been leveled and a concrete slab poured. From the looks of it, Cliff surmised, a gas station and convenience store were planned for that corner of the property. He shook his head and reached in the window of the truck for another beer. An old red pickup turned off the highway and headed up the road. He watched it pass by, then the driver hit the brakes and stopped dead in the middle of the road. Its transmission whined as the driver shifted to reverse and backed up until it came to a stop in from of him.

"Well I'll be damned," Alice Hilliard exclaimed through the open passenger-side window. "I heard you were back in these parts."

"Yes ma'am. Been back a while."

CHAPTER 23

ALICE HILLIARD PULLED over and parked. When she stepped out of her truck, she paused, hands on hips and an appraising look in her eye. "I see you got rid of all that baby fat." She eyed him as if she was grading a steer. "You look like a *man* now."

Never comfortable with compliments, Cliff glanced down at his beer. He raised the can to his lips and took a swallow before he spoke. "Thirsty?"

"I should say so."

He handed her a beer and nodded toward the construction site. "They've made a lot of progress since I left."

"If you call that progress." She took a drink and squinted at him. "You come through all that stuff I read in the paper okay?"

"The paper made it sound worse than it was." He gazed toward the hills above the construction site. "I put it all behind me."

She took another drink from her can. "Come on up to the house. I want to show you something."

Cliff followed in his truck, waiting while she opened an iron gate and drove in. When both trucks were inside the gate he hopped out and closed it, then followed another hundred yards to her house.

It was cool inside despite the scorching temperature outdoors. Alice took her hat off and hung it on a hook by the door, revealing blonde hair cut short. She pointed to her right as she walked away. "Go on out to the patio, where it's nice and breezy. I'll be there in a minute."

Cliff was surprised by the place. He had expected a ranch house, dusty and slightly rundown. Instead, it had thick walls, broad porticos, and marble floors. He was impressed by the rich furnishings and finely crafted woodwork as he made his way down a wide hall toward the patio. To his left, he noticed a row of framed vintage photographs on the wall. The first was of a Union soldier with a faded inscription in the corner that read: Lieutenant Horace Hilliard, Fort Tejon, 1860. He was braced at attention, his uniform immaculate, his eyes focused intently on the camera. The firm set of his jaw bore a resemblance to Alice Hilliard's.

"My great, great grandfather," she said from behind Cliff.

"Very distinguished," Cliff said. "I presume this is your great grandfather." He pointed to the next portrait. It depicted a man with a drooping moustache dressed in western gear, a wide sombrero on his head and the same stern expression as his father.

"Yes. Henry Hilliard. Follow me." She led him out a pair of French doors. The shaded patio looked westward, toward the valley. Highway 101 was a ribbon in the distance and the hills beyond appeared to be slumbering in the hot sun.

Cliff took in the impressive view. His eye followed the highway below, from south to north. To the right lay the Buffum Ranch construction site. From where he stood, it looked like an ugly scar on the land, dotted with bright orange tractors and the dark mound of dead trees.

"When this house was built, that highway was a wagon trail," Alice said. "When I was a girl, it was a two-lane road." She put a hand over her brow, shielding her eyes from the sun. "Then it became a highway and for a good long while it remained that way, until the Buffums sold out. There'll be no stopping the developers now." She sat in a wicker wing-back chair that faced the valley. "I'll be damned if I'm going to sit here and look at that eyesore every afternoon for the rest of my life."

Cliff thought of his own home in Avila Beach, with its spectacular view. He would have been incensed if that view had been spoiled by a strip mall. "I understand, Ms. Hilliard. I'm sorry I had a hand in that project."

"Call me Alice, or Al if you like."

Cliff gazed at the construction site and pondered what might be done. "You could plant trees there." He pointed to the land sloping down toward the job site. "Eucalyptus are fast-growing. It wouldn't take long for them to grow tall enough to block the view."

"They wouldn't block the noise, or the smell." She turned her attention to an old dog, an English setter, that had wandered out of the house and sat next to her. "Woody, you old hound, we've got to move," she said, rubbing the dog's ears. "Woody used to go everywhere with me, but he's gotten too old to jump in the truck anymore," she said to Cliff.

Satisfied, the dog rose stiffly, gave a perfunctory wag of its tail, and went back into the house.

"You're thinking of moving from this beautiful place?" Cliff asked. "Where to?"

"Well, that's what I wanted to talk to you about."

"Me?" Cliff wasn't sure he heard her right.

"Yup." She rose from the chair. "Come on, let's take a ride."

They took Alice's truck and got back on Buffum Ranch Road. Half a mile up the hill she turned off and Cliff jumped out and opened a steel gate. Alice talked as they drove.

"My great, great grandfather started buying land back in the 1860s. His son and grandson bought more. At one time the H-Bar ranch, as it was called back then, covered 24,000 acres." She slowed the truck, going around a tight turn in the gravel road. "They ran cattle and horses in those days. The country needed beef and horses then. My grandfather, Herbert Hilliard, bought a good deal of land east of here, around McKittrick. Ever heard of it?"

"Nope." Cliff was still processing the idea of 24,000 acres.

"We called it East Ranch. Anyway, they discovered oil out there and before long the majority of the family income came from oil instead of ranching." The truck topped a hill and turned south through a grove of oaks and cottonwoods.

"So, we're still on your land now?" They had been driving for fifteen minutes and Cliff wasn't sure.

"Yes, 'course the ranch isn't nearly as big as it used to be. We've sold off pieces of it for one reason or another. Now we're down to about 18,000 acres."

"Do you manage all of this land yourself?"

"Oh heavens, no." She downshifted as the truck emerged from the woods onto a narrow plain and rolled to a halt. She turned off the engine and gazed out at the landscape to the south. The hills were brown and dotted with trees. Below, a dense line of trees hid a creek. A hawk soared above the hillside, hunting. The air was crystal clear and the silence was broken only by the ticking of the truck's engine cooling.

Cliff was awed by the scene.

"This is why I brought you here," Alice said, staring at him.

"I don't understand." Cliff fidgeted in his seat.

"This is where I'm moving to, and I want you to design the house." She got out of the truck and started walking.

Cliff jerked the door open and caught up to her at the edge of the plain. "You want *me* to design a house for you?"

"Yup."

"You barely know me. Haven't you been reading the papers? People think I'm a drug dealer. Hell, I got fired from my last job!" He held up a thumb and forefinger an inch apart. "A few months ago I was this close to being in jail."

"I'm aware of all that."

"Every architect in the county would jump at a project like this," he exclaimed. "Why me, of all people?"

"Don't underestimate me," Alice said. "I've done my homework. I know the work you did for Larsen Haines. They may not have been the kind of buildings you wanted to do, but no one ever criticized the quality of your work. And I appreciate that you tried to save that tree in Buffum's pasture. You sacrificed your job for that. It meant a lot to me." She pulled the brim of her hat down and stared at him. "Well, will you do it?"

Cliff turned and gazed at the landscape and imagined a home among the trees. He looked southward at the beautiful view, his thoughts racing. He turned back to Alice. "I'm working for a construction company. Framing new houses over in Baywood Park. It'll take another month to finish the contract, and they're depending on me to help get it done on time. I can start when that job is finished."

Alice solemnly reached out and shook his hand. "Thank you. I believe we're going to work very well together."

On September 4th, Cliff collected his last paycheck and said goodbye to his boss.

"You're a damn good carpenter," Phelps said, "If that gig up in the hills doesn't work out, you've got a place in my crew anytime you want it."

Cliff was restless and edgy over the long Labor Day weekend, eager to get started on the Hilliard Project, as he called it. He had already filled a couple of notebooks with sketches, notes, and ideas. When he arrived at Alice Hilliard's house the following Tuesday morning, he was ready.

Alice drove him a mile up the road to a vacant house next to a creek. It was a wood-frame structure with a peaked roof, a big brick fireplace and a barn behind it. "This used to be the ranch foreman's house but nowadays ranch hands would rather live in town. They say it's easier that way. Schools and stores are more convenient." She gave him a brief tour of the home. "You can set up your office here. No one's using the place anyway." They walked out onto the front porch where the sound of the creek was louder. "It's mighty peaceful here. Hell, you could live here if you want to."

"I'll rent it from you. If that's agreeable to you, I'll move in next week."

Cliff wasted no time setting up an office in the house. He worked on the design of Alice's new home during the day and in the twilight hours, he sat alone on the front porch, listening to the babbling creek and watching the deer come quietly through the trees to drink from it.

Summer turned to autumn and the leaves on the trees fell while Cliff drew the plans for the new house, hiring an engineer for the structural work. The crisp evenings turned cold and each night he built a fire in the big fireplace. The long winter nights were lonely, and he often thought of Lena, wondering if she ever made it to Chile. Did she free her parents, or just run off with the money in her backpack? He couldn't break himself from asking that question. It was like a wound that wouldn't heal. He had not heard a word from her in the nine months since that night in Catalina. *Surely,* he thought, *she's forgotten me by now.* The white-hot passion he once felt had turned to ashes in his heart. He fought his loneliness by throwing himself into his work. Aside from the house, Alice Hilliard had presented him with half a dozen other projects on her vast property, leaving him with little time for loneliness.

On a warm Saturday in the spring he drove a mile out on the freshly graded and graveled road to Alice's new house for a quiet inspection of the roof structure that had been completed the day before. The rafters were all in place, revealing the final shape of the house. Alice had been adamant that it blend in, rather than stand out from the surrounding landscape. Though some trees had been removed to accommodate the house, she ordered a new tree planted for every one that was cut down. Now he walked around the building and studied it from all sides, comparing the reality to what he had envisioned.

Satisfied by what he saw, he followed a rocky trail from the house to an overlook at the edge of the plain, where nature had provided a perfectly formed bench: a slab of granite that had split off from a larger rock eons before. The tall grass on the hillsides waved in the breeze and poppies bloomed in infinite shades of orange, yellow and gold under the brilliant sun. *Alice is going to love this view from her porch,* he thought as he sat and gazed at the panorama before him. *There won't be any roads or mini-marts to spoil this view in her lifetime, or mine.* Butterflies flitted by on bright yellow wings and honeybees buzzed among the wildflowers as the faint sound of Alice's truck rose and fell, then disappeared. Cliff leaned back and closed his eyes, letting the sun warm his bones.

The sound of footsteps came down the gravelly trail. *That'll be Alice,* he thought, eyes still closed.

"Cliff?"

The voice was not Alice's, but it was one he knew. His mind stumbled a second before his eyes snapped open and he turned to see its owner. *Lena!*

Their eyes locked as he struggled to find his voice. His heart started thumping like a drum. After all this time, he wasn't sure if he was glad or angry that she had suddenly appeared.

"You're not an easy man to find," she said. She maintained her distance, her backpack still on her shoulder.

"How did you get here?" he stammered.

"Alice brought me," she said with a roguish smile.

Cliff glanced back toward the house, where Alice usually

parked her truck, but it was gone. "I didn't think I would ever see you again."

"I was in Chile caring for my parents until two weeks ago." She lowered her pack to the ground. "I have been searching for you since I got back to the States."

Like rewinding a film, Cliff's mind went back to *Staghound*, the *Tortuga Negra*, and the purpose of the voyage. In his anguish over missing her, he had forgotten her single-minded drive to liberate her parents, but it came back to him now. "Did you find them? Are they safe?"

"They are at peace." She took a tentative step toward him.

"That sounds ominous. Where are they?"

She looked away, across the valley, and watched a vulture circle in the sky. "My mother died six weeks after they were released. My father was very weak, but he fought until death took him a month ago. They are buried together in the *Cementario Disidentes*, in Valparaiso."

As the weeks and months passed, Cliff had imagined what he would say to her if he ever got the chance: Harsh words that expressed his hurt and bitterness over her disappearance. But now he could not muster them. "I am sorry," he said instead. Gazing at her now, he struggled with his feelings. *I finally got over her, and now, out of the blue, here she is, as if it is perfectly normal for her to be standing there, without notice or explanation.* "What do you want?" he asked coldly.

"When I left you that night in Catalina, I told you I would come back, remember?"

"I remember a lot of things. I remember the number you gave me to call, which I did at least a hundred times." He shook his head slowly. "You just disappeared. That was a year ago."

Lena took another step toward him. "I saw in the papers that you were talking to the FBI and I was afraid they would be pounding on my door any minute, so I fled. I caught a flight to Lima, then took a bus to Santiago."

"I told you I would keep your name out of it."

"I was afraid they would force you to talk, I couldn't take that chance."

"So...Mission accomplished. You got them out."

"Yes." She stepped forward and reached for his hand, but he didn't respond. "And I told you that when they were safe, I would come back and find you." She studied his face. "But you are not glad to see me." She lowered her eyes. After a moment of silence, she turned and reached for her pack. "I have been dreaming all this time that when I came back, we would finally be together." She lifted the pack to her shoulder. "I see I was mistaken."

Cliff watched her start back on the trail. "Was it hard?" he called after her.

She stopped and half-faced him. "Was what hard?"

"Getting them out of prison."

"No." She started walking again.

"Wait. I want to know how you managed it."

She stopped and faced him again. Even forty feet away, he could see tears glistening on her cheeks.

"I really want to know." He took a couple of steps toward her, then broke into a run. She threw her pack to the ground just in time to fling her arms around him as they crashed together. He held her so tight he lifted her off the ground, so tight he felt her heart pounding against his own. She wrapped her legs around him and let the tears run down her cheeks to his collar.

After another minute, he eased her down and gazed into her eyes. "It's been hard as hell waiting for you. In fact, I stopped waiting. Now you've shown up and completely knocked the wind out of my sails."

They stood that way, talking in whispers as the sun shifted westward, until he led her by the hand back to the stone bench.

Looking out at the vista, he said, "I think I've found a home here." He swept his arm across the landscape.

"I know." She took his hand and held it in her lap. "Alice told me."

"Speaking of whom, how did you find her?"

"I assumed you were still in San Luis Obispo, so I came here, opened the phone book and called every architect in it. All of them had heard of you, but none knew where you were. But one person said there was an architect working as a carpenter in Baywood Park. I wandered around that big construction site until I found someone who knew you. A Mexican man who had worked with you, framing houses. He led me to Ray Phelps, who told me you were building a house on the Hilliard Ranch. He said you were a very good carpenter."

Cliff smiled. "It was actually fun working with Phelps's crew. Good to work outdoors, too. But how did you get Alice Hilliard to bring you here?"

"I drove out early this morning and saw some workers planting eucalyptus trees along the road. There was a woman in a Stetson hat pointing out exactly where she wanted them planted, and I knew that was her."

Cliff shook his head and smiled again. "That's Alice Hilliard."

"When I explained who I was and what I wanted, she invited me up to her house for coffee. We talked all morning. She told me about the construction project across the road and how she met you." Lena squeezed his hand. "She's quite fond of you."

They sat in silence as the sun moved farther west and the shadows lengthened. A cottontail meandered down the trail, unaware that they were there. Cliff put a finger to his lips and pointed it out to Lena. They watched it browse until it disappeared into the brush.

"How did you get your parents out of that prison?" he asked.

Lena grew solemn. "Everything in Chile has changed.

Pinochet's government is tottering, ready to fall. To save face, he offered to support a plebiscite later this year. He will surely lose, then we'll see if there is a peaceful transfer of power, or if there will be more fighting. I am not hopeful." She paused, gazing westward toward the sun. "My parents were among the last to leave the Villa Granada because they would never sign a statement in favor of the government. In the end, they had become an embarrassment to the CNI, the Secret Police, who were glad when we took them out of the prison, my mother on a stretcher and my father barely able to walk. I held my mother's hand every day until she died. I walked in the park with Papa every day, until he was too weak to stand." She heaved a bitter sigh. "It is my most fervent hope that when Pinochet is gone, his Gestapo will be brought to justice." She glanced at Cliff, her eyes glittering with anger.

"Did you hear anything about the *Tortuga Negra*?"

"It sank somewhere off the coast, near Coquimbo."

"And Yori, lost at sea?"

"Hardly. He and Antonio managed to transfer the guns to the skiff and make it to shore. Parga has them, and he is something of a legend among them now." She shook her head ruefully. "MIR is not happy about that and they are already skirmishing with Parga. After the fight against Pinochet is over, I'm afraid the next war will be between the cartels for control of the drug trade," she said sadly. "Chile can never get a decent break."

They sat together on the bench and watched the sun touch the western hills, sending fiery rays through the scattered clouds.

"So, you're building a house," Lena said. "I knew you would." She rose, pulling him with her. "I want to see this house of yours before it gets too dark." She slung the backpack over her shoulder and they hiked up to the construction site.

Hand in hand, he gave her a tour of the place, then drove her back to his house by the creek. She looked around the home, admired the fireplace, and gravitated to the big drawing board

Cliff had set up in the living room. On it lay the plans for Alice's house. Lena perused each page, asking questions about the details. Then she turned over the last page, revealing a scale drawing of a sailboat that Cliff had drawn. "What's this?" she asked.

"Well, someday I'm going to build a boat and go cruising. Visit Polynesia, Fiji, and New Zealand. Then I'm going to Lombok and Bali, the Indian Ocean and up the Red Sea to the Lycian Coast, and on to the Balearics."

Lena studied the drawing. "How big is this boat you're planning? Big enough for two?"

"Of course."

"So you're in the Balearics, Ibiza I presume."

"Yup."

"Then where?"

Cliff went to a corner of the room and retrieved a globe on a stand.

Lena watched as he set it on the desk and spun it so the Mediterranean Sea was visible. He put his finger on the island of Ibiza, then traced a course across the Atlantic as he spoke. "We'll go through the Straits of Gibraltar and across the Atlantic to the Antilles, then through the Canal and up the west coast of Central America and Mexico, and back to California."

"A round trip?" She let her finger follow the course he had traced on the globe.

"Yup."

"And what are you going to do on this round trip?" she asked, gazing into his eyes.

"Aside from seeing the sights, meeting the people, tasting the food, and surfing the waves?"

"Yes, aside from all that."

"Make love to you."

"I see." Her eyes grew larger, more intense. "And how are you going to pay for this boat, and the round trip."

"Well, that's the part I haven't figured out yet. Just the boat will cost a couple hundred thousand."

Lena stared at him a moment, then reached for her backpack. It was the same one she had when she dove off *Staghound's* stern. "The prison guards were so eager to be rid of my parents they didn't even demand a ransom." She turned the bag upside down and shook it.

Cliff watched, speechless, as twenty familiar bundles of hundred-dollar bills tumbled onto the table.

"We can start on that boat whenever you're ready," she said, smiling.

THE END

Glossary of Sailing Terms

Abeam: 90 degrees from dead ahead, or directly from the side.

Aft: Toward the stern.

Afterguy: Rope used to pull the spinnaker pole aft.

Backstay: Wire or rod connecting the masthead to the stern.

Backstay adjuster: Hydraulic device used to exert tension on the backstay.

Batten: Fiberglass strip used to stiffen a sail.

Beam: The width of a boat.

Bear off: To turn away from the wind.

Berth: A bed or bunk.

Bilge: The area of a boat located beneath the floor.

Bimini: Canvas shade over the cockpit of a boat.

Block: Pulley

Boom: Metal beam attached to the mast and used to support the foot of a sail.

Bosun's chair: A sling or seat that can be attached to a halyard to hoist a person up the mast of a

Sailboat.

Broad reach: Sailing with the wind coming from 50 to 70 degrees aft of abeam.

Bulkhead: A structural wall in a boat.

Bulwark: A raised barrier along the perimeter of the deck.

Cheek block: A pulley that is mounted on another object so it lays on its side.

Cleat: A T-shaped device mounted to another object to which ropes can be tied.

Clew: The part of a sail where the sheet is attached.

Coaming: A raised perimeter around a hatch or cockpit.

Cockpit: A recessed area in a boat's deck in which the crew works or takes shelter.

Coffee grinder: A pair of handles mounted on a pedestal and mechanically linked to a winch.

Companionway: Passageway from above deck to below deck.

Dodger: A metal-framed canvas structure mounted on deck to protect crew from wind and water.

Draft: The depth of a boat below the waterline.

Flake: To fold a sail with alternating folds like an accordion.

Foot: The bottom edge or area of a triangular sail.

Fore: Forward.

Foreguy: A rope used to pull a spinnaker pole forward and down.

Freeboard: The vertical distance from the waterline to the deck of a boat.

Genoa: A large jib used in light winds.

Genoa lead car: A pulley on a track mounted to the deck that can be adjusted forward or aft.

Gunwale: The upper edge of a hull or bulwark.

Halyard: A rope used to hoist sails.

Hank: A metal device use to attach the leading edge of a sail to a mast or stay.

Head: Toilet aboard a boat or the top corner of a sail.

Headstay: A wire or rod that connects the top of a mast to the bow of a boat.

Jib: A triangular sail attached to the headstay.

Jib lead block: A pulley mounted on deck through which the jib sheet passes.

Jib sheet: Rope used to control the jib.

Lazarette: A space in the stern of the boat and accessed from above the deck.

Lazy sheet: A rope used to control a sail that is not currently in use. Opposite of working sheet.

Leech: The aft edge of a sail.

Line: When a rope has a purpose such as controlling the jib, it is referred to as a line.

Luff: The forward edge of a sail, usually attached to the mast (mainsail) or headstay (jib).

Nav Station: A part of the interior of a boat dedicated to navigation tasks.

Noon Sight: Using a sextant when the sun is at its zenith to determine a vessel's latitude and
longitude.

Outhaul: A rope or wire used to pull the clew of a mainsail aft on the boom.

Pilot berth: A bunk located against the hull, usually outboard of a seating area.

Rudder stock: The central structural shaft of a rudder.

Settee: A long seat that can be used as a berth.

Sheet: A line used to control a sail.

Shroud: Metal wire or rod used to hold the mast in position in the lateral direction.

Sole: Any floor in a boat.

Spinnaker: Large balloon-shaped sail with the tack attached to the spinnaker pole.

Spinnaker pole: A long pole with one end attached to the mast and the other end attached to the

tack of a spinnaker.

Tack: The forward lower corner of a sail that is attached to the mast or headstay.

Transom: The aft-facing part of a hull.

Vang: A hydraulic device connected to the base of a mast and to a point on the boom used to control the shape of a mainsail.

Staghound

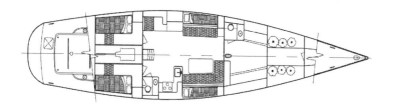

Staghound's Accommodations

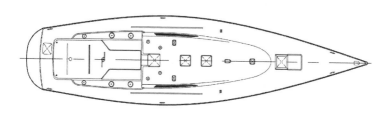

Staghound's Deck

Tortuga Negra

ACKNOWLEDGEMENTS

When I began writing VOYAGE TO CRUSOE four years ago, I had never written anything longer than a magazine article, nor any fiction at all. My first chapters were, even to my inexperienced eye, pretty awful. I thought about giving up on the idea of becoming a writer, but then I met George Snyder and everything changed.

George was in his late seventies when I showed up at the little writer's critique group he ran in the basement of the Barnes & Noble bookstore in Long Beach, California. He was no Hemingway, but he had written over forty novels and knew a good story when he saw it. He urged me to rewrite the opening chapters of the book and submit them to his group. Slowly, my work began to improve, and over the next couple of years the manuscript took shape. I am profoundly grateful to George, Mary Frances, Neil, Moss, Lance, and the other members of the group for their help and advice.

George Snyder built his own boats and sailed them as far north as Alaska and south to the Sea of Cortez. It was fitting that he was aboard his boat when he passed away recently, at the age of eighty. He was a mentor and inspiration to me, and he did what he loved to the very end.

I also owe a debt of gratitude to my beta readers and critics, who found the errors I missed. Because of them, the burden on my editors, William C. Hammond III and Sheree Fenwick was eased a bit as they tightened up the prose and punctuation. Thank you, Bill and Sheree for your help and suggestions, and for your generous contributions to causes that are dear to me. Any mistakes remaining in the manuscript are entirely my own.

Last and most importantly, I want to thank Lisa. Without her patience and forbearance, encouragement and wise counsel, this book would not have been possible.

❧

ABOUT THE AUTHOR

Leif Beiley is best known as the designer of fast and beautiful sail-boats. His designs have earned for him a large following of sailing enthusiasts, and his blog is read by a global audience.

Based in Southern California, when Leif is not busy working on his next novel, he's usually traveling or on his boat, but you can always find him on Facebook, his blog (www.cruisingboatdesigns. blogspot.com), and his website: *www.LeifBeiley.com.*

51821025R00186